After graduating from Hertford College, Oxford, Martin O'Brien joined Conde Nast and was British *Vogue's* travel editor for a number of years. As well as writing for *Vogue*, he has contributed to a wide range of international publications. He was editor of *Sixty Years of Travel in Vogue* and is the author of *All the Girls*. His highly acclaimed novels *Jacquot and the Angel*, *Jacquot and the Waterman* and *Jacquot and the Master* are also available from Headline.

Praise for Martin O'Brien:

'A wonderfully inventive and involving detective story with vivid French locales creating the perfect backdrop. *Jacquot is top of le cops*' *Daily Express*

'O'Brien creates a sexually charged atmosphere that is as chilling as it is engaging' *Sydney Morning Herald*

'Fans of Agatha Christie's technique in *And Then There Were None*, in which trapped characters are thrillingly knocked off one by one, will appreciate the strategy. O'Brien, as always, makes effective use of his chosen setting – a sunny place for shady people' *Daily Mail*

'A strikingly different detective, Jacquot walks off the page effortlessly. And O'Brien seems to bend the plot at will, each time leading readers up an alley only to dart away into the shimmering heat' *Good Book Guide*

'You can practically feel the sun of the Mediterranean beating down on your head as the mystery unfolds along the gilded French coastline' *Time Out*

'An enjoyable tale set
Review

Also by Martin O'Brien and available from Headline

Jacquot and the Angel
Jacquot and the Waterman
Jacquot and the Master

JACQUOT AND THE FIFTEEN

Martin O'Brien

headline

First published in 2007 by
HEADLINE PUBLISHING GROUP

First published in paperback in 2008 by
HEADLINE PUBLISHING GROUP

1

Cataloguing in Publication Data is available from the British Library

ISBN 978 0 7553 3508 4

Typeset in New Caledonia by Palimpsest Book Production Limited, Grangemouth, Stirlingshire

Printed and bound in Great Britain by
Clays Ltd, St Ives plc

Headline's policy is to use papers that are natural, renewable and recyclable products and made from wood grown in sustainable forests. The logging and manufacturing processes are expected to conform to the environmental regulations of the country of origin.

HEADLINE PUBLISHING GROUP
An Hachette Livre UK Company
338 Euston Road
London NW1 3BH

www.headline.co.uk

For Rosie,
who spotted Daniel
and said yes

Part One

THE FIFTEEN

1	Paul DRUART	(Loosehead prop)
2	Antoine PEYROT	(Hooker)
3	Patric SOUZE	(Tighthead prop)
4	Guy MAGEOT	(Second row)
5	Théo PELERAIN	(Second row)
6	Jean-Baptiste THIERS	(Flanker – blindside)
7	Olivier TOUCHE	(Flanker – openside)
8	Louis CABEZAC	(Number Eight)
9	Bernard SAVRY	(Scrum-half)
10	Pierre DOMBASLE	(Captain/Fly-half)
11	Sidi CARASSIN	(Left wing)
12	Luc VALADIER	(Inside centre)
13	Valentine CALOUX	(Outside centre)
14	Gilles MILLET	(Right wing)
15	Jean-Charles RAINS	(Full-back)

SUBS
Daniel JACQUOT
Simon TALAUD
Marc FASTIN
Claude LORRAINE

September

It was the rugby player, she was certain of it. The one with the ponytail. He was broad in the shoulder, tall enough to have to bend his head when he reached the top of the stairs, and, as he turned on the landing, Camille Rives saw him reach out a meaty hand and flick his fingers at the silken rump of his companion.

Madame Rives had arrived at Club Xéro with her husband a couple of hours earlier. Jean-Claude had parked in the usual place – a small courtyard off the canal where workers from a nearby laundry played hoops in their lunch hour. After dark the courtyard was silent and still, and a suitably discreet distance from the club. It didn't do to advertise, Jean-Claude always counselled, but as they walked along the tree-lined towpath with only city lights across the canal to guide them, Camille sensed her husband's quickening pace, his declared sense of caution superceded by the impetus of anticipation.

Camille and Jean-Claude made the trip out to Club Xéro on the last Thursday of each month. Camille's sister looked after their three children, or they brought in a babysitter. It was important to have time alone with a husband, Camille told her sister – a film, a bite to eat somewhere, just the two of them. And her sister agreed, wishing only that her own husband felt the same way. What Camille's sister didn't know was that these monthly nights out were not devised to take in a film or a restaurant. They were spent in an old four-storey granary on a cobbled quay set back from the Canal du Midi in the north-east of the city, a building whose quayside windows had been barred and blacked out and whose front door was a solid metal rectangle scrawled with graffiti. There was no handle on this door, and no sign advertising Club Xéro's presence, just a small spyhole in the centre of the door and a bell push set into the stone door-frame, no indication to the casual passer-by of the particular commercial enterprise carried on behind the granary's flaking, rose-coloured brick façade.

Camille and Jean-Claude had been club members for only two years. Before that they'd had to drive a half-hour out of Toulouse to an old converted *mas* on the road to Carcassonne in the brooding shadow of the Montagne Noire. After a police raid, it had taken them six months to secure alternative arrangements. Unsurprisingly perhaps, Jean-Claude had been more proactive than Camille in searching out these arrangements; the couple's introduction to, and membership of, Club Xéro was initiated after Jean-Claude attended an avionics conference in Paris.

Camille knew very well that it was her husband who took the greater enjoyment from the diversions on offer at Club Xéro, hence his quickening pace whenever they visited. Not that she didn't avail herself of the pleasures it provided when she felt in the mood. The last two visits she'd enjoyed a strangely intense, if painful, partnering in a basement Correction Room with a bank manager from Bordeaux, and an hilarious marijuana-fuelled group session in one of Club Xéro's three jacuzzis.

On this particular evening, however, Camille Rives had stayed at the bar while Jean-Claude paired up with a thirty-something blonde in a Chinese cheongsam. So far as Camille could see, the tight split-skirt dress did the woman no favours, but that hadn't deterred Camille's *husband. With a consenting 'do-as-you-please' smile, she'd watched him buy* Madame la Chinoise *a drink, take her for a dance, then five minutes later return alone to the bar to say he'd be back in an hour and did she want to join them?*

If the woman had been ten kilos lighter, Camille might have been tempted. Instead, she waved Jean-Claude off with a laugh, told him to enjoy his 'takeaway' and ordered another whisky-and-soda. Perhaps a few drinks would loosen her up, she thought, wondering how Jean-Claude could manage an hour with La Chinoise *yet only twenty minutes with her. Or maybe he was just being optimistic.*

She was on her third drink when she spotted, in the mirror behind the bar, the rugby player, the one with the ponytail. She turned on her stool in time to see him swirl his companion in a rock 'n' roll spin before hurrying her up the stairs. As Camille well knew there were only two options on the floors above the bar – the playrooms or the Black Hole.

Which one, she wondered idly, would the rugby player choose? The playrooms – a doctor's surgery, a classroom, a nursery, an office, a monk's cell, each equipped with the appropriate furnishings and costumes – were located directly above the bar and each of the rooms had a glass viewing panel set in the door for those who didn't mind being watched, with a curtain behind the door for those who did. Privacy or performance. At Club Xéro all tastes were catered to.

On the top floor, however, the action was definitely communal and, in the complete and utter darkness that prevailed beyond the locker and shower rooms, thrillingly anonymous. Not a chink of light, just a pleasing mix of wave music or jungle soundtrack to cover the moans and the sighs rising up from the oiled and quilted plastic surface that comprised floor and walls.

Stubbing out her cigarette and finishing her drink, it struck Camille that it might be interesting – and possibly fun – to find out the rugby player's preference. Scribbling a note for her husband and leaving it with the barman – 'I'm upstairs. See if you can find me' – she left the bar and climbed the stairs to the playrooms. Four of the five 'sets' were empty, the viewing panel of the fifth – a classroom – discreetly curtained but occupied, as Camille knew only too well, by the couple who'd struck up a conversation with her after Jean-Claude disappeared with La Chinoise, *suggesting a vacancy for a second naughty schoolgirl, an invitation she had politely declined.*

Which meant that the rugby player – what was *his name? – and his companion could only be on the floor above. In the Black Hole. Climbing the stairs, Camille felt the first prickling of excitement. Twenty minutes earlier she'd pretty much concluded that an evening at the bar would suit her mood perfectly, yet the next thing she knew she was heading for the Black Hole. That's the kind of place Club Xéro was.*

In the locker room, she bagged her jewellery, stripped off her clothes and set the locker's combination code with the day, month and year of her birth, keys in the Black Hole being something of an encumbrance. Pushing through the set of double doors, closing the first before opening the second, nipples hardening, thighs trembling, Camille got down on to her knees and eased through the final opening that gave the Black Hole its name. It was also, she knew, a useful safety device; you didn't want to go prancing in, blind as a bat, on a surface that was as slick as oiled ice. In the Black Hole you slithered naked like a snake . . .

In the complete, blinding darkness, three things struck Camille: the swaddling warmth of the chamber, a musky scent of vanilla and oak, and the thick, sliding, springiness of the floor. To the screeching of distant howler monkeys and the closer cackling of what sounded like a toucan or macaws, Camille slid over the oiled and quilted floor like a predator searching out its prey.

Judging by the two other secured lockers she'd seen in the locker room, there were only the rugby player and his companion in the chamber, the sound of their panting and the soft tremors of their squirming almost immediately indicating their presence and position, directing Camille into the furthest corner of the room.

Reaching out in the darkness she felt a foot, a large foot, a man's foot, but as she slid her hand up the leg she felt it tense and spasm, heard a muffled grunt and realised that, for the moment, the game was over. The deed done. Not that it worried her. In the warm, oiled darkness, to a jungle soundtrack of screeching parrots and low nocturnal growls – not to mention the goading presence of an unknown hand – it was often extraordinary how quickly the male of the species recovered, and the games began again.

By now Camille had found the second foot and was sliding herself up between the man's legs, wondering where his companion might be. It was then, with the tips of her fingers, that she felt a hot stickiness against the insides of his thighs. Not sweat, not juices, but a flowing pulse of liquid as though hot soup was being poured too fast from a narrow-necked flask.

She found the opening moments later, the source of

the flow. In the darkness it felt like a meaty gash, what had once stood there slashed away, reduced to a wrinkled scrap of oozing tissue still connected to the abdomen by a thread of flesh.

Camille knew she screamed. Heard a high, excitable whoop-whoop-whooping response from the monkeys in the trees high above her and, as she pushed back from the body, she felt something hard and cold and sharp press into her left breast.

1

October

'I don't want to go,' said Daniel Jacquot, burying a cigarette end into the sand and staring out over the inky water. 'It's as simple as that.'

'You have to go,' replied Salette, pushing at the circle of stones that held the embers of their fire. Above the dark sides of the *calanque* where Salette had moored his sloop, stars glittered like a twisting stream of twinkling light heading out to sea. 'You made the run. You scored the try. Without you—'

'It's not my thing, you know that, Sal. Reunions? *Bouff!* For people who can't let go of the past. I'd just prefer . . .'

Salette started to chuckle as though he'd never heard anything so ridiculous. 'It doesn't matter what you prefer or don't prefer,' said the old harbour master. 'It's something you have to do. You can't walk away from it. You can't pretend it didn't happen.'

'I played just the once, remember? One cap. Maybe ten minutes on the pitch. The rest of them, the team, they played together for years. The reunion's for them. Not me.' Jacquot knew it was a weak argument and that the old man would not be persuaded.

He was right.

Reaching forward, Salette stirred the embers with a length of driftwood. A final, weak flurry of sparks weaved up between them and the dying heart of the fire momentarily lit their faces – Salette's drawn cheeks and age-freckled scalp, Jacquot's gently broken nose and light green eyes. The old man tossed the stick beyond the glow of light and then leaned forward in his seat.

'*Écoute*, Daniel, this man Pierre Dombasle didn't send you that invitation because he was being polite. He wants you there. You're a part of it all, whether you like it or not.'

'It's not even a proper anniversary, did you know that?' countered Jacquot. 'Just eighteen years. Not even that. Not twenty. Not twenty-one.'

'So maybe he wants to get you all together while you've still got your marbles, while you're all still around. Or maybe it's his birthday and he wants to see his old friends.'

Jacquot snorted. 'Old friend? Me? I doubt very much that Pierre Dombasle would recognise me if we bumped into each other in the street. It's eighteen years, Sal. A lot can happen in eighteen years.'

'Tell me about it,' the harbour master replied. 'Eighteen years ago I was in my fifties and having fun. Now I need a winch to pull up the anchor. And I'm not just talking sailing . . .'

'Come on, old timer,' said Jacquot, getting to his feet. 'I'll row you back to the boat and you can open up that bottle you've been hiding in your cabin.'

'God help us . . . you row, and we'll end up in Corsica. I may have trouble with my anchor but I can still pull a pair of oars.'

Kicking out the fire, they gathered up their things – griddle, plates, two empty wine bottles, Salette's striped picnic chair – and loaded them into the tender they'd come ashore in, pushing away from the narrow belt of sand where they'd spent the last three hours. Salette was first in, slipping the blades into the rowlocks and taking the first pull before Jacquot was properly settled. The tiny boat rocked and the old man laughed. 'You might be able to run and score tries, my young friend, but your sea-legs are shite,' he crowed. 'You shouldn't stay away so long.'

Some time later, cabin lights doused, *bonnes nuits* exchanged, Salette took the single bunk and Jacquot spread the cockpit cushions on the stern deck of the old man's sloop. This time of year, there was every chance of a chill and maybe dew settling, but he didn't care. The half-bottle of Armagnac they'd polished off would keep him warm and as he made himself comfortable, watching the stars blink out and reappear as the mast swayed across them, listening to the pleasing hypnotic lap and suck of the sea on their hull, Jacquot remembered what the old man had said. 'You're a part of it all, whether you like it or not.'

They reached Marseilles's Vieux Port before the sun had shown over the jagged ridges of Montredon, fishermen still swinging their catch-crates on to the Quai des Belges where aproned wives had set up a line of trestle stalls. There were some early cars coming down the slope of La Canebière, a baker's lorry unloading at the Café Samaritaine but otherwise the traffic lights around the old harbour were signalling to empty roads.

Salette teased the sloop between two of the fishing *pointus* and Jacquot, his skin and scalp still salty-tight from his early morning swim, stepped up from the bow on to the quay.

They bid each other '*adieu . . . à la prochaine . . .*' and Salette, engaging reverse, steered his way clear of the *pointus* and began his turn.

'Hey,' Jacquot cried out, 'you still got that old dinner jacket?'

'Let me know when you need it,' replied Salette with a smile and salute. 'I'll take out the mothballs and give it a brush.'

2

'The cop?' Delphine's voice was suddenly breathless with surprise. 'The guy I met at Sydné and César's that time in Marseilles? The one I set you up with? Only he didn't show?' And then, with mock annoyance, she said, 'So why didn't you tell me?'

'It's early days,' replied Claudine, the phone clamped to her shoulder as she rinsed out the brushes in her studio.

'How early?'

'Three months, give or take.'

'And? What's he like? I mean, I know he looks good, but what's he . . . you know . . . like? I mean, have you . . . ?'

'*Del*phie,' protested Claudine, feeling her neck and cheeks flush, 'just because you're a big-deal TV journalist up there in Paris doesn't mean you can give your little sister down south the third degree. I'll let you know when I have something to tell. And not before.' And with that, she wished her sister an abrupt '*adieu*', and cut her off. That'd teach her.

Through the studio window, the sky above the Grand and Petit Lubérons was darkening as much with cloud as with the approach of night. The days were getting shorter, and there was a briskness in the sun's progress as though it was in a hurry to do its job and be off somewhere else. It was not, Claudine reflected, a time of year that she looked forward to – she felt as though something dreadful and unexpected might happen at any moment. And it wasn't as though she had no good reason to imagine this. Her mother had died in October; she'd found her husband in bed with another woman in October; and her darling aunt, Sandrine, had had her big stroke in October. October, she'd decided, was not her favourite month.

Yet somehow Claudine didn't feel quite as cowed as she had in the past, weighed down with her sadness and her loss, alone in the big house with only her memories for company. This year, October felt somehow different. Lighter. More comforting.

Turning off the tap in the studio sink, flicking the water from her brushes and slotting them brush end up into the old paint can where they lived, Claudine switched off the studio light, closed the door and stepped into her kitchen.

Three men, thought Claudine Eddé as she whisked some eggs for an omelette, set the skillet to heat and opened a bottle of wine. She wondered if her sister knew. Thirty-eight years old and she'd slept with just three men. Loved just three men. Married two of them. No wonder Delphie had wanted to know more.

The lawyer, Paul Bécard, had been first. His parents had moved to Cavaillon from Lyon and he'd attended the same Lycée as her for their final year. At the end of that year, Claudine was pregnant and three months later they married. Five years later, the day after their daughter's fourth birthday party, Paul had driven into a barrier on the A8 somewhere between Lyon and Valence. It wasn't the crash that killed him but the heart attack that preceded it.

The property broker, Sebastien Masson, had come next. She'd met him in the check-out at a Champion superstore. He'd been playing tennis and he looked energised, as though the game had somehow enriched his blood, flooding his cheeks with health. He was tanned and tall, his legs were long and finely toned and his smile was pure salesman – big and broad and engulfing. It made your mood lighter just looking at it. He'd started it, letting his sweater drop from his shoulders then reaching down for it in the narrow aisle, coming up with it and letting his eyes travel over every inch of her before the smile blinked on. Of course her daughter, Midou, hadn't liked him one bit but what nine-year-old was ever going to like a new dad, some stranger making a space for himself in the nest she and her mother had shared between them for the previous five years? She'd sulked through the wedding ceremony that followed in due course and when she discovered that her stepfather had been cheating on her mother, Claudine knew she'd been hard pressed not to say 'I told you so'.

And now the policeman, after all this time. Daniel Jacquot.

Claudine wondered what Midou would make of him, what she would say. Nineteen years old and starting her second year at the Institut Océanographique in Toulon, she had a mind of her own and a tongue to match. In typical Eddé/Bécard fashion, Midou said what she thought and rarely kept her opinions to herself. Claudine had managed to keep the two of them apart during the long summer holiday – it was too early to bring them together, she'd decided – but now she regretted it. Three months into this new affair, she needed to talk to someone about him. But not Delphie. Never Delphie. Or at least not yet.

Her omelette dispatched, her bottle of wine half-empty, Claudine curled her legs under her and thought about the three men in her life. Just as different as could be. Paul, with his bowties and coloured waistcoats, his soft hands and uncertain smile. Sebastien, two years older than her, with his weekend trainers and T-shirts and baseball caps. When he dressed in his shiny double-breasted suits for work, she hardly recognised him.

And now this Jacquot. This policeman in Cavaillon. They'd met in Marseilles the previous summer, although 'met' was maybe too strong a word to describe their encounter. He'd come to the gallery where she'd held her first-ever exhibition, bought one of her paintings and that was that. And then by chance, four months ago, they'd met again. And both of them had known, she was certain, that it had all been meant to be. He was working, investigating a missing person at a luxury hotel on the other side of the Calavon Valley, but late one night he'd played the piano for her, a few smokey tunes, and she felt like the last eighteen months hadn't happened. The way his fingers stroked those keys, the low hum as he tried to remember the lyrics, the way his eyes closed to the music.

And then he was gone, just his business card and a lyrical note – '*Let there be oysters/Under the sea . . .*'

A week later, having spent six days convinced that as

a policeman he was sure to be able to find her, and six days idling around Cavaillon pretending to shop in the hope they might bump into one another, she'd finally picked up the phone and called the number on his card. She hadn't expected it to be a direct line but of course it was. The moment she heard his voice – '*Oui? Allô?*' – she knew there was no turning back.

Outside a flurry of rain spattered against the window and she glanced at the time. It was late – time to tidy the kitchen, and head upstairs. She had some packing to do.

3

Jacquot had cleared the weekend away with his chief, Rochet, and over an after-work pastis with his assistant, Jean Brunet, at Fin de Siècle on Cavaillon's Place du Clos, he'd simply said that he'd be back in the office on Monday morning. Brunet had nodded. It was Brunet's weekend on call so there was no suggestion that his superior was seeking a favour.

'*Pas un problème*. Do you have a contact number? Just in case?' Brunet shot Jacquot a quizzing look, wanting to know more.

'I don't,' replied Jacquot. 'But I'll keep in touch.'

And that was that. Back in his apartment under the eaves of Cours Bournissac, just a few minutes' stroll from the canopied terrace and smoke-dulled chandeliers of Fin de Siècle, he'd packed a bag, watched an hour's TV, then switched out his bedside light, listening to the sounds of the street below and thinking about the following day, the weekend ahead and the new woman in his life, the woman he'd be picking up at nine o'clock the following morning, the woman who'd be joining him for the weekend away.

He knew as certainly as he could that he was in love with Claudine Eddé. His previous lover, Isabelle Cassier from the *judiciaire* in Marseilles, who'd helped him move to Cavaillon and had kept him company those first few months, had been right. His heart had been somewhere else while they were together and she'd correctly judged that there was no future in their liaison. And though Isabelle couldn't possibly have known it, the reason for his lack of attention had been that sales assistant at the Ton-Ton Gallery in Marseilles. The sales assistant who was actually the artist though she'd been too shy to admit it when he bought the picture that now hung in his hallway, a plate of lemons. Ten minutes in that gallery, choosing the picture (the only one he could reasonably afford), writing the cheque and handing it to her – that was all it had taken for her to lodge in his mind. And that's where she'd stayed, until June, just four months earlier, when they'd bumped into each other at the Hôtel Grand Monastère des Évêques up in Luissac.

He remembered the way she wiped the rain from her

face the first time he saw her, that sharp challenging tongue of hers, the way she smoked her cigarette and sipped his calva while he played the piano. He remembered, too, the first time he kissed her, in the hotel restaurant, holding her by the arms, leaning forward and planting a lopsided kiss on her mouth. And the first time he took her to his bed, right here in Cours Bournissac, not two weeks later. On their first date. The urgent shedding of clothes in his narrow hallway as they stumbled down the corridor to this room, and the long, slow hours that followed. Lying there he thought of her warm, soft body, her teasing stroking fingers, the way her lips fitted gently to his, their whispers and giggles and her long surrendering sighs.

A beam of light from a passing car in the street below lit up the sloping roof above his head, sped across the ceiling and slanted away to the floor, leaving the room in darkness again. By the time the car turned into Cours Victor Hugo, Jacquot was asleep.

Eight hours later he woke to the hiss of rain outside his bedroom window, drumming lightly on the slant of roof above his head. It was the first rain in weeks and when he opened the window to check the sky – a low scud of grey cloud coming from the north – he could smell the dusty, metallic odour of the street below, mixed with the sweet scent of melons from the *marchand des fruits et légumes* on the next block.

Showered and dressed, Jacquot felt the tiniest worm of irritation as he stepped from his front door and hurried to Auzet's on the corner for a croissant and coffee. Judging by the dripping trees, shiny street and sodden awnings the rain had started sometime in the night – unexpected and unwanted – and didn't look as though it had any intention of moving on. There was, Jacquot decided as he sipped his coffee, something deliberate and malign about it.

You're going away for the weekend? With your lover? the rain seemed to say. Well, why don't I just keep the two of you company?

An hour later, his overnight case on the back seat, Salette's old dinner jacket in a plastic dry-cleaner's wrap stowed away in the boot, Jacquot climbed in behind the wheel and took the Apt road out of Cavaillon, the sky blackening with every kilometre he drove. Twenty minutes later, he turned to the left and started up a rutted, rain-streaming *impasse*, at the top of which stood the house, an old mill, where Claudine Eddé lived.

Five minutes later, they were backing out of the drive and heading down the slope.

'Two days together. Do you think you can handle it?' she asked, reaching out a hand to his leg.

'I will try my very hardest.'

'I'd expect nothing less.'

4

There'd been fifteen of them on that sodden, churned-up London pitch when the final whistle blew. Fifteen bruised faces and worn bodies, fifteen muddy, rucked and torn blue shirts. And steam. Steam rising off them like cattle in a dawn milking shed as they clasped each other, coming together at the halfway line as the coach, the trainer, the physios, leapt from their benches and bounded on to the pitch, dancing and leaping and punching the air at their victory, the Dax band blaring out a triumphant 'Marseillaise' into a floodlit Twickenham evening. They'd won. Against all odds. In the final minute.

Playing the wheel between his fingers as they slid past Aix, Jacquot went through the names. Druart and Souze, the front-row props, heads stubbled, necks thick, and socks around their ankles; Antoine Peyrot, the hooker, with his bulging cauliflower ears and four missing front teeth; Mageot and Pelerain, the second row, tall and gangly in their leather scrum caps and loose shirts; Cabezac, Number Eight, with his head bandaged, nose bleeding and eyes just blue pinpricks in a muddy face; Jacquot's friend Olivier Touche, the other flanker, his left eye already clamped shut and his split bottom lip spilling blood on to his shirtfront.

And then the line of backs – tiny Bernard Savry the scrum-half, with as many tricks as a bagful of weasels the Scottish commentator had said, though they wouldn't hear that particular description till later, when they watched the replay in the dressing room, and wondered what a weasel was, let alone a bag of them. Beyond Savry was the skipper and fly-half, the magnificent Pierre Dombasle, shoulders as wide as a mantelpiece, running strapped and muddied fingers through a thatch of sweat-streaked blond hair; Luc Valadier, the medic from Agen, at inside centre, hands on hips, still panting from that last long run in support of Jacquot; Caloux, Valentine Caloux, wearing the Number Thirteen shirt, relieved to hear the final whistle, hobbling off the pitch with a cracked rib, broken thumb and stretched cruciate ligament. And there, clapping raised hands together, falling together in a hug, the two wingers Sidi Carassin and Gilles Millet, slim and speedy as whippets, joined by big old Jean-Charles Rains, the safest pair of hands on the field, sixty-four caps and this his last game, the man who converted Jacquot's final try – the ball spinning between the posts through the floodlit rain, the crowds rising, the referee checking his watch and blowing the whistle. Over.

Jacquot could see every face, the whites of their eyes in their masks of mud, remembered every one of them. Eighteen years. Eighteen years since he'd seen or spoken to any of them. But what would they be like now, he wondered, as the speckled, chalky slopes of Mont Ste Victoire slipped away to their left and he slowed for the *péage*? Eighteen years on. Would he recognise any of them?

'It's stopped raining,' said Claudine.

'I'm sorry?' said Jacquot, coming to. For the last ten minutes they'd been driving in silence, Claudine humming along to Stan Getz and watching the countryside slide by, Jacquot's eyes fixed on the road ahead, his mind lost in the past.

'I said, it's stopped raining,' Claudine repeated. 'You can switch off the wipers now.'

Jacquot gave a chuckle, not a spot of rain on the windscreen, and switched them off. He glanced at her and smiled.

'So. An evening with Pierre Dombasle,' she began. 'You've heard of him?'

'Difficult not to,' she replied. 'What's he like?'

Jacquot shrugged. 'It's been twenty years. Apart from what I read in the newspapers . . .'

'But you played with him. He was your captain.'

'Once. One match only. He was a few years older than me. And a great player. A great skipper, too. Me, I was just a reserve, a substitute. Sat on the bench for four internationals before anyone noticed I was there. I doubt I ever said more than a half-dozen words to the man. I remember once, coming off the pitch at Stade de France in Paris, he said to me, 'Next time, Jacquot. We'll get you on next time.'

'And did he?'

'Nope. Not that time.'

'So you weren't any good then?' she taunted him. 'Sitting on that bench all by yourself.'

He gave her a look and grunted. 'There was a man in the squad called Thiers, Jean-Baptiste Thiers, who played my position. The only way I was ever going to get on the pitch was if someone broke his leg.'

'And did they?'

'*En effet*, they pulled him off in that last match. He was exhausted, but they still had to drag him off. I was sent on in his place, for maybe ten minutes, most of it injury time.'

'And you scored?'

'I was lucky. I was also fresh, don't forget; running against men who'd been on that pitch for eighty minutes.'

'So why didn't you play again? I'm right, aren't I? That's what you said. Just the once.'

'*Écoute*,' said Jacquot, switching to the inside lane and coming off the autoroute. 'You hungry? Why don't I tell you over lunch. There's a little place I know . . .'

'Now why doesn't that surprise me?'

The rain may have stopped but they took a table inside. Out in the restaurant's garden, the leaves were still dripping and chairs had been leaned against tables. Over a platter of local charcuterie, omelettes *fines herbes* and a bottle of white Bellet, Jacquot told Claudine how he'd come to sit on that bench all those years ago, and how, having secured his first cap, his career was brought to an abrupt and painful end when his achilles tendon snapped in a club match just a week later.

While he spoke, picking his way through the sliced meats, the olives, the cornichons, Claudine watched his eyes, the way they drifted away from her as he told his story, looking back into the past, somewhere over her shoulder, through the window. And his voice, low and confiding, warm and seductive, seemed to spread between them, drawing her in.

As the first plates were cleared from the table, Jacquot

refilled their glasses. 'A short distance from here, over that line of hills there,' he began, nodding across the fields, 'is a small farm, a vineyard, where my mother grew up. When she died, it's where I went to live with my grandparents. And where I learned to play rugby. My grandfather loved the game and taught me to love it too.'

'So you're a local boy.'

'Marseilles. The first fifteen years. After that, yes. A local boy. Over those hills.'

'Do you ever go back?' asked Claudine. 'Is the farm still in the family?'

Jacquot nodded. 'My uncle lives there now. With his family. A long time ago he made it clear I wasn't welcome.'

'Nice man. Does he play rugby too?'

'He used to. Now, like me, he probably just watches.'

'And remembers.'

'Of course. Even him. Because, you know, it is hard to forget. The more you play, the further you go in the game . . .'

'But it's so violent. So rough . . .'

'When you have fifteen men facing another fifteen men, and each one wants to get that ball in his hands, it's never going to be easy. So sure, like you say, it's rough. A rough, relentless, unforgiving game. Sometimes you get hit so hard you lie on the turf and . . . and you wonder how you will ever get to your feet again. But you do, and you play on. Because when you have that ball in your arms and you're running, and there's a space, or you make that perfect pass, or you sidestep an opponent, there is a kind of . . . a kind of elegance to it, you know? In all the grunting and the pain and the sweat there is what my grandfather used to call *poésie*, which . . . which just lifts the heart and makes your blood sing. You feel, just for a moment, the . . . the breath of God, and below the roar of the crowd, in your ear, the whisper of angels.'

'So I'm sleeping with a man who's heard the whisper of angels,' she said, running a finger across his knuckles. 'I better watch out.' And then, 'You must miss it.'

He levelled his green eyes on her and she felt him take her in, his lips finally stretching into a smile that showed no teeth but put a double line of brackets into each cheek. A pause. And then, 'Only when you're not around.'

5

It may have stopped raining but summer, even on the Côte d'Azur, was gone. The sun still shone, the waters of the Baie des Anges still glittered and shifted with silvery splinters of light, and milky waves still turned on to the sand, but the parasols that buttoned the *plages* all summer in neat, orderly rows, casting cool shadows over plump *matelas*, had been stowed away, and the stuffy stuccoed fronts of the grand hotels had a glum deserted look about them. *Le Saison* was past, five degrees – maybe more – below the previous month. As Jacquot turned off Nice's Promenade des Anglais, threaded his way past the port and followed the corniche road round Mont Boron towards Villefranche, the open windows of his old Peugeot filled with a breeze that still smelt of salt and pine but carried with it a certain teasing chill. It was a little past four in the afternoon, they had missed the worst of the local traffic and were only minutes now from their destination.

'How long since you've seen any of them?'

'Years. Most of them not since that last match. Olivier Touche played the same club as me, was there when I was carried off the pitch, came to see me in hospital. But that's it. TV, sure, when France played. But not being on the team any more, I lost touch. Work, you know. Going back to Marseilles. It happens . . .'

'So how do you feel about it? Seeing them all again.'

Jacquot let out a deep sigh. 'A little uncomfortable, as though I don't deserve to be a part of it. As though, somehow, I don't quite belong.'

'But you scored the try. You won the match. You have as much right to be here as any of them.' There was a certain pleasure and pride in the way she spoke which Jacquot noted and enjoyed.

'Perhaps you're right,' he said, leaning forward, looking out for road signs.

'Are we lost and you're too embarrassed to tell me?' she teased. 'I mean, you do know where you're going, don't you?'

'Only roughly. Apparently it's off the old coastal road . . . down through Beaulieu, past Eze-Bord-de-Mer, keep the tunnel on your left and cross the rail tracks. That's what the invitation said.'

Ten minutes later they found the turning, crossed the Nice-Menton rail tracks and sloped up an ill-kept single-lane strip of split and potholed tarmac. For a moment it seemed unlikely that a billionaire businessman would choose to live anywhere near such a stretch of uncared-for approach road, but a half-kilometre further on the track swung abruptly round a jutting wall of cliff, and a pair of massive wood gates attended by a pair of looming maritime pines rose up ahead of them.

Jacquot slowed and turned towards the gates, now richly gilded as a lowering sun dropped towards a distant Cap Ferrat. Blazing in the last of the sunshine, he could see a brass plate mounted into the left hand pillar, set with a button and speaker grill. He stopped the car, opened the door and was about to get out and state his business when the gates started to move, silently swinging open.

'There's a camera,' said Claudine. 'Up there on the other pillar. I think they've seen us.'

6

Guy Mageot watched the main perimeter gates swing open and chuckled to himself. He loved making visitors stop their cars and start to get out before pressing the button that opened the gates. Just a little joke of his. If it had been Dombasle, the gates would have been opened as he turned the corner. No delay for the big man. But anyone else? Fair game, Mageot reckoned.

He watched the old Peugeot enter the estate. Only three guests left to arrive – Pelerain, Jacquot and Druart. Mageot wondered which of the three it would be. He should have waited a moment longer before opening the gates. The car, now swinging round the first of the four terraced hairpins that led down to the house, spoke either of an easy disregard for material things or an aching void in terms of financial achievement. But was it the postman? The cop? Or the pig farmer? Any one of them might drive a Peugeot. Sitting in front of the monitors that covered Monsieur Dombasle's estate, Mageot tried to get a view of the driver as the car negotiated the final bend and headed down the main drive. All he could manage was a glimpse of a rather beautiful-looking woman on the passenger side.

So not Druart then, he thought with a grin. Twelve years earlier, the last time Mageot had seen the loose-head prop-forward from Lisieux, Druart had been almost twice the size he'd been on the pitch, his big round face as red and shiny as a tomato, his chins too numerous to count. Of course, Mageot knew the reason well enough; they'd all been through it at some stage or other: accepting too many congratulatory drinks and attending one too many testimonial and civic dinners. In Druart's case he hadn't known when to stop. The man had let himself go, just intoxicated by the celebrity, the recognition. There was no way that Druart – then or now – was going to bag the beauty even now getting out of the Peugeot.

Which meant, Mageot realised, it was either Pelerain, the lofty second-row man from Perpignan, or the *flic* Jacquot – a big deal in his Marseilles days but sidelined, so Mageot had heard, to some country posting just the year before. Both had been good-looking lads, and either one could be sitting in the driving seat. A postman and a cop. In an old Peugeot. As good as it was likely to get for either of them, Mageot suspected.

But the woman. From his seat in the security room Mageot watched as she closed the car door and looked around her, tall and lean and effortlessly elegant in simple blue jeans and a wrap-around sweater. A little like Madame Dombasle, in fact. But years younger, and raven-haired not blonde. But then Mageot's attention flicked across the car roof to the driver now hauling himself from the driving seat. The ponytail was the first thing Mageot saw and he knew immediately that it was Jacquot, Daniel Jacquot, the sub brought on to replace brave old Jean-Baptiste, the sub who scored one of the greatest tries ever just five minutes later. His first time out, playing for the national squad. And his last.

Daniel-bloody-Jacquot! Still well-built, still fit-looking, Mageot noted. And still that ridiculous bloody ponytail.

Mageot shifted around in his seat and reached for a bottle of water. He unscrewed the cap and took a swig, turning to the other screens – single views of four of the six *cabanes* set through the wooded headland, angled views of the main house itself, and more single views of the garage block, tennis courts, jetty and pools.

Down at the front of the house, he watched Manolo glide down the front steps to greet the new arrivals, a houseboy on each side and one step behind him. He was glad that Manolo and the house staff were seeing to the guests. He wouldn't have wanted the lads to think he was working for Dombasle in any domestic capacity. Security, yes; door-opening and bowing, no. Let Manolo and the boys do the welcome and the luggage and directions. When he made his appearance a little later, there would be no doubt in anyone's mind that Guy Mageot was a lot more than just hired help.

Things had never really gone right for Mageot. When he hung up his boots, after fourteen years playing for his country, there had been a sudden vacuum. He'd tried his hand at commentary but his twangy southern accent had let him down. A bull on the pitch, he was suddenly nervous of the studio lights and the cameras, and stammered and missed his cues. Three matches in the commentary box and that was the end of Mageot's TV career. The next obvious move had been coaching, but all the top clubs were fully manned. Two seasons after his final match, he was hired by the University of Toulouse as Assistant Coach to their first team, but was let go after a stand-up fight with the Director of Sport. He'd been minding the door at a club in Antibes – banging heads and strong-arming drunks – when finally his luck had turned. One night he'd popped out back for a cigarette to find a young woman being assaulted by three sailors from the port. In short order, he'd put two of them in hospital and the third through a shop window. The following night he found out the girl's name when her stepfather called by to thank him for his intervention. Nonie. And Nonie's stepfather was none other than his old skipper.

An hour after shaking his hand and hugging him tight, Dombasle had persuaded him to pack in his job as a nightclub bouncer and start work for SportÉquipe. A week later he had three new suits, a company car and was Dombasle's personal bodyguard. Ten years on he was head of security.

Down in the driveway, Mageot watched Manolo guide Jacquot and his squeeze away from the house and down a path towards one of the *cabanes*, the houseboys scurrying behind with the bags.

Daniel Jacquot, thought Mageot grimly.

Daniel – bloody – Jacquot.

away from work, away from Cavaillon, away from October sadness. Later, having her hair cut in Apt, she'd picked up an old copy of *Regarde Sud* and seen Pierre Dombasle – and his film-star wife – on the front cover. Inside, the lead eight-page feature showed them at their home in Cap Corsaire – its lush airy salons, its landscaped grounds, a dark-marbled infinity pool cantilevered into a cliff and a sea pool that acted as a jetty cut into the rocks of the headland. When Jacquot drove between the lofty white pillars of the estate, she'd thought she would know what to expect. She'd been wrong. The pages in *Regarde Sud* had signally failed to adequately convey the complete and utter splendour of the Dombasle estate.

From the gates down to the drive, the four hairpins cut through stone-walled terraces that followed the line of the coast, planted with groves of olive, fig, aloe and cactus. From the last of the hairpins, a curving drive led another two hundred metres to the house, a cream gravel pathway set between a tightly manicured border of lawn. Beyond this, fenced in by a sentinel line of cypress, their tapered ends shaved to a formal brush cut, loomed a forest of red-barked maritime pine, balooning aleppo and ribboned eucalyptus. And the house . . . Claudine whistled under her breath as she gazed up at its cream, stuccoed grandeur: a flight of blue-runnered stone steps rising grandly to an open loggia, a further two terraced floors above, each terrace shaded by wide matching blue awnings, each with nine shuttered windows, and each corner buttressed by a thin circular tower.

'Some of our other guests are up by the pool,' said Manolo, nodding towards a distant sound of shouts, soft laughter and the splash of water, then stepped through a tunnel of white hibiscus and ushered them across a small tiled terrace and into what looked like an ivied seaside *cabane*.

Inside, Manolo showed them round – floors tiled and laid with rugs, walls bare white stone, its furnishings extravagantly low-key, the large double bedroom set with sliding glass doors which opened on to a small plunge pool. There was no fan, no air-conditioning in the *cabane*, Manolo explained, but in both salon and bedroom one wall was made up of wooden louvres. A dozen floor-to-ceiling mahogany panels – Claudine counted them – each panel set at an angle to catch and direct the slightest breeze, their position controlled electronically using the remote by the sofa or the bed. Manolo showed them how to use it, then handed it to Claudine.

'If you want to join your friends, Monsieur Jacquot, just follow the path,' said Manolo, gesturing to a sloping stand of pine beyond the *cabane*. 'Otherwise, Monsieur Dombasle is looking forward to greeting you all at seven-thirty on the lower-deck terrace.'

Manolo went to the door, waving the houseboys away, then paused and turned back.

'I nearly forgot. In the dresser there is a small welcome gift for each of you from Monsieur Dombasle. He hopes you will enjoy it.'

As the door closed and Manolo's slippers slapped away across the terrace, Jacquot and Claudine looked at each other.

'So who's going to do the honours?' asked Jacquot, glancing at the dresser.

'Me, me, me please. Me please,' and before he could stop her, Claudine was across the room and sliding open the dresser drawer. She pulled out two small square-shaped parcels, examined them, shook them, and then passed one to Jacquot.

'No names,' she said and started unwrapping hers. The ribbon and paper fell away from a wooden box. She flicked the clip and opened the lid. Inside were two columns of gambling chips. And a note: '*Bienvenu à Cap Corsaire*,' it began. 'Here are ten thousand francs to use on the tables which will open in the main salon at 12 p.m. What you lose will be mine. What you win will be yours.' It was signed simply 'Dombasle'.

'Now that's what I call a host,' said a stunned Claudine, running a finger over the chips. 'Can you believe it?'

By this time, Jacquot had opened his own box. The

same two columns of chips. The same signed note. All Jacquot could think of was, a home on the Côte d'Azur that could easily accommodate – what? – thirty people? And ten thousand francs worth of chips for each guest, to play with or simply cash in. He wondered if any of them would do such a thing without laying a bet.

Putting down the box, Jacquot picked up the remote and turned the louvres to their narrowest setting. The room became shadowy as the slats closed.

'Don't you want to go and see your friends?' asked Claudine, watching him, a smile settling across her lips.

'Later,' he said, as though he had more important things on his mind. It turned out he did. 'Right now I can think of nothing I want more than to stay here with you, undress you, marvel at you, make love to you.' Kicking off his shoes and pulling off his T-shirt he crossed the room to her, drew her towards him, felt her body soften to his and the gentle warmth of her lips.

'That's good,' she whispered. 'I'd like that . . .'

8

All three men in her life had been good lovers. At least, Claudine wasn't aware that any of them had been bad. Different, of course, but not bad. Not that she would know. Three men. That's all she'd ever had. Maybe, for all she knew, they were terrible lovers and every other man better than them. And she had been shortchanged and didn't know it. But something told Claudine that this time, with this man, she'd been dealt a special hand. All three men, in their different ways, suited her. But Daniel . . . Daniel Jacquot . . . the new man in her life, sleeping beside her, hair loose on the pillow, arms flung up around his head as though someone had a gun pointed at him, fingers curled over open palms, the hard ridges of his ribs and belly rucked in a tangle of white linen sheets – this man was special.

Even with his eyes closed the web of laugh lines were there and just the faintest ghosts of a crease at the corners of his lips. How many women had he slept with, she wondered? How many lovers had he had? Yet somehow he made her feel that she was the first: the uncertainty as he reached for the ties of her wrap-around sweater; the way his knee pressed between her knees, then withdrew, unsure, only to press home again; the way he led without leading, like a dancer who allows for the occasional hesitancy of someone unused to the dance floor, unfamiliar with the moves and the steps and the flourishes. She tried to think, was there any way he might know she hadn't been with a man for nearly two years? Was there anything she'd said, or done? Or anything he'd picked up in the time they'd been together? That it was eighteen, no, nineteen months since she'd felt the urgent pressing weight of a man on her? She couldn't think. She couldn't remember. And who cared, anyway?

What had begun to surprise her was that she should have fallen in love with him. And that he, she was certain, was falling in love with her. That part she hadn't expected. Not that she was complaining.

She moved quietly away from him and glanced at her watch on the bedside table. A little after six. She'd have to hurry. Sliding from their bed she found the bathroom and closed the door softly.

Jacquot awoke to the sound of a shower. Or rather, the switching off of a shower. It was the sudden stopping of the spatter of water, not the shower itself, that had woken him. For a moment he didn't move, thinking of the rain that morning, tapping on his roof and window on Cours Bournissac. He knew instantly where he was and who he was with and he felt a great lift of pleasure and delight. Two days. Two nights, if she invited him in when he got her back to Cavaillon on Sunday. The longest time they'd spent together. He turned his head and saw where she had lain beside him – the dented pillow, the fall and fold of the sheet – and he thought about her, just next door, silent in the bathroom bar a click and clink, a tap, cleaning her teeth.

Twice married. He knew that. He wasn't a cop for nothing. In the four months they'd been together, he hadn't even needed to ask. He'd just watched and listened.

She'd married young. In her first year at the École des Beaux Arts in Aix, to a law student at the university. Her first real love, Jacquot guessed. His name was Paul but he'd widowed her four or five years later, leaving Claudine to bring up their young daughter.

Later, much later, as far as he could determine, Claudine had married again, her daughter Midou's stepfather a property developer who'd got in early on the Lubéron boom, big bucks to be made from wealthy outsiders who wanted to live the Provençal dream. As far as he could discover, this second husband had played fast and loose for much of their time together. Though he didn't know the man, Jacquot felt a bitter twist of anger at the way she'd been treated, the way her heart had been broken. For it surely had been.

But what did Claudine think of him, Jacquot wondered? He knew she liked him, but somehow that wasn't enough. He wanted her to feel the same as he was already beginning to feel for her. The starter's gun had fired but had he sprinted off too soon, would he be brought back? He rolled over in the bed, to her side, and drew in the smell of her from the sheets and the pillow, like a tracker dog taking the scent of a quarry, burying its nose in the source.

Forty minutes later, arm in arm, they left the *cabane* and set out for the lower terrace, just as Manolo had directed.

'Your suit looks like an old friend,' she said, tugging at his sleeve.

'It belongs to an old friend,' replied Jacquot.

9

They found the lower-deck terrace after a lengthy hike through Dombasle's headland gardens. Unlike a hotel where directions would have been posted at the head of every path, Cap Corsaire offered no such notices. The first path they followed – the one they were certain that Manolo had pointed out – ended at a small two-lounger sun-deck built into the rocks with a view of Cap Ferrat and, ghosting its silhouette, the higher, more distant promontory of Mont Boron.

Retracing their steps, they found another path that led to a circle of raked gravel in a walled enclosure of giant ferns. In the centre was a round pond, its dark waters filled with the gliding shapes of koi carp, gold and ivory and speckled torpedoes slowly circling a mossy statue of the Buddha.

Jacquot and Claudine glanced at one another.

'Makes my garden back home look like a parking lot,' she said.

'You don't have a dozen gardeners.'

'True. And even if I did –' she cocked her head, looked at the combed stones, the carp, the Buddha, at the wall of ferns – 'it's not quite . . .'

'What you mean is, you wouldn't want to paint it.'

She looked at him, surprised. 'You're quite right. Just a little too . . .'

'Perfect?'

'*Exactement*.'

After the Buddha pool they gave up on paths and wandered through the trees, as though they had nothing better to do than stroll together in the twilight, the last of the daylight seeping over a sloping carpet of knotted roots and scattered pine needles.

And then they heard it, a soft susurrus of voices, somewhere to the left and below them. A moment later they came to the edge of the trees and looked down at the sea pool, three of its decked sides levered into the rock, the fourth stepped down to a narrow jetty.

For a moment Jacquot stayed where he was, holding back. There were far more people than he'd expected. For some reason he'd been thinking of the men he'd played with in that match. Fourteen of them, not counting him, and he was surprised to see at least fifty people gathered beside a tented pavilion, white-jacketed waiters and waitresses moving among the black ties and lounge suits and cocktail dresses. Wives, of course, he thought. Or maybe, like Claudine, girlfriends, companions. But from where he stood, on this rise above the pool, at the edge of the treeline, he could make out not a single face or figure he recognised.

And then he heard Claudine whisper in his ear – '*Allons-y, Monsieur Timide*. What are we waiting for?' – and she tucked her arm into his and pulled him forward.

10

'. . . Limousine from the front door to the airport at Pau, then a private jet to Nice, and then – wait for it – not another limo, not a helicopter, no-sireee, just a bloody great yacht – I'm telling you, you wouldn't believe the size of it. Launch tied up at the end of the runway, out to the *Belle Lydie* and we get dropped right there, down on the jetty there . . . *eh, merde alors, c'est pas possible. Mais oui*. Danny! Danny Jacquot, as I live and breathe!'

The man who was speaking looked as tall as a tree, ears rubied and swollen. His jawline appeared to be the widest point on his head, his grey hair was cut short enough to show every bump and depression and scar on his skull, and his drink was clamped in a fist the size of a bunch of pink bananas.

'What on earth has he done to his ears?' whispered

Claudine as the giant strode towards them. Before Jacquot could explain the man-mountain reached them, swung his arms round Jacquot, and lifted him off his feet.

'Well, how long's it been, eh?' he bellowed, kissing Jacquot loudly on both cheeks before putting him down and stepping back to better admire him. 'Looking good, looking good. Still got the ponytail then . . .' The giant pushed a meaty hand across his own greying brush then looked down at Claudine who reached no higher than halfway up his upper arm.

'Ah, and still the girls, eh? Never short, our Danny. Never short in the old days, madame, but he's found himself a princess this time and no debate.'

In an instant her hand disappeared in his meaty paw and he lifted it to his lips, her arm stretched upwards almost as far as it would go. A brush of stubble and wet lips and it was returned to her.

'Who's your friend?' she whispered, as the man-mountain turned to the scrum behind him and announced Jacquot's arrival.

'The Bear. Lou Cabezac – Number Eight . . .' But that was all he had time to say before Cabezac turned, gripped Jacquot by the shoulder, and steered him into the crowd, leaving Claudine to follow behind.

Accepting a Kir royale from a passing waiter and a curried lobster claw from an accompanying waitress,

Claudine spent the next ten minutes following Daniel through the crowd, only to be pounced on by one after another of his old team-mates.

'Peyrot, Antoine Peyrot. Number Two shirt. Hooker . . .'

'Gilles Millet. Right wing. Number Fourteen . . .'

'Jean-Charles Rains. Number Fifteen. *Rains Les Mains*. Full-back. *Enchanté, madame* . . .'

'Valentine Caloux, madame. Val. Outside centre. Number Thirteen. Unlucky for some . . .'

And so it went, each member of the team qualifying his name with the shirt number and position as though somehow it placed him, as though Claudine would know what they were talking about and know immediately the kind of men they were. Of course she didn't, although it didn't take long to work out that the small round ones with no necks and the big, beefy ones like Jacquot probably belonged in the scrum, while the more slender and athletic were probably the ones who did all that running and fancy footwork, all lean and narrow-hipped.

But for all their eager and earnest introductions, their names and numbers and positions, it was immediately clear to Claudine that most of them were more interested in talking to one another, rather than one of their team-mates' partners.

'It's always the same,' said a tall blonde woman in a flower-patterned dress and snappy bolero jacket. She sounded, Claudine thought, a little less than delighted to be there, maybe a little bored, as though she could think of many better ways to spend her time. '*Les veuves de rugby*,' she continued wearily. 'Any more than two men in the room and it's just rugby, rugby, rugby. My name's Maryvonne, by the way. Maryvonne Pelerain. And that's my husband over there, Théo, the big brute with the grey whiskers. Or maybe I should say Second Row, Number Five.' She laughed a brittle little laugh and tipped back the last of her drink. 'So what's your number?' she asked.

Claudine found the woman's tone discomforting, and sensed a certain hostility – not towards herself, but towards the world in general. Also she wasn't quite sure how to respond. Her own name or Jacquot's? She settled for her own.

'Claudine,' she replied. 'Daniel Jacquot. Number . . . Six?'

'Jacquot! The one who scored the try? *Ooh là là.* Is he here?' Maryvonne looked around, craning her neck. 'Does he still have that ponytail?'

'He certainly does.'

'Suits him though, don't you think?' confided Maryvonne. 'Well, you would, I suppose. Being married to him.'

Claudine was about to correct her when another woman joined them and introductions were made. Her name was Nathalie Rains and, apart from some of the waiting staff, she must have been the youngest woman there, more a girl really, schoolgirl-slim but clearly pregnant. She had high-pointed cheekbones, almond eyes and wore very little make-up. A pale blue Alice band held back a fall of fine black hair, and she looked as nervous as a fawn who's lost its mother.

Maryvonne frowned. 'Rains, *Rains les mains*? So you must be wife number two, then?'

Nathalie blinked. 'That's right. Jean-Charles and I were married in February.'

Maryvonne put a hand on Nathalie's arm and leaned forward. 'Well, you're a far sight prettier than the first Madame Rains, I can tell you that, my sweet. And quick off the mark too, by the look of you,' she added.

A waiter passed, a tray of drinks in the palm of his hand. Maryvonne exchanged her empty glass for a full one and took a swig. Dabbing her lips with the linen coaster, she looked at her two companions with a confiding smile. 'At some stage tonight I'm probably going to fall over,' she confessed, 'so I might as well make it as painless as possible.'

As she was speaking Maryvonne's voice rose, the last four words almost shouted as an aircraft suddenly roared overhead no more than fifty metres above them, wing-lights flashing against the starlit night sky, the sound of its engines finally dying away as it disappeared behind the trees. For a moment all conversation halted, then gradually it picked up again, only to falter a few moments later as the sound returned, a growing blast as the aircraft swooped around the headland even lower than before, its curved silvery hull actually touching down on the water and sending up a spraying bow-wave, a set of landing lights below the wings casting racing pools of diamond brightness across the black sea. As its speed lessened, it settled itself into the water and turned towards them, tipping on a side float, props spinning, exhaust fumes belching from its hooded engine cowlings.

'Now that's what I call an entrance,' said someone behind Claudine.

'Who do you suppose it is?' asked another, one of the small round men pushing forward to get a look.

'The skipper, got to be,' came another voice.

Down on the jetty one of the houseboys jumped into a launch and sped out to the aircraft. By the time the launch slid between float and fuselage, the propellors had spun to a stop and a hatch had opened below the wing. Standing in the open doorway, gripping its edges, was a tall, blond-haired man in a white tuxedo. As the houseboy steered in towards him, the man leapt effortlessly on to the bow and stood there as the launch returned to the jetty.

As it closed on the quay the new arrival raised his hands to his mouth and shouted out, 'What's happening here? Who the hell are you lot? And what do you think you're doing on my land?' A metre from the jetty, he leapt from the launch as easily as he'd leapt on to it and hurried up the steps.

Beside Claudine, Maryvonne peered between the shoulders in front of her and shook her head. 'Here we go,' she sighed. 'Always the showman, our Pierre.'

A cheer rose from behind them and someone started clapping.

Claudine, who hadn't the faintest idea what was supposed to be happening – was this some kind of party entertainment? – suddenly recognised the man from *Regarde Sud*. Pierre Dombasle. Coming up to greet his guests.

'Guy. Manolo. We've got trespassers. Should we call the police?' Dombasle trotted up the last few steps and stopped in front of them all, hands on his hips, tall and broad, his face a flattened oval of pock marks, scar tissue and broken bone. 'Ah, no need,' he continued. 'I see one here already. The Number Six shirt. Daniel Jacquot.'

He came up to Jacquot, took his hand in both of his,

shook it warmly, and embraced him like a long-lost brother. 'How wonderful, how wonderful to see you, Danny. And still the ponytail I see.' He looped it affectionately through his fingers, then turned to the crowd, slinging his arm round Jacquot's shoulders. 'So, my old friends. What an extraordinary coincidence. How very good to see you all.'

11

If everyone on the terrace, drinking their Kir royales and whisky sodas and crème de menthe frappées (whatever you wanted, you just had to ask), had imagined that Pierre Dombasle's dramatic appearance at the party could hardly be bettered – his latest acquisition, the 1953 Grumman HU-16 Albatross in which he'd arrived, now floating serenely offshore – they had failed to consider his wife.

No one really knew when the flambeaux leading to the house had been lit. One minute the trees rose above the terrace like a bank of giant red stems, the path between them a canyon of darkening shadows, the next, flames flickered along its edges, and concealed uplighters discreetly illuminated the trees and undergrowth. And then, along its course, a bichon frise clasped in her arm and another, like a fluffy snowball yapping and gambolling around her gold-sandalled feet, came Lydie Dombasle.

Jacquot had just introduced Claudine to a man called Bernard Savry – 'Scrum-half. Number Nine' – the size of a grasshopper and just as agile, according to Jacquot, when a hush fell over the crowd. Someone had heard the yapping dog, looked up, and noticed Lydie, and the whisper had spread. Lydie Dombasle. Lydie Dombasle. Standing there above them. Lydie Plessis as was. Star of *L'Affaire Meysett*, *Donnes-Moi La Folie*, *Les Derniers Après-Midis* and a dozen other French classics. In her time she'd worked with Truffaut and Berri, Malle and Auteuil, Depardieu, Sarti and Demarchemain; she'd been shot, raped and deserted; been a mother, daughter, killer and thief, and picked up a silversmith's shop-window of awards and tributes. But she'd never made it to Hollywood. Never wanted to make it to Hollywood. Lydie Plessis was an icon of French cinema – as familiar as Deneuve, as mysterious as Adjani, as beguiling as Moreau – and French cinema was her home, where she had wanted to stay.

And Claudine, who knew her cinema, actually felt a shiver of excitement when she, too, looked up and saw Lydie standing there. Her hostess for the evening had made her first brief appearance in Sarti's *Voyage Triste* before Claudine was born, and retired forty years later to marry, after a long and scandalous list of legendary screen lovers, the billionaire businessman Pierre Dombasle. Five years on, and closing on sixty, she stood silently on that rise, with the trees arching above her and the flambeaux licking at the fairy-wing drapes of her pearl-grey crêpe de Chine wrap, waiting there until every eye was on her. Strangely amplified by a sea breeze that appeared as if on cue to carry her words to her guests, she spoke in her low, signature fracture of a voice.

'*Mesdames. Messieurs. Mes amis. Le dîner vous attend.*'

Raising her chin, resettling the fluffy cushion of her bichon frise in the crook of an elbow, she beckoned to her husband and he sprang up to her, took her hand, kissed her fingertips, and slid an arm around her waist. Turning back to his guests, he flung up his other arm for them to follow – 'Come on, it's getting cold. Dinner too.'

The house glowed through the trees, as though warm honey was spilling from every window, the tutored, toothbrush lawn spread around it sprinkled with cupped pink camelia petals. As they emerged from the trees it was suddenly clear to the players and their wives that they were not the only guests that the Dombasles had invited.

Standing around the steps leading to the loggia, waiting for them, glasses in hands, sleek, tanned and tuxedoed, were another hundred guests, applauding as the players and their consorts approached. As the Dombasles reached this second knot of guests, Claudine began to recognise faces – Jean-Claude Guilhem, who'd appeared with Lydie in her last film, *Pas Pour Toi;* the old crooner Montrichard, who'd given Aznavour a run for his money; a tall, tanned gentleman, who looked remarkably like the Mayor of Nice; a couple of ministers, who regularly appeared on the evening news; a television anchor-man; and other no doubt equally elevated figures, their wives sheathed in sparkling gowns, teetering on tiptoes so their heels wouldn't sink into the lawn.

Like currents of water the two groups slid together, introductions were made, hands shaken, shoulders clapped, cheeks offered, and then, slowly, like a river turning upstream, the guests moved up the steps to be shown to their tables, fifteen of them spread easily across the open ground-floor loggia, nests of white linen and flickering candles and sprays of mimosa and lavender and sparkling glass and cutlery. At the far end of this loggia a string quartet bowed and leaned behind their stands, not Bach or Handel or Mozart but a medley of rock and pop that sounded appropriately late seventies, the kinds of songs that might have played when the team played.

It was, thought Jacquot, settling Claudine into her chair, a clever touch.

There appeared to be no pre-arranged *placement* – sit where you wish had been the word during drinks on the lower terrace – which pleased Jacquot as much as the crowd that chose the same table: Jacquot's friend and fellow-flanker Olivier Touche and his wife, Sophie; Bernard Savry, on his own; the *conservateur* of the Musée des Arts Provençaux, Charles Rémy, who was soon in deep and delightful conversation with Claudine; Rémy's wife, Josette, in a knotted Guadeloupe turban; the fisherman Sidi Carassin ('Left-wing, Number Eleven'), looking stiff and uncomfortable in a shiny lounge suit but trying to make the most of it, and his wife Mathilde; and Lydie Dombasle's twenty-nine-year-old daughter, Nonie, whose full parentage had exercised gossip columnists since Lydie fell pregnant. And in all that time Lydie had never once named the father, though the young woman's looks, Jacquot decided – her lanky, angular frame, her full lips and droopy eyes – bore a remarkable resemblance to Jean-Claude Guilhem, sitting at the top table with Pierre, Lydie, the Mayor of Nice and others.

As much as the guests at Jacquot's table, it was the seating that complemented the mix. Everyone seemed, as though by design, to be seated in exactly the right place: Claudine with the curator, Charles Rémy, on one side and Olivier, a terrible flirt, on the other; Nonie and Sophie Touche either side of Jacquot, which would have put a smile on any man's face; the curator's wife, Josette, between Sidi Carassin with his beaming smile and twinkling Berber eyes, and Bernard Savry whose bald head appeared almost at a level with the considerable décolletages of Josette Rémy on one side of him, and Mathilde Carassin on the other. It was immediately pointed out by Olivier, who, sitting exactly opposite the three of them, had the best view of what he referred to with a wave of his finger as 'les cinqs seins'. When Bernard realised what Olivier was referring to, he lowered his head sportingly and there were, indeed, five breasts. The cheer was so loud that guests on other tables turned to see what the clamour was about, and Bernard, even more sportingly, repeated the exercise.

Savouring every mouthful of his millefeuille St Jacques almost as much as Nonie's scandalous stories from the catwalk and studio, not to mention Sophie's outrageous indiscretions about celebrated customers at the Touches' restaurant in Gorbio, Jacquot realised with a mix of surprise and delight that he was enjoying himself. Apart from the time he would be spending with Claudine – who also appeared to be having fun – Jacquot had not

of badly secured barrels in his warehouse; while the surgeon Luc Valadier, inside centre and a bull of a man, had been killed in a hit-and-run accident in Paris. Only a few minutes later he'd learned from Bernard Savry that, just three weeks earlier, the lawyer Marc Fastin had argued his last case. Ponytail Two, they used to call him though he was the one who'd first worn his hair in that style.

It was Bernard, Jacquot discovered, who'd written the three obituaries. 'And all in the last seven months,' said Bernard, who was actually following up the latest death with regular reports in the papers.

'Marc and a ladyfriend in an exchange club in Toulouse. His throat'd been cut and his tackle removed. According to the police, it's the ladyfriend did the deed, then kills herself. I tell you, it just doesn't stack up. And with all due respect, Danny, your boys haven't got a fucking clue.'

It was these three names that Pierre Dombasle graciously and movingly eulogised in a short speech he gave as the remains of the millefeuilles were removed from the tables. After introducing all the players one by one, which meant each of them standing to receive a round of applause, Dombasle's voice dropped a notch and slowed as he spoke those three names, recalled some sporting prowess for each, then raised his glass and wished them well on whichever pitch, on whoever's side they were now playing.

'*Et maintenant, mes chers amis*,' he continued, 'after the surf, the turf – a suitable tribute, I am sure you will agree, to our esteemed English opponents, none of whom I saw fit to invite here this evening.'

Over a rousing cheer of delight, the string quartet started up a lively 'Marseillaise' that seemed to signal the arrival of the main course – a silver domed trolley trundled out to each of the fifteen tables, chefs in high, white toques following each one, sharpening their blades on steels.

'*Mes amis*,' Dombasle shouted out from the top table. '*Je vous présente – les rosbifs!*'

As one, fifteen silver domes were whipped away to reveal fifteen broiled, blood-red ribs of beef which the chefs set upon with a flourish of slicing blades.

'Let us do to them now', continued Dombasle over the howl of appreciation from all his guests, 'what we did to them all those years ago . . .'

It was late, sometime around three, when Jacquot and Claudine left the dance-floor and, after cashing in their chips (a thousand francs up on the night) and getting directions from one of the staff, made it back to their *cabane* without losing their way.

'What does it feel like?' asked Claudine, sliding into the bed beside him.

'What does what feel like?' replied Jacquot, grunting softly and turning to her across the pillow. He'd been about to fall asleep. She was still wide awake.

'What does it feel like to know that you could have slept with any of the women there tonight? Any one of them.'

'I'm sorry. I was asleep. What are you saying?'

For a moment Claudine didn't know herself what she was saying, what she was asking. For all its whispered lightness, the gentle tease, this could be dangerous ground. Four months only. Surely it was too soon for such boldness. But she carried on, albeit in a softer tone: 'I said you have a way about you, Daniel. Every woman there tonight . . . they all wanted to talk to you, to touch you, to be with you. If you'd wanted, there wasn't a woman there who wouldn't have—'

But he interrupted her with a patient smile and a sigh and a searching hand. 'There is only one woman I want. Only one woman I'm meant to be with. And that woman, thank God, is lying just centimetres from me. That's all I know. And that, my darling, is all I need to know.'

12

It was the distant sound of a siren that woke Jacquot. A long, blue wailing that seemed to slide into warm, linen dreams. A siren drawing closer, as the dreams faded. Beside him Claudine stirred, but stayed asleep, not as finely attuned as he to that low whooping sound. And what it signalled.

For a second or two he held his breath, confirming first that it really was a siren, and then the direction of the sound. Close enough to be worth investigating. Swinging his legs from the bed, draping the displaced sheet over Claudine's long brown exposed flank, he reached for his clothes. As he pulled on the jeans he'd driven down in the day before, a T-shirt and espadrilles, the siren lost its power and subsided into a slow, trailing whoo-whoo-whoop that sounded no more than a few hundred metres away.

Glancing at his watch – a little before six – Jacquot stepped from the *cabane* and closed the door quietly behind him. The sun had yet to rise above the headlands of Cap Martin and through the trees he could see a long salmon-pink fillet of cloud lining the horizon, a half-dozen slices of golden sunlight slanting through it. For a moment he stood there in the tiled courtyard and tried to decide where the sound had come from. To his left was the gravelled path that curved through the trees to the main house, on the right the path to the pool and terrace, the steely glint of the sea showing through the trees, and ahead a slope of headland that led to the nearest *cabane*, hidden by a walled stand of shifting, creaking bamboo. The house, it had to be the house, he decided, and as if to confirm it, he heard what sounded like a car door slamming shut.

A few minutes later Jacquot stepped out into the turning circle at the front of the house. Parked at the bottom of the steps was an ambulance, its back doors swung open, and a white Peugeot patrol car with its signature blue stripe and crown of lights. As he drew nearer he could hear the squawk and buzz of radios, unanswered, since no one was there to respond.

Jacquot looked around. His first thought was that someone in the house had been taken ill. A heart attack? Food poisoning? Or maybe Nathalie's unborn child had decided to make an early and unexpected appearance. But why the squad car, thought Jacquot? And as he peered into the back of the ambulance – the gurney gone – he heard the front door of the house open and close and footsteps hurry down, gravel crunching when they hit the drive.

Jacquot looked round the rear door of the ambulance. It was Guy Mageot, pulling a sweatshirt over his head, arms flailing to find the sleeves. When his head popped out through the neck of the shirt, his eyes immediately latched on to Jacquot. A look of surprise was followed by an amused acknowledgement that, of all the guests, it should be the policeman nosing around.

'Daniel, *bonjour*. Now why shouldn't I be surprised?'

Jacquot spread his hands. 'Sirens. What can I say? It goes with the job. So what's the trouble?'

Mageot took a deep breath, looked around as though checking that no one was within earshot.

'It's Bernard. Bernard Savry. One of the ground staff found his body this morning. He called me and I called the emergency services.'

'His body? He's dead?' Jacquot was stunned. Just a few hours earlier he'd been talking to the man, laughed with the rest of them when Bernard lowered his head to make the fifth breast.

'Oh yes, he's dead.'

'Jesus . . . Bernard? How?'

'Suicide.'

'Suicide? Why would he want to do that? He was so full of it last night!'

Mageot took a deep breath. 'Your guess, Chief Inspector, is as good as mine.' He gave Jacquot a look, his piggy eyes glinting out from a face that seemed to sink directly into his shoulders. 'I suppose you'll want to take a look?'

'If I can help.'

'Then you might as well come with me, and see for yourself,' said Mageot. 'It's probably nothing that you haven't seen before and you'll know the drill. The garage is this way, through the trees.'

Without any further delay, Mageot crossed to the side of the house and turned down a wood-chip track. 'At the moment,' he said over his shoulder, 'all we've got is an ambulance crew and a gendarme from Beaulieu. I came back to the house to bring in someone a little more senior.'

And possibly someone a little more co-operative? wondered Jacquot. Someone in the local *judiciaire* with a little more *piston* than some night-duty *flic*, someone who could take matters in hand and, with a delicate touch, make sure that the Dombasles and their guests were caused as little inconvenience as possible? Jacquot didn't doubt it for a moment. The last thing a business billionaire like Pierre Dombasle, or indeed his celebrated film-star wife wanted, was a body.

As far as Jacquot could establish, the Dombasles' garage was housed in what looked like a stable block, its flag-stoned yard surrounded on four sides by single-floor wings and accessed through two arched gates. Each of the four wings had four double doors of blue chevroned planking. On one side of the yard three of the double doors were open and, concealed in their shadows, Jacquot caught a glimpse of a wired Bentley grille, the black snout of a Ferrari and the curved wheel arches of a Shelby Cobra. An impressive collection, thought Jacquot, wondering what other cars Pierre Dombasle kept stabled there.

'It's through here,' said Mageot, hurrying across the yard and indicating the second arch. Beyond, parked on a stretch of gravel beneath a palm-thatched canopy roof, were a dozen or more cars. Jacquot saw his own Peugeot and assumed that this was where the guests' cars had been brought following their owners' arrivals the day before. Three cars along from the Peugeot, towards the end of the row, was a blue Audi, its boot lid, rear passenger door and driver's door all open. A couple of paramedics in green reflective waistcoats and red trousers were packing away their gear, and a single gendarme, his képi on the roof of the neighbouring car, was smoking a cigarette. When he saw Mageot and Jacquot come through the arch, he stubbed it out and reached for his cap.

'There was nothing we could do,' said one of the paramedics. 'I'd say he's been gone no more than a couple of hours. We'll move him as soon as we get the OK.'

Mageot nodded. 'Good. We've got someone coming up from the *judiciaire*. I'd be grateful if you could wait. Shouldn't be long now.'

'Do you mind if I take a look?' asked Jacquot, and stepping past Mageot without waiting for an answer, he approached the car. After the sweet resinous morning scents that had greeted him when he stepped out of his *cabane* and the rich red oaky smell of the pathway through the trees, the sinuous shafts of exhaust fumes seemed doubly strong, still lingering in the chill air.

The Audi's engine had been switched off but the length of garden hose coiling round from the car's exhaust to the rear passenger window was still in place, one end sealed into the tail pipe with a plug of what looked like quick-drying fire cement, the other end wadded into the top of the rear window with a length of oily towelling. Jacquot looked into the boot – a plastic oil can, an old map, a twisted length of charging leads, and a squeezed-out tube of fire cement – then moved to the rear passenger window and pulled gently at the material. It didn't give, and Jacquot could see where Bernard's fingers had pushed the towel between window and door frame for a close, sealing fit. It was clear he meant business. He had come prepared.

Wiping the grease from his fingertips, Jacquot moved round the passenger door and knelt down beside the body. Bernard Savry was slumped across the steering wheel, the pale skin on the back of his skull folded into thin pleats, his arms hanging either side of his legs, reaching, ape-like, almost to the floor of the footwell. His head was turned to the front passenger seat where an open and almost empty bottle of brandy had leaked on to the cloth seat. He was wearing what looked like cream-coloured sweats, as though he'd been out for a jog before he fixed the hosepipe, took a swig of the brandy and switched on the engine.

'Well?' said Mageot, when Jacquot rejoined him.

'Who found him?' asked Jacquot. 'You said "ground staff".'

'Hamid, over there.' Mageot nodded to a figure in a white T-shirt and blue dungarees. He was sitting on the ground, leaning against the wall of the stable block. When they'd come through the second arch they must have walked right past him.

'Do you mind if I ask him some questions?' asked Jacquot.

Mageot shrugged. 'Be my guest.'

Jacquot walked along the row of cars, aware that Hamid was watching him. Five metres away, Hamid got to his feet. As he did so, Pierre Dombasle strode through the arch. He was dressed for tennis – a sleeveless jumper over a white open-necked sports shirt, shorts, white socks and tennis shoes.

'Daniel. Is it true?' he asked, coming straight over to him. Lines of anxiety were carved like scars across his forehead.

'I regret to say it is.'

'You're sure? Bernard?'

Jacquot nodded.

'Jesus. That's terrible. Last night he seemed so . . .'

'I know. I know. The life and soul . . .' Jacquot gestured towards Hamid, who was kicking at the dirt with the toe of his shoe, shoulders slumped, hands in his pockets, waiting for Jacquot. 'One of your groundsmen found him. I was just going to ask him a few questions, if that's all right?'

'*Mais bien sûr*, of course,' replied Dombasle. A tiny smile slipped across his lips. 'Once a policeman, always a policeman, *n'est-ce pas*?' Then the smile vanished and the frown returned. 'You go ahead. I'll have a word with Guy.'

Jacquot nodded and the two men parted, Dombasle

heading for the Audi and Jacquot turning towards the gardener.

'You're Hamid, right?'

Hamid nodded. 'That's me.'

'Monsieur Mageot says you found the body?'

'*Oui*. About an hour ago.'

'What's your job here?'

'One of the gardeners. Work on the grounds. Came down to pick up some gear from the shed there' – Hamid nodded to a low stone blockhouse behind the row of parked cars – 'and heard an engine running.'

'And?'

Hamid shrugged, pushed back a tangle of black hair. His deep, dark eyes swept the ground between them. 'Didn't think much of it, to tell the truth. Someone leaving early, warming up the car. I went to the shed, found what I wanted, then came back out.' He nodded to a wheelbarrow and a sack of wood-chips standing close by. 'The motor was still running so I go to take a look. That's when I see the hose, what's happening, you know, and called Monsieur Mageot.'

'You open the car doors?'

Hamid nodded. 'Just the driver's door. Leaned across and switched off the engine, checked the guy, you know? But didn't touch nothing.'

'Where did you call Monsieur Mageot?'

'There's a phone in the garage block. Servicing bay.'

'How long did it take Monsieur Mageot to get here?'

'Pretty quick.'

'What about the back passenger door and the boot lid? Was it Monsieur Mageot who opened them?'

'The back door, *oui*. That was Monsieur Mageot. But the boot lid was open when I got here. Like whoever it was was loading luggage.'

'What about the hose? Does it belong to the house?'

Hamid shook his head. 'We use yellow pipe, monsieur. MagnaLine. It's bigger, stronger.'

'So no green hosepipe?'

'Like I said . . .'

'And fire cement?'

Hamid's mouth turned down. 'No such thing that I know of.'

'OK, thanks,' said Jacquot. And then, as Hamid turned towards the wheelbarrow, '*Dites-moi*, *copain*, you live here, on the property?' He gestured to the stable block.

'Just the head gardener, monsieur. He's the only one. The rest of us, we're down in Eze or Beaulieu. Come up every day.'

Jacquot took this in, nodded, thanked him again and was on his way back towards Mageot, thinking about what he'd found, when a red Suzuki trail-bike came thundering through the arch. Twenty metres ahead, in a plume of swirling dust, the rider drew up beside Dombasle and Mageot, cut the engine, swung off the saddle, and was pulling the bike up on to its stand when Jacquot reached them.

13

Chief Inspector Laurent Murier of the Nice *judiciaire* looked as though he had just stepped off a yacht. He wore mirrored sunglasses on a cord necklace, deck shoes over bare feet and a cobalt-blue sports shirt tucked neatly into a belted pair of shorts. He was tanned and lean, somewhere in his late thirties, Jacquot guessed, and looked more like an off-duty, well-to-do lawyer than a policeman.

'Monsieur Dombasle. A pleasure to meet you, sir. Laurent Murier of the Nice *judiciaire*.' Murier pulled off his sunglasses and the two men shook hands. 'Philippe Corneille asked me to drop by, to see if I could be of assistance. A suicide, he said. One of your guests? Please accept my condolences.'

'Thank you,' said Dombasle. 'Most regrettable. A dear

and old friend. And thank you for coming so swiftly.' With the merest flick of the eyes, he took in the man's clothes and added, 'I hope we haven't interrupted anything?'

'A day's sail. My wife's brother – Charles Rémy, *conservateur* of the Musée des Arts Provençaux? – is going out to Sainte Marguerite. He asked us along.'

'Charles? Charles Rémy?' exclaimed Dombasle. 'But of course, of course. He was here just last night. A fine fellow and a fine sailor too, I hear. Does he still have that beat-up Oyster?'

'Not any more,' replied Murier. 'Which is why he's asked us on board. An Oyster still, but a little more . . . *confortable, n'est-ce pas*?'

'Well, I hope he finds his sea legs. He was partying till late.'

Standing to one side, Jacquot caught Mageot's eye, gave him a look. So this is what you call police procedure Côte d'Azur-style? Mageot clearly knew what Jacquot was thinking, but returned the look with a thin smile as though to say: This is Monsieur Dombasle. How else do you suppose these things are done?

'So,' said Murier, gesturing towards the car, 'would you mind?'

'Of course, please. The poor man's name is Bernard Savry. We had a reunion party last night. As you say, he was a guest. Early this morning, one of my staff found him here, called in the paramedics. It's a most terrible thing.'

Murier went to the Audi, glanced at the hose, stepped around it and bent down to peer at the body. He nodded, sniffed, put his hand to the crumpled skin on Savry's skull as though to reassure himself the man was actually dead and then, as though everything was just as he would expect, he walked back to Dombasle. Sliding on his sunglasses, he glanced across at Mageot and Jacquot.

Dombasle stepped in with the introductions. 'Chief Inspector. This is Guy Mageot, head of my security, and another of my guests from the party last night, Daniel Jacquot. In fact, Chief Inspector Jacquot. The *judiciaire*, it would appear, is well represented.'

Murier shook hands with Mageot and then turned his mirrored lenses on to Jacquot. He did not extend his hand. 'Jacquot? Jacquot? Marseilles, *n'est-ce pas*?'

'*En effet*, Cavaillon. Regional Crime Squad,' replied Jacquot.

'So a little off your beat then, monsieur.' The honorific, Jacquot was quite certain, was deliberate, and the message and smile that went with it luminously clear. My turf, it said, so stay out of my way.

Abruptly he turned to the paramedics. 'You can move the body now. I've seen all I need.'

'You're not calling in Forensics? Surely . . .' Jacquot could not help himself, the words tumbling out of his mouth before he could stop them.

Murier turned back to him, a slow deliberate turn, possibly to give Jacquot time to reflect on the wisdom of his outburst.

'Forensics?'

'It's just—'

'To a suicide?' Murier gave a little grunt of amusement. '*Non*, *non*, *non*, monsieur. I don't think so. A post-mortem, of course, but nothing more. What has happened here, tragic and regrettable though it may be, is, in my opinion, exactly what it appears to be.' He waved his hand to the Audi. 'Monsieur . . . Monsieur . . . ?'

'Savry,' volunteered Mageot with another sly grin for Jacquot.

'Monsieur Savry, *c'est ça*. For me it is quite clear that Monsieur Savry has taken his own life. For whatever reason.'

'But there's no note . . .'

Murier sighed. 'As is so often the case in circumstances such as these, monsieur. Not everyone feels an urge to explain or apologise.'

By now the paramedics had wheeled their gurney to the Audi and were manoeuvring the body from behind the steering wheel. It was not an easy job. A black body bag was unzipped, the small, bent body cradled within it and the zip pulled up with a jerking, bee-buzzing sound. Jacquot watched the paramedics hoist the bag on to the gurney, and strap it down.

As they wheeled it away, Murier turned to Dombasle. 'Monsieur. May I ask how many guests you have staying here at Cap Corsaire?'

'Twenty-five – not counting . . . poor Bernard.'

'And staff? Resident staff?'

'Four in the house. Another two above the garages. The groundsmen and other house staff come in.'

Murier took this in, seemed to think about it, then turned to Mageot. 'And who found the body?'

'One of the groundsmen. The fellow over there.' Mageot nodded to Hamid. 'He called me up and I came right down. It was immediately clear there was nothing we could do.'

Again Murrier nodded.

'Was Monsieur Savry alone? Is he with anyone? A wife? A companion?'

Dombasle shook his head. 'Bernard was not married. He came by himself. Maybe you have heard of him. Bernard Savry. The sports writer?'

Murier shook his head. 'Not unless he writes about sailing.'

Dombasle and Mageot chuckled; Murier gave a smug little grin. For all the world they could have been having a chat at a cocktail party. Jacquot could hardly believe what he was seeing and hearing. Or rather he could. He'd seen it often enough and knew only too well that homicides were often put down to suicide by an overworked, understaffed *judiciaire*.

'Do you happen to know his next of kin?' asked Murier. 'Parents? Maybe children?'

Dombasle shook his head. 'As I said, he wasn't married. I have a home address, of course, but for anything else I suggest you contact *Monde Sportif*, the magazine he writes for. Or his publisher? Or agent?'

'Do you happen to have any names?'

'Gauchon Fils is the publisher. I'm afraid I don't have names for his editor or agent,' replied Dombasle.

Murier nodded, then glanced at his watch. Dombasle noticed the look and took his cue.

'So, Chief Inspector. Thank you for coming out so promptly on a weekend, and for handling all this . . .' Dombasle waved his hands, '. . . this matter so . . . sensitively.'

'Monsieur. The very least we could do.'

The two men shook hands. 'And I trust we haven't held you up? Your brother-in-law . . . Sainte Marguerite . . . ?' continued Dombasle.

'So long as I make it by—' Murier glanced at his watch again, as though for the first time. '*Dieu*, I must hurry. I hope you will excuse me, monsieur.' And with a final nod and smile he walked over to his bike.

By the time Jacquot reached him, Murier had swung himself on to the saddle, started up the bike and kicked away the stand. As Jacquot approached, Murier gave the throttle a threatening twist. He held it until Jacquot reached him, then released it.

'Monsieur?'

'Is that it?' asked Jacquot, keeping his voice as low as he could over the sound of the engine.

Murier frowned. 'I'm sorry?'

'Is that all there is? All you're going to do?'

'What else, monsieur? It is a suicide. It can be nothing else.'

'You're telling me you think this is a suicide?'

'What exactly are you trying to say?'

Jacquot cast around, then fastened his eyes on Murier. It was time to dispense with official courtesies and meaningless pleasantries. 'Are you blind? Didn't you see his hands?'

14

Jacquot was trying his best, but Claudine could see that something was bothering him.

'You were up early,' she began, pouring him a coffee. In his absence she'd showered, her hair slick to the shoulders, the collar of her gown drawn up. She was sitting outside their *cabane* at a laden breakfast table brought down from the house. Jacquot was slumped in a recliner, away from the table, brooding. She stood and brought the coffee over to him. 'There's fruit, yoghurt, some ham, scrambled eggs, croissants and baguettes. I ordered for the two of us.'

'Just coffee will do fine,' replied Jacquot, taking the cup and leaving her with the saucer. He sipped the coffee and put the cup down on the table beside his recliner.

Claudine went back to her seat and, wrapping her

gown around her legs, settled herself. She broke off a piece of crusty, warm baguette, buttered it, spooned on a smear of *abricot* and took a bite. Something told her that she should wait, not push him. Whatever was bothering him, she suspected, he would tell her soon enough. Just so long as it had nothing to do with her.

Clasping his hands behind his head, Jacquot sighed. 'You remember the man with the bald head? Bernard Savry, the one at our table?'

'Number Eight? Full centre?'

'Number nine. Scrum-half.'

'The sports writer.'

'That's the one.'

Claudine waited for more but nothing was forthcoming. 'And? What about him?' she asked at last. 'I like him. He's funny.'

Jacquot reached for his coffee, sipped it again, then cupped it in his hands as though to warm them. 'Well, I'm sorry to tell you that he's dead.'

It took a moment for Claudine to register what Jacquot had said. 'He's dead? You're joking?'

Jacquot shook his head. 'I'm afraid not. One of Dombasle's gardeners found his body earlier this morning. In his car. A hosepipe in the exhaust.'

'He killed himself? Suicide? Oh no . . .'

'No, indeed.'

Claudine caught Jacquot's tone, frowned. 'I don't understand. You said—'

'I said he was dead. I didn't say he committed suicide.'

'But he was in his car. A hosepipe, that's what you said. The exhaust . . .'

'That's right. That's how he died. But he didn't do it himself.'

Claudine put down her baguette, looked across at him. 'You sound very sure, Daniel.'

'I am very sure. Very sure indeed.'

'So what makes you so certain?'

'His hands.'

'His hands? What . . . ? They were tied?'

Jacquot gave her a big smile and grunted. 'They were clean.'

'How do you mean, they were clean? *Je comprends pas*.'

'One end of the hose had been plugged into the exhaust with fire cement – to keep it in place, so it wouldn't work loose. The other end was wadded into the gap in the window with an oily rag – like a towel, like a mechanic's rag, you know? Something you'd find in the boot of a car. To seal it tight. I touched it, pulled at it. And it made my fingers greasy, dirty.' Jacquot held up a hand and Claudine could see a shadow of black on his fingertips.

'And?'

'As I said, Bernard's hands, his fingers, the fingertips, none of them showed any trace of grease or oil. Or the cement worked into the exhaust.'

Claudine frowned. 'He could have wiped his hands on his clothes.'

'Yes, he could have. In which case I would have seen marks, *n'est-ce pas*?'

'Not necessarily. I mean, if he was in his suit from last night . . .'

'He was wearing cream-coloured jogging trousers and a white sweatshirt. No sign of oil, or grease, or cement. Nothing.'

'The car upholstery?'

'Cream again.'

'Grass?'

'There was no grass. The car's parked on gravel. And anyway, if you're about to commit suicide, are you seriously going to worry about cleaning your hands?'

Claudine fell silent. Jacquot watched her. He could see she was thinking it through, coming soon to the same conclusion he had reached as he left Dombasle and Mageot at the stable block and walked back to the *cabane*.

'If what you're saying is true . . .'

'It is.'

'Then, that means . . . that means there's a murderer here. Among the guests. Or staff.'

'Not necessarily,' said Jacquot. 'Someone could have come on to the property. A thief, burglar. Maybe Bernard, out for his morning jog, surprised them. Maybe there was a fight. Maybe the burglar killed Bernard. Or maybe, in the struggle, Bernard had a heart attack. These things happen. And to conceal the crime the attacker made it look like a suicide. No investigation. Easy. Off the hook.'

'Or it could be one of the guests? Or staff,' Claudine persisted.

'It could indeed,' agreed Jacquot, finishing his coffee and putting the cup on the table.

'So what are you going to do? Are you the one handling the case?'

Jacquot smiled and shook his head. 'I'm afraid not. This is outside my jurisdiction. A Chief Inspector Murier from Nice has already called by. Seen the body, the car. And confirmed a suicide. If he's not too busy, I'm sure he'll have someone contact the next of kin . . .'

'But won't he want to speak to us? The guests? Find out what we were doing last night. Where we were. Ask what kind of mood Bernard was in. If we suspected anything . . .'

'If this was TV, he would certainly do that.'

'Did you tell this Murier about the hands?'

'Of course I did. But he chose not to listen. This is his turf, remember. Not mine.'

'But that's terrible.'

'For the police, a suicide is often easier to deal with than a homicide.'

'That's even more terrible.'

'It's also, *ma chérie*, a fact of life.'

Despite her dismay at Savry's death, and her horror at what she considered a shocking miscarriage of justice, Jacquot's 'my darling' warmed her.

'You have to remember', Jacquot continued, 'that our host, Monsieur Dombasle, is a very wealthy, very powerful man. With important friends. You saw some of them last night. Also, his wife is a very famous actress. It would not do to cause such people any inconvenience. Or embarrassment. And Chief Inspector Murier knows that.'

'So he's turning a blind eye?'

'That is exactly what he is going to do. As I said, it is the reputation and the convenience of people like Dombasle and his wife, and his other guests here last night, set against the life of a sports writer. *En effet*, a journalist. And Murier knows what's expected of him. If he doesn't want his superior howling down the phone, or if he's not looking to get a swift transfer to Cavaillon, he'll play the game and swear suicide.'

'Does Pierre know about this? About the clean hands? That Bernard didn't kill himself?'

'It doesn't matter any more. As far as the authorities are concerned, the matter is closed. *Enfin* . . .' Jacquot spread his hands.

'Closed? How can it be closed? If you suspect—'

'Know . . . I don't suspect. I know.'

'So what are you going to do about it? You can't just let a murderer go free.'

'I don't intend to, *chérie*.' He reached for his cup, held it out. 'Some more coffee?'

15

Up at the house, Jacquot found Antoine Peyrot, Olivier Touche and Jean-Charles Rains on the loggia. Just a few hours earlier, a hundred and fifty people had sat here for dinner; now there was nothing to indicate that the party had ever happened. The fifteen tables from the night before, along with the tree ferns and flambeaux, had been cleared away, the awnings drawn back, and the tiled loggia floor had been swept and polished, a slight astringent citrus scent in the air. Antoine and Olivier were sitting at a single long breakfast table, and Jean-Charles was helping himself to toast and scrambled eggs from the buffet.

'You hear?' asked Peyrot, legs sprawled out in front of him, as Jacquot joined them.

'I heard,' said Jacquot.

'What a mess,' continued Peyrot. 'What a terrible, terrible waste.'

'Such a fantastic player,' said Olivier, shaking his head. 'Seventy-three caps. Slippery as oiled grapes. *Quelle tragédie*.'

'A good writer too,' added Rains, coming back to the table, setting down his eggs and pulling back a chair. A waiter came on to the loggia with a pot of fresh coffee. Jacquot said no, but the other three took refills. While the waiter poured, they remained silent. 'You ever read any of his stuff?' Rains asked after the waiter withdrew 'Just . . . beautiful.'

'Rugby?' asked Olivier.

'Any sport. He'd do an interview, a feature – golf, boxing, football, whatever – and he'd just drag you in. You'd be there, wherever it was – on the seventeenth hole in Augusta, at Longchamps, for a penalty shoot-out at L'Olympique, in a Tour de France chase-car . . . Jesus, he could write.'

'Where was he staying?' asked Jacquot lightly. 'Here in the house?'

'Not here,' Olivier replied.

'He had a *cabane* somewhere over there,' said Peyrot, waving his hand towards the drive. 'That's the last time I saw him. Staggering back to his pit.'

'He was drunk?'

'Who wasn't?' chuckled Rains. 'And he was just a little fellow, remember. Not much bigger than a jockey. It wouldn't have taken much.'

The four men fell silent, contemplating Savry's demise.

Rains broke the silence. 'I remember we had a sailor on the *Sainte-Agathe* one time. We'd been on manoeuvres in the South Pacific, a few years back now, and were heading for Noumea. We'd been at sea maybe a couple of weeks, and the crew couldn't wait to get ashore. If you've been to Noumea, you'll understand why. Anyway, the night before we docked, this lad just strung himself up from the barrel of a 100mm anti-aircraft gun and jumped over the side.' Rains shook his head. 'Good-looking kid. Popular, too. A real joker. Everything to live for. But something made him knot that rope round his neck and climb the rail. I've never been able to understand it. Suicide. It just doesn't make sense.'

Jacquot nodded but said nothing.

'Then you've lived a lucky life,' said Peyrot. 'Never been down there where the black dogs snap at your heels. Maybe that's where Bernard was, and none of us knew it. Maybe he'd lost his job, or he'd been diagnosed with some killer disease, or a girlfriend'd left him. Sometimes all it takes—'

'He was gay,' said Olivier quietly. 'There wouldn't have been a girlfriend. Never was.'

'Gay? Savry?'

Olivier looked surprised. 'You didn't know?'

'How? How could I know that?' asked Peyrot, clearly shocked by the news. 'How do you know?'

'He told me,' replied Olivier, sipping his coffee. 'Years ago. It was no secret.'

Jacquot watched Peyrot's shocked expression turn slowly to disgust, falling like a shadow over his face.

'Shit!'

'I didn't know either,' Rains added. 'He seemed—'

'He played rugby,' said Olivier with a wry smile. 'Who'd expect a rugby player to be gay?'

Just then, from the front of the house, came the sound of footsteps on gravel. Jacquot peered over the balustrade and spotted Guy Mageot crossing towards the garden terrace where the night before a Calypso band had played Rasta-style covers.

'Back in minute,' said Jacquot and, pushing back his chair, he got to his feet and headed for the steps. Down on the gravel he called out to Mageot who turned and waited for him.

'*Tout va bien*, Daniel? Everything OK?'

'Fine, fine,' said Jacquot. 'I just wondered . . . there's a security camera in the corner of the loggia looking over the garden.'

'That's right,' said Mageot, lightly fingering a swollen,

bunched ear. 'We have cameras all over. It doesn't pay to take chances.'

'Is there a camera down by the cars?'

Mageot gave him a long dark look, pursed his lips as though he was considering the implication of Jacquot's questions, and the answer he should give. 'In the garage block there are two cameras – where the skipper keeps some very valuable and precious automobiles – but nothing outside the courtyard. Nothing where Bernard's car was parked.'

'What about the drive?' asked Jacquot.

'We have a camera at the gates, a couple on the terraces, one right behind you' – he nodded to a discreetly placed camera by the front door that Jacquot hadn't seen – 'and that's it.'

'You've run the tapes, of course?'

Mageot smiled. 'Of course,' he replied, glancing at his watch. 'For the last forty-seven minutes. While you were having breakfast.'

'And there was nothing?'

'Nothing beyond Savry weaving his way down to his *cabane*.'

'About what time was that?'

'Just after three.'

'Odd that he should consider a jog when he was "weaving"?'

Mageot's eyes hardened. 'Who said he was jogging?'

'Well, what he was wearing, for starters. The sweats, the trainers.'

'Evening dress can be an uncomfortable uniform. Maybe he got to his *cabane* and changed into something more comfortable.'

'At three in the morning? Drunk?'

Mageot sighed. 'Daniel. I know what you're thinking . . .'

'What am I thinking?'

'You're a policeman. There's a body. It would be remiss if you didn't cover all the points.'

'Unlike your Chief Inspector Murier, you mean.'

'Murier is a good man,' said Mageot a little too swiftly, a little too sharply. 'He may appear a little laid-back, I grant you. But I've heard he's highly thought of. What, do you suppose he's going to call by in full dress uniform? It is a Sunday, after all. The weekend. He's going sailing.'

Jacquot was about to continue when a walkie-talkie, attached to Mageot's belt, squawked. Mageot held up a hand to Jacquot and switched on the receiver. He listened a moment, glanced at Jacquot and said, '*Immédiatement*.'

Slipping the walkie-talkie back on to his belt, he turned to Jacquot. 'If it's OK with you, the skipper would like a word. I'll show you the way.'

somewhere near sixty paintings in all. Jacquot was no expert, but he recognised quite a number of them – a wild blue Dufy promenade, a rose Signac sunset, a speckled Derain, and what looked like a fractured Vilotte beach scene.

At the double doors, Mageot lifted his hand to knock, then paused. In a low voice he said, the hand still raised, 'It's sorted, Daniel. OK? Right now we don't want the skipper to be caused any headaches. So why don't you just leave it be?'

Before Jacquot could reply, Mageot rapped the frame of the door with big meaty knuckles, leaned forward to open it, and stepped aside for Jacquot to enter, leaving just enough space for him to avoid squeezing past.

Dombasle's study was long and high-ceilinged, one in a line of four fans gently stirring the air, the walls to left and right decorated with sporting memorabilia – trophy chests, team photos, a still-muddy blue shirt with the gold *coq* insignia framed and spotlit, a pair of boots in one square glass case and the cast bronze equivalent in a second. And there, at the end of the room, behind a glass and chrome desk, stood Pierre Dombasle himself, still in his tennis kit. He was on the phone, his back to Jacquot, his eyes fixed on the view beyond the house.

Behind him Jacquot heard the door close and he started forward, a good twenty paces, to reach Dombasle's desk. As Jacquot drew closer the view from the study came properly into focus. Beyond sliding glass doors and a balustraded terrace a broad boulevard of lawn stretched away between the red-barked pines like a tapered green candle to the sea. Over its shadowed cobalt depths and milky emerald surface, white sails bent to the wind, a speedboat chalked a line that faded into a sun-glistening wake and in the far distance a container ship shivered on the horizon. Green grass, red tree trunks, and numerous shades of blue between sea and sky. The colours were extraordinary. Vibrant.

As Jacquot took in the view, Dombasle turned, smiled, held up a hand. Through the glass surface of the desk, Jacquot could see that he was barefoot, his toes curling and uncurling on the tiled floor. It was a strangely intimate observation and reminded Jacquot, for some absurd reason, of the team changing room: the rich, truffley smell of sweating bodies and sodden kit, with Dombasle conducting a half-time pep talk – eyes on fire, pounding one fist into the other, snarling encouragement or insults at his team.

And then, giving Jacquot a jolt of surprise, Dombasle began speaking. In Russian.

'*Ya znayu, ya znayu*. It's a ridiculous price.' He laughed lightly, waved his hand, rocked back on his heels. 'But he said he'd pay it. And I'm taking him at his word. Can you arrange delivery? I'd be very grateful. You're a true and good friend, Nikolai, *spasibo*, *spasibo*. See you on the twelfth. And please give my love to Katya. Bye now. *Poka!*'

'The Russians,' said Dombasle, putting down the phone. 'They have been on the Côte d'Azur since the eighteenth century. We lost them for a bit, of course, but they're coming back. They're coming back. And in a big way, you mark my words.' He gestured to the terrace and indicated that Jacquot should follow him. 'Did you know that the last Czar actually visited this estate? In 1909, when the headland here was still a defensive position.'

The two men settled themselves in a pair of rattan armchairs and Dombasle chattered on. 'Napoleon was the first to use this site, you know? And over the years the military added to it. Until twenty years ago, there was a naval platoon here – coastal defence, keeping watch. Would you believe it? *Incroyable. C'est à dire, absolument incroyable.*' Dombasle chuckled at the absurdity of such a thing. 'When they realised there wasn't much to watch beside pleasure boats, water-skiers and topless bathers, the place was put up for tender as a real estate development.' Dombasle's voice lowered a notch, the tone conspiratorial. 'I was fortunate enough to secure the deeds.' A strong, satisfied smile was directed in Jacquot's direction. 'The military? *Boufff!*' continued Dombasle.

'They might know how to fire guns but they don't know shit about property. Anyway, enough of that. So, what did you think of the entertainment last night? And the *rosbif*? A nice touch, I thought. And, of course, you are comfortable? You and your wife? Your *cabane* was once an ordnance store. You'd never know it now, would you?'

And then, for the first time since he put down the phone, Dombasle suddenly fell silent. As though he could think of nothing more to say – every possible subject exhausted. It had been a stream of idle chat – deflecting, disarming – but Jacquot had known there'd be something to follow it.

There was.

With a clearing of the throat, Dombasle set to: 'I was talking to Chief Inspector Murier . . .'

Jacquot nodded.

'He called from the port . . .'

Jacquot smiled.

'It seems there was possibly a misunderstanding. Between the two of you?'

'No,' replied Jacquot. 'Not "possibly". There was, very definitely, a misunderstanding.'

'Apparently you think that Bernard's death was not suicide?' Dombasle's tone suggested that such a possibility was as absurd an idea as coastal defence on the Côte d'Azur.

For a moment, Jacquot felt just the tiniest whisper of intimidation, sitting there in front of his old skipper. But it was nothing more than that. He held his ground. 'That's correct,' he replied. 'Bernard Savry did not take his own life.'

Dombasle frowned. 'And what makes you so certain, Daniel, when Chief Inspector Murier . . . ?'

For the third time that morning, Jacquot explained about Bernard's hands. 'They were clean. They should have been dirty. He couldn't have blocked the exhaust or wedged that cloth into the rear passenger window without dirtying his hands. Someone did it for him. As simple as that.'

'So you think someone lured him to his car, made him sit at the wheel, connected a hose to the exhaust pipe, sealed the back window, then switched on the engine and asked him to sit there until he died?'

Dombasle's voice was low and disbelieving, a skipper's voice, quizzing one of his players about a dubious move, a costly error.

Jacquot noted it, but paid not the slightest heed. 'I don't know how he got there yet. As far as I could see there appeared to be no wounds, but I'm still certain – *absolument* – that Bernard was either dead or unconscious when he was put behind the wheel of that car.'

'By the killer?'

Jacquot nodded.

'Here at Cap Corsaire?'

For a split second Jacquot knew what it must have been like to be that player, trying to explain how he'd failed to make a tackle or given away a penalty beneath the posts, waiting for the skipper to give him a piece of his mind.

Which Dombasle proceeded to do.

'I'm going to tell you a story,' began Dombasle, steepling his fingers and tapping them against his chin. He glanced at Jacquot. The way he locked his eyes on to Jacquot's made it immediately plain that the 'story' was to remain confidential. 'Last year Bernard Savry got in touch with me. He said he wanted to write my biography. About my sporting past and my subsequent success in the world of business. The takeovers, the gambles . . . that sort of thing.' Unsteepling his fingers, Dombasle waved his hands modestly then placed them on the arms of the chair, resettled himself, crossed his legs, a bare foot swinging to some unheard melody. Jacquot had seen the same move countless times in countless police interview rooms. He always read it as nervousness – guilt or innocence yet to be established, but nervousness, for whatever reason, all the same.

'He told me that mine was an inspirational story,' continued Dombasle, 'and that his agent was very excited about it and had already approached a publisher who, as these things go, was also very excited about it. As far as Bernard was concerned, it was a done deal. I would agree. Old team-mates and so forth. All he needed was the go-ahead, the green light from me. All that remained, as far as he was concerned, was finalising terms. Percentages etc.'

'And you told him "no"?'

'That's right. Absolutely. I did.'

'For what reason, might I ask?'

Dombasle gave Jacquot a look. 'Don't get me wrong, Daniel. I liked Bernard. He was a great player. If you dropped a ball he passed to you it wasn't because his pass was bad. You know that as well as I. No one faster, and no one tougher. Didn't matter how big they were, he went at them. If he could latch on to a leg or an arm or a scrap of shirt, you'd never shake him loose . . . and after the playing, he turned out to be a very popular writer. A real talent . . .'

'So why did you say "no"?'

'Have you ever read any of his stuff? In *Monde Sportif*? In the papers? He likes to dig the dirt. Which is probably why he's so popular.'

'And you have dirt to dig up?'

Dombasle smiled a weary smile. 'Doesn't everyone?'

Jacquot spread his hands, but made no comment.

Dombasle continued, his voice dropping again; a

confessional tone: 'As you may know, I was married before Lydie. Maybe you remember her? Annette?'

Jacquot shook his head.

'After your time, then. I met her in South Africa. On tour. It was her father who got me started, loaned me the money I needed.' Dombasle looked down into the garden.

'And?'

'She was a drunk, Daniel. A terrible, terrible drunk. Alcoholic.'

'Did Bernard know that?'

'If he didn't, he'd have certainly found out. She, too, committed suicide. In a car. Just like him.'

Jacquot felt a jolt at the coincidence. 'Do the police know that? That that was how your first wife died? Chief Inspector Murier, for instance?' It seemed a long shot, but . . .

Dombasle gave him a look. 'You surely don't think there's some connection?'

'Or are you saying that Bernard was trying to make a point? That you were responsible for what he was going to do? That you had driven him to suicide? That he had chosen this method to remind you. To make you feel guilty.'

Dombasle shook his head. 'I don't pretend to know what Bernard was thinking. But I do know he was desperate.'

'Desperate how?'

'Two months ago, he contacted me, asked me to reconsider. I told him my position hadn't changed and we had words. Or rather, he did. He was not pleased. Afterwards, I was certain he would stay away from the reunion, just to make a point.' Dombasle smiled. 'So I was surprised when I saw him on the terrace last night. And he was charming. As if we'd never had that conversation. Even joked that the Graumann landing on the water, the reunion, would have made a great opening scene for the book. He still wouldn't let it go.'

'But you made it plain that this was not going to happen. Ever.'

'*C'est ça, exacte.* After dinner.'

'And you think that's why he committed suicide?'

'Not just because of the book, no. A combination of things. After that telephone conversation, I had Guy check him out. Bank, credit cards – the usual sources. And he was broke. Or as good as. He'd also been sacked from *Monde Sportif*. Been given notice.' Dombasle shrugged. 'It appeared our good friend was on his uppers.'

'So you believe he had cause? And why not make a point of it, while he's about it?'

Dombasle nodded. 'That is how I read it.' He might have been commenting on a passage of play.

'Well, it may appear that that's the case, and that Bernard had good reason to consider suicide. But that doesn't alter the fact that someone killed him.'

'Mmmmh,' was all Dombasle said, nodding his head as though accepting that Jacquot was entitled to his opinion, of course, but that he, Pierre Dombasle, remained unconvinced, unmoved by Jacquot's certainty.

'So what do you intend to do, Daniel?' he asked at last.

'Everything I can.'

And then the most extraordinary thing happened. A seagull landed on the balustrade no more than a metre or two behind Dombasle's chair. But rather than fly off when it spotted the two men, it ruffled its wings, stretched its neck and made itself comfortable, settling a beady, contemplative yellow eye on Dombasle. Without bothering to turn, Dombasle simply waved his hand over his shoulder as though dismissing a member of staff. The bird tensed and sprang, gone with a squawk and a clatter of wings.

As he lowered his hand, Dombasle's eyes latched on to his watch. The next instant he sprang to his feet.

'*Merde*, I didn't realise the time. The team photo. You haven't forgotten?'

17

There was a crowd on the loggia and around the front steps – Jacquot's team-mates, their wives, and two houseboys with trays of drinks and canapés. Out on the sweep of gravel drive, a photographer had set up his tripod and Hasselblad. Though there was no real need for it, a beach parasol had been erected to provide some shade, and an assistant crouched among a nest of aluminium cases. On the lawn behind them, Olivier Touche threw a rugby ball at Jean-Charles Rains. The old full-back caught it cleanly, elbows up, ball clasped to his chest, and dug in his right heel. 'Mark!' he cried and with a laugh he tossed it back to Olivier.

Nodding and smiling, trying to recall the last time he had picked up a rugby ball, Jacquot pushed his way across the terrace until he reached the top step and caught sight of Claudine coming up the path from their *cabane*. His breath caught in his throat. She looked radiant – a sleeveless cream dress, a light blue cardigan draped over her shoulders, flat cream shoes – the soft pastels bringing out her colour – lustrous dark hair in waves to her shoulder, bare brown legs, arms folded in front of her.

Over on the lawn, Olivier spotted her and shouted her name. Jacquot saw her look up, to the left, and then he saw the ball in Olivier's hand, back behind his shoulder, and knew what would happen next.

When he had her attention, Olivier launched the ball through the air, a twenty-metre throw, fast and high, no quarter, the ball spinning in an arc between them. And without breaking step, Claudine reached out a hand and swept the ball into the crook of her elbow.

'C'est ça? C'est tout? Le rugby?' she called out, almost mockingly.

Beside Jacquot, Lou Cabezac, Paul Druart and Théo Pelerain clapped appreciatively, and Sidi Carassin and Maryvonne hooted and cheered.

Out on the path it looked for a moment as though Claudine was thinking of kicking it back.

Please don't try to kick it, thought Jacquot. *Leave it at that catch. You'll only make a fool . . .*

But Claudine didn't kick it.

Instead, holding on to the shoulder of her cardigan with one hand, she leaned back, ball balanced in the other . . .

Please don't throw it . . . Please don't try to pass it . . .

. . . And threw it back at Olivier . . .

Jacquot winced, looked away, then saw Simon Talaud, the butcher, put two meaty forefingers in his mouth and let out a piercing whistle of approval. Jacquot looked back in time to see the ball spin through the air, just as straight and high and fast as Olivier's, and drop cleanly into his waiting arms – hardly a step to retrieve it, scoop it up. Except it seemed that Olivier had misjudged the speed and accuracy of Claudine's throw. He seemed to totter, wrong-footed, fumble for the ball, then drop it and trip over his ankles. He landed heavily and the ball trickled away from him.

There was a roar of delight from the terrace, and feet stamped. Out on the lawn Olivier shook his head and Claudine curtsied to her fans with a low sweep, one ankle behind the other. In an instant, Jacquot felt the fiercest surge of pride he'd ever felt for anyone in his life, man or woman. A moment or two later, she came up the steps, saw Jacquot and came over to him. He slipped a hand round her waist and drew her to him, smelt the soft warm scent of her. She looked so beautiful, he couldn't quite think what to say.

'You didn't tell me you played,' he managed.

'You didn't ask,' she replied and smoothed the palm of her hand down his cheek.

If there'd been no thought given to *placement* at dinner the night before, it was abundantly clear that Dombasle had given the seating plan for the team's reunion photo the most minute consideration.

Eight chairs had been set out on the gravel at the bottom of the front steps. Standing with his back to the photographer, tossing an inscribed rugby ball from hand to hand, Dombasle shouted out names as though he was selecting a team which, Jacquot reflected, was exactly what he was doing. It wouldn't have surprised him if Dombasle had shouted out their numbers too.

'Valentine . . . far right, front, *s'il vous plaît*.'

'Antoine . . . next to him, please.'

'And Gilles . . . there.'

Caloux, Peyrot and Millet took their places as instructed and got themselves comfortable.

'Olivier . . . Olivier? Touche, where the hell . . . get over here,' called Dombasle, waving Olivier to his place. Olivier loped over with the ball in his hand, to a chorus of boos and catcalls at his shameful performance with Claudine.

In just a few precise, ordered moments, before he took his own seat between Olivier and Claude Lorraine in the middle of the front row, Dombasle had everyone where he wanted them, Cabezac, the tallest man on the team, standing directly behind him.

But if Dombasle, checking that the writing on the rugby ball he held in his lap was properly lined up, professed himself satisfied with this arrangement, the photographer clearly was not.

After checking his viewfinder and asking them all to move a little closer, he pointed to where Jacquot and Sidi Carassin stood in the back row. With only a single cap to his name – at least twenty caps less than anyone else in the team – Jacquot had been placed on the far left of the back row, while Carassin's forty-eight caps ensured a position closer to the heart of the team.

Except the photographer didn't see it like that.

'You, monsieur, the one at the back there . . . with the hair.'

Jacquot straightened, looked expectant, and heard Caloux at the far end of the front row chuckling, presumably at the hair reference. But there was no time to speculate.

'If you could just change places with the man on your left, monsieur? The coloured gentleman, that's right . . .'

With a quick shuffle Jacquot and Sidi swapped places so that Sidi was now on the outside. As the photographer bent down to his viewfinder once more, reaching for the button cable, both men knew why the change had been made. In terms of symmetry, the reunion team photo would have been thrown out of kilter with Sidi standing between Jacquot and the equally tall Talaud. The heights of the players in the back row always rose from the outside. With Jacquot nearly a foot taller, Sidi was the natural choice for end man.

'And please, messieurs, if I could ask you to fold your arms in front of you . . . *Bon. C'est ça, et . . .*'

As though to draw their eyes, the photographer held up his hand, thumb poised to press down on the button cable. The team held their breath, the breeze dropped, the cicadas seem to soften their static buzz and . . .

. . . Click.

It was over. The players started to disperse.

Except . . .

'Messieurs, messieurs, if you could please stay in your places,' he called out, pulling a film plate from the back of his camera and waving it in the air to dry. 'This was just a polaroid . . .'

In the back row, Jacquot groaned. Jesus, he thought, they were going to be there all damned day.

18

As it turned out, Dombasle's photographer took only a few minutes more to finish the job. Three more whirring clicks and, much to Jacquot's relief, it really was over. Hands were shaken, hugs and good wishes exchanged, like players at the end of a match, and the team paired up with wives and drifted towards the loggia where a buffet had been laid out.

Not surprisingly perhaps, conversations were muted and appetites, save Lou Cabezac's, Druart's and Maryvonne Pelerain's, were in abeyance. Word had spread fast of Savry's 'suicide' and there was a sober atmosphere at the buffet. At no time, however, had Jacquot made any attempt to express his doubts – for which Dombasle saved him a special smile. Even Mageot was friendlier than expected. 'Don't worry, Daniel. I'll make sure you're kept posted on everything that happens down here.'

Jacquot thanked him, not really worried one way or the other. He fully intended doing that all by himself. First thing Monday morning.

As lunch came to an end ('I don't think I've ever seen so many broken noses and false teeth in one place,' Claudine had confided to Jacquot. 'And what have they done to their ears?'), the Dombasles' guests began their farewells. It was time to be getting home. Most of the locals – Olivier and Sophie Touche, the Peyrots from Antibes, the Lorraines from Monaco and the Millets from Grasse – had their own transport, but there was a rumour going round that the others, the Cabezacs, the Pelerains, the Druarts and Talauds, would be airlifted to Nice airport in Dombasle's Graumann to make their various connections.

When it was their time to say goodbye, Jacquot and Claudine were treated by the Dombasles as though without them there the party really was well and truly over. How could any party work with Daniel Jacquot and Claudine Eddé not present? Or at least that's how it felt to Jacquot. Pierre Dombasle embraced him like a father seeing his son go off to war, while his wife, Lydie, kissed him affectionately and clung to his arm all the way to their car.

The warmest sentiments, however, were reserved for Claudine.

As Pierre Dombasle kissed her hand, he congratulated her on her throw to Olivier, declaring that on the strength of that single pass, he'd have had her on any side he skippered.

Suitably complimented, she'd turned to Dombasle's wife only to have Lydie finally release Jacquot's arm in favour of hers.

'*Ma chère*,' Lydie stage-whispered for all to hear. 'My husband has only now seen fit to tell me that you are a most remarkable artist. It is the one talent I wish I had. All I will say is that, with such beautiful eyes and such effortless elegance, your choice of career is nothing less than a tragic loss to cinema. *Vraiment, une catastrophe.*'

'Did you hear that?' said Claudine, as they swung through the gates and joined the Nice road. 'Beautiful eyes and effortless elegance. From Lydie Dombasle, no less. It was worth coming just to hear her say that.' Claudine leaned across to plant a kiss on Jacquot's cheek. 'And you, Monsieur Daniel Jacquot, Number whatever, you should think yourself a very lucky man to have me.'

'I do. I do. Any woman who can throw a ball like that deserves only the very best.'

Part Two

days before contacting Murier for his report and findings, to give the man a chance to sort out his social life first.

As expected the police and medical reports gave Jacquot nothing particularly useful to work with. All three deaths had been filed as 'accidentals', only Valadier's hit-and-run left open should further information come to light. Seven months after his death, nothing had turned up and Jacquot doubted it ever would. Apparently Luc's body had been found in the gutter of a residential street in the Marais at a little after midnight, a short distance from his clinic. According to his staff, he'd been working late and had been walking to his car when the accident occurred. On that dark and silent Marais street there had been no witnesses, and no descriptions of the vehicle which had hit him, just a neighbour who had heard a mighty thump in the road – no squeal of brakes, Jacquot noted – and gone to investigate. In the pathologist's report it was stated that the nature of the impact wounds suggested a high-fronted vehicle, possibly a van, causing multiple and considerable upper-body fractures that Luc might conceivably have survived had it not been for the back of his head striking the kerb and breaking open. Since the vehicle had clearly been driven at considerable speed – how else to explain Luc's body more than ten metres from his briefcase – local garages had been asked to report any vehicles with significant damage to bonnet, radiator and front wings. But nothing had come of it. The driver, and the vehicle, had vanished. It wasn't the first time – and it wouldn't be the last – that a terrified or drunken driver had simply raced away, leaving their victim sprawled on the roadside. Sometimes these drivers were traced, but most of the time they got away with it, either putting it out of their mind or living with that terrible uncertainty and a crippling guilt that never eased.

But then, of course, there were those who did it deliberately . . .

In the case of Patric Souze, the Bordeaux *négociant* and the team's front row prop, Antoine Peyrot's version of events was wildly off-course – much like some of his passing if Jacquot remembered correctly. Rather than being crushed beneath wine barrels in his warehouse, the report from the Bordeaux *judiciaire* stated that Souze had died in his own *cave*, at home. Apparently a wine rack had toppled on to him and one of the broken bottles had severed an artery in his leg. Trapped beneath the weight of the rack, he'd slowly bled to death. His wife, Amélie, had found his body the following day.

As for Marc Fastin and the swingers club in Toulouse, the police had been called to an address on the outskirts of the city at 11.33 p.m. Two bodies had been found in one of the communal 'play' areas. Fastin's throat had been cut and his genitals partially removed with a long-bladed kitchen knife. A Sabatier. The same Sabatier that had been plunged into his companion's heart, her hands still gripping the handle when the police arrived on the scene. Bernard Savry might have thought differently, that a 'tryst' murder and suicide simply didn't make sense, but as far as the Toulouse *judiciaire* was concerned the evidence at the scene of crime was solid enough to have the case swiftly closed and shelved.

And that was it – pretty much what Jacquot had expected.

Looking up from the reports, Jacquot saw Brunet stroll into the squad room and he waved him through to his office.

'I want everything you can get on these guys,' said Jacquot, writing out the four names – Valadier, Souze, Fastin and Savry. 'Everything I won't find in their medical and police reports which, apart from Savry's, I've already sourced. I'm looking for something else, Jean . . . you know the sort of thing. Leads, links, anything suspicious, anything that doesn't add up.'

Brunet swung round a chair and settled on to it, its seat between his spread legs, his arms slung over its back. Somehow he managed to make an office chair look as comfortable as a cushioned sofa. Tipping forward he slipped the paper off the desk and read through the list.

'They're all footballers, right? Team-mates of yours, boss?'

Jacquot nodded. 'I knew them, and played with them. But that's it. I haven't seen or spoken to them in years.'

'You said "medical and police reports". They in trouble?'

'They're dead,' said Jacquot, pushing the files towards Brunet. 'Four of them in seven months. And the last one, Bernard Savry, was most definitely not a suicide.'

'Savry? Not the sports writer? *Monde Sportif*?'

'The same. You've heard of him?'

Brunet nodded. 'He did a story on the *Tour* last year. Best piece of sports writing I ever read. I mean you were there, right there. He put you in that saddle, made your legs ache like you were doing the Alpe d'Huez. Fantastic stuff.' Brunet shook his head sadly. 'What a loss.' And then, getting back to business, 'Any thoughts?'

'Right now. Nothing. *Rien*.'

'How long do I have?'

'Are we busy?'

'The bodies didn't particularly pile up while you were away, so just another Lubéron week. Someone's helped themselves to a consignment of candied fruit from a depôt in Apt; there's a joy-rider taking other people's cars for a spin around Bonnieux then torching them; and some *Anglais* over in Lourmarin reported a break-in Saturday night.'

'What was taken?'

'A dog. The intruder left a note. Fifty thousand francs and you get the mutt back.'

'Give me the files. I'll leave the names to you. And do it from home, why don't you? Keep a lid on it for now . . . unofficial.'

'Sounds good to me, boss.'

20

For the first few weeks of their liaison, Claudine had been happy enough to have a dinner date with Jacquot in town and to make do afterwards with his one-bedroom *atelier* on Cours Bournissac. There was something youthfully, urgently romantic about it, in an under-the-eaves sort of way, which Claudine found utterly irresistible. This arrangement also ensured that she was able to keep some distance between Jacquot and Midou during her daughter's summer break. She didn't want Midou asking too many questions until she was confident she had the right answers. But by the end of that summer, once Claudine became more sure of Jacquot, once she was certain of her feelings for him – and his for her – the cramped apartment, the noise of traffic and a temperamental supply of hot water soon began to jar and their time together shifted to Claudine's old house.

Claudine's home was a large, rambling old mill-house that she had shared with her aunt, Sandrine. What was now Claudine's studio had once been a ground-floor annexe for the old lady who, two years earlier, in October of course, had suffered a crippling stroke. After a month in hospital Sandrine had been transferred to a hospice near Salon and since then, having sent her husband packing, Claudine had lived in the house alone.

After eighteen months of her own company – save the occasional visits from Midou – having a man around the place suddenly seemed like a good thing. The mill had a fine old fireplace which Jacquot knew how to stoke to a roaring blaze as the days began to shorten, and there was always a handful of small jobs that needed a man's touch before winter set in. Jobs that Jacquot seemed happy to undertake, while she prepared a suitable reward in the kitchen. And not once did Claudine ever get the feeling that Jacquot was taking advantage, his feet under the table, making the most of his good fortune and a soft billet.

'Why don't you come over for dinner?' she'd phone and say, when Midou finally returned to college. Or, 'You couldn't do me a favour, could you?', and he'd jot down a shopping list for wine, or fruit, or vegetables –

whatever it was she wanted – and bring it out to her. And stay the night. Two or three evenings a week, as autumn crept up on them, Jacquot would leave his office at police headquarters, take a quick shower in his apartment, and then drive out on the Apt road to the turn-off for Claudine's home.

He did exactly this on Tuesday evening, three days after Dombasle's reunion and two days after letting Brunet loose on the Savry, Valadier, Souze and Fastin files. In that short time Jacquot had traced the dog-napper (the ransom demand had been written on a till receipt from a local supermarket, an itemised receipt that included rump steak and dog food, the customer identified from security tapes, and his address tracked through his credit card), and had also managed to catch the Bonnieux car-torcher and sort out the candied fruit supplier in Apt. An hour after Claudine's call, Jacquot left headquarters, took a quick shower at his apartment, and headed out to her house. She had made a *cassoulet* – good winter fuel – and the two of them polished it off with a pair of Isolettes that Jacquot had picked up on his way out of Cavaillon.

After they'd cleared away the dishes, they settled on cushions by the fire and Claudine hesitantly brought up the subject of Savry's 'suicide' at the Dombasles'.

'I thought you had a house rule about me never talking

about work after hours?' said Jacquot, wiggling his toes in front of the fire. He loved it when he caught her out; it wasn't easy to do.

'This is different,' replied Claudine. 'I met the man. I was there. And he made me laugh. I liked him. I just wanted . . . I just want to know what's happening. If you've found anything out.'

Jacquot smiled, put an arm around her shoulder, and pulled her to him. 'It's early days,' he replied. 'These kinds of investigation take time. You have to remember it's not my jurisdiction down there and I have no authority to barge in and question another officer's performance or findings. I'll have to work by myself until I have something more substantial to show. Then, maybe—'

'More substantial! But it's as clear as spring water. The filthy cloth, the fire cement, the clean hands. What more could they possibly want?'

'A great deal more, I'm afraid. Right now, it's Murier's investigation . . .'

'But you're not going to let it go, are you? If you think someone killed him? If it's murder?'

'I won't let it go, *chérie*, but there are ways and means.'

Claudine sighed, calmed. 'I know you won't. I know. I'm sorry. It's just . . . it's just so dreadful. That something like this could happen and no one do anything about it. Just sweep it under the carpet because it's inconvenient, because Pierre Dombasle . . .'

'I know. I know. It all seems crazy. But we'll get to the bottom of it, you'll see. It will all work out in the end.'

21

If there was any inconvenience involved in spending the night at Claudine's house, it was the twenty-minute journey to work the following day, rather than a quick stroll through the old town.

As he drove into Cavaillon that Wednesday morning, Jacquot was glad he'd said nothing about the other deaths when Claudine had started in with Savry. He'd thought about it, but had held back. The less she knew at this stage, the better. Leave it at Savry for now.

Arriving at headquarters and parking the car in the car park, Jacquot wondered if Brunet would come up with something, provide him with a lead that he was certain must be there – something that might help explain what had happened to Savry. Maybe even something that would link his death with the others.

Four deaths. In seven months. Each of the victims a member of the same team.

It was too much.

There had to be something else that tied them all together.

And if there was, then Brunet was the man to find it.

After only a year in Cavaillon, Jacquot had reached the conclusion that Brunet was possibly one of the best assistants he'd ever come across. Up there with Rully, Jacquot's right-hand man at the *judiciaire* in Marseilles. There was nothing that Brunet couldn't find out, as relentless and thorough in his work as he was in his pursuit of pretty women. When he wasn't sniffing out a felon, he was on the scent of other prey. Indeed it surprised Jacquot that after twenty years' committed philandering there should be any women left in the Lubéron for Brunet to conquer. Or any time for police work.

'Morning, boss,' said Brunet brightly, when Jacquot appeared in the squad room. 'I put everything on your desk,' he continued, tapping away at his keyboard.

'You did what?' asked a stunned Jacquot. He hadn't expected to see Brunet back so soon; he'd been about to call him that very morning to tell him to take his time, everything in the office was under control. As indeed it was – thanks to a forgetful van driver, a car-mad kid who got carried away with the petrol, and a dog-napper who might as well have left his calling card. Not that Brunet need know any of that.

'I went as far as I thought you'd want,' replied Brunet, an eyebrow raised, just the ghost of a smile. 'What was needed.'

Jacquot frowned. Brunet turned back to his keyboard.

'There isn't much,' he said as Jacquot headed for his office, pulling off his coat. 'But I reckon there's enough.'

'Let me read it through,' said Jacquot over his shoulder. 'I'll give you a shout.'

Settling behind his desk, Jacquot reached for the file that Brunet had left for him, swung his boots up on to the window sill, and flicked it open. Across the car park, a flight of pigeons swept past the belfried spire of Église St-Jean and swooped away over the rooftops. Jacquot licked a fingertip, turned a page, and down in the street someone pushed an elbow on to a horn – a long impatient blast and two swift follow-ups.

Six pages. A page and a half for each of the victims – names, addresses and telephone numbers.

Jacquot caught Brunet's eye out in the squad room and waved him in.

'So what's your take?' asked Jacquot, as Brunet swung out a chair and settled himself in his customary manner.

'It didn't start to ring bells until that Fastin guy,' explained Brunet. 'Some club, by the sound of it.' Brunet raised an eyebrow. 'Anyway, I just don't buy this *crime passionnel* theory. Murder then suicide, she does him then kills herself . . .' Brunet shook his head. 'There's a third party missing from the action, *c'est certain*. Which is why, if you add said missing person to the other "accidentals", well . . . I'd have to say there definitely seems to be a pattern . . .'

'Murders that look like something else. Murders made to look like something else.'

Brunet nodded. 'You could say.'

'Thanks, Jean, I appreciate it.'

'There's something else,' said Brunet. 'It's not in the file, and it might be nothing . . . who knows?' Brunet fell silent.

Jacquot was used to this little piece of stagecraft from his assistant, keeping something up his sleeve. A little goading was all that was needed.

'And? You said "something else"?'

'As I say, it might be nothing, who knows? But each of the victims had some kind of dealings with another member of that team of yours.'

Another brief pause.

'And that would be?'

'Your skipper. Pierre Dombasle.'

22

Five days later Madame Chantal Valadier opened the door to her apartment on the slopes of Paris's eighteenth *arrondissement*, held out her arms and smiled. 'Daniel, it's been a long time.'

They exchanged kisses, their hug held a moment too long by the widow.

'It has, indeed,' replied Jacquot. 'But you haven't changed a single scintilla.'

And she hadn't. Dressed in a cherry-coloured Chanel skirt and a cream shawl-necked sweater, Chantal Valadier looked as radiant as she had when Jacquot first met her, at the team dinner after the Twickenham match in London. She had just finished a degree course in Political Science at INSEAD and she and Luc were due to marry at the end of the season. She'd been bright and sharp and bubbly with long curling blonde hair, the bluest eyes and the widest smile. She reached Luc's shoulder, which made her about the tallest girlfriend that the looming inside centre had ever had. The last time the three of them had seen each other was at their wedding in Agen at the Church of Notre Dame and at the celebrations afterwards at the Maison du Sénéchal. The following week, while they honeymooned in Martinique, a Béziers prop-forward stamped on Jacquot's heel and snapped his Achilles tendon.

'*Entré. Viens, viens*,' said Chantal, drawing him in and closing the door behind him, her heels clicking on the parquet floor, softening when they hit a rug, as she led him down a wide corridor. 'It was so lovely to hear your voice after all this time,' she continued, showing him through to the salon. 'And it's just so lovely to see you again.'

The Valadiers' apartment, Jacquot decided, was simply stunning, seeming to float like a perfumed cloud above the city spread out below. On one side of the room the view from four draped windows seemed to take in the whole of Paris below the Butte de Montmartre, a thin mist wreathed around a thousand rooftops and chimney-pots, pierced by the square towers of Notre Dame, the soft dome of Opéra Garnier, and the fretted spire of the Eiffel Tower. If that was not quite enough, the windows at the far end of the room were filled with the glaring white slope of one of the domes on the Basilica of the Sacré Coeur, seen over a line of plane trees and framed by the end of the street. It must be a fabulous view at sunset, thought Jacquot, wondering just how successful a doctor had to be to afford such a billet.

Although the salon was suitably grand and formal, it was comfortable and homely, stylish too, the nineteenth-century mouldings and ornate panelling painted a uniform white rather than highlighted in gold. The floor was a dark herringbone parquet patched with rugs, the mantelpiece set with what looked like a branch of grey-weathered driftwood, and the alcoved bookshelves on either side stacked with books, CDs and a Niermeyer stereo, almost hidden behind a pair of thick-limbed ficus trees. Wherever windows allowed, the walls were hung with colourful abstract splashes and, set between three long sofas and the fireplace was a tapestried ottoman loaded with books and magazines.

The only things missing – on the mantelpiece, on the walls, on the shelves and on occasional tables – were framed photos of children. There hadn't been any. Jacquot couldn't decide whether that was a good thing or not. Better the loss of a husband, than the loss of a husband and father.

Settling herself beside Jacquot on one of the sofas, Chantal put on a brave face as though simply seeing

Jacquot was enough to bring back a host of forgotten-till-now memories.

'I'm only sorry I didn't hear about Luc's death in time,' Jacquot began. 'You know I would have come.'

'*Mais, bien sûr*, Daniel. I know you would have. I tried to find you, to let you know what had happened. Or rather, my mother did. She arranged everything. I was just too . . . *distraite.*' Chantal spread her hands as if only this empty gesture could possibly convey the shock, the misery.

'One day,' she continued, 'somehow, somewhere, they will find who did this dreadful thing.'

'Sometimes that's how it works,' said Jacquot softly. 'But you shouldn't raise your hopes.'

Chantal sniffed and nodded. 'I know, I know . . .'

From far below came the distant hum of traffic on Rue des Abbesses.

'And thank you for your note,' began Chantal again, as though anxious to fill the silence with words, conversation. 'It was the sweetest thing . . .' She leaned over and patted his hand. 'Luc thought highly of you, you know? When he heard about your injury he was terribly upset, said you had a great career in front of you. That France had lost a great player.'

Jacquot wasn't sure whether to believe her, but he felt a certain pleasure in hearing it. Valadier had been a giant of the game in more ways than one. More than forty outings in the blue shirt and white shorts.

'I'm afraid I only found out a couple of weeks ago,' continued Jacquot. 'At Pierre Dombasle's reunion. I had hoped to see you both. It was a shock when I heard.'

'The party, yes. Was it good? Was Lydie there? And Nonie?'

Jacquot nodded, smiled. 'Everyone was trying to work out who her father was.'

'Oh Jean-Claude Guilhem, for sure.' Chantal clapped her hands, chuckled delightedly. 'They look so alike, don't you think? Pierre always tried to pass Nonie off as his, but it's simply not possible. Can you imagine? That great jaw? Those close-set eyes? Poor Nonie, *non, non, non, c'est pas possible. Mais quelle bonne chance pour elle, n'est-ce pas?*'

'You knew them well? The Dombasles? You stayed in touch? Afterwards, after the playing was over?'

'Of course. Almost more than before. Luc and Pierre, they were like brothers. Just the two caps between them. Or was it three? And only a few months in age. Very close, anyway. But back in those days, you know, it was Annette. Not Lydie.'

'Annette? Annette?' Jacquot put on a suitably puzzled expression.

'Maybe it was after your time, Daniel. After your accident. They met on tour. South Africa. The Springboks.

Her father was immensely wealthy – hotels, casinos, vineyards. And she was very, very beautiful – in that kind of fey, waif-like sort of way.'

'Sounds a little like Lydie.'

'Yes. Yes, you're right. Maybe he goes for women like that. They say we do, you know? That we always go for the same type.'

Jacquot wasn't sure he agreed. Claudine was unlike any woman he had ever met.

'*Et toi?* You are married, Daniel?'

'No. I'm not.'

'A partner, a girlfriend?'

Jacquot nodded, turned down the corners of his mouth, glanced at his hands.

Chantal watched, smiled a little sadly. 'I know that look. Enough said. But anyway, I was telling you about Annette, wasn't I?'

'And?'

'Well, she was the most terrible drunk. *Affreuse.* Whether she was before they met, who knows? But poor Pierre had an awful time with her. The captain of the national squad – all those receptions, charity events, TV – and more often than not his wife would be . . . *hurlante*, howling.'

Jacquot looked suitably sympathetic. 'They divorced?' Sometimes his facility for deception surprised him.

Chantal shook her head. 'No need – though I'm certain Pierre must have thought about it. She committed suicide. Conveniently. It was kept quiet, of course, but we all knew about it. She plugged a hose into her car exhaust. It was Pierre who found her.'

A silence settled between them as though to give them a chance to consider the horror of such a discovery.

'Tell me,' began Jacquot, 'why didn't you come to the party?'

Chantal's lips tightened and she looked down at her hands. Her earlier softness, that evanescence, seemed suddenly to desert her and he could see a chill creep through her.

'Because . . . I wasn't invited.'

'Not invited?'

'I'm a wife not a player, Daniel. And now I'm a widow. Why would Pierre want me there?'

'But you are friends. You said—'

'I said we *were* friends. But not so much now. Now that Luc has gone.'

'But Pierre . . .'

'Pierre plays his own game. Always has and always will. When Luc died, I knew it was over. Believe me, Daniel, I never expected an invitation. You were never going to see me there.'

'"Over"? What was "over"? The friendship?'

'That, of course. But the business too.'

'The business?'

'Two days after Luc's death Pierre Dombasle called with his condolences. At the funeral, he stood up in the church where Luc and I were married and spoke so movingly of his friend that there was hardly a dry eye in the house. Me too. It was—'

'He has a way with words,' said Jacquot quietly, remembering the toast to the *rosbifs* a couple of weeks before.

'Spoken and written,' replied Chantal, sharply now. 'A week after the funeral – it must have been drafted the following day – I received a letter from his lawyers asking if I wanted to buy back their client's shares.'

'Shares?'

'Shares in Luc's business. The clinic.'

'Dombasle had a financial stake in Luc's clinic?'

Chantal smiled. 'But of course. How else do you suppose . . . ?' Chantal waved at the room they were sitting in, the view they enjoyed, the obvious trappings of wealth and success. 'It was Pierre who put in the initial start-up capital. If he hadn't done that, it would have taken us simply years to raise the funding. Pierre had faith in him.'

'And?'

'As I said, his lawyers – lawyers, mark you – wanted

to know if I'd be prepared to buy Dombasle's shares back. I'd been rather hoping he was going to make an offer for mine.' Chantal gave a little laugh.

'And?'

'When I told them I couldn't afford to settle at that time, it appears that Pierre – their client and our old friend – simply instructed them to cut his losses. The shares were dumped and the holding company which Pierre had set up to administer the loan – 'loan', mind, not investment – was dumped. Everything we had was suddenly worthless. The company was Luc. Without Luc, it was nothing. We all knew, Pierre too.' Chantal sat forward on her seat. 'But you know what? He wasn't even prepared to give us the time to regroup, to work out a strategy to keep the practice going. The senior shareholder simply walked away. Suddenly the banks foreclosed on other loans, staff were laid off . . .' Chantal took a breath, sighed, clasped her hands in her lap as though to keep warm. 'In January I will be leaving this apartment. It's sold. It's gone – the home Luc and I shared.' Chantal took a deeper breath. 'In seven months, *cher* Daniel, I have lost everything.'

23

Jacquot wasn't sure how he felt about Paris. He'd arrived that morning on the TGV from Cavaillon, snatched a late lunch at the station brasserie, and taken the Métro to Abbesses. Huge mistake. He should have jumped in a taxi. The journey would have been much slower and cost more but at least he'd have been above ground, had a chance to reacquaint himself with the capital.

When he left Chantal's apartment, promising to stay in touch, Jacquot didn't make the same mistake. Two blocks from her apartment building he flagged down a cab and had it take him to his hotel. The sky had darkened, the clinging mist and low cloud denying any possibility of a glorious sunset – just a bruised smudge of terracotta that suddenly changed into night. But Paris was undeniably Paris, and jouncing round in the back seat of the cab Jacquot felt a lift of excitement at the names and the places – Place de l'Opéra, Rue du Rivoli, the Louvre's pyramids, the Tuileries, Pont Neuf, Notre Dame and, after the grand and glorious Boulevards of Haussmann, the burrowing medieval streets of the Left Bank – could there really be a need for so many antique shops on a single stretch of pavement? – streetlights twinkling in a thin drizzle that turned, in the time it took him to check in, shower and step out again in search of somewhere to eat, into a determined downpour. Pavements shone, cars swished past and people hurried along hunched under umbrellas. Five minutes later, brushing the rain from his jacket and settling at a restaurant table no more than twenty metres from the steps of his hotel (this was Paris after all), Jacquot, if not actually feeling quite at home, felt . . . comfortable. A *pichet* of red, a confit of duck with Sarladaise potatoes that didn't look as if they had been reheated, a *plateau* of interesting-looking cheeses, and delicious home-baked bread with creamy Isigny butter was all it took.

As he waited for the confit Jacquot remembered the last time he'd been in the city. Four years earlier he'd come here to spend a weekend with a girlfriend. (He'd been younger then, he thought ruefully, even if it was just the four years ago.) But on the flight home, the late one, he'd met Boni Milhaud. She was the stewardess. Two hours after landing at Marseilles's Marignane airport, he was taking her stockings off and the girlfriend in Paris was history.

As he worked his way through the confit, Jacquot also thought of Chantal, alone in that apartment. He'd stayed far longer than he'd meant to, unwilling to leave while she looked so down. But eventually she had glanced at her watch and exclaimed. She was taking up so much of his time . . . she hadn't thought . . . 'Should I call you a cab?' she'd asked.

The choice she was offering was stay if you'd like to, which would be nice, or go if you must. The decision was his. He knew it and she knew it. When he told her not to bother with a cab, he'd walk, he saw the expression on her face – delight that he didn't want her to call a cab, an almost immediate but well-concealed regret when he said he'd walk.

But Chantal Valadier had been a delight. He did really like her. And he would try to keep in touch. He felt sorry for her, too – the loneliness, no children, just friends and a mother to see her through, help her cope. But Chantal Valadier was no loser. In the end she'd win through. It was only seven months after all . . .

What really annoyed Jacquot was just how badly Pierre

Dombasle had behaved – to strong-arm Chantal so soon after Luc's death. There was no excuse for it, surely? None whatsoever. Of course, Pierre's lawyers might simply have acted on their client's behalf without considering the social implications, doing it without reference to Dombasle – just the way SportÉquipe business was conducted; certain smaller decisions taken on his behalf without consultation. But that didn't sound like Dombasle. Dombasle was the kind of man who knew exactly what was going on – every single second of the day.

Though he was annoyed at the way Dombasle had behaved, Jacquot couldn't altogether say he was surprised. He could even, in a strange sort of way, understand it. Dombasle was a billionaire for one very good reason. Being sharp. Maximising his assets. Just like a skipper on the pitch. You do what you do – replace a player, drop a player – without regard to sentiment, loyalty or friendship. Team comes first, individuals last. Because you have no choice. It goes with the territory – no room for emotion.

But a friend, a widowed friend? In Jacquot's book that was different. (Which was maybe why *he* wasn't the billionaire, he decided.) If Luc and Pierre had been so close, the least Dombasle could have done was postpone the inevitable – he could certainly afford to (there you go, thought Jacquot; billionaire buinessmen don't get where they are by *giving* money away). Or at least try to work things out – arrive at some solution that was more practical, positive and, maybe, just a little more sensitive (there you go again, Jacquot reprimanded himself, finishing his cheese and calling for *'l'addition, s'il vous plaît'*). Luc's practice might have been fronted by him, relied on him, but according to Chantal there were partners, staff, and a large clinic with extensive surgical facilities which, judging by their apartment, appeared to be providing a profitable return. No wonder she was angry. It may have seemed like petty cash to Dombasle – but, billionaire aside, why couldn't he simply have left his money where it was?

24

First thing the following morning, Jacquot took a cab from Boulevard St Germain to the Marais and a tree-lined street off Rue de la Roquette. Asking the cabbie to wait – a newspaper was out and a cigarette was in the driver's mouth before he'd hauled himself from the springless back seat – Jacquot strolled down the street. Halfway along, the pavement carpeted with damp brown leaves, Jacquot found the Clinique Valadier set behind a fence of high spear-tipped black railings, the name incised on a shiny brass plaque on one of two pillars bracketing extravagant wrought-iron gates.

As far as Jacquot could see, Luc's clinic was the only business on an otherwise residential street and, save the brass plaque at the gate, its ground-floor windows furnished with venetian blinds not curtains, and the upper-floor windows mirrored to reflect back the clear November sky, the property was indistinguishable from its neighbours. Beyond its gates and railings, there was no movement, no sign of life, and it struck Jacquot that the clinic had already been closed down.

Even at this time of the morning the street was quiet, just a gentle drumbeat of traffic from Place de la Bastille. At night Jacquot had little doubt that it would be even quieter. With its trees, garden shrubbery and bordering hedges it was no surprise that none of the residents had seen anything.

According to the police report, Luc had been hit approximately ten metres from the gates of the clinic, walking to his car. Since Jacquot didn't know where Luc had parked, whether he had turned left or right on leaving the clinic, and since there was nothing to indicate the likely impact spot, Jacquot checked both directions, and both sides of the street. His first impression was that this was not a likely scene for an accidental hit-and-run. The road was long and straight, restricted to one-way traffic and, despite the trees, would have been well-lit at night with its regularly spaced streetlights. For whatever reason parking was only allowed on one side of the road, across from the clinic, which meant that the approaching driver must have been blind not to see Luc walking along the pavement or stepping out into the road to cross to his car. Either that, or ruinously drunk. And even then the road was easily wide enough for any driver, even a drunk, to take avoiding action, to make a last-minute swerve, maybe even mount a pavement or crash into parked cars. And being one-way, with no approaching traffic, sudden movements like that, even at night, would not have been a problem.

And what about Luc? Surely he'd have looked before crossing the road? Surely he'd have waited for any approaching car or van to pass? Even if he was tired, or preoccupied, he'd surely have heard the sound of a car approaching, or seen sidelights or headlights? Unless, of course, the lights had been doused and the driver had waited until he was in the middle of the road before putting his foot down.

As he walked back to his taxi, Jacquot decided that if he had been the investigating officer, he'd certainly have put it down as a hit-and-run incident – but not necessarily an accidental one.

Late at night this quiet residential street, just a stone's throw from La Bastille, would have been a perfect execution ground.

Visiting the scene of a crime wasn't the only reason that Jacquot had stayed overnight in Paris. Dropping into the back seat of the cab, he asked the driver to take him on to Porte des Lilas and, a couple of blocks beyond it, Espace Cligny. It was here, exactly on time, that Jacquot pushed through a set of double doors into the reception area of *Monde Sportif* and asked to see the editor, Monsieur Lousard; he was expected.

Ten minutes later Jacquot was sitting in Gabriel Lousard's office, looking at a line of framed *Monde Sportif* covers on the wall, watching the magazine's staff at work through the glass panel behind Lousard's head and waiting for the man to get off the phone.

'It's three thousand, a piece that length. Always has been. Won't change now. Yeah, it's tough. I know, I know. *Dites moi . . .*' Lousard glanced at Jacquot, eyes rolling under a thick mono-brow while his finger made a few lazy turns against his temple. '*Oui, c'est tout. Trois. Oui ou non? Bon. Jeudi. Et c'est Jeudi matin, compris?*'

Lousard jammed down the phone in its cradle, the hooped cable hopelessly, irretrievably knotted. 'Thank God these guys aren't cops,' he said with an energetic clearing of the throat. 'You'd never catch anyone. The only question they'd be asking is when are you going to raise my wages. So. You wanted to talk about Berne.'

'That's right.'

'Is this part of an investigation?'

'Investigation? Should there be one?'

Leaning back in his chair, Lousard loosened his tie and undid the top button with a snarling grimace. 'Course there should. Berne? Killing himself? Give me a break.'

'Why do you say that?'

'Because it wasn't his style. Not Berne. And no reason either.'

'Have you told the police that?'

'I'm telling you.'

'*En effet*, it's not my case.'

'So what are you doing sitting in that chair?'

'He was a friend. We played together once. Team-mates.'

Lousard squinted at Jacquot for a moment or two. 'You're the one who scored that try, aren't you?'

Jacquot nodded.

'Thought it was you. The name, the ponytail. I was in the crowd, would you believe? Watched it. Jesus, we got smashed that night.'

'*Moi aussi*,' said Jacquot.

'I'm not surprised,' said Lousard with a grin.

'So tell me, have the police been in touch with you?'

'Just a call from down south,' said Lousard. 'They were looking for next of kin. Said they needed an address for someone to come and claim the body. Funeral, I suppose.'

'And that's all?

'That, and your man asking questions. And you, sitting there.' Lousard leaned back in his chair, eyeing Jacquot. 'So, what do you want to know about Berne that you don't already know?'

'Why you sacked him?'

'Who told you that?'

Jacquot shrugged, spread his hands.

'Well, they're right. I did. Every time the little bald bastard had a fucking story to write. Whatever it took to get his copy. He liked it when I shouted at him, threatened him. If he was sitting there, he'd just give me a smile. On the phone, he'd start whistling the fucking "Marseillaise". And then, right up to the wire, in he'd saunter and just drop it on the desk. The best fucking stuff you ever read. Jerk-offs, like that guy,' Lousard jabbed his finger at the phone, 'they don't come close. But Berne . . . just magic. Pure bloody magic. Every single word. Every single time.'

'So you didn't sack him?'

'And lose half my readership? You've got to be fucking kidding.' Lousard shook his head.

'What about money? I heard he was broke.'

'Same source?'

'Same source.'

'And the same shit. Sure he had problems with money. He liked to gamble – horses, dogs, mice if you could race them. Always subbing him for this and that – the next story in advance. But he always bounced back – picked the winner. And paid back.'

'Were the bets large?' asked Jacquot, finding himself drawn to the man across the desk. There was something dog-eared but resilient about him, the kind of man who'd made his way round a few blocks in his time and probably had a few good stories to tell, the kind of man Jacquot liked.

'Never more than he could afford. I mean, there's no wife or kids to bleed him, you know what I'm saying?' Lousard gave him a look. Jacquot nodded. 'Sure he went short, but don't we all?'

'Did he have a regular partner? Anyone important?'

'I wouldn't know. He was very quiet about that.'

Jacquot took this in. 'Tell me about Pierre Dombasle.'

'The man or his advertising budget?'

'SportÉquipe advertises with you?'

Lousard grunted. 'Big time. Maybe twenty per cent of revenue.'

'You ever meet him?'

Lousard shook his head.

'Did you know Berne wanted to write a book about him? A biography.'

Lousard nodded. 'He'd been talking about it, sure. Got a load of stuff on the guy. But if there's one thing

Berne knows, it's strings and bows. Suddenly Dombasle's out of the picture. It doesn't matter any more.'

'Why?'

Lousard gave Jacquot a deeply satisfied smirk. 'Because Berne just goes and lands the biggest bloody publishing contract you can imagine. Football's future heroes, that kind of thing. Big publisher, big advance. Starting with a guy called Zidane. Plays for Marseilles. If you haven't heard of him, you will. Even if Berne's not going to be the one who writes the official biography.'

'So, what do you think happened?' asked Jacquot, trying to tally what Lousard was saying with what Dombasle had told him.

The phone started ringing. Lousard gave him a look. 'Isn't that why we got you guys? To find these things out.'

25

From Paris Jacquot caught a train to Bordeaux. He arrived at Gare St-Jean on a chill, blustery afternoon that was relieved only by the scent of a distant sea, a sharp salty Atlantic tang that almost scorched the lungs with life. Picking up a hire car, Jacquot bought a road map at a service station and headed south on the A62. At St Selve he stopped at the side of the road, consulted the map and fifteen minutes later he reached the entrance to Patric Souze's driveway.

Unlike many of the properties that Jacquot passed – wine-label chateaux with witch-hat towers, and ivied country mansions – Souze's home was breathtakingly modern. The first frosts had still to come to these open gentle slopes south of the Garonne and the vines glowed a golden brown as far as the eye could see, splashed with patches of sunlight yellow. A kilometre from the road, at the end of a gravelled drive, Jacquot could see what looked like a long sheet of glass encased in thick concrete.

Five minutes later he parked his car, walked up the steps to the house and rang the bell. Through the sliding glass panel that constituted a front door, Jacquot saw a tall young man jog across a marble hallway towards him. He was dressed in sweat pants, trainers and wore the blue-and-white chequered strip of the Bègles-Gironde rugby club.

The lad looked about eighteen or nineteen, and had a thatch of unruly brown hair and a surly, distrustful look. As the door slid open, Jacquot detected the stale green scent of dope on him. Unlike his father, who had come no higher than Jacquot's shoulder, the son, even slouching, was as tall as Jacquot, his frame, thin and reedy, waiting only for the muscle to catch up with the growing. Only the eyes – one of them badly bruised – and the wide jaw were Patric's, a pair of features that stopped the son, despite the spots and slouch, being a handsome young man. As it was there was something low-browed and intimidating about him.

'Bonjour,' said Jacquot lightly. 'I wondered if Madame Souze was at home?'

The boy's eyes narrowed. 'Not right now,' he answered. 'She's out.'

'Any idea when she might be back? You're her son, right?'

The boy frowned. *'Oui. C'est moi.'*

'I was a friend of your father's,' said Jacquot by way of introduction. 'We played together.'

It was as if a light had switched on. Apart from the brow and eyes and jawline, the boy might not have looked like his father or be built like him but it was clear that the son knew his rugby. A smile of recognition suddenly spread across his features. 'I don't believe it,' he said. 'You're Jacquot. The ponytail, right? Daniel Jacquot. Number Six.'

The glass front door which had until then been held to the young man's shoulder and opened only wide enough to accommodate that shoulder suddenly swung open.

'It's great to meet you. Come in, come on in. *Maman* won't be long, should be back in a while. And yeah, I'm François. François Souze. Glad to meet you, Monsieur Jacquot.'

'Call me Daniel,' said Jacquot, pulling off his coat.

'Here, let me help you,' said François, taking it from Jacquot and laying it reverently over a Charles Eames recliner that stood just inside the door.

'Quite a place,' said Jacquot taking in the open-plan hall which seemed to occupy the entire floor. Apart from the recliner, there was a nest of steel-framed sofas in one corner, and a glass dinner table set with a dozen high-backed chairs in another. It felt, thought Jacquot, like some futuristic stage set.

'Come on down,' said François, leading Jacquot to a spiral staircase in a third corner. 'Everything's down here. It's three levels – four if you count the wine cellar – except you just see the one from the drive. It used to be a small quarry, until the old man got his hands on it.'

Stepping off the spiral stairway François showed Jacquot into a sleekly trim kitchen-dining area.

'Coffee? A beer?' asked François, and as he set to work on the coffee maker to produce the espresso requested, Jacquot looked around. As in the room above, one whole wall was glass, the ranks of vines trooping west towards a distant misty sun. Somewhere vine cuttings were being burnt and a scarf of smoke stretched across the fields like a low blue cloud.

'I was sorry to hear of your father's death,' began Jacquot as the espresso-maker started to whistle and whine. 'He was a great player.'

François nodded as he worked the machine, pouring the coffee into a small cup and handing it to Jacquot. 'It was a shock. *Maman* . . .' He shrugged, as if there was nothing he'd been able to do to make it any easier for his mother.

'It takes time,' said Jacquot softly, sipping the hot coffee carefully.

'I guess,' said François, opening a fridge beside the coffee machine and pulling out a Coke.

'And you? How're things with you?'

For a moment, François was silent. 'Sure, it's hard. And I miss him. I really do. But . . .'

'He was a tough one,' said Jacquot, encouraging the lad.

François grinned. 'You could say. Nothing I ever did seemed to work with him. And now . . . well, now it's too late.'

'You play?' asked Jacquot, nodding at the shirt. The number on the back was 10. Dombasle's position.

'Of course. Fly-half with Bègles-Gironde. The B team, but I'm keeping my fingers crossed for next season.'

'Not bad,' said Jacquot. At Bègles-Gironde even playing the second team was good work.

François pointed to a kitchen table. 'Here, take a seat. Make yourself comfortable. You come far?'

'From Paris,' replied Jacquot.

'You live in Paris? That's a long way to come.'

'I was visiting with friends,' replied Jacquot. 'I was on my way home and thought I should call in, say hello, pass on my condolences.'

'*Maman* would like that,' said François pulling the tab

on his Coke and sucking up the frothing overflow. He wiped his mouth, gave a tiny burp which he covered with his hand.

'So what are you doing now? Apart from the rugby. Lycée? University?'

'That's what *Maman* wants – university. This time next year. But, you know, it's not going to be so easy to play. Study, exams. It's just, it's just I think I'm good enough to give it a go . . . and concentrate on my game. I've spoken to Monsieur Dombasle and he was very encouraging. He's come to see me play a couple of times. He wouldn't waste his time if he didn't think there was a chance. And I know Papa wanted me to try.'

'But your mother doesn't?'

'In one. It's all "who's going to run this place, now your father is gone, if you're off playing rugby somewhere".' François chuckled. 'She tends to forget that I'd be away at university too.'

'That's what parents do. Cut down the risks.'

'Not Papa. Sometimes you've got to take risks, he'd say.'

'Mothers are different,' replied Jacquot.

'You have kids of your own?'

Jacquot shook his head. 'Too busy playing rugby and then being a policeman.'

As Jacquot had expected, François's face paled and

his jaw almost dropped. 'You're a *flic* . . . I mean a policeman?'

'Chief Inspector. Cavaillon Regional Crime Squad. But I'm on holiday, off duty,' he lied smoothly. 'So you don't have to worry about that dope you've been smoking.'

François's wide blond face reddened in an instant. Jacquot could almost see the blood spread in a wave across his cheeks.

'Hey, it's OK. It's OK. In fact, I'm partial to a smoke myself. And like I said, I'm off duty.' Jacquot made to press his hand against his heart, but thought better of it and pretended to reach up to pull his ponytail through his fingers. 'I'm just sorry I didn't make it to the funeral,' he continued, changing the subject.

'It was big,' said François, almost proudly. 'Seemed like pretty much the whole town turned up. *Vignerons*, *négociants*, and some of the old team of course.'

'Oh yeah?' said Jacquot, finishing his coffee. He took out his cigarettes. 'Is it OK . . . ?'

'Sure, sure. Go ahead. *Maman* smokes. It's just me that's not allowed.'

'Mother or club?'

'Both.'

Jacquot offered his pack. 'You want a cigarette?'

'Sure. I'd love one.'

Jacquot handed over the packet, flicked his lighter and lit both cigarettes.

'So you were saying some of the team turned up.'

'Not everyone,' said François, taking a deep drag and letting the smoke out in a series of coiling rings – one, two, three. 'Guy Mageot, Antoine Peyrot, Gilles Millet. And Monsieur Dombasle, of course.'

'So how long have you been here?' asked Jacquot. Not long, he thought to himself; he could still detect the faint, occasional scent of plaster and paint.

'Just a year or so . . . Papa bought the land five years ago but it took a while to build. It was his pride and joy.' The lad looked around forlornly.

'He was a *négociant*, *n'est-ce pas*?'

'Still is . . . I mean was. *Maman* runs it now. Three days in Bordeaux, four days here.'

'She stays there?'

François nodded. 'There's an apartment above the office.'

'Warehouse accident, wasn't it? That's what I heard.'

François shook his head. 'Not at the warehouse, no, no. It was right here. In the wine cellar.'

'Here? In the house?' said Jacquot, feigning astonishment. 'But I thought—'

'Nope, right here. I'll show you, if you like.'

26

The cellar was another two floors down, reached through a door high enough to admit Patric Souze without too much trouble but too low for François and Jacquot.

'Mind your head,' warned François and he clattered down a steep flight of stone steps.

Just as Jacquot would have expected, Patric Souze's cellar – the private cellar of a successful *négociant* – was no mean or tawdry stash of bottles.

Down here in the bowels of the old quarry, it was warmer than outside, the still air filled with the dusty smell of gravel, a corky whiff of stale wine and the smokey scent of burning candles. Stretching back into the bare rock of the quarry was a single tunnel wide enough to accommodate wine racks on each side, set out back-to-back like library bookshelves. There were easily a dozen rows each side, and at the entrance to the tunnel was a long refectory table, with a half-dozen chairs drawn around it and six silver candlesticks. Jacquot could picture the scene: Souze, a brutal prop-forward but one of the jolliest men Jacquot had ever encountered, hosting some intimate little wine-tasting. And old Souze had always liked his wine, red the best, even when he played – never beer, never spirits. Back then he'd guzzle a bottle of *cru bourgeois* at the end of very game.

Crunching over the gravel floor Jacquot and François made their way past the table and down the central aisle, Jacquot noting the names at the entrance to each racked alleyway: Côtes de Nuit, Côtes de Beaune, Côtes de Chalonnaise and Mâconnais; Médoc, St Emilion, St Estèphe, Pauillac, Pomerol, St Julien, Margaux. Magical names.

'No new worlds, I see.'

'Oh yeah. He kept them down here, out of sight,' replied François with a grin, turning to the right and standing aside for Jacquot to see yet another length of tunnel, this one with whitewashed stone bins fixed to the wall. 'Papa got these from the old Château Dasimes. The bins.'

'And this . . . this is where your father died? Down here? I don't see how . . .' Jacquot looked around, suitably perplexed and shamefaced to be asking – curiosity getting the better of him, just as it would anyone. Natural.

'One of the racks,' replied François. 'The Sauternes back there. It just collapsed on him.'

'But how could that be?' asked Jacquot as they walked over to the offending rack. There was nothing to see save a patch of fresh new gravel raked into the old. 'The racks look so solid.'

'It's easy enough. If you're taking a bottle from the top shelf and you don't pull it out cleanly. Especially if you're my father's height. Look, I'll show you.'

Stooping down to approximate his father's size, François reached out an arm and stretched up for a bottle on the top row. He grasped it by the neck and dragged it down rather than pulling it out smoothly. Jacquot could see what François meant. Just this small snag made the rack sway minutely, but sway enough for other bottles to rattle dangerously in their metal nests.

'That's how they reckon it happened,' said François. 'Reaching for the top row. He just pulled everything down on top of him.'

Or, thought Jacquot, maybe someone had been standing the other side of the rack and had given it some encouragement, a push. Must have been someone Souze knew, Jacquot reasoned; how else would they get down here with him?

'He kept saying he'd fix it. But he never got round to it,' continued François. 'But it wasn't the rack that killed him. One of the bottles broke. Cut through an artery. An Yquem '61. Papa would have liked that.'

'So who found him?' asked Jacquot, hoping his questions didn't sound too like a police interrogation. He needn't have worried. It was as if François had told the story so many times that if Jacquot hadn't asked the questions François would, in all likelihood, have still provided the answers.

'*Maman*. The following day. She'd stayed over at the apartment. Came back, saw the door open . . .'

'And you?'

'Me? I was in hospital. Someone in the Brives scrum thought my head was the ball. They thought the retina had detached so I was laid up for days.'

And then, from above, an anxious voice came floating down to them.

'François? François? *Où es-tu? Tu es là-bas? Dites-moi.*'

'Down here, *Maman*. We have a guest.'

It was just as well that Jacquot hadn't booked a hotel for the night. Even if he had, Amélie Souze would have made him call and cancel the reservation.

'But you are staying here, Daniel. That's all there is to it. If you think you're going to disappear again after all this time, you've got another think coming. So I don't want to hear another word. It's settled.'

Unlike Chantal Valadier, Amélie had changed in the years since Jacquot had last seen her. Her hair had been extravagantly dyed the rusty colour of a good *rouille*, and where she had once been round and sexy in a bubbling, barmaid sort of way, she was now stocky and stout with a couple of jowly chins and swollen ankles. But the twinkle in her eye was still there and she had little trouble persuading Jacquot to stay.

Up in the kitchen, the sun already gone and the line of smoke from the bonfire lost in a darkening sky, Amélie set about preparing a dinner. 'I have some steaks, some wine, some cheese. *Ça marche?*'

For the next few hours, Amélie kept up a lively chatter, keeping the conversation pinned down around Jacquot. Where did he live? Was he still in the police? Was he married? And why not? It was only after François cleared the table, stacked the dishwasher and left them for his bed that Amélie felt able to open up about her husband.

'He was so young, you know. Fifty-two. And there was so much he wanted to do.'

'It looks to me as though he had everything he could

possibly want. Your home here, the business. You and François.'

'Ah, François. Patric was so proud of him. So proud. Might not have told him all that often, but he was.'

'And it looks as though François is going to follow in his father's footsteps. Bègles-Gironde is a good club. Patric must have been very pleased.'

'Patric maybe, but not me, Daniel. It's a vicious game – no need to tell you that. A few days before Patric died the boy was kicked so badly he nearly lost an eye. Just like that.'

'He told me.'

Amélie nodded. 'Like most of them, of course, he thinks he's indestructible. But there are terrible accidents, Daniel. Last season, one of the backs in the A team was trapped in a maul and broke his neck – won't ever walk again, *le pauvre*. Everything, gone, like that.' She clicked her fingers. 'I just can't bear it. That one of these days it might happen to François.'

'You can't protect them all the time.'

'But you can try,' she countered.

'He looks like he can handle himself,' tried Jacquot.

Amélie gave a little laugh. 'That's what Patric always said. You're all alike, you lot. And Dombasle the worst, offering all manner of encouragement. If only he'd let it be.'

'Dombasle? Pierre?'

'The same. Been up here a couple of times to see François play. Always encouraging him. All his kit from SportÉquipe. New boots. New this. New that. Talk of sponsorship, modelling contracts. It's enough to turn any kid's head, giving them ideas like that.'

Amélie reached for the wine bottle, held it to the light and when she saw it was empty had Daniel open another. 'Maybe he is a good player. Maybe he could make it,' she said, as Daniel pulled the cork and filled their glasses. 'But he needs an education too, Daniel. Ten years playing and a lifetime trying to deal with it.' She shook her head. 'You see it so much. They just can't settle. When their time's up, they try to hang on. Or they can't seem to operate like the rest of us. Patric and I were lucky. So were you. You had the police. And Rains, too – being in the Navy.'

'We weren't the only ones. Luc Valadier, Gilles, Olivier. They all did well after the playing. Dombasle especially.'

'They were the lucky ones. Most don't manage it. They hit the bottle or beat their wives. And things are different now, Daniel. Selection is tough and there's not much time for anything else.'

'Like university . . .'

'*C'est ça, exacte.* He can play all he likes but he can't quit his studying. There's a business here for him to run if he wants it. But he's got to know how. I'll not see him squander everything Patric and I worked so hard to get. He needs to understand that. He needs books not boots.'

And so it went, sitting at the kitchen table, listening to Amélie's concerns, sharing memories with a laugh and a tear until, at a little after midnight, with a goodnight peck on the cheek from Amélie, Jacquot slipped into his bed and reached for the light. Which was when he noticed the envelope on his bedside table and a familiar smell.

Jacquot opened the envelope, looked inside and smiled.

'Good boy,' he thought.

27

The third day out of Cavaillon, two hundred and forty kilometres south of Bordeaux, Jacquot was starting to feel tired. He'd left Amélie and François after breakfast that morning, thanking Amélie for her hospitality and, very discreetly, François for his gift, driven back to Bordeaux, dropped off the hire car and taken another train to Toulouse. At Gare Matabiau, beside the Canal du Midi, he'd waited in line for a taxi and given the driver the address he'd taken from the police report into the club killings. Twenty minutes later, on the far side of town, the taxi pulled into a smartly kept suburban street, its edges fringed with pink oleander, a grassed island down its middle and more than one garden proudly sprouting palms.

Jean-Claude Rives lived in a long, low-slung, one-floor villa halfway down the street. The roof tiles were a bright terracotta, the walls a glaring white even in the November sunshine, but the front lawn and flower beds looked unkempt and uncared for. Somewhere down the road Jacquot could hear kids playing in a garden. He looked around, hoping someone would answer the door, hoping the man was at home. There was no car in the driveway, the garage doors were shut, and in the windows either side of the front door, the venetian blinds were closed. Pressing the bell a second time, he turned on the stone porch and looked up as a large Airbus roared overhead, coming in to land at nearby Blagnac.

How could anyone live with jets taking off and landing so close, wondered Jacquot? It would drive him insane.

'Monsieur? Can I help you? Monsieur?'

Thanks to the Airbus Jacquot hadn't heard the door open but he heard the last of the voice, raised against the diminishing whine of jet engines.

The man standing in the doorway was in his late forties, maybe early fifties, but could easily have been older. He looked gaunt and haggard, as though he'd spent the previous night working hard at a bottle, and a shadow of black stubble on his neck and cheeks exaggerated the puffy pallor of his features. His hair was grey and extravagantly tousled as though he had just lifted his head from a pillow, and his eyes were bleary and unfocused. It was a wonder he'd managed – or even bothered – to answer the door.

'Monsieur Rives?' Behind Jacquot the sound of the jet had finally receded.

'Who's asking?'

'Detective Jacquot,' he said, flashing his badge and pocketing it swiftly, saying his name quickly and dropping himself a few ranks. He had spoken to Chantal Valadier and Amélie Souze as an old friend paying a social call. He couldn't play the same game with Rives. 'I'm sorry to bother you, Monsieur Rives. I wondered if we could have a few words?'

The man's eyes narrowed. He gave Jacquot a cursory once-over. 'Don't tell me you're taking it seriously all of a sudden?'

'I'm afraid you have me at a disadvantage.'

'You work with Rudolfe, right? The *judiciaire*?'

'Regional Crime,' replied Jacquot obliquely.

At the word 'crime', a caterpillar eyebrow raised itself slightly.

'Monsieur, maybe if I could come in . . . some questions?'

'Come on then. Come on in,' said Rives, turning away and leaving Jacquot to close the door behind him.

The first thing Jacquot noticed was the smell. A dark airless atmosphere rich with the scent of flat beer and cigarettes, body odour and cold pizza. And the place was a mess. Mail lay in a pile behind the door, a bunch of flowers in a glass vase on a window sill had wilted, the water a murky green, and takeaway boxes in some numbers littered the floor in the salon.

'I'm in the kitchen,' came Rives's voice. 'You want a coffee?'

Jacquot pushed through a set of saloon-bar swing doors and stepped into a kitchen that was in much the same state as the salon. Newspapers littered the kitchen table, the sink was stacked with dirty dishes and a bottle of whisky with no more than a couple of measures left in it stood by an empty wine rack. A line of plants on the window sill above the sink looked as healthy as the flowers in the salon, but the blinds were up and, for all the mess and smell, a thin slant of wintery sunshine gave the room a certain cheering brightness. Sliding doors leading to a narrow patio and a stretch of sun-dried lawn were open, a climbing frame and a plastic playhouse in bright, primary colours the only furnishings in a garden as ill kept as the front.

Rives caught Jacquot looking at the climbing frame and the pictures of the children pinned haphazardly on to the fridge door. Beside the children was a polaroid of a middle-aged woman in a red party dress, a party hat on her head and a glass in her hand.

'The kids are with my sister-in-law. It's been difficult . . .'

Lifting the kettle he slopped water into two mugs and handed one of them to Jacquot. 'It'll have to be black. I'm out of milk. Sugar, too.'

'That's fine, no problem,' said Jacquot.

'So,' Rives continued, 'what's new? You changed your minds yet?'

'Why should we change our minds, Monsieur Rives?'

'Suicide pact? Rudolfe's got to be taking the piss. How could anyone see it that way?'

'Which is why I'm here, monsieur,' said Jacquot, following Rives to the table and taking a seat. Rives swept an open newpspaper on to the floor so that Jacquot could put down his mug of coffee.

'You taking over from Rudolfe then? Someone ought to.'

'Why would you think that?'

Rives gave Jacquot a look, wiped a hand on his shirt and started counting off on his fingers.

'Number one: you don't take part in a suicide pact with someone you don't know.

'Number two: my wife's youngest sister – her favourite sister, as it happens – was getting married five days later. No way she was going to miss that.

'Number three: if she was going to kill herself, or the

man they found her with, she wouldn't have used a knife – just hated knives, she did.

'Number four: she sure as hell wouldn't have sliced the guy's dick off, and I can't see him doing it himself, can you?

'Number five: Camille doesn't wear perfume. Got a skin condition that makes her flare up at just a squirt of the stuff. But the guy she's with stinks of it.

'Number six . . .' Rives shook his head, dropped his hands on the table. 'I could go on and on. But Rudolfe and his boys aren't having any of it. More interested in shutting the club down than finding a killer. Or maybe they reckon it's just too difficult a case for them to handle. Since they're all as thick as cow shit, it wouldn't surprise me.'

Overhead another jet came in to land at nearby Blagnac and the surface of Jacquot's coffee rippled. Rives looked at the ceiling with a faraway look.

'So how long were you and your wife members of Club—'

'Here we go, here we go again,' sighed Rives and shook his head. 'Just because the wife and I liked a bit of action, just because we went to Club Xéro, it's like it's our fault when something goes wrong, that we've got no one to blame but ourselves. I mean, anywhere else and you lot would have been a bit more sympathetic, a little more keen to get to the bottom of it. But Club Xéro . . . *Tant pis*.'

'So maybe you'd just run me through the evening?' asked Jacquot. Police reports, as he well knew, only went so far. 'Exactly what happened?'

'Again? How many more times?' Rives sighed, wiped a hand across his eyes, and blew out a wad of stale breath that Jacquot could smell across the table.

Jacquot stayed silent, sipped a coffee that was already cool.

'Once a month, me and Camille take a night out, right? Away from the kids, away from the house. Time's short, and Club Xéro makes the time count.'

'And that night?'

'We got there about ten, parked the car, walked the last bit. No point advertising.'

'Was it busy? Many people?'

'Thursday night, maybe seven or eight couples. It's busier weekends, more choice, if you know what I mean, but Friday and Saturday nights are difficult for us.'

'You know the people there?'

'That's the point. You don't know anyone. Sure there are regulars – staff – a few locals, but Toulouse is big enough not to see too many familiar faces.'

'And that night?'

'One couple I'd seen before. Camille didn't like him,

but the wife was a cracker. Dressed up like a Chinese, you know? So I make a move, buy her a drink, have a dance and then clear it with Camille.'

'And where was she? Camille?'

'Sulking by the bar. Slotting back the whiskies. But she's cool. Says "go ahead". So I do. Maybe an hour or so later I'm back in the bar . . .'

'*Un moment, s'il vous plaît.* Where did you go with your friend?'

'Jacuzzi to start. It's a good place to break the ice, if you know what I mean. Then one of the rooms down on the lower floor.'

'You see anyone you knew?'

Rives shook his head. And then, 'Hey, you got a cigarette? I'm out and busting for a smoke.'

Jacquot pulled out his pack and Rives took one, saw that it was filterless and tapped it against the table top.

'Can you remember anyone particularly?' Jacquot continued. 'On the dance floor, at the bar, in the jacuzzi?'

'Just the guy they found her with. Had a ponytail just like you.'

'You saw him?'

'Dancing. With this chick. Tall, she was. Darkish too. Either got a hell of a tan on her or she's a *noire.* All over each other, they were. Then, next minute they're gone.'

'Did you see them leave the room?'

'Nope. One minute there, the next . . . and I'm busy, remember? So I'm not looking around too much.'

'At any time, after the dance floor, did you see them again?'

'Just the once. Him. In the Hole with the wife. When they found them.'

'And his companion?'

Rives gave him a look. 'No. Nowhere. Not once. She was gone. Told Rudolfe a hundred times – "What about the girl he came with?" But he just shrugs. She went home by herself. Someone saw her, he tells me all the time. It's a pact, he says; face it. But clubs like Xéro don't like one of a couple just leaving. You come in as a couple, you leave as a couple – either your own or someone else's. But whatever happens, the numbers are always even, you know what I'm saying? And you have to be let out. The door's locked. But Rudolfe didn't even bother to chase it up. Didn't talk to the doorman, didn't bother with descriptions, nothing. Just let the bitch walk.'

'So you think the killer is the woman he was dancing with?'

'I haven't changed my mind, you know. It's what I've been saying all along but no one's listening. It's the darkie. Has to be. Camille, somehow, just got in the way.'

'This club. The members. You pay a fee to join?'

'A password. That's all it takes. You have the password, it means you know someone who's been there. That's all the recommendation you need. You pay your *entrée* – a thousand each, say – and that's it. You're in. And everything laid on – at a price.'

'So the management doesn't have a list of names? Members? Guests?'

Rives gave a bitter little chuckle at that. 'If you had to sign in, there wouldn't be a real name there. That's the point, right? *Anonyme, n'est-ce pas?*'

'So tell me, what happened when the police arrived?'

'Not much. When the bodies were found, word spread. Everyone was gone. By the time your boys arrived the place was pretty near empty. Except me. I couldn't find Camille.'

'So what do you think happened, monsieur?'

A look of resignation settled over Rives's stubbled features. 'You want to know what I think? I think there's someone out there walking round, free as a bird, with my wife's blood on her hands. And if your man Rudolfe's got anything to do with it, she'll stay free as a bird and do it all over again. To some other poor bastard, that's what I think. For whatever insane reason she might have. You ought to sack that fat fucker, Rudolfe, before she does any more damage.'

'You think the killer might be mad?'

recognition was established with a flurry of smiles and nods before they were close enough to shake hands.

'Mademoiselle Talleyran, it is good of you to see me.'

'Chief Inspector Jacquot. Anything I can do to help. Should we get a coffee? Maybe a drink? There's a place I know nearby.'

'A drink would be good,' said Jacquot with conviction. Though the sun shone, a fresh afternoon breeze had started up.

Five minutes later, as the two of them settled at a table at the back of Café des Jacobins on Place St-Georges and ordered a *chocolat* and pastis, Jacquot took her in. Just a couple of swift glances were enough to confirm Brunet's take on her. They'd only spoken on the phone, but he'd got her just right. She looked to be in her early thirties, with a sweetly sculpted nose, bright intelligent eyes and a firm jaw, these last two features suggesting the kind of focused dedication you'd need in an *advocat* pleading your case before magistrates. Yet despite the eyes and the set of her jaw, Jacquot also sensed a fragility about her – the thin bony hands, the almost translucent skin, the delicately turned ears peeping out from loose wisps of hair at her temples. There was a sense, too, of disappointment about her, as though life had not quite delivered on her dreams. According to Brunet she lived with her mother across the Garonne in St Cyprien. 'She sounds like a little bird,' Brunet had said. 'All a-twitter. But I'd guess underneath . . .'

'It doesn't look much,' said Mademoiselle Talleyran, casting around the low, beamed room, a swish of steam billowing from the Gaggia behind the bar, 'but they serve wonderful salads and omelettes at lunch. And for the centre of town it is very reasonably priced.'

Jacquot said he had no doubt she was right, and there was nothing like a good omelette for lunch, especially an omelette that was reasonably priced. But time was pressing. He still had one more call to make before catching his train back to Cavaillon. When his *petit jaune* and the *chocolat* arrived he got straight down to business.

'My colleague tells me you knew Marc Fastin at Lafranc-Fastin?'

'Your colleague was a most persuasive and persistent man.' Monique Talleyrand smiled. 'I have no doubt that the senior partners at my firm would have no hesitation in using his services were he ever to leave the *judiciaire*. I probably told him far more than I should have. I have a feeling I was very . . . indiscreet.'

'Jean Brunet is a very persistent man,' agreed Jacquot. 'And a very fine officer.'

'But not an officer with the Toulouse *judiciaire*,' she

said with a twinkle in her brown eyes. 'Cavaillon, I believe he said. And you as well?'

'You're quite correct. We are out of our jurisdiction here, but this is really just a matter of tidying things up. From our end. Some of Monsieur Fastin's . . . friends, contacts, you understand.'

'Tidying things up? But the case is closed, is it not?' She gave him an arched smile.

Jacquot spread his hands.

'But you're not happy with the findings?' she persisted.

'That's correct. It all seems—'

'Too convenient?'

'C'est ça, exacte.'

Monique Talleyran nodded as though she couldn't agree more, then gestured to Jacquot's ponytail. 'He wore his hair just like you,' she said. 'At first, when I saw you coming towards me . . .'

There was a wistful softness in the observation, the suggestion of an intimacy, which encouraged Jacquot to wade in when otherwise he might have been less abrupt. 'Tell me, mademoiselle, how long were you and Marc Fastin lovers?'

It came out so unexpectedly that Monique Talleyran gasped. 'Chief Inspector, are you always so direct?'

Jacquot spread his hands. 'Sometimes, mademoiselle, in situations like this it is the best way.'

She took up her *chocolat*, pursed her lips, and blew across its foamy surface. Holding the cup with the fingertips of both hands she took a sip. 'If we are going to talk about my love life, then perhaps we should dispense with formalities. My name, as you know, is Monique, but friends call me Nikki.'

'Nikki,' repeated Jacquot, as though savouring the sound of the name. 'It suits you.' And as he said it, Jacquot was suddenly aware of Mademoiselle Talleyran as a woman. Not as a lawyer, not as a source of information, but as a woman – an attractive and, he suspected, easily seduced woman. But a needy, lonely woman too. The kind of woman who would love with a desperate, devoted passion, and cling tragically when things started going wrong. The kind of woman a man should be careful of. All or nothing. Marc Fastin would have learned that.

Nikki put down her cup, settled it neatly in its saucer and, without any kind of embarrassment, began. 'I will tell you all I know, Chief Inspector. To help you find his killer.'

'So you do believe he was murdered?'

'There can be no other explanation, even if Chief Inspector Rudolfe, here in Toulouse, chooses to think differently. He is well known to my firm, of course. We have had dealings with him before, on other matters. In case you do not know him, he has maybe five years to go until retirement and is clearly not anxious to put himself out. Anything I can do to make life, shall we say . . . uncomfortable for him, would be enormously gratifying.' She gave Jacquot a smile, sharp little teeth bent slightly inwards towards a tiny pink tongue.

And so Nikki Talleyran began her story, staring up at the beams above their heads and working at her bony knuckles as she recalled her affair with Marc Fastin, pausing only to sip her *chocolat*. And Jacquot listened.

'Marc was a brilliant advocate. He could argue the hind legs off a donkey. If you were up against Marc, you had your work cut out, and no mistake. He was like your colleague – persuasive, persistent. Sooner or later he got whatever it was he wanted.' She smiled, looked down at her cup, and Jacquot knew she wasn't just talking about work.

'I believe one of his clients was SportÉquipe. Pierre Dombasle?'

'That's right. Marc did a lot of work for them. Licensing, franchises, commercial leases. And not just here in Toulouse. All over.'

'And how did the two of you meet?'

'Professionally. Two years ago. At a deposition at his offices. We were lovers within a week, and for the next eighteen months.' Without being able to do anything about it, a blush swarmed across her cheeks. 'He was one of the most extraordinary men I had ever met. So full of life. So energetic, enthusiastic. There was nothing I wouldn't have done for him – even if, sometimes, I was uncomfortable with it.'

She looked at Jacquot, caught the frown.

'At first, he was a kind and considerate lover . . . if rather more experienced than I.' The blush returned. 'And I was happy, happier than I had ever been. But then, slowly, he began to change. Little things. He'd get impatient with me, get cross, sulk. Once or twice we'd make arrangements to meet after work and he'd call at the last moment to cancel. Then, in bed, sometimes, I felt he was just . . . going through the motions, you know? His heart wasn't in it. Not so considerate any more, a little distant, as though he was bored with me, as though what we had wasn't working for him any longer but he couldn't think how to get out of it.'

Jacquot sipped his drink, said nothing, waited for her to continue.

'And I would have done anything to avoid that . . . him leaving me. The thought of not having him, of losing him. It was round then that he told me about this club, Club Xéro, told me what happened there. "If you don't want to try, you might as well die", he used to say. It was a kind of mantra with him – anything from eating Japanese food to snorting cocaine. And every time he suggested something, I knew I had to go along with it or risk losing him, that we'd be finished. Which is why I said "yes", why I agreed to go there with him. How silly can you be? I should have just told him "no" and damn the consequences.'

'And what of Club Xéro?'

Nikki grimaced, clamped together her sharp little teeth and sucked in a breath through tightening lips. 'It was . . . horrible. Sleazy. So . . .' She paused, shook her head as though she couldn't think of a suitable word to describe it. 'The men there, the women. And the things that went on . . . it was too much for me.' She gave a sad little laugh.

'How many times did he take you?'

'Three times,' she replied. 'I don't know how I managed. To have other men . . . just assume I was available. Because I was there. As if they had some kind of right. The . . . familiarity.' She looked at the table, hunched her shoulders and shuddered. 'And worst of all, of course, was to see Marc behaving like that. With other women. Wanting other women. It was as though I wasn't enough. I was so . . . jealous. So angry. Yet still I persevered.' She started to shake her head. She sniffed, turned it into a deep breath, as though to gather herself. 'But I lost him anyway.'

'When was this?' said Jacquot, knowing she wanted

to cry, knowing the effort it was taking her to hold it back.

'Seven, eight months ago now.' She finished her *chocolat,* put the cup back in the saucer, fingers playing with the handle. 'Suddenly there was someone else.'

'Do you know who?'

'I don't know her name, but I saw them together. Once. Out of my office window, would you believe? He was walking along La Pomme with her, arm around her waist. And she was . . . nuzzling him. I nearly died. My knees . . . my stomach . . . it was such a shock.'

'Age?'

'Mid to late thirties. Around there.'

'And do you remember what she looked like? Anything about her?'

'Everything I'm not, Chief Inspector. Blonde, for a start. And tall. I only ever came up to his shoulder.'

'Tanned? Dark skin?'

'Not that I could see.'

'Long hair? Short hair?'

'She was wearing a beret. I couldn't tell.'

'So how do you know she was blonde?'

Nikki gave a sharp little laugh at being caught out. 'A guess. A woman's intuition. Marc liked blondes.'

'Club Xéro?' asked Jacquot, recalling that Camille Rives was a brunette.

She nodded. 'Club Xéro.'

'So you think she was the killer? The new girlfriend?'

'Yes. That's what I believe. Although killing that other woman too, and setting up that . . . that charade . . . ?'

'Did you tell the police all this?'

'Rudolfe? *Mais bien sûr.* As soon as I heard about the deaths, I phoned him. Even if, as a lawyer, I was taking a risk. Telling them about my affair with Marc . . . my going to that club. If it had somehow leaked to the Press, it would have been very embarrassing for me – personally and professionally. And I think Rudolfe played on that, the risk I was taking, when he concocted his convenient little *mise en scène*. As far as he was concerned, it was the woman Marc was found with. She was the one who did it.'

'But you don't believe that?'

Nikki gave him a look.

'And have you seen her around? This girlfriend? Since Marc's death?'

Nikki shook her head. '*Non, jamais.*'

29

The last address took Jacquot back to the train station. Crossing the railtracks a couple of kilometres further down the line, the taxi dropped him along a length of canal. According to Brunet, the manager of Club Xéro lived on the fourth houseboat along from the old laundry.

Chez Nous, the name painted on the blunt bows of an old canal barge, was a mess. A table and chairs had been set on deck but had fallen over, three bulging bin liners had yet to be taken ashore, and a sagging length of cable stretched from a half-open deck hatch to a TV aerial roped to the rigging above the pilot house. A line of washing had been hung on it to dry – a pair of combat trousers (beige-spotted desert issue) and a selection of tank top T-shirts.

It was therefore no surprise to Jacquot to find that the owner of the barge – Silvio Robillant – was dressed in exactly that: combat trousers (green and black jungle issue) and a red tank top. Emblazoned in black across the front of the vest was the word '*Quoi?*'.

Which is probably why Monsieur Robillant chose not to say anything when he eventually appeared in the pilot house from below deck and slid open the door. He just lifted his chin as though to give a clearer look at the message on his chest.

'Daniel Jacquot,' said Jacquot, and lying smoothly, 'Jean-Claude Rives gave me your address.'

'You a *flic*?' said Robillant, glancing to left and right along the towpath as though expecting an ambush.

'Yes. But this is unofficial.'

'I like unofficial,' said Robillant, and he slid the door open just wide enough for Jacquot to step past.

'Beer?' he asked, shuffling down a set of steps into the cabin below.

'Not for me, thanks,' said Jacquot, following more carefully, feeling for each step with his heel. By the time he reached the bottom, Robillant was pushing a fridge door shut with a bare foot and popping a Grolsch. There was something seedy and tousled about the man – paunchy, late forties, fat lips glistening in a rash of grey stubble.

'Take a seat.' He waved at a leopard-skin banquette and a table heaped with magazines, a couple of spilling ashtrays, and an empty bottle of wine on its side. 'Sorry about the mess. You just can't get the staff . . .' He tipped the can, took a swig.

'It won't take long, monsieur,' said Jacquot, sliding between the table and banquette.

'Go ahead. No rush,' replied Robillant, leaning back against the fridge and letting out a tiny burp.

'It's about Monsieur Marc Fastin.'

Robillant nodded. 'There's only so much I can tell you. Even if I have already told it a million times. I knew Monsieur Fastin from previous visits. Not that name, of course. Came in once or twice a month. Always a different girl. And always pretty too. Didn't swing so far as I know, just came for the facilities. Which was cool. We didn't mind that.'

'But the woman he was found with?'

'Wasn't the woman he arrived with.'

'What about her – the one he arrived with? Where was she? Did you see her that evening?' Three questions at once, thought Jacquot. Not correct police procedure. But he knew why he'd done it. He wanted to get out of there. The cabin was so stale and stuffy you could hardly take a breath – a warm conjoining of dirty bedding and damp carpets.

Robillant shook his head. 'Didn't let him in so I didn't get a good look at who he was with. Saw them down in the disco, but they were shadows. Didn't see them go upstairs.'

'And what do you suppose happened to her? Fastin's companion. The woman he arrived with.'

'Skedaddled, most likely. With the rest of them.'

'Did you tell the police about the house rules – couples only? And there was Fastin with Camille Rives. And Jean-Claude on his own. Three of them?'

Robillant shook his head. 'They didn't seem too bothered. Open and shut as far as they were concerned. Can't say I blame them, to tell the truth. After I saw the pair of them, up there in the Black Hole. Him with his throat sliced and his tackle gone. Her with her hands still gripped tight round the knife handle. You wouldn't believe it. And blood everywhere. Looked just like what they said it was. Suicide pact.'

'Not quite that.'

'Well, you know what I mean. She cuts his throat, slices off his *couilles*, then does herself. Murder/suicide then. That better?'

Jacquot nodded.

'I mean, he's not going to cut his own dick off, then cut his throat and hand her the knife, is he?'

Jacquot nodded again. 'Tell me, did they know each other? Madame Rives and Fastin? Had they been at the club at the same time before?'

'Might have. Who knows? There's a lot of people came through Xéro. You can't remember every set, you know?'

'But you knew Madame Rives?'

'Saw her a few times, you know? She was a regular. Comes with her husband like once a month. Liked a drink too. Her husband played more than she did. But she was no prude, you could see that. Great structure on her, you know what I'm saying?' Robillant gave Jacquot a leery grin.

'But you never saw them together? Fastin and Madame Rives?'

'Not at Xéro I didn't.'

'Somewhere else?'

Robillant shook his head. 'Nope. I'm just saying, they could have met up someplace else, is all. They could have been an item.'

'So what do you think happened that night?'

Robillant crossed from the fridge and sat at the table. 'I think they knew each other. Don't ask me why. I think they were having a thing and it was going wrong. He wanted out and she didn't.'

And then, calling down the passageway, came a

woman's voice. 'Sylvioooohhhhh. *Qu'est-ce que tu fais? Qui est là? Viens ici, petit méchant. Maintenant.*'

Robillant rolled his eyes, then gave Jacquot a stubbly grin. 'Time's up, Monsieur *Flic*. 'Fraid I got business to attend to.'

30

Jean Brunet was already in the squad room when Jacquot arrived at Cavaillon police headquarters the following morning.

'Good trip?' he asked as he followed Jacquot into his office.

Going behind his desk, Jacquot flicked through the stack of paperwork – usefully edited down – that Brunet had put there in his absence. For some strange reason, the newspaper clipping on top of the pile failed to register.

Jacquot looked up. 'Just as you said, it looks like there's someone missing.'

'And each one . . . there's Monsieur Pierre Dombasle. SportÉquipe. Valadier's clinic, Souze's boy getting sponsorship, Fastin and his law practice, Savry and the book.'

Jacquot nodded. 'And each death neatly signed off. No action. Hit-and-run, falling wine rack, suicide, and a pact-style murder/suicide.' Jacquot tugged at his pony-tail. 'If I didn't know better, I'd say the various *judiciaires* were in on it.'

'What about drowning?' asked Brunet. 'How do you feel about drowning?'

'Drowning?'

'There's been another one. Two nights ago. Antoine Peyrot.'

For a moment, the words meant nothing. And then, 'Peyrot? Antoine Peyrot?'

An image of Peyrot, the team's hooker, sprawled out at Dombasle's breakfast table, sprang into Jacquot's mind, and then, just as quickly, the look of disgust that had spread over the yacht-broker's face when Olivier had mentioned that Savry was gay.

Brunet gestured to the newspaper cutting on Jacquot's desk. 'The bare bones of it are there,' said Brunet. '*Nice-Matin*. This morning.'

Jacquot snatched it up. The story was a page three, bottom right corner report, two edges of the paper frayed, the other two scissored, the page number visible. Under a headline that read *Noyade à Antibes*, the story had been neatly squeezed into two short columns. Accompanying the story was a black and white photo of Antoine standing by the prow of a yacht. He was dressed in a dark sports shirt that was probably blue, wore white shorts and held a rope. He looked as though he was taking the yacht behind him for a walk. The caption read *Peyrot: Port Vauban*.

'He was found early yesterday morning floating between two boats on the new *quai*, Antibes' harbour,' continued Brunet. 'Cause of death established as drowning, but badly beaten up too. That's not in the story by the way. I got that from a contact in the pathologist's office.'

'So there'll be an investigation,' said Jacquot. A death following a beating meant only one thing. Skimming through the story, he looked for confirmation. He couldn't find any.

'Apparently not,' said Brunet. 'According to my sources the injuries sustained to head and body have been judged compatible with "hull friction", the body knocked around by the boats along the *quai*. Apparently there was quite a swell the other night. And there was nothing stolen. Rolex watch, a wad of notes in his wallet, a gold bracelet. All where they should be. Oh, and alcohol. He'd been drinking. Must have stumbled, fallen in, they reckon. As of nine o'clock this morning, it's down to accidental death. No suspicious circumstances. Nothing to follow up.'

31

If Claudine Eddé had a fatal flaw, it was the irresistibility of Déscharme's art supply shop on Cavaillon's Place Lombard. That Thursday afternoon, flush with her winnings at Pierre Dombasle's gaming tables, she'd pushed open the door, breathed in the scent of dusty floorboards, fresh canvas and linseed oil, and felt the same hungry rush of excitement that another woman might feel in a couturier's *salon*.

Old man Déscharme was on duty behind the glass-topped counter. Perched on a stool and poring over a copy of *Art France* like Rodin's *Thinker*, he was dressed in his usual cords, brown apron and hand-knitted cardigan. He looked up when he heard the doorbell jangle, acknowledged Claudine with a flirting 'Mam'selle, *bonjour*, *entrez*, *je vous en prie*,' before turning back to his magazine. He knew she'd be at his counter soon enough.

And she was. But not that soon. Forty minutes after entering the shop she placed the last tubes of paint on Déscharme's counter and reached for her purse. In exchange for several hundred-franc notes she received a few centimes and a carrier bag that bumped against her leg as she swung across Place Lombard.

And there he was. Daniel. Heading for Cours Bournissac, twenty metres ahead and turning the corner out of sight.

For a moment Claudine wasn't certain what to do. He'd phoned once, from Paris, but that was the last time she'd heard from him. She had hoped he would call again, but she'd heard nothing. Now he was back (without telling her) and she surprised herself by suddenly wondering how long it would be before he got in touch. She decided to save herself the anxiety of waiting for the phone to ring and for it to be him. Instead of heading for Sadi Carnot where she'd parked her car, she followed after him.

She caught up with him as he fitted the key into the lock and pushed open the door.

'So you're back, and you haven't called yet.'

Just the look on his face was enough to tell her all she needed to know. It split into a huge grin that showed his teeth and hid his eyes in a web of laugh lines. Before she knew it, she'd been swept up in his arms and his lips had brushed past hers to nuzzle at her neck.

He held her away from him and looked at her hard. A woman walking past glanced up at them. Jacquot pulled Claudine further into the hallway and closed the door with his foot.

'I could eat you up,' he whispered. 'I really could.'

'Upstairs,' she told him, pushing him away, already panting lightly. 'Upstairs you can.'

Later, the room dark now, lying on his bed, Jacquot told Claudine about his trip. And how it wasn't just Bernard Savry any more. There was Valadier too; and Patric Souze; and Marc Fastin. He told her about the street where Luc died; he told her about the wine rack that Souze had been meaning to fix; and the missing partner at Club Xéro. But he didn't say anything about Antoine Peyrot, and he didn't say anything about Pierre Dombasle – how he'd 'helped' Luc with start-up capital and now withdrawn it; how he'd secured Marc a partnership at his law firm; and his interest in François Souze.

'So you think they could all be murders?' she asked.

'They certainly *could* be.'

'And? What next?'

'Right now?'

'Right now.'

'Right now I'm hungry and Baie d'Halong is just a few doors away.'

It was on their way out that Jacquot stopped in the hallway to check his mailbox. A fistful of circulars which he crumpled up and stuffed in the bin provided, and a large, stiff-backed envelope.

'Aren't you going to open it?' asked Claudine as they settled at their table five minutes later. He'd brought the package with him, tucked under his free arm, and had put it down by the side of his chair.

'I know what it is.'

'Well, I don't.'

He looked at her, stunned for a moment, then saw her slow smile. He'd been away from her too long. They both laughed.

But he did as he was told.

Leaning down he pulled out the envelope and slit it open with a chopstick. Inside was a framed photo. He glanced at it, then handed it over.

Her eyes widened. 'It's the team. It looks great.' And holding it out in front of her, turning it for some light, she said, 'Quite a production, too.'

The photo was an old-style black and white – standing

players, seated players, arms crossed, grouped around their skipper and the inscribed ball.

The focusing was pinprick-sure and Claudine could read the writing easily:

L'Équipe,
Côte d'Azur, 1996

Beneath the photo she read the names of the players, lingering on Jacquot's – full initials and position – all extravagantly copperplated and clearly embossed on to the mounting. And somehow, thought Claudine, the photographer – with his assistant and silver suitcases and sunshade – had, amid the horseplay and discomfort in front of a camera, captured the fifteen of them perfectly. Fifteen middle-aged men, doubtless looking less fresh-faced and energetic than they might once have been, a little paunchy here and there, balding too, and some with spectacles. She wondered if they'd gone for black and white to soften down some of the louder shirts and jackets. She suspected she was right.

Jacquot took the photo back, tucked it away again, seeming to push it even further under his chair. 'Maybe I'll forget it when we leave.'

'No you most certainly will not,' she replied, looking horrified.

Jacquot gave her a look, then laughed. It didn't take long to get back into the mood.

Menus were brought, dishes chosen and Claudine came back to the picture.

'So when they position you like that, for a team photo, is there any kind of order? You know, protocol? About who sits or stands, or where?'

Jacquot shrugged. 'Often it's based on the size of the player, a kind of symmetry for the photo,' he replied, thinking of Sidi Carassin. 'Or sometimes they put more experienced players, the older guys, on chairs in the front row, as a sign of seniority. The number of caps they hold. Only the Captain remains in the same place. In the centre. Why do you ask?'

'It's funny,' she said, as though musing to herself.

Just then their food arrived, two bowls of thin, steaming soup scented with coriander and lemon grass. Then rice, noodles, satays. Finally, their table crowded with dishes, the staff bowing their retreat, Jacquot gave in. 'What's funny?'

'Looking at that photo, I see it now. I didn't at the time, but I do now.'

'See what exactly?' he asked, drawing his soup closer.

'You know, the guys around Pierre. Olivier, Lorraine, Millet, Peyrot, Jean-Charles with the pregnant wife, and that rather smarmy Caloux.'

'What about them?' asked Jacquot, pleased that she should have spotted Caloux for what he was.

'Then there's the Curé, of course,' Claudine rattled on, 'so he'd have to be in the front row, I suppose – like a kind of team mascot, really.'

'And?' Jacquot sipped from his china spoon, tasted the soup, almost not listening as the chillies hit his tongue and puckered the insides of his mouth. '*Dieu, Dieu, si délicieuse*,' he thought, exactly what he wanted.

'And all the rest at the back, standing – Sidi, you, Simon, Théo, Lou, roly-poly Paul, and the one with the ears – Mageot. Fisherman, *flic*, butcher, postman, teacher, farmer, bodyguard. And all of you poor. Or rather, not as rich as the ones in the front row.' Claudine chuckled. 'The poor standing, the rich sitting.'

Jacquot put down the china spoon, and frowned. She was right, dammit. What an observation. Rich sitting, poor standing.

'Bet you anything you like, if those other guys were rich – Valadier, Savry, Souze and Fastin – if they had shown up, they'd have been sitting too,' Claudine continued, putting into words exactly what Jacquot was thinking.

'They were. Rich, I mean. Savry had just lined up a big publishing deal, Luc was a successful surgeon, and Patric was a Bordeaux *négociant*. As for Marc Fastin, he was a partner in a big-deal firm of corporate lawyers. Five men. All team members. All in the last seven months. And all of them wealthy.'

Now it was Claudine's turn to frown. 'Five? There're just four, surely.'

Jacquot took a deep breath. He'd got carried away. Said more than he should have done. He looked across the table.

'As of two nights ago, there're five. Antoine Peyrot. Sitting in the front row.'

Claudine's face paled. 'Well thank God you're poor, is all I can say.'

That night, while Claudine slept, Jacquot slipped from their bed. In his small galley kitchen he poured himself a calva, sat at the table and reached for the team photo.

If Claudine was right – and her theory seemed as likely a runner as any other – then who would be next? wondered Jacquot. The tax expert Claude Lorraine, with a lucrative consultancy in Monaco? The *notaire* Caloux? Gilles Millet, the architect in Grasse? Jean-Charles? Olivier? Or, maybe even Dombasle himself?

Jacquot looked at their faces, one by one – Olivier, smiling of course, the other five looking suitably stern and square-jawed.

32

Antoine Peyrot's funeral service was held the following Monday morning in the hills above Golfe Juan, in a small chapel at the top of a sloping olive grove, on the outskirts of a tiny village called Sainte-Fione that was far enough away from the coast to have avoided the developers, yet still close enough for a narrow triangle of blue sea to sparkle between the green hills.

Like Luc and Chantal Valadier, Église Sainte-Fione was the church where Antoine Peyrot and his wife, Isabelle, had married, and the church where his three children had been baptised. That bright, high, blue-skied November day, his widow and sons sat together in the front pew, Isabelle's rounded back hunched between their broad shoulders and straight, suit-clad backs. No more than two metres away Antoine's coffin, raised on a shrouded trestle, stood on the altar steps between the twin balustrades of an ancient communion rail. The bare wood of Antoine's casket glowed in the cool, dusty air of the chapel and the flowers laden across its lid smelt of summer – hot, thick-petalled and waxy.

The chapel was full, eight rows each side beneath simple stained-glass windows, the space by the font and double-planked chapel doors, and the aisles between the pews and walls providing standing room for those, like Jacquot, who had arrived too late to claim a seat.

Jacquot had left Cavaillon at dawn, crossing the still dry and reedy banks of the Durance, and followed the route south that he and Claudine had taken for Dombasle's reunion, heading first for the harbour at Antibes where the body had been found. The new *quai*, Brunet had said, and he found it easily enough, a long finger of piled stone and smooth concrete pathway decorated with a squadron of yachts drawn up each side, stern ladders out, rigging snapping in the breeze, gulls screeching, wheeling and hovering in the off-shore breeze. Despite himself, Jacquot understood how a verdict of accidental death could have been reached. The quay was not long enough for the boats moored to it, their hulls crammed together railing to railing, fender squeaking against fender, the stones of the quay's pilings sharp and sloping. Any body trapped there, between hull and rock, with a swell to push it, would soon be ragged and bruised from contact.

The service had started by the time Jacquot completed the hairpin drive up to Sainte-Fione from Antibes and finally located the chapel, at least a kilometre from the cobbled streets of the village. From the arched black shadow of its open doors, the ponderous beat of an organ reached out to him across the dry grass and stony earth, a small patch of land that in summer would crackle with the buzz and static of a million crickets but was now, save the low drawling notes of the organ, silent.

Even with their backs turned to him and their heads bowed, Jacquot could see them – Olivier, Millet, Lorraine, Jean-Charles Rains, Mageot and there, in the front pew across from the grieving Peyrot family, Pierre Dombasle and his wife Lydie. From the back of the chapel Jacquot could see that Dombasle, head bowed, was wearing a stiff, formal morning suit, his wife, Lydie, swathed in black, the wide brim of a black straw hat casting her face into shadow.

Beyond the coffin, a priest in a lacey white surplice led the congregation in prayer – a low murmur of responses to his quavering voice. He looked as ancient as the chapel he served, his shoulders rounded like the vaulted ceiling, his skin the colour of the stone walls, eyes black as the flagstones and wispy hair as white as the altar cloth.

'*In nomine Patris et Filii et Spiritus Sancti* . . .' he intoned, raising a crooked hand to bless the man he had married to Isabelle, the man whose three children he had baptised and confirmed, the man he had maybe baptised as well. Jacquot had a feeling that the old fellow was as sad as any of the mourners there. Beside him a knot of shawled women and local men in black berets and tight jackets and buttoned-up shirts mumbled their responses and crossed their brown, creased faces. Jacquot glanced at them, not one as high as his shoulder, and he knew what some of them would be thinking. So young, and so dead. And me thirty years older, and still here. I'm ahead of the game, thanks be to God. It was only human nature, surely?

With the final blessing given, Olivier Touche, Pierre Dombasle, Gilles Millet, Claude Lorraine, Guy Mageot and Jean-Charles Rains stepped out from their pews and, arranging themselves around the coffin, they lifted it from the trestles and up on to their shoulders. Slowly, first steps uneven, they moved down the aisle, the foot of the coffin tipping slightly to make contact with the shoulder of the stringy architect, Gilles Millet, from Grasse.

No one in the congregation spoke as they followed

the pallbearers to the Peyrot crypt behind the church, just a nod, a sharp gloved wave, and swift sad smiles when eyes met.

Gathering around the crypt – stone-built like a small *borie* but bare of any decoration save a necklace of flowers set around its edge and the family name chiselled into a stone block above the door – the mourners watched as the casket was lowered down the steps and manoeuvred inside. It was here, Jacquot noticed, that Gilles came in handy, dashing forward from the foot of the coffin to go ahead, into the crypt, helping his larger team-mates to squeeze through the opening. Somehow Jacquot knew that the boys had practised this move.

And then, with a final splash of holy water from the curé, the squeaking of rusty hinges as the crypt gates were swung closed, followed by a thin heart-rending wail from Isabelle, it was over.

Jacquot had positioned himself well. When Olivier Touche came out of the crypt Jacquot's fellow flanker had made for the far side of it, hands clasped in front of him, head lowered. In those last moments Jacquot edged over to him and reached for his friend's elbow, holding him back as the rest of the mourners turned to go.

A big grin lit up Olivier's face. 'Daniel. So good of you to come. Antoine would be very pleased.'

'Maybe . . . but you know we were not the greatest friends, Antoine and I. We had our moments.'

'Whatever,' replied Olivier. 'At least you're here. So, shall we go to the house? Antoine's mother's place. The family home. About two or three kilometres up the road?'

'I can't,' replied Jacquot. 'I have to be in Nice within the hour. But I need to talk to you. As soon as possible.'

Olivier nodded. 'I'll pass on your condolences, *mon ami*. As for talking, how long will you be in Nice?'

'An hour – if I'm lucky.'

'Then come out to the restaurant. Come to dinner. Sophie will be thrilled to see you again so soon and I will be just as thrilled to show off my little empire. In fact, why not stay the night? There are rooms. And you can't possibly drive all the way back to Cavaillon. *Non, non, non.* Come to us and then we can eat and drink as well as talk.'

33

'Chief Inspector Murier will be with you shortly, Monsieur Jacquot.'

Each time they said it, Jacquot nodded, quite unsurprised that he was being made to wait. He wondered if Murier had told all his various messenger boys to address him by name and not rank. He thought it almost a certainty.

For the last forty minutes, Jacquot had been sitting on a bench in the main reception hall of the Nice *judiciaire*. He'd watched the usual cast of characters come and go – felons, cops, lawyers; striding, huddled, threatening, pleading – and was thinking about stepping out for a cigarette when he noticed a young woman coming towards him. She wore a pinstripe trouser suit, blonde hair tied back, sensible heels clacking on the marble. A few steps from the bench she reached out her hand and Jacquot got to his feet to take it. Firm and dry and businesslike.

'Chief Inspector Jacquot?'

'*Le même. C'est moi, mademoiselle,*' said Jacquot, surprised and gratified to hear his rank. Maybe they were starting to take it all a bit more seriously. Or maybe Murier had not been able to brief the young woman now standing in front of him. Jacquot couldn't have been more wrong – on both counts. Title aside, she was all business.

'*En effet*, Detective Inspector Ambert. Christine Ambert,' she replied. And to Jacquot's surprise, she levelled twinkling blue eyes on him and gave him a look, a very direct, unmistakable look. A blind man could have seen it. Or certainly felt the waves that accompanied the look. 'But you are right – mademoiselle, also. Shall we . . . ?'

Reaching for his upper arm, she turned him expertly and steered him into the middle of the hall. She didn't waste any time. 'I regret to say that Chief Inspector Murier has been called away. He apologises, of course, and he has asked me to see how we . . . I . . . can be of help to you.'

The two of them stopped in the middle of the hall and faced each other – one more huddled conversation.

'He's been called away?' said Jacquot with a smile.

'Regrettably. Just moments ago. I am so sorry. But how may I help?'

For a moment Jacquot felt like walking away, giving up, just not bothering. But something held him back. He needed someone on the Nice *judiciaire* to know what was happening, what might be happening.

Jacquot took a deep breath and wondered if she would hear him through. He'd find out soon enough.

'Three weeks ago, a friend of mine called Bernard Savry was found dead. Chief Inspector Murier judged it a suicide; I did not. In the last seven months, four other men, all members of the same rugby team, have died in what could be considered . . . what I believe to be . . . suspicious circumstances. The latest victim was found floating in Port Vauban last week. I have just been to his funeral. Chief Inspector Murier needs to be aware of this. He needs to know what might be happening, and I believe he must take the matter seriously.'

'And what exactly are these suspicious circumstances? Don't tell me – suicide we know. Drowning? Hit-and-run? You know as well as I do, Chief Inspector, that if we put a spin on every hit-and-run and every drowning and turned it into a full-scale investigation, there wouldn't be a cop left to direct traffic; and the bad boys would have a field day.'

'As I said, they were all team-mates. Members of the same squad.'

'How long ago, Chief Inspector?'

'How long ago? Seventeen, eighteen years . . .'

'So they'd be in their fifties, or thereabouts?' she asked with a twinkle in her eye.

'Close enough.'

'And where do they all live?'

'Paris, Toulouse, Bordeaux . . .'

'So all over the country, then?'

Despite what appeared to be indifference, her implied disbelief, Jacquot sensed a kind of understanding behind her questions. She was playing by the book, but also, like him, playing from the gut. He suspected she knew what he was trying to get at, and wanted to help.

'Hardly all over . . .'

'Any evidence – threatening letters, tapes, photos, something to link them, back up your . . . your . . . ?'

'"Speculation" is the word you're probably looking for, Detective Inspector. And I understand why you should use it. My case is weak, maybe, but I would still be grateful if you would pass on everything I have said to your Chief Inspector. My . . . concern. Here is my card,' he said, reaching for his wallet and pulling one out, knowing his time was up. She'd given him more than he'd expected. 'I will leave it to him to call me.

But if anything further crops up, I will call him to let him know.'

'And here is my card, Chief Inspector,' said Christine Ambert, producing her own from a jacket pocket and flourishing it under his nose.

He made to take it but she held on to it a second too long.

'Let *me* know, Chief Inspector. And I will do *all* that *I* can to be of assistance.' And with that she released her card, but left him holding his. '*À la prochaine*,' she said and turned on her heel.

34

Streetlights were blinking on in Nice's apartment-canyoned dusk as Jacquot drove along Boulevard de Riquier, following signs for Rue Bischoffsheim and the Grande Corniche. At that time of day, Olivier had told him, it was the route to take out of Nice. The Middle Corniche would be hellish in the rush-hour and the Corniche Littorale was closed because of roadworks after Eze. A section of cliff had dropped on to the road – it would take a month to clear . . . *tant pis*, Olivier had shrugged. At least it wasn't summer any more.

But it wasn't just directions on his mind. Since leaving the *judiciaire*, Jacquot had been thinking about Detective Inspector Christine Ambert. He knew it was a terrible thing, but if it hadn't been for Claudine Eddé sitting in her mill-house outside Cavaillon he'd have called Olivier and cancelled their evening, or invited Mademoiselle Ambert along with him. A few years back, he would have found it impossible to walk away from a woman like that. She reminded him of Boni Milhaud, the Air France stewardess on that long-ago flight from Paris to Marseilles. There was, Jacquot knew, exactly the same charge about the two women, the same burst of electricity that seemed to make the air shiver around them, both women strong, both determined, both of them out to get whatever it was they wanted and God help anyone who stood in their way. As a policewoman, Jacquot suspected that Christine Ambert would be formidable. As a lover . . . equally formidable, Jacquot had no doubt.

If Claudine hadn't been a part of his life, then he would certainly have acted on that look she'd given him.

Or maybe, he thought ruefully, he was fooling himself. Maybe he wanted that spark of electricity to be there, even if it wasn't. Such an attractive woman. Long blonde hair, pulled back into a tidy enough squad-room chignon, her skin pale, no touch of the sun, her frame long and lanky in that almost too tight trouser suit, the three buttons of the jacket and frilled undershirt not enough to cover the rise and swell and promise of her breasts. He hadn't looked, but he knew that she knew that he'd wanted to . . .

Or maybe . . . maybe he was too old?

Too old to bother. Or, worse still, too old to count?

How old was she, he wondered? Thirty-two? Thirty-four? Whatever, it hadn't seemed to dilute her interest.

So maybe it was a case of too old to bother. Already taken. Claudine in her mill-house.

But as Jacquot swung the wheel into the first bends leading to the Grande Corniche, his eyes settled on his bare ring finger.

No wonder women had men wear rings.

Leaving Nice behind and below him, pulling past Lézardière towards the Grande Corniche, Jacquot drove on until the approach road levelled out five hundred metres above the coast. From sea level to mountaintop in less than fifteen minutes, the lights of Villefranche and Beaulieu and St-Jean Cap-Ferrat winking like a scatter of orange stars far below.

Level it may have been but the road was still dangerously sinuous and driving east, Jacquot noted uncomfortably, meant keeping to the outside lane, with just a low stone wall no higher than his hub-caps between him and thin air. Keeping his eyes firmly on the road – Jacquot didn't like heights at the best of times – he welcomed the settlements of Col d'Eze and La Turbie where comforting pavements and buildings concealed the drop. A few kilometres out of La Turbie, with its Christmas lights set out across the main street but not yet switched on, the road began to slope again, barrelling down towards Roquebrune, Cabbé and Menton. And then, up ahead, a few kilometres from Roquebrune, Jacquot spotted the narrow cut he'd been told to look out for and branched off into a forest of scrub oak and aleppo, heading for Gorbio and Ste Agnès.

Jacquot knew all about Touche's restaurant. Every newspaper or magazine he looked at seemed to carry a review or story. On the Côte d'Azur, the name Touche came as high as La Terrasse and Le Moulin in Mougins, Le Cagnard above Cagnes-sur-Mer, the Colombe d'Or in St-Paul-de-Vence and Jacques Maximin in Vence. In a wider sense, Jacquot wondered if it might even eclipse Le Réfectoire at Hôtel Grand Monastère des Évêques in Luissac, where Jacquot had recently enjoyed what he considered to be some of the finest meals he'd ever been served. He could almost taste them now – the *ris de veau*, the cutlets and that slim tranche of calf's liver.

Unforgettable.

Suddenly, coming round a bend, Jacquot spotted a single floodlit post driven into the side of the road. Hammered into the post at about head height was a single silver letter – 'T'.

'You'll know when you get there,' Olivier had told him. And Olivier was right. Around the next bend was another post, another floodlight, and this time a silver 'O'. And so it went. Another four bends and Jacquot had arrived, dropping through the last trees to pull up in front of a long stone façade that reminded him of a Lubéron *bastide*, its shuttered length gently uplit by a line of cool green spotlights, a pair of sleek Mercedes limousines drawn up to one side of the entrance.

As he handed over the keys to a valet, he was thinking he should have opened the windows on the drive, to get rid of all the cigarette smoke, when he turned to see a familiar figure coming down the steps towards him.

35

'Daniel, Daniel, how lovely to see you,' said Sophie Touche as the valet started up the old Peugeot, buzzing the window down as he did so. The next instant, Sophie had taken his face in her hands, smacking three perfume-laden kisses on his cheeks. She was pert and petite and her face was pixie-like with fun and mischief. Her nose was long and sharp, her eyes almost oriental and her cheekbones high and pointed.

'Twice in a month,' she continued, patting his face with her hand. 'It's a record. And I'm so thrilled Olivier managed to persuade you to stay.' Her words came in a low mocking voice gravelly from too many cigarettes, but warm and welcoming. 'I'm so sorry I wasn't there,' she added, voice dropping lower and more gravelly, referring to that morning's funeral service. 'I didn't know Antoine well, but he and Olivier had been seeing a lot of each other. Olivier was even thinking of buying a boat. Can you imagine? *Ooh là-là. Quelle horreur.*'

If Jacquot had thought Lubéron *bastide* when he arrived, he was in for a surprise as Sophie led him into the restaurant. Beyond the wooden door, they passed down a minutely sloping flagstoned hall before turning into what Jacquot could only think of as a glass box supported by rust-coloured wooden posts that seemed to jut out into the same thin air that he'd studiously avoided all the way there. He wondered if Patric Souze had seen this. He'd have loved it.

The next thing Jacquot knew, an arm slid round his neck and pulled him backwards, turning him into an embrace. Olivier.

'So you made it. Good, good. Welcome to our little home,' he continued. 'So, are you set? Are you ready?'

'I even have a tie,' said Jacquot, the same one he'd worn for the funeral. He realised he hadn't eaten all day and he suddenly felt hungry. Dinner at Touche. It didn't get much better. He looked around the dining room, an opaque glass floor, he was grateful to see, and wondered where they would sit. Already, at only a little past seven, it looked as though every table was taken.

'Well, you can take that off right away,' Olivier told him. 'They don't wear ties where we're going.'

Jacquot knew he hadn't misheard and felt a twist of disappointment. So he wouldn't be eating at the restaurant after all.

'Michel. Michel,' said Olivier, waving over the maître d'. 'Make sure Monsieur Le Ministre and his friends have everything they need – maybe some *digéstives* on the house – and if Mademoiselle Collins turns up late, tell her we would stay open if it meant waiting for the dawn. Sophie,' he said, turning to his wife, 'we will not be late. I promise you.'

'Even if I minded, would it worry you?'

Olivier thought for a moment. 'No. No, it wouldn't.'

'Just be careful, you hear?'

'*Pardon, pardon? Je m'excuse?*' he said, cupping a hand to his ear as though hard of hearing.

'Away with you. *Va-t'en*. Daniel, you're in charge. And don't encourage him.' And with that she leaned up to both men, kissed them, and turned back to the restaurant.

'Here,' said Touche, leaning behind the maître's desk and pulling out a sheepskin flier's jacket. 'You'll need this. And give me that tie, for God's sake. You look like a schoolteacher.'

The motorbike had been drawn up where Jacquot's car had stood not five minutes earlier. It was red, as red as a bloody knife, and looked twice as dangerous. The bodyguards beside the two black Mercedes watched with interest as Touche swung a leg over the machine and pressed the starter switch. The engine growled like a guard dog catching a scent and Touche kicked the bike forward off its stand. With a couple of twists of the throttle that rent the air, he patted the seat behind him.

'You are joking?' said Jacquot, who hated motorbikes even more than he hated heights. As far as he could remember, the last time he'd swung a leg over the saddle of a motorbike, he'd been sixteen, riding pillion, and the 50cc engine had puttered along well enough in the back streets of Le Panier. This bike was quite another kettle of fish. 'I suppose a helmet's out of the question?' he continued, scrambling up on to the saddle and looking down to see where he could put his feet.

'No, no, put them there,' said Olivier, twisting round and pointing to a pair of silvery metal twigs somewhere below and behind Jacquot. Rather than feel with his feet, Jacquot tried to look where Olivier was pointing and the bike swayed dangerously.

'Whoa . . . easy, easy. There, you got it. And now just wrap your arms round me. There, that's it. OK, hold tight . . .' and with a seismic snort of power, the bike sprang forward with an incredible energy, weaved past the bodyguards and Mercs like a current of water streaming past an obstruction and shot off up the drive.

Seconds later, the bike braked with such force that Jacquot felt himself ride up Olivier's back. Less than a second after that he was flung backwards as Olivier swung round to the left and headed down to the Corniche turning.

Jacquot kept his eyes closed for most of the journey. On only two occasions did he open them. On the first, he was in time to see a pair of car headlights slice past only inches from his left knee, and the second time was when he dared a glance over Olivier's shoulder to see the centre line cross from left to right of the machine as Olivier swung out to take a blind corner, actually shifting his backside to bring the bike down, swooping around the bend as if there was an empty autoroute – all six lanes – waiting just for them. There wasn't. Instead, there was a van coming straight at them. In that split second, Jacquot knew they were both going to die – the bike embedded in the van's radiator grill, the whole broken mess toppling over the side of the road and tumbling five hundred metres to the beach. But they didn't die. With a whoop of delight that Jacquot could actually hear over the blast of the klaxon and the roar of the engine between their legs, Olivier powered the bike into a brake-slide-throttle-up manoeuvre that shook Jacquot like a giant doll.

After that Jacquot kept his eyes firmly shut, and only

when the bike finally slowed, turned off the road, and the surface became rougher, did he judge it safe to open them.

'Did you see that van?' cried Olivier over his shoulder, bringing the bike to a halt in a small square of trees. In the headlights, Jacquot could see a narrow path weaving upwards.

'I'm assuming you know that road very well?'

'Maybe ten times a week, if the wife'll let me. I can do Lézardière to the Roquebrune turning, eighteen kilometres, in seven and a half minutes,' he crowed, as he held the bike steady for Jacquot to clamber off.

'Is that night-time or daylight?' asked Jacquot, legs trembling a little as he put weight on them.

'Night-time, of course. Night-time's much faster. And safer. If it hadn't been night-time, I wouldn't have seen that van's headlights and we'd have been history.' Olivier dismounted and rocked the big red machine on to its stand.

'You mean, you knew that van was coming?'

'Of course. That's the whole point.' Olivier clapped Jacquot on the shoulder and laughed mightily. Jacquot shook his head in disbelief. That was Touche. One second you wanted to kill him (before he killed you), the next you wanted to have his babies. Leaning forward, Olivier switched off the engine, the headlight died and the small dusty path ahead of them was lost in a complete and utter blackness, just a low breeze licking through the trees. Moments later a torch switched on.

'So, off we go,' said Olivier, beckoning him on towards the path, flashing the torch ahead and backwards as they climbed up through the wood.

'There's a restaurant up here?'

'The best in the world. Believe me. Only the very best for my old friend Daniel Jacquot.'

36

What seemed an age later, the two men came out of the trees and Jacquot could see in the torchlight a pitch of sloping land covered in a low scrub no higher than their knees. Halfway across, Olivier turned and pointed behind them. There, far below, a jet was taking off from Nice's Côte d'Azur airport, banking over the sea, away from the brilliant necklace of light that stretched from St-Jean-Cap-Ferrat directly below them to the distant orange glow of Théoule and the jagged bulk of the Esterel.

'The best view in the world,' said Olivier, wrapping his arm round Jacquot's shoulder, switching off the torch so they could admire it without distraction. Jacquot felt as though he was floating on air, high above the earth.

'And there, there is the greatest smell in the world,'

continued Olivier, tipping back his head and flaring his nostrils into the breeze.

And though he didn't expect to smell anything so high up in the hills – another one of Touche's elaborate charades – Jacquot caught the same scent, the warm, sinuous aroma of roasting meat.

Olivier switched the torch back on and started across the slope. Up ahead, he cupped hands to his mouth, the torch beam splitting the night sky with a column of light and shouted, 'Ahhhh-Bel! Ahhhhh-Bel!'

A moment later came a distant response. '*Ici, tout droit. Tout droit.*'

And there, up ahead, Jacquot saw the swing of a lantern raised in the air, like a lighthouse guiding a ship into port. The light was yellow and faint but as they drew closer, Jacquot could make out the man holding it. He was tall and lean, dressed in a long skin coat that came to the tops of his boots, and he stood in the entrance of a low cave, more a scoop of an opening in the slope, its roof offering no more than a metre or two of cover. At its mouth, a metre or so behind the man, two fires burnt. A large cookpot blackened with age and battered with dents hung over the smaller fire and on the other, what looked like a small brown carcass turned over a bed of glowing embers. His old friend, Salette, the Marseilles harbour master, would have loved something like this.

'Abel, *ça va*? *Ça marche bien?*'

'*Très bieng*, M'sieur Olivier.' The man's voice was as low as the murmur of the breeze in this high place and as Jacquot stepped forward into the circle of light thrown by the lamp and fires he saw an old face as brown and wrinkled as a pickled *cailletier* olive.

'Abel, *je vous présente mon vieux ami ici*, Daniel,' said Olivier as an introduction.

No hand was offered, but the old man nodded at Jacquot and his eyes took him in, tiny glowing pinpricks of light set straight and level in a web of creases under curling, wiry brows.

'M'sieur Daniel. *Plaisir. Vengez, asseyez.*'

His accent was rough and southern, as though the words were torn from the sides of his throat, but his smile was big and his perfect white teeth shone against his dark skin. Stepping back he pointed out a length of worn tree trunk set against the slope a few metres from the fires, half the trunk under the roof of the cave, the rest in starlight.

Olivier made himself comfortable and patted the log for Jacquot to join him. 'How's that for a view?' he said once more, sweeping his hand proudly down the slope. To the west were the brighter lights of Nice's Promenade des Anglais and airport, stretching away through Cagnes, Antibes and Cannes. Below them the lip of the slope cut all light from the settlements of Villefranche, Beaulieu and Eze save the far headland tip of Cap Ferrat but, to their left, from further along the coast, came the glow of Monaco and distant Menton. Far below, the Cap Ferrat lighthouse blinked its message and another tiny plane banked above it.

Now that they weren't climbing, both men felt the chill and Jacquot was grateful for the closeness of the fires and the jacket that Olivier had given him.

'So what's the story, Olivier? I know you're dying to tell me.'

'Abel, you mean?'

The old man looked up when he heard his name but then dropped his eyes to the fires, the bubbling pot and hissing meat.

'Abel is an old friend,' continued Olivier. 'His grandfather worked for my grandfather, and his father worked for mine. When it was his turn in the kitchen he lasted four days. According to my father he was nineteen. He's been up in these hills ever since. He has a donkey to carry his kit, he has twenty goats – one of which we're going to eat in a minute – and he moves from cave to cave. This, believe it or not, is his summer camp. He's been here four months, grazing his herd, but by the end of next week he'll have moved on. He's never seen a television and he's never been in a car.'

Jacquot was stunned. So close to the richest, most sophisticated and probably most crowded stretch of coastline in the world. Close enough to see it far below. Yet so far away from it all. He shook his head.

'Is he married? Does he have a family?'

'He has a wife on a smallholding beyond the Col d'Eze, and two girls at university.'

'So how do you find him? How do you let him know you'll be . . . just dropping by with friends?'

'He has a son in my kitchen. One of our best chefs. But not as good as his father.'

Over by the fires the old man lifted the lid of the cookpot and a billow of steam curled up over the lip of the cave-mouth. A warm sweet aroma of garlic suddenly filled the air around them and Jacquot felt his cheeks pucker. Picking up a long wooden spoon Abel pushed it into the pot, stirred, then replaced the lid.

He looked at them, held out five fingers. '*Cink 'nutes*,' he said and, reaching for a jug, '*Du ving?*'

More than an hour later, as he smeared the last of a fresh young *chèvre* on to a last crust of his bread, Jacquot could not think of a better meal. All the others paled compared with the one he had just eaten, here, out in the open, five hundred metres above the sea, their 'table' lit by more stars than he'd ever seen. The chicken lentil soup served in mess tins was the best soup he'd ever tasted and the roast kid with its stone-baked olive bread and mixed leaves simply supreme. The warmth of it, the taste of it, the smell of it on this open hillside. Simple, but sensational. Jacquot had never felt so contented in all his life. He wanted to laugh out loud at the sheer bursting delight of it all – being there, having it.

'So now let's talk,' said Olivier, breaking into Jacquot's satisfied reverie. 'This morning you looked and sounded very serious.' He pulled two cigars from his pocket, handed one to Jacquot and reached forward to the edge of the fire for a glowing branch stub. 'So go ahead and ruin my evening.'

For the second time that day Jacquot told almost exactly the same story he'd told Inspector Ambert, somewhere beyond the slope, down there in that patch of golden light. And after only the shortest pause to consider Jacquot's story, Olivier then expressed pretty much the same doubts that she had.

'And how, exactly, are these circumstances suspicious? Hit-and-run? Drowning? Suicide?'

'It wasn't suicide. Bernard did not take his own life. And I very much doubt that Luc's hit-and-run was an accident, or Souze's getting trapped under his wine rack, or Antoine drowning. As for Fastin, well . . .'

'So you are honestly telling me that you believe someone is out there stalking us and killing us off one by one? Daniel, don't say it.' Olivier shook his head and chuckled. '*Et pourquoi? Quelle raison, dites-moi?* No, no, no, my friend. I think you've had too much of Abel's *vin de table*.'

'Olivier, I don't know why, and I don't know who – don't ask me. But what I can tell you is that the feeling right here in my gut is telling me that this is not right. None of it.'

'With the greatest respect, *mon vieux*, is there anything more than your venerable gut to back all this up? Is there any hard evidence, *mon ami*?'

Jacquot shook his head. 'Not a thing. Just circumstances, possibilities, theories. But Bernard was right. It doesn't add up. None of it.' He decided not to mention Claudine's observation that it appeared that only the richest members of the team were the ones being targeted – or maybe targeted first. And Olivier was certainly rich and, by the sound of things, destined to become even richer. Over dinner he'd run Jacquot through their planned expansion. Not just Touche Côte, but Touche Campagne and Touche Cité, with a franchised chain of shops named Touche Terroir.

Olivier took a swig of his wine. '*Écoute*. We live all over the place. We all do different things. And we're of an age, Daniel. Heart attack, forgetting to look right and left when we cross the street, getting drunk and falling in the water, getting depressed – our jobs, our lives, money, women, whatever. Sure, it's terrible, but shit happens, you know? At our ages, maybe we're lucky it's just five of us. Come on, old friend, it's late. Time to thank our friend here and head back to the bike.'

As Olivier went to push himself up on to his feet, hands pressing down on his knees, Jacquot reached for his arm and the wine in his cup slopped over Olivier's sleeve. Maybe Olivier was right. Maybe he had had too much of Abel's wine. But Jacquot knew he had to finish what he wanted to say. And just as Jacquot had sensed a certain quiet agreement or understanding in Christine Ambert that he might possibly be on to something, so did he too in Olivier. Despite what appeared to be a teasing disbelief.

'I just want you to know, Olivier. That's all. I want you to know what might be happening. And I'd like you to warn Pierre and Gilles and Claude too. You're closer to them than I am. They might listen to you.'

'They might,' replied Olivier, licking the spill of wine from his wrist. 'And they might also think – with good reason – that I've gone *completement fou*. But I promise you I will tell them, Daniel – just what you have told me tonight.' Olivier caught hold of Jacquot's hand and hauled him to his feet. 'I see Claude on Wednesday evening, and Pierre is having dinner with Gilles and I at the restaurant next week. To discuss our plans. I will pass on your warning.'

'Your plans?' Jacquot asked. 'You are all in this together?'

'Gilles and Claude of course – Gilles on design and building and Claude creating all the corporate stuff we need. Pierre too, of course. Well, Pierre's the funding. *Qu'est-ce qu'on peut dire?*'

After they bade farewell to Abel, the strongest handshake Jacquot had ever received, and thanked him for their dinner, the two men retraced their steps down the mountainside. And as Jacquot followed the beam of Olivier's torch, he tried to make sense of all he'd learned. Dombasle, the funding, old team-mates benefiting from their skipper's largesse, and his ruthlessness when things went wrong.

At least, thought Jacquot as he pulled a quilt around himself later that night, Olivier seemed to have taken his warning on board. There was no question that the ride back along the Peille road had been far more sedate than the journey out. Maybe Olivier had done more than listen.

37

The phone call came through on Thursday afternoon at a little before three o'clock. Fifteen minutes earlier Jacquot had switched off his telephone ringtone so that he could get some peace, but there was no way to stop the red flashing light that also signalled incoming calls. Jacquot had just read through Chief Inspector Murier's brief report on Bernard Savry's 'suicide' – cause of death attributed to suicide by gassing – and had started on the pathologist's report that Brunet had managed to get hold of. It was immediately clear that if Murier needed any evidence to support his 'cause of death', it was all there in the report from the Head of Pathology – a Doctor Nicolas Arbuthepas. According to the good doctor, Savry had a widespread cancer at the time of his death. Jacquot had reached the paragraph noting that it was unlikely that Savry would have had long to live, when the flashing light got the better of him.

With an irritated *tsk-tsk* he flung the file on the desk and tipped forward to reach for the phone.

'*Oui? Allô?*'

'Daniel? *C'est toi?*' It was the smallest voice, distant, little more than a whisper.

'*Oui, c'est moi.* Is that you, Sophie? Sophie?' It sounded like her but he couldn't be sure.

On the other end of the line, he heard a great intake of breath. The words that followed came in a controlled exhaled rush – the only way to get them out. '*Oui. C'est* Sophie. I'm calling from Hôpital Saint-Saëns. Olivier had a crash. That dammed bike of his. He was coming back from Villefranche when it happened. On the link road between Eze and La Turbie. He was with Claude Lorraine. Claude's dead and they're not sure if Olivier's going to make it.'

Jacquot reached Hôpital Saint-Saëns first thing the following morning. It was dark when he left Cavaillon and he drove towards a sky that turned from blue to grey to red and pink and gold. By the time the sun reached above the hills he was searching for somewhere to park.

Getting out of the lift on the fourth floor, he was

headed towards the reception desk when he caught sight of Sophie looking out of the window in a small waiting area.

'Sophie? It's me, Daniel,' he called out quietly, and when she turned and saw him her face dissolved in tears.

'Oh Daniel, Daniel. Thank you for coming. I'm afraid I called everyone, but you're the first. The kids are on their way from Paris, Pierre and Lydie are still in the States. There was no one . . .'

'I'm glad you did. I'm only sorry I couldn't get here sooner. How is he?'

'Stable, they say. But not good. He's . . . he's lost a leg. Somewhere above the knee. They operated last night, after we spoke. Apparently there was no alternative. The damage . . .'

'But he's alive, that's the main thing.'

Sophie nodded. 'Alive. Just.'

'So what happened? You said he was on his bike?' Taking her arm he led her to a sofa.

'He was going to have dinner with Claude Lorraine. At Touche, apparently. But he changed his mind. Just like he did with you. When Claude arrived, he got out that blessed motorbike and they rode down to Villefranche – La Mère Germaine. At about midnight, just as we were closing up, the gendarmerie called. There'd been an accident. Olivier's bike had left the road on the La Turbie slip, jumped the barrier, and ended up twenty metres down the slope on someone's terrace. Olivier was still alive but they found Claude in a tree . . .'

Sophie bent her head and sobbed.

Jacquot put an arm around her and for the next twenty minutes they sat there together, Sophie thinking of her husband, Jacquot feeling a hot coil of anger twist in his guts.

38

After spending most of the morning with Sophie, Jacquot left the hospital a little after midday and drove across town to the Institut de Pathologie Criminelle off Rue de Lestes. It was easier to find than he had expected and, even more welcoming, was well furnished with empty parking spaces. As a result Jacquot was ten minutes early for his appointment with Doctor Nicolas Arbuthepas, ten minutes to find somewhere to park.

Jacquot had made the appointment the previous afternoon but his punctuality did not appear to make much difference. A further twenty minutes after their agreed appointment time, Dr Arbuthepas had still to make an appearance.

'It's always like this towards the end of a week,' said his secretary, a motherly, middle-aged lady in a pleated tartan skirt, bringing Jacquot a coffee by way of recompense for the inconvenience. 'He's thorough, is the doctor,' she continued, going to her desk and reaching into a drawer for sweeteners. 'You want sugar?' she asked. 'Or these?'

A calva would have been good, thought Jacquot, but it wasn't the time or the place.

'No thanks,' he replied and smiled at her.

He'd just about finished his coffee when suddenly the double clanging of the cage-lift doors could be heard outside in the corridor. Another double clang followed as the gates were drawn closed and footsteps headed in their direction.

'Here he is now,' said the secretary, and as she turned to the door a tall, stoop-shouldered man lumbered into the office. He pulled off a scarf, unbuttoned himself from a beige overcoat, and hung coat and scarf on a hook behind the door. Under the scarf and coat he was wearing surgical scrubs. On his feet were a pair of scuffed white clogs.

'You're Jacquot?' he said, starting forward and shaking Jacquot's hand.

'Chief Inspector Jacquot, that's right.'

'Not of this parish, though, are you?'

Jacquot shook his head. 'A general inquiry, possibly tied in with a killing in Cavaillon – which is my parish.'

Arbuthepas released Jacquot's hand, then clapped him on the shoulder and led him through to his office. Arbuthepas was in his late fifties, Jacquot judged, his gaunt frame relieved by a wide, honest smile. Jacquot liked him immediately. He liked him even more a few moments later.

'You know Chief Inspector Murier?' asked Arbuthepas.

'We met just the once,' replied Jacquot, giving the words the edge they needed.

'My condolences,' said Arbuthepas, settling behind his desk and gesturing Jacquot to a chair. 'Dreadful man. Every time I see him, I experience an aching desire to explore his prostate wearing gardener's gloves. Now, where were we? Have you had coffee? Can I get you anything?' Arbuthepas's smile was even wider than it had been before. 'So. How can I help?'

'I'm following up on a suicide. The last week of October. The man's name was Bernard Savry.'

Arbuthepas pushed back in his chair and reached for a drawer in a tall cabinet beside the desk.

'Savry . . . Savry . . .' His fingers danced over the files and then slipped one out. 'Here we are. Savry.' He turned back to the desk and opened the file. Without looking up, he said, 'Computers are all well and good, Chief Inspector, but I still believe my system is faster. The old system. When Madame Barel outside can get me what I need on the computer faster than I can find it in that cabinet will be the day I bury my scalpels in a tub of wet cement and take up golf. So, what exactly . . . ?'

Jacquot smiled, paused a moment before speaking again. Arbuthepas's eyes latched on to him.

'I believe Monsieur Savry had a cancer?'

'Several, as a matter of fact,' corrected Arbuthepas, looking back to his notes. 'An initial presentation in the liver had probably gone unnoticed and spread. Liver to stomach to bowel.'

'When you say "unnoticed" . . . ?'

'. . . I mean that there was nothing in Monsieur Savry's medical records that indicated the cancers had been recognised. No complaint had been made by the patient, no examination had been carried out, no treatment had been recommended and no medical process initiated . . .'

'You mean, he didn't know he had the cancers?'

'That is what I mean. He might have gone to another doctor, another practice, rather than consulting his own; things like that often happen – particularly with sexually transmitted infections, you'll be surprised to hear. But in this case, I doubt it. The spread had been swift. A few months, maybe. He could have been one of the lucky ones who suffer no more than a certain listlessness, maybe an accompanying loss of weight – symptoms one might normally ascribe to age or work or stress. We all know about that. However, given the spread of the infection, it wouldn't have been very long before he felt compelled to seek help.'

'And this is what you said to Chief Inspector Murier?'

'That's correct.'

'And his response?'

'When I told him about the cancers he couldn't have been more delighted. The presence of the cancers was reason enough for suicide. Case closed.'

'But you weren't happy?'

'I'm a pathologist, Chief Inspector. I examine and I advise. But I am not privy to the workings of investigations unless further input is requested from investigating officers. In this case Murier made no further call on my services. He had all he needed – the cancer, I mean – to confirm suicide as a probable cause and that, as far as he was concerned, was that. There was nothing I could say or do to change his reading of the case. It was his call.'

Arbuthepas slapped the file shut and returned it to its drawer in the cabinet.

'But the death was suicide?'

Arbuthepas, who had answered Jacquot's questions

swiftly so far, now paused to consider his reply. 'The patient was gassed in his car. He died of gas inhalation. Given the "presence" of cancers it would appear there might also have been a credible motive.'

'And?' Jacquot felt there was more. He was right.

'The patient's blood/alcohol reading was staggeringly high. How he managed to drink so much and still manage to set up the car for a suicide simply astonishes me.'

'There was a bottle of brandy beside him.'

'That's what Chief Inspector Murier told me.' Arbuthepas pulled out a large Paisley handkerchief and blew his nose with a thunderous gusto. A couple of flourishes and the hankie was back in his pocket. 'To which I replied that a bottle of brandy was not the only thing he'd drunk that night. It would have taken a great deal more than that to reach the levels I recorded.'

'You're saying that he might have been so drunk that someone else might have been involved? Someone to . . . "help" him into that car?'

Again Arbuthepas paused. 'He would have been very drunk, Chief Inspector. Very drunk indeed.' Arbuthepas spread his hands. And smiled sweetly. 'I doubt very much he could have done it all by himself.'

Five minutes later, Jacquot was waiting for the lift

and going over what he'd learned. He was so preoccupied that he failed to notice who was standing in the lift as it wheezed to a stop at his level.

'Chief Inspector Jacquot. *Quelle surprise*,' came a familiar voice through the latticework of the lift doors.

39

Of all the people . . . Detective Inspector Christine Ambert of the Nice *judiciaire* smiling at Jacquot and looking even lovelier than he remembered. This time she was in blue jeans, with moccasins, a white T-shirt and hair loose over the collar of a denim jacket.

'Chief Inspector, what a surprise,' she said, pulling open the doors so that he could step into the lift. 'How nice to see you. Are you going down?' As if that was the direction in which she was headed.

'Detective Inspector. Sure, that'd be fine. And yes, it's nice to see you again too,' replied Jacquot.

The lift should have smelt of polished wood panelling and lubricating grease and worn carpet, as it had on the way up, but as he drew the doors closed behind him Jacquot could smell the perfume she wore, light musky notes with a hint of oranges and sandalwood that seemed to fill the space around them. It was a close, warm, intimate scent and as they started to descend Jacquot was about to remark on it when the lift came to an unexpected stop on the floor below. An old lady in a veiled cloche hat, fur-collared coat and pinching black shoes stood on the landing and waited for Jacquot to open the lift doors for her, looking at the two of them as if she hadn't seen their like before, then indicating with her many chins that they should make proper room for her and the pair of shivering Pomeranians tangled around her ankles. Whatever perfume Ambert had been wearing was immediately overcome with a stronger mix of lavender and old rosewater. Exchanging looks behind the old lady's back and taking care not to step on her dogs in the cramped confines of the lift cage, Jacquot and Ambert made the rest of the descent in silence, which gave both of them an opportunity to collect their thoughts. When they reached the ground floor, Jacquot leaned forward and drew open the double doors, stepping back so that 'Madame Lavande et Rose', disentangling the leads of her two dogs, could get out of the lift first. With a tight little nod, jerking the dogs after her, she hobbled off across the institute's entrance hall, the paws of her Pomeranians clicketty-clicking and sliding across its marbled floor.

'In Peru they eat dogs like that,' said Jacquot, ushering Ambert out of the lift.

'I thought it was guinea pigs,' replied Ambert.

'You may be right, Detective Inspector. You may be right.'

There was a moment's pause, and then, 'So what brings you to—' they both began.

Christine laughed, then looked at her watch. 'Talking of food, why don't I take you to lunch,' she said.

'I'm not interrupting anything?' he asked, pretty sure he knew where she'd been going in the lift, and whom she'd been planning on visiting.

'*Pas de tout*. Not at all,' she replied. 'I'm starving. What about you?'

The place she took him to was not a restaurant but, like Abel's cave, it was no worse for that. The proprietor was a man named Louis and his premises comprised a narrow doorway in the old quarter of town, a low three-legged milking stool, a portable gas cooking ring and a deep-fat fryer with a battered lid. Despite the season he wore a flower shirt open to the band of his trousers and a pair of leather espadrilles. The sleeves of his shirt were rolled up to the elbow, and arms and chest displayed a luxuriant pelt of grey hair.

'Two for me, three for my friend,' said Christine by way of a greeting, and without any consultation. It was clear to Jacquot that the two of them knew each other. Then she said, 'Maybe make it four, Louis. He's an old rugby player. Needs to keep his strength up.'

At which Louis's eyes sprang open. 'Jesus. I knew it. Knew it as soon as I saw you turn the corner. The pony-tail. It's you, isn't it?' Since it would have been too much of a performance to haul himself off his low stool, the *friturier* made do by reaching up a pudgy hand to shake Jacquot's.

'It was a long time ago,' Jacquot replied.

'Still,' said Louis, 'that try . . .' He shook his head and gazed off into the past.

'When you've got a moment, Lou,' chipped in Christine. 'Time's a wastin'. And a girl's gotta eat.'

While Louis busied himself with his frier, turning up the gas and pulling a string of ringed *colinots* from a wicker basket, Christine Ambert turned to Jacquot. 'So, Chief Inspector, you were going to tell me what brings you down to Nice . . .'

'No, no,' interrupted Jacquot. 'If I'm not mistaken, you were about to explain to me what you were doing, calling on Doctor Arbuthepas.'

One by one the floured *colinots* were dropped into the frier with a hiss of bubbling oil and the lid replaced. It was years since Jacquot had tasted them, the fleshy baby hake traditionally served as a *friture* with its tail in its mouth. Held in a napkin, it was like eating a hot fish doughnut – perfect street food.

'You first, Chief Inspector,' said Christine Ambert.

'After you, Detective Inspector, I insist,' replied Jacquot.

She took a breath. 'Very well. I'll start. And you're right. I was calling by to see the good doctor. After you expressed your unhappiness regarding the circumstances of your friend's suicide I called up the pathology report and took a look. As far as I could see everything seemed perfecty straightforward. Death by gassing. Suicide.'

'But?'

'But there were two things that concerned me.'

'And they were?'

Before she could reply there was a clatter of movement from Louis. Two bags were punched open, the lid of the fryer was shovelled aside and one by one the deep-fried *colinots* were fished out with a pair of wooden tongs.

'Know who catches these?' said Louis, as he twisted the bags and handed them over with a fistful of paper napkins and a split lemon. 'That team-mate of yours. Sidi Carassin. Brings in the best there is.'

'You get them from Sidi?'

'Him or his wife. Whoever delivers. He keeps his *pointu* down in Villefranche. Been there years.'

'Then they'll be good,' said Jacquot.

'Now here's a man who knows his fish and his rugby,' said Louis to Ambert. 'You got to take care of a man who knows his fish and his rugby,' he continued with a sly smile. 'Isn't that right, monsieur?'

A fifty-franc note changed hands and the two of them bid Louis farewell. Knowing the fish would be too hot to eat right away they headed down to the Promenade des Anglais, dodged through the traffic and settled on the low retaining wall between promenade and beach. Joggers, skateboarders and cyclists passed them by as a thin November sun sparkled weakly over the bay.

Without needing to be reminded, Christine Ambert carried on from where she'd left off. 'What wasn't clear in the doctor's report was whether your friend, Monsieur Savry, knew he had cancer. I mean, was he in pain? If not, then the cancer didn't really stand up as a reason for taking his own life.'

Jacquot nodded as though the thought was interesting. 'And the second reason?'

'Apparently he was very drunk. A huge quantity of alcohol and such a small man. So how did he sort out the hose and the fire cement?'

'Have you mentioned these doubts to Chief Inspector Murier?'

'I thought—'

'That you'd have a chat with the pathologist before you went any further? Make sure your suspicions could be backed up?'

'That's correct,' she said, opening up her paper bag and taking out one of her *colinots*, wrapping the joined head and tail in a napkin. Jacquot watched as her lips curled back and her white teeth bit into the coiled belt of white flesh. 'Mmmmh. Just the best,' she said, wiping a flake of fish from her lips. 'And now it's your turn. So what brings you here?'

He gave her a look. 'Exactly the same as you, Detective Inspector. You and I, young lady, have reached the same conclusion but from different directions.'

'Different directions?'

Jacquot opened his bag and selected the largest of the four rings. The heat in the bag had yet to dampen the *colinot*'s floured skin and his first mouthful was a crackle of flavours – good olive oil, crisp peppered skin, and silky white meat. If the *colinots* were good because they were Sidi's, they were also good because Louis knew his *friture* and hadn't overcooked them. Jacquot hunched his shoulders and took a second bite, teasing the flesh off the white needle-like ribs in one looping mouthful. Christine Ambert noted the clean execution and nodded approvingly. It was clear the Chief Inspector knew how to handle his *colinots*.

Jacquot didn't speak until he'd swallowed those first mouthfuls, licking at the salt on his lips. 'For me,' he began, 'it wasn't the cancer or the drink where I started from. It was why Bernard didn't have any traces of fire cement from the exhaust pipe or grease from the rag in the window on his hands. That's what alerted me. His hands were clean.'

Ambert looked impressed. 'I didn't know that. Did you mention it to my boss?'

'Yes I did. But he seemed . . . disinclined to consider it as any kind of evidence.'

'So what did Doctor Arbuthepas have to say about the cancer?' she asked with a sly smile, 'since I wasn't able to ask him myself.'

'Just what you were hoping for. According to the good doctor, it was unlikely that Savry knew about the cancer, unlikely that he would have been in any pain. Arbuthepas even called up Savry's medical records and checked. No visits to his doctor, no complaints of any pain, no lumps, bumps or other questionable indications. So hardly a reason to commit suicide.'

Jacquot removed the napkin from the clenched head and tail of his *colinot* and sucked discreetly on each.

'The sweetest part,' said Christine Ambert.

'That's what my papa always told me.'

'He knew his fish too, did he?'

'He was a fisherman. Out of Marseilles. Like Sidi, he knew where to find the *colinots*.'

'So you're Marseillais?'

'I am. *Exacte*.'

'Rough boys, the Marseillais.'

'Pussycats,' he replied with a smile he regretted as soon as he gave it to her. Quite unconsciously he had started to flirt with her. And she was responding. He reached into his bag for the next *colinot* and started in on it.

'There's something else you should know, Detective Inspector.'

Her mouth was full. She cocked an eyebrow.

'On Wednesday evening there was a motorbike crash on the slip road between La Turbie and the Corniche Moyenne. The man riding pillion was killed. His name was Claude Lorraine. He, too, was one of the team.'

Christine stopped chewing, swallowed, but said nothing.

'And the man driving the bike was Olivier Touche. He is presently in a critical condition at Hôpital Saint-Saëns. He owns a restaurant up near Gorbio.'

'Touche? I know it, of course.'

'He was also a member of the team. He may or may not survive. So, we now have six deaths in just eight months – six out of fifteen, three of them in the last month alone, not to mention my friend Olivier fighting for his life.'

Christine Ambert whistled. 'So what are we going to do now?'

Jacquot noted the 'we' and felt an unexpected jolt of relief. At last. Someone was taking him seriously.

'You are going to mention all this to your boss and let me know what he has to say. As for me,' he glanced at his watch, 'it's time I was going. I have to drive to Cavaillon and I'd like to call in again on Olivier. See how he is. At this rate, I'll be lucky if I make it home for dinner.'

'So stay over,' she said lightly. 'I'll give you a guided tour of Nice by Night.' This last was said to soften the directness of what Jacquot recognised as a particular kind of invitation.

'Maybe next time,' he said, without thinking.

Inspector Ambert gave him a smile, wrapped up the bones of her fish, and lobbed the bag into a nearby bin.

'Next time, then.'

40

After parting company on the promenade, Jacquot returned to the Pathology Institute, retrieved his car and then headed back to Hôpital Saint-Saëns. On the fourth floor, the intensive care ward hummed with a quiet efficiency, a dozen windowed rooms filled with patients it was hard to make out beneath the tubes and wires and bandages. At reception Jacquot showed his badge and asked if Sophie Touche was still there. The nurse in charge told him that she'd left for home an hour earlier, but was expected back later. Poor Sophie, he thought. He wondered if the restaurant would be open that night. Knowing Sophie, it probably would be.

'Do you want to see him?' asked the nurse, remembering Jacquot from his previous visit.

'Is he conscious?'

'In and out,' she replied, pushing away from her computer screen and coming out from behind the desk. 'You may be lucky. I'll show you where he is.'

When Jacquot had visited earlier, he had stayed with Sophie, taken her to the cafeteria for a coffee and croissant, comforted her. Since Olivier had still to shake off the anaesthetic there'd seemed little point in visiting him.

'I'll let you have five minutes,' the nurse told him as she led him down a window-panelled corridor. She stopped at a glass door and pushed it open. 'If he wakes, just smile a lot, joke, but don't tell him about the leg. Or his companion. And please don't sit on the bed.'

As the door hissed closed behind him, Jacquot looked at the bundle of bandages on the bed and could hardly recognise his old friend. The room was uncomfortably warm and close. A monitor blinked its rhythmic green static, two drips were attached to Olivier's arms and a third bag slung beneath the bed bulged with blood-speckled urine.

The bottom of the bed was hooped beneath a sheet and Olivier's chest was bare. It was the only part of his body – badly bruised and patched with dressings – that showed. His arms were bandaged from above the elbows to his fingertips and his head was swathed in a tight wrap of bandaging. His bruise-blackened eyes were closed, his cheeks lacerated and painted with iodine as orange as the urine in the bag, and his nose was pushed dramatically to one side. A light dusting of grey stubble showed on the cleft of his chin and on the edge of his cracked top lip. A breathing tube had been inserted into his nostrils and his swollen grey lips were bared over a line of broken teeth. It seemed a miracle, given the evident damage, that the man had survived at all.

Pulling over a chair, Jacquot sat beside his friend and wondered what to do next. Should he say something? Should he reach out a hand and stroke a cheek? In the event he didn't have to do anything. A few minutes after sitting down, Olivier's eyes fluttered open and then squinted in the light. The sinews in his neck stiffened and Jacquot knew he was trying to lift his head from the pillow, but the effort was wasted.

'It's OK, it's OK,' said Jacquot gently. 'Don't try to move. It's Daniel. Daniel Jacquot.' He stretched out a hand and touched his fingertips to Olivier's shoulder. The eyes closed and a thin sigh escaped between the parched lips.

For a while it seemed that Olivier had drifted back into unconsciousness but then his eyes fluttered open again and his lips moved. The sound that came from his mouth was somewhere between a grunt and a whisper. Not a word. Just a sound.

Jacquot saw the lips close and the throat constrict as though Olivier was trying to swallow, or draw a breath, or lubricate his vocal cords. He was wondering if he should call the nurse when another dry grunt worked its way through Olivier's lips. This time it sounded like a word.

Getting to his feet, Jacquot leaned over the bed so that Olivier could see who was there without having to turn his head. At first the eyes seemed to look straight through him – the whites viciously reddened beneath the puffed lids, the pupils like two blue waistcoat buttons staring sightlessly ahead. As he watched his friend's face, smiling gently, Jacquot could see the effort it took for Olivier to focus.

'It's Daniel. Danny Jacquot. Sophie's gone home but will be back soon,' he said, trying to load his words with as much care and softness as he could.

Another grunt. A slow, tired blink.

'You took a fall on that bike of yours,' whispered Jacquot. He spoke slowly, carefully enunciating each word. 'You're in Hôpital Saint-Saëns. It's Friday. You're a bit bashed up, my old friend, and you had them worried for a while. But they told me to tell you that they need the bed so can you hurry up and get well?'

There was another low grunt and a flickering at the corner of Olivier's mouth.

Was he trying to smile? Jacquot wondered. Had he understood Jacquot's little joke?

Behind him Jacquot heard the door-seal part with a hiss and the same nurse who had brought him to the room was now stepping round the bed to the monitor. She, too, leaned over the bed, but a lot more confidently than Jacquot, and when she spoke her voice was a great deal louder than Jacquot's earnest whispering.

'So you're back with us, are you, *mon brave*? And about time too.'

It was as if the nurse knew that her voice had to carry a long, long way. Had Olivier heard anything he'd said?

The nurse caught Jacquot's eye. 'Maybe, Monsieur . . . ?'

He knew what she was asking. It was time for him to go.

He looked back at Olivier and smiled as big a smile as he could muster for his old team-mate. 'I think they want to change your nappy, *copain*, and that's a treat I think I can do without. But I'll come back soon, you hear me? I promise.'

And then, as Jacquot leaned away from the bed and out of Olivier's field of vision, his friend's body seemed to stiffen, his chin raised and his lips bared. Slowly, painfully, his chest rose. For all the world he looked as if he was dragging in his very last breath. Across from Jacquot, the nurse looked suddenly alarmed and glanced at the monitor. The speed of the beeps had certainly increased.

'I think you'd better—' the nurse began.

But she was interrupted by a great gurgling exhalation from Olivier that had a certain cadence, a certain form and rhythm. Jacquot was suddenly convinced his friend was trying to say something.

'*Grais . . . Grais. Chew . . . ah . . . grais,*' was what it sounded like.

'Monsieur, please,' said the nurse.

'*Un moment plus, s'il vous plaît,*' replied Jacquot, as Olivier tried to drag in another huge breath. His chest rose, his eyes squeezed shut, and his fingertips fluttered at the ends of his bandaged arms as though he was trying to play a tune on a piano that wasn't there.

And then the lips parted, the rubied eyes opened wide and the same gargle of sounds tumbled through broken teeth into the space between them – the 'g' sounds now a rolling 'r' – as close to a death rattle as Jacquot had ever heard.

'*Rrrrais . . . Rrrrrais. Raissss . . . Tchu . . . Tew . . . ah . . . rrrais . . . unh . . .*'

And then the eyes closed, the fingertips stopped their fluttering and a low sigh drifted from his lips. Whatever he'd been trying to say, it was clear the strength had finally left him.

It was ten minutes later, unlocking his car, that Jacquot finally made sense of what his friend had been trying to say. All the way down in the lift, Olivier's 'words', the sounds he had made, had repeated themselves in Jacquot's head.

Was it something? Or was it nothing?

And then, pulling the key from the doorlock, he had it. Suddenly the sounds, the words, reassembled themselves into something that could be guessed at, maybe even understood.

'Tu as raison. Tu as raison.'

'You are right. You are right.'

41

It was nearing seven o'clock when Jacquot finally crossed the Var river and joined the Autoroute Provençale. It had grown dark and all that remained of the day was a deep purple streak on the hilltops that rapidly thickened into night. On Jacquot's left a stream of headlights slid past, heading east, bound for the coast. Ahead lay the rise and the fall of the autoroute, a glittering pathway of red tail-lights, four glimmering strands of rubies that disappeared round a bend, then reappeared again. Holding his speed at around a hundred kilometres an hour, Jacquot kept to the second lane and decided to take his time. Claudine was at a gallery opening in Avignon that evening and would not be returning until the following day so all he had to look forward to was a nightcap at Fin de

Siècle and his lonely *atelier* on Cours Bournissac. So there was no rush.

It was warm in the car and Jacquot was soothed as much by the steady speed as he was by the interpretation he had given to Olivier's garglings. He lit a cigarette, opened the window a fraction to clear the smoke, and felt a blast of chill air. He smoked quickly and closed the window.

In Jacquot's world there were certain times and certain places where he thought best. When he woke in the morning, those first few languorous minutes when his brain raced so fast he could hardly keep up; over an early morning café-calva and that first, reviving cigarette; at lunch at what was rapidly becoming his favourite corner table at Gaillard's Brasserie on Passage Cabassole; and, when the weather was fine, in the garden at Le Tilleul on the road to Apt.

And in his car, of course.

A car was surely the perfect place for conjecture, for speculation and for the weaving – or unravelling – of conspiracies? After visiting a scene of crime – in the Lubéron or in Marseilles – Jacquot always liked his assistant to drive, so he could think of what he had just seen, get everything in order, achieve some kind of perspective. It was the way he worked and his assistants soon learned to accommodate their boss's whim. And though Jacquot didn't let on, it worked just as well – if not better – when he drove himself, alone in the car.

And driving at night seemed the most fertile time of all – dark and enclosed – the questions crowding in, but the answers always tantalisingly elusive. That November evening, with another two hundred kilometres to drive before he reached home, the lights of the Baie des Anges dwindling behind him and the darkness of the countryside closing in on him, Jacquot went back over the events of the last few weeks, from the moment he'd seen Bernard Savry's hands and known something was not quite right.

His meeting with Chantal; with Nikki; with Savry's editor at *Mond Sportif*; with Patric's son, François; with a grieving Jean-Claude Rives and that fat, stinking scumbag Robillant – trying to find a thread, trying to see beyond the obvious links: all men; all members of the same rugby team, albeit eighteen years earlier; and all, as Claudine had observed, wealthy.

And now, in the space of a single day, there appeared to be others who seemed to be coming round to his way of thinking. The pathologist, Arbuthepas, clearly had doubts; Christine Ambert too; and now, not an hour earlier, scrabbling on the brink of life and death, his old friend Olivier Touche had, he was certain, confirmed those suspicions.

Tu as raison. Tu as raison.

Slowing for a *péage* and tossing the coins into the scarred plastic scoop, Jacquot waited for the light to change from red to green and the barrier to rise. And as they did so and Jacquot pressed the accelerator, went through the gears and settled once more at his steady and satisfying 100kph, he felt sure he was right about those three repeated words. *Tu as raison. Tu as raison.* It was Olivier trying to tell him that his suspicions were well-founded, and that he should have paid more attention to Jacquot's warning.

Away from the lights of the *péage*, shrouded once more in a warm, petrol-scented darkness save the glow from his instrument panel and the headlights of oncoming vehicles, Jacquot wondered what had happened to Olivier and Claude on that winding slip road between the Grande and Middle Corniches. Given that it wasn't an accident, given that Olivier had not misjudged the traffic or the bends, then it seemed only reasonable to conclude that someone had made him crash, had caused his bike to flip over the barrier and tumble down the slope. Had the brakes been tampered with? Had someone tried to ram him off the road? Had he swerved to avoid something? Until Olivier recovered more fully from his injuries and was able to give an account of the incident there was little point in further speculation.

Except . . . except . . . there was a certain irresistibility about speculation no matter how weak or far-fetched. Put a drop of sparkling water to your beaten eggs and you had an omelette; make it with milk and serve it with toast, and you called it scrambled eggs. Once you started the mixing and the matching, it was hard to stop. And often it yielded some unexpected insight – usually unproveable, of course – but insight all the same, something to work on. A direction to follow.

For instance, all the deaths had happened at night, under cover of darkness. It was, of course, a good time to kill; a time that Jacquot would have chosen himself had he been so inclined. But was there something else to be read into it? Perhaps a killer who was occupied during the day? Someone whose job precluded the hours of daylight?

Also the killer – for it had to be a single killer, surely? – had to be able to drive; not just to get around from one place to another but to drive the van that hit Valadier, to reach Souze's isolated home, to get away from Club Xéro and, possibly, to set up an ambush on that corniche slip road. Also a killer who had time to reconnoitre, a killer who had time to learn the victims' habits, their daily routines: the Souzes' apartment in Bordeaux and Amélie staying there to visit her son in hospital; Luc

Valadier given to working late on a tree-lined residential street; Marc Fastin and his taste for swingers' clubs; Antoine Peyrot who liked a drink or two and had access to super-yachts for assignations his wife would never find out about; or Olivier, who rode like a demon on roads where a single misjudgement would mean almost certain death.

But what was the motive? Why was it happening? Why murder these six men? What bound six middle-aged rugby players – apart from their wealth, their various affiliations with Pierre Dombasle, and the fact that they were all men who had, eighteen years earlier, played on the same team?

However many times he considered the angles, the possibilities, Jacquot knew that he currently had no sure motive – beyond the possibility of Claudine's rich list.

Just as he had no sure suspect.

And no firm, concrete evidence.

Try as he might Jacquot knew he was still a very long way from saying who was behind Olivier's crash; Luc's hit-and-run; Peyrot's battered drowning; Savry's 'suicide'; Souze's crushing; and Fastin's meaty, bloody castration.

But by the time he reached Cavaillon, even the prospect of an empty apartment waiting for him failed to dilute the comforting sense of satisfaction that Jacquot felt as he turned into Cours Bournissac. After two hours of teasing speculations at the wheel of his car Jacquot was now certain of two things.

That the killer was a woman.

And that she would almost certainly strike again.

The question was – who and when?

42

'The boss wants to see you,' said Brunet, when Jacquot called in at Cavaillon headquarters the following morning. The night before he'd stayed at Fin de Siècle longer than he'd intended, and drunk too many contemplative calvas. He'd woken with a dry mouth and a tight head. Not even a sweet milky latte from Auzet's had eased the pain. He'd walked to headquarters slowly, each cautious footstep setting up a rattle of resentful drumbeats in the back of his skull.

'Take a seat,' said Rochet, when Jacquot knocked and entered the Chief's office. 'You look like you need it,' he added, standing behind his desk, tamping tobacco into a pipe.

Jacquot thanked him and eased himself gently into a chair. 'I keep forgetting I'm growing older.'

Rochet grunted. 'Just wait,' he warned, putting the pipe between his teeth and searching the pockets of a woolly cardigan for a box of matches. He found it, shook the box and, after picking out four dead matches in a row which he placed in an ashtray, he finally found a live one. The head scratched across the side of the box and a flame flared. He waited for the flare to subside then set it to the bowl of his pipe, sucking away contentedly. Jacquot may have been feeling fragile but he knew what Rochet was playing at.

'You've been busy, I hear,' Rochet finally began, pulling his chair round and sitting in it.

For a moment Jacquot thought the old man must be referring to the candied fruit merchant in Apt, or the torcher, or the old Englishman whose dog had been snatched – three small cases that Jacquot had put away in a couple of days.

But that wasn't what Rochet meant at all.

'Complaints, Daniel. As well as not spending too much time at your desk in the last few weeks, it would appear that you've been upsetting people. Important people.'

Murier was the first name that came into Jacquot's throbbing head. 'Don't tell me. Chief Inspector Laurent Murier, Nice *judiciaire*,' he said with a sigh.

Rochet nodded. 'And Chief Inspector Félipe, eighteenth *arrondissement*, Paris; and Chief Inspector

Lasquet, in Bordeaux; and Chief Inspector Rudolfe in Toulouse. Four chief inspectors in four separate jurisdictions, each one asking me what you thought you were doing – trespassing on their turf, upsetting people – and what was I going to do about it?'

Jacquot waited. Crossing jurisdictions was taken seriously. No cop liked someone else on their turf, questioning procedures.

'I told them I'd have a word,' continued Rochet. 'What I didn't tell them was that you're too good a cop to do something like this without a very good reason. So, what's going on?' Rochet took a few hopeful puffs from his pipe but the load was out. He laid the pipe in his ashtray and clasped his hands behind his head.

Very quickly Jacquot ran Rochet through the story.

'And you reckon the killer's a woman?'

'Has to be. Fastin in the club, Souze, Peyrot . . . Also, Souze was reaching for a white wine, not a red.'

'Meaning?'

'Meaning women tend to drink whites, and Souze always preferred red.'

'My wife used to like Burgundy. Red.'

Jacquot spread his hands. 'I know it's weak, but . . .'

'But you say she's made a mistake?'

'She shouldn't have killed Savry at the party. Sure, it could have been someone trespassing on Dombasle's estate, breaking in, being surprised by Savry, but it's unlikely. I think she saw an opportunity and took it.'

'Which means?'

'She has to be one of the guests at Dombasle's reunion party. One of the wives.'

'Or staff?'

Jacquot shook his head. 'No link.'

'You said Savry was gay. Maybe one of the house-boys . . . ?'

Jacquot shook his head. 'All straight. All accounted for.'

'Fast work,' said Rochet.

Jacquot nodded. It was Brunet who'd thought to check that one out.

'Still,' Rochet persevered, 'maybe Savry didn't know that, made a play when he shouldn't have. Some people can get very upset . . .'

'Savry was last seen leaving the house alone, very drunk, heading back to his *cabane*.'

'And you think someone followed him?'

'That's what I think. Then, or later.'

'How far from his *cabane* to where his car was parked?'

'Hundred metres, give or take.'

'And how exactly did your killer, this woman, get him there? I mean, he's not exactly going to go for a stroll to the car park when he's pissed, is he?'

'I think she carried him there.'

'Carried him? You're kidding.'

'He's a scrum-half. They don't come much smaller.'

'So it's a woman with a bit of muscle?'

Jacquot smiled. 'Cuts it down, don't you think?'

'How many in the frame?'

'Maybe six.'

Rochet unclasped his hands and reached for his pipe. He dug out some ash from the bowl, found his matches and reapplied a flame. The last of the tobacco crackled and spluttered.

Rochet settled his eyes on Jacquot through the smoke. 'Don't tell me. You'll be needing some time off?'

43

It had come as something of a shock to Claudine when she suddenly realised that her underwear was sadly lacking. Eighteen months alone and all she had was old and worn or carried memories. It was time to go shopping, she decided, and the morning after the gallery opening in Avignon she stayed in the city to replenish her stock.

She couldn't say for sure whether Daniel was a stocking man or not – he'd certainly not mentioned it – but Claudine reckoned he couldn't be that different from other men. So she started with black silk stockings and a small panelled suspender belt with prettily ruched straps at a shop she remembered off Cours Mirabeau. Then some bras, a silk camisole top with lace bodice and spaghetti straps, knickers that were frilled and plain and, as much for her own amusement as Daniel's, a trim white bustier that rested ticklishly on her hips and turned her breasts into golden brown globes. And everything bar the stockings white. Even Claudine thought she looked good. Say what you like about having your heart broken, it sure kept you in shape.

The first thing Claudine did when she arrived home from Avignon was pour herself a glass of wine, take a long perfumed bath, and then try everything on. Sitting on the edge of her bed, drawing on the stockings, clasping them to the suspender, made her feel strangely excited, and very, very feminine. She hadn't seen Jacquot in three days and wanted him there very badly.

He arrived a little later than usual, his headlights flickering through the trees as he came up the hill, the beams passing over the salon ceiling as he pulled into the drive. Claudine had lit candles in the salon and a tepee of logs blazed in the hearth. For a moment, when she heard the knock on the door – she had yet to give him a key – Claudine felt a flutter of anxiety. Was it too much, the candles, the fire, what she'd finally decided to wear? She felt suddenly self-conscious in the tight wool skirt that she'd bought, the new silk blouse, and her underwear.

But she needn't have worried. When she opened the door to him, his smile was as warm as ever and even though she could feel his eyes take her in from behind that wrinkled web of laugh lines – the tight line of her skirt, the low-buttoned blouse with just a peep of white lace beneath – there was something comforting and thrilling about it.

'You look beautiful,' he told her, dropping the bag he was carrying, taking her hands and drawing her to him.

But that was it. The kiss was not swift and unthinking, but neither was it lingering or curious. As she closed her eyes and before she could press herself against him, he turned away to shut the door, picked up his carrier bag and went through to the salon, pushing at the logs with the toe of his boot, flicking through the CDs for some music, then collapsing on the sofa. It all happened so quickly, so naturally, that she wasn't upset. It could wait.

'Tough day?'

'Interesting day,' he replied. 'It seems, *finalement*, as though we might be getting somewhere. The Savry case. There's a possibility I might be away for a few days.'

'Possibility, or probability?' she asked, sliding on to the sofa beside him.

'No more than a week,' he answered with a smile.

'It will cost you.'

'I thought you might say that. Which is why I bought',

he said, 'a very, very expensive bottle of wine for dinner.' And with that he lurched off the sofa in search of his carrier bag.

For a moment Claudine was taken aback, as much at his distance, as at her own increasing desire for him. If she hadn't known better, she'd have said it was another woman. But this was Daniel, she told herself, watching him unwrap the tissue from the bottle and present it to her. Not her cheating second husband, Sebastien. There was no way Daniel would do that. She was certain of it. Absolutely certain.

But that single, fleeting, unsettling thought – so swiftly, so easily dismissed – was enough to cool her, draw her back. So much so that she pulled on an apron to serve their kitchen supper and kept it on while they ate. And the moment Daniel got up to clear the table, she'd dashed to her bedroom to change, coming down in long woolly socks and her favourite striped pyjamas. It was Savry, she told herself, winding a woollen scarf round her neck as they returned to the salon. He was just thinking about Savry and Peyrot and all the rest of them and she shouldn't worry about it. This was the man he sometimes was. She had better get used to it.

And then, of all things, when she was least expecting it . . . in her old cotton pyjamas, hunkered down beside him in front of the fire, he let a hand stray to her leg, and she felt the backs of his fingers brush against the inside of her knee.

Men, she thought, feeling herself warm as those green eyes settled on her, letting herself ease back as he turned and leaned towards her.

And all that underwear . . .

Maybe another time.

Part Three

44

On the drive down from Cavaillon to Nice that Sunday morning, Jacquot had been too preoccupied to think too much about Claudine. By the time he reached the bottom of the *sans issue* leading to her home his mind was firmly focused on business. After his meeting with his station chief, Rochet, Jacquot had set about planning his next moves. The old man was behind him, Jacquot knew, and he was grateful for it. Phone calls would be made, excuses and apologies offered where necessary, and assurances given that it would not happen again – the heavy treading on important toes. In the meantime, Jacquot had just the five days Rochet had given him to come up with something concrete, five days to find a killer, or provide clear and persuasive evidence of murder in any of the six deaths.

Given that Jacquot had decided the killer had to be a woman, and discounting the other female guests whom Pierre Dombasle had invited to the team reunion party – the sequin-sheathed, coiffed and jewelled wives of the actors, singers, TV anchormen, government ministers, local dignitaries and assorted SportÉquipe corporates – there had been thirteen team wives or partners staying the night at Dombasle's home on Cap Corsaire. Thirteen contenders whom, by a simple process of elimination, Jacquot had cut down to a more manageable seven.

Claudine had been the first to go, of course – not just because she hadn't known a single one of his old team-mates before the party, but also because, if he couldn't account for her whereabouts when Souze and Valadier had died (they hadn't known each other back then), Jacquot knew exactly where she was when Savry, Fastin, Peyrot and Lorraine had died.

In bed with him, on all four occasions.

And anyway . . . Claudine? It simply wasn't possible.

Jacquot had also eliminated Isabelle Peyrot, Marie-France Lorraine and Sophie Touche. Each of these women had suffered at the hands of the killer – two of them were widows already and, if Olivier didn't make it, Sophie would soon be joining their ranks. It didn't seem conceivable that one of them could possibly be a killer. Why? For what possible purpose?

Also, since it was likely that the killer had either dragged or carried Savry to his car, Jacquot had felt able to cross a heavily pregnant Nathalie Rains from his list. And Lydie Dombasle, too. She was nearing sixty years old, thin and bony enough to be described as frail, with hardly enough strength to support a bichon frise in the crook of her elbow.

Which left Jacquot with seven suspects: Druart's beefy wife, Martine; the edgy Maryvonne Pelerain; Sidi Carassin's wife, Mathilde; the red-cheeked and jolly Pierrette Cabezac; the butcher Simon Talaud's wife, Florence, one of the best rock 'n' rollers Jacquot had ever danced with; Fabienne Millet, the interior decorator married to Gilles Millet; and Corinne Caloux whose husband Val was a *notaire* in Théoule.

Of course, if Claudine's conjecture about the victims being wealthy was correct then maybe he could also rule out Fabienne Millet? She was a successful interior decorator with her own practice and her husband Gilles was an award-winning architect, part of the team working on Dombasle's Touche project – one of whom was now dead, another critically injured. Which would bring the number down to six: a farmer's wife; a butcher's wife; a fisherman's wife; a teacher's wife; a postman's wife; a *notaire*'s wife.

One of these six, Jacquot was now certain, had to be the killer.

As he swung off the Promenade des Anglais and burrowed through its grandly stuccoed façade into the bustling sun-slanted streets of Nice, heading for Hôpital Saint-Saëns, Jacquot wondered about the *notaire*, Valentine Caloux. How wealthy could a *notaire* become? Depending on the elasticity of their scruples, wealthy enough, Jacquot supposed. And Valentine, Jacquot recalled, had left Dombasle's home on that Saturday morning in a brand new BMW.

So maybe the odds – given the killer's preference for wealthy targets – ruled out Corinne as a suspect? If her husband Valentine, like Millet, Rains and Pierre Dombasle himself, was a possible target, then it surely seemed unlikely that Corinne would turn out to be the killer? Unless, of course, Valentine was the only one left. Then they might have a clearer idea of the killer's identity.

As he drove round the hospital's car park looking for a space, Jacquot knew what he had to do: in the next five days he would visit Rains up near Valbonne, Millet in Grasse, Caloux in Théoule and Pierre Dombasle now just a few kilometres down the coast, warn them what might be happening, advise them to keep their eyes open, and have them call him if they noticed anything suspicious.

He had also asked Brunet to check out Mesdames

Druart, Pelerain, Cabezac and Talaud. Means and motives. Their whereabouts when the murders were committed – subtly, of course; without arousing their suspicions. He had left Brunet to work out the 'how', but Jacquot had no doubt that his assistant, as usual, would come up with something ingenious.

As for Mathilde Carassin, the last of the suspect wives, he had decided to do that himself. Her husband, Sidi, the fastest wing-three-quarter ever to play for France, who'd stood beside Jacquot in the team photo, kept a fishing *pointu* in the harbour at Villefranche. And Villefranche was where he'd be spending the night.

45

'So tell me about Pierre Dombasle,' said Jacquot. He sipped the wine that had been poured for him, nodded to the waiter, and watched him fill their glasses.

He and Sophie Touche were having lunch in a small brasserie close to Hôpital Saint-Saëns. Earlier, Jacquot had found her at Olivier's bedside. Her husband was sleeping, and she was watching a silent TV with wide, tired eyes. Outside in the corridor, she broke the bad news. First it was the leg – which she knew Olivier knew about even though nothing had been said to him – and now the head. They'd found a swelling. They were going to have to operate again. The poor woman looked shattered, as though she hadn't eaten or slept since the crash.

'The kids arrive?' asked Jacquot.

She nodded, smiled. 'Pascal's in the kitchen and Louise is looking after front of house. And one of them is always here when I'm not.'

'Which doesn't look as though it's often enough. You need a proper break, Sophie. Let me take you to lunch. Something to eat. If only to keep your strength up. There are only so many cafeteria paninis or croque monsieurs one should have to suffer.'

At which she'd looked through the panel of glass at Olivier, still asleep, and then turned back. 'You're right. Exactly right,' she said. 'I need something to eat. And some good company.' Instinctively, she put a hand to her bob of black hair, brushed down the front of her T-shirt, and pulled the woolly cardigan around her. 'Let's go, before I change my mind.'

Now, twenty minutes later, dipping their bread into a bowl of *grossanne* olive oil, they sat together over a gingham cover.

'Pierre?' asked Sophie. 'You need *me* to tell *you* about Pierre?'

'It's been a long time, remember. And I only played the once.'

'For you once was enough, *n'est-ce pas*? There are players out there who'd have killed their mothers to make a run like that – and score. In the last minute, no less.'

'Didn't you hear what Caloux said at Pierre's reunion?' Jacquot asked.

'No. What?'

Jacquot told her about the fresh legs and dry hands.

'*Eh voilà*,' she said. '*Pré-ci-se-ment*. The man is jealous. Mad with it. Even after all these years, he still can't forgive you. You have what he doesn't have. And just the one game, when Caloux had years on the pitch and a cabinet full of caps. All of which he'd happily trade for that one try.'

'Maybe, maybe you are right,' Jacquot deferred, waving it aside. 'But coming back to Pierre, no, I did not know him. Not like Olivier, Luc, the ones who'd played with him a long time.'

Before Sophie could reply a small dish of seafood charcuterie was served – a pile of *soupions* like glistening white pearls, surrounded by lobster claws, *bulots*, mussels, oysters and clams; shells removed, everything laid on ice.

'I'll never be able to eat all this,' Sophie exclaimed.

'You don't have to. We share it. The next course is the one you eat by yourself.'

And so, with the first real laugh he'd heard from Sophie all morning, they set to, Jacquot watching her hesitate, then plunge in – a lobster claw first, then a mussel, and then one . . . two . . . three *soupions* speared on her fork and tucked away in a bulging cheek.

'I can't believe I'm so hungry. Come to think of it, I probably *can* believe it. And I probably can eat the whole plate.'

'You'll regret it,' warned Jacquot with a smile. 'There's still the *dorade* with that *sauce mousseline*.'

'If I explode, all you have to do is find my ring finger and give this . . .' she spun her wedding ring in the sunlight '. . . this ring to the kids. But I'm chattering on. It's just a relief, I suppose, to talk to someone. To hear a friendly voice. So, Pierre . . . well, what can I say? He has ambitions. For Olivier, for me, for *la famille* Touche. Olivier probably told you all about it – Touche Côte, Touche Campagne, Touche Cité.' She tossed off the names with a heavy disdain. 'A franchise even . . . who knows?'

'You don't sound very happy about it.'

She shot him a narrow look. 'If I'm honest, I'm not. Touche is our restaurant, Daniel,' she continued, spearing the last of the *soupions* an instant before the waiter removed the plate. 'We love it and we don't want to expand. Even if Olivier says he does.'

Jacquot noted the steeliness in her voice.

'And why should we expand?' she continued. 'Why should we bother? It's the way to go, of course, if that's the kind of thing you're looking for. But we're not. We're happy there, Daniel. We've got our customers, we've got our reputation – and a family business that provides a very comfortable living. Remember, *Les Touches* have worked that spot a long time. Olivier's father, his grandfather. It's changed, grown, too, I grant you, but it's still as good as it ever was. And, you know what? Sometimes I even cook myself, and then it is truly great!' She took a deep wistful breath. 'It's just . . .'

'Just what?' pressed Jacquot.

Sophie leaned back as her *dorade* was served, a tiny copper pan filled with the *sauce mousseline* put down beside her plate. 'Sometimes, I just wish he'd mind his own business – Pierre, I mean. And there's enough of it to keep him busy, let's face it.'

'So why don't you say something? Tell him.'

'It's not so easy, believe me. Once he's involved it's difficult to shake free. He kind of . . . takes over. It's like he can't let go. He's the skipper again, coming up with all these tactics, plans, schemes . . . it's like – all the boys together once more, prepping for a match or something. You should see them when he phones or drops by. Olivier, Gilles, Claude, Antoine . . . they all jump when they hear the skipper.' She shook her head. 'A lot of kids, that's all they are.'

'Antoine? You said Antoine?'

'Well, it probably won't happen now,' she said, 'but

Pierre was going to back Antoine in some venture the two of them were cooking up. Like Touche, only boats.' She held up her hands. 'Don't ask,' she said, then picked up her knife and fork and set to work on the *dorade*. 'Just delicious,' she said, licking her lips. 'And so much more delicate than your *loup*,' she added.

But Jacquot wasn't thinking about the difference between *dorade* and *loup*. He was thinking about Chantal Valadier. If Chantal's experience following her husband's death had anything to do with it, Sophie was probably right when she suggested that Antoine's widow, Isabelle, would remain in the dark about her husband's proposed business dealings with Dombasle. And if anything happened to Olivier when they opened up his skull, then he suspected that the same would happen to Sophie, even if it meant that she would get what she wanted. Dombasle's interference would tail off. Touche would stay where it was. Just Touche – no Côte, or Campagne, or Cité. Jacquot was sure of it.

'So enough of Touche,' said Sophie, tucking away a mouthful of *dorade*. 'What about you, Daniel? How are things with you? And what about that gorgeous, gorgeous Claudine? I want to know everything about her. Every last detail. You owe me.'

And so he told her about Claudine – how they'd met first in Marseilles, met again on a recent case, how she was an artist, and how it was still early days. But the more he said, the more he was aware that Sophie was smiling gently . . .

'You're teasing me,' he said, halfway through a funny story about Claudine's early attempts at sculpture.

'*Non, non. Pas de tout. Je te promets*,' said Sophie. 'It's just . . . it's just nice to see a man so in love.'

'Who said anything about love?'

She gave him a tired look. 'Daniel. Please . . .'

Two hours after leaving Hôpital Saint-Saëns, Jacquot took Sophie back there.

'Please don't remind me how much I ate,' she kept saying, hugging his arm as they walked along. 'I was a pig. I can't believe it. I can hardly breathe.'

They parted on the hospital steps. 'Are you staying down here?' she asked. 'Why not come to Touche? Even with the kids, there's loads of room.'

'I'd love to, but there are some things I have to do. Work. I need to be . . .' He tried to think of something appropriate.

'I understand, I understand,' she said. 'Just keep in touch. I'll see you when I see you. Come soon.'

She reached for his arm, squeezed it, smiled. 'And thank you, Daniel.'

Then she turned and was gone.

oak that rose above the Baie des Anges, following signs for Roquefort-Les-Pins.

Despite only playing together in squad training sessions and for those ten minutes on that pitch at Twickenham, Jacquot and Jean-Charles had been good friends. Along with Olivier and Sidi, Jean-Charles was one of the few team members who had not, at some stage or another, made some cutting remark about Jacquot's last-minute dash for the English line, the winning try. That long-ago winter's day in London, it was Olivier who'd pulled him from the mud, Sidi who'd jumped on his back and Jean-Charles who'd grabbed his shoulders and planted those three exuberant muddy kisses on his cheeks – an image captured by a side-line photographer and sold around the world. All three players had been delighted by Jacquot's performance, more concerned that France beat the English than how it was done, or why it hadn't been one of them making that run down the length of the pitch.

And then, as these things happen, the four of them had lost touch with each other: Jacquot working his way up through the Marseilles *judiciaire*, Touche returning to his father's restaurant above Menton, Sidi out on his fishing *pointu* and Jean-Charles as a serving naval officer. Yet when they met up at Dombasle's reunion party, it felt as though they had never been apart. Touche still had that mischievous grin, Jacquot still had his ponytail, and Sidi was as wiry as ever with a face as dark and creased as an oiled nutmeg. Only Jean-Charles had really changed. He looked older, somehow more patrician, more responsible. With a straighter back. They'd teased him about it, of course. Maybe it had something to do with command, Jacquot decided, the discipline of the services.

And now, Jean-Charles Rains was going to become a father for the first time. The swelling closeness of his lovely wife and the prospect of looming fatherhood had made him smile at Dombasle's, but there was a look of terror in the eyes too. They'd teased him about that as well, though Olivier was the only one among them who'd actually been a dad, with grown-up children.

Jacquot was negotiating the *rondpoint* outside Rouret and watching out for the sign to Domaine de la Côte that Jean-Charles had told him about when the Peugeot's petrol gauge gave a bleep-bleep warning. Jacquot knew from experience that this warning was only triggered when the tank was pretty much running on vapour so at the first petrol station he came to, a few kilometres past the *rondpoint* on the road to Jean's house, he pulled into the forecourt and waited his turn.

Little did Jacquot know, as he paid for the gas, that the delay would save his life.

47

As the sun threw long shadows over the Magnan golf course, halfway between Rouret and Valbonne, Jacquot passed through a set of unmanned security gates into Domaine de la Côte where Jean-Charles and Nathalie Rains lived. Jean-Charles had given him the security code for the main gate but somewhere along the line Jacquot had forgotten what the number was or where he'd written it down. In the event, he didn't need it. There was enough traffic coming in and out of the Domaine for him to squeeze in while the gates opened for someone who did have the number.

Jean-Charles and Nathalie lived at the end of a narrow cul-de-sac at the very top of this gated hillside community, with views south to the coast and north to the rearing bookend massifs of Roquefort. The house was modern, a terracotta-roofed villa with two floors and five windows a floor. A balustraded porch was set around the whole of the ground floor, there was a closed double garage to one side, and the property was bordered by a line of wind-break shaved cypress and leaning palms, with a terraced lawn that sloped down to the road. A lately discovered talent for software programming – and a naval pension – certainly appeared to pay well, thought Jacquot, as he drew up at the foot of the lawn and switched off his engine.

Getting out of his car, Jacquot pulled his scarf round his neck and, remembering the slack security at the entrance gates, paused to lock his car. He knew how these things happened and wasn't prepared to take any chances. Jean-Charles would greet him at the front door, take him through to a terrace at the back of the house and his car would be left for anyone to ransack or drive away. Two hours later he'd find the Peugeot trashed at best, or simply not there. And given Rochet's five-day limit he didn't have time for inconveniences like that.

Crossing the pavement, settling his overcoat around him, Jacquot was halfway across the lawn and no more than fifteen metres from the porch steps when suddenly, in a disconcerting kind of slow motion, the long rectangular frame of the villa seemed to bulge. In the millisecond in which Jacquot registered this, a pulsing orange light seemed to fill every window, there was an explosive crack of wooden doors, shutters and window frames, a shattering smash of glass and the whole house erupted in a vast balloon of flame that washed over the lawn with an ear-numbing *whumph*.

Before he had time to understand what was happening, a wave of heat and wind caught Jacquot square in the chest, lifted him off his feet, sucked the breath from his lungs and sent him sprawling backwards. In the seconds before he hit the ground there was time enough to see the roof rise up like a fiery fountain and shatter into a thousand shingle tiles, the walls break outwards and a plume of angry flame and smoke billow up into the evening sky. Hurled back on to the sloping lawn of Jean-Charles' and Nathalie's house, Jacquot saw what looked like a pram soar overhead and crash down into the road somewhere behind him.

And then there was darkness.

48

'Attention! He's got a gun,' came a voice. The words sounded oddly distant and muffled, as though his ears were packed with cotton wool.

'Stay back. Stay back. Don't go near him.'

Who? thought Jacquot, coming to his senses. Who had a gun?

What gun? Where?

He opened his eyes. High above him the sky had darkened, stars twinkled. He could see a pulsing lighthouse flash of red and blue sweeping across his field of vision, from somewhere the distant sound of sirens, and the closer familiar sound of voices. There was a strange, unpleasant chemical smell in the air, in his clothes, in his hair. Without touching it he knew his face was wet, his cheeks hummed with heat and he seemed to have no strength in his arms or his legs. He could tell that he was lying on his back, the knot of his ponytail digging into the back of his head, and that his head was lower than his feet. He was lying on a slope and pegged, like Gulliver, to the ground. He closed his eyes, opened them again, tried to concentrate on what he could see, what he could hear, what he could smell and what he could remember – the car, the lawn, the slow-motion blasting disintegration of Jean-Charles's home; being caught up and flung back like a shred of useless litter caught in a gust of wind; the hollow, deafening *whumph*; the lung-tugging smash of his body on the ground . . . but it was all too much.

'I'm a cop,' he whispered, scraping up a voice from somewhere. 'I'm a cop. I've got a badge. In my pocket. Somewhere . . .' and as he closed his eyes he saw again the baby's pram cartwheeling through the air.

He woke up crying. He knew he was crying, knew there were tears, could feel their cool twin tracks on his scorched cheeks. It was the crying that brought him round.

Jean-Charles.

Nathalie.

The baby.

Above him a pram soared through the air.

'You OK?' A soot-smeared helmeted face came between him and the stars. They seemed brighter now, the sky even darker. The sooty face looked like a backlit shadow. 'Can you hear me?' The voice was loud, urgent. 'Say something.' And then the face disappeared.

A minute later . . . an hour later . . . another face – no helmet this time – broke into his vision. A woman's face, hair tied back, a green reflective waistcoat that seemed to glow in the flashing lights. He closed his eyes again.

'Will you move your fingers for me?'

Jacquot tried. The trying seemed to stretch into eternity, but he was aware of no response.

'If you can hear us,' came the woman's voice, 'but you can't speak, just squeeze my fingers . . .'

He was aware for the first time of his hand being held. He tried to squeeze. He couldn't tell if he'd managed it. Couldn't tell if . . . He opened his eyes again. He saw a smile.

'Or you could blink your eyes,' the woman said.

He blinked.

And then, 'I'm OK,' he said, wondering where the words had come from. He didn't feel all right at all, but at least he could speak. Or could he? Had they heard him?

'You're Daniel Jacquot, is that right? Chief Inspector Daniel Jacquot?'

'I'm Jacquot,' he managed, aware as he spoke that his throat was as rough and sore as a deathbed, Bourbon-drinking, sixty-a-day rock-and-roll singer. 'Daniel Jacquot.' The name, when he finally succeeded in getting it out, seemed somehow unreal, unfamiliar. Just a tag. A title. Nothing to do with him. And where the sounds came from . . . who could tell? He wanted to cough, tried to cough, and felt a lance of pain shoot through his chest and throat. He also realised his neck was braced. He couldn't move his head, his lips were crumpled, his jaw clenched, his ears bent . . .

'Easy. Easy,' came the woman's voice and he felt a soft, cold hand on his forehead, saw her face float in front of his. 'You took a fall. You're OK. You're going to be fine. Maybe a broken rib, but everything else seems OK. Now I'm going to give you a small injection. You're going to feel a sting.'

'Jean-Charles. Tell me . . . My friends. Nathalie . . .'

And then his body sank away from him, into the wet grass, and one by one, very quickly, the stars blinked out and the pulsing beams of light faded.

49

'Daniel?'

It was a strangely familiar voice.

'Daniel, it's me.'

Jacquot wanted to open his eyes but it felt as though the lids were somehow stitched together.

'He should be coming round,' said another voice. It was a woman speaking.

'Daniel, can you hear me? It's Jean-Charles. Jean-Charles Rains.'

The name registered slowly. Jean-Charles. But he was dead, surely? And Nathalie too.

Carefully, slowly, Daniel tested his body – feet first, then legs; fingers, hands and arms. Willing movement into distant muscles. Without much prompting they did as he wanted, flickered with life. He was alive. Everything seemed to be working. Everything seemed . . . and then he winced as he tried to sit up.

'Take it easy, big boy. That's a cracked rib there and they can bite.'

Daniel opened his eyes. A fluorescent tube, a curtained cubicle. He was on his back still, but in a bed. He tried to focus on the woman. She was wearing a blue tunic with a name tag on her lapel. He tried to read it but the letters seemed smudged, somehow out of focus.

She saw what he was trying to do and smiled. 'For your information, you're at the Centre d'Urgence in Rouret. Fractured rib, minor facial abrasions and a slight concussion, but you'll live. Your friend here said you were a tough one.' She looked across the bed.

Daniel carefully turned his head. The neck brace was gone and his head moved surprisingly easily on the pillow. He squinted, tried to focus. There was another figure standing there at the bedside. The other voice. Jacquot had forgotten it.

'Used to be tough is what I actually said. But probably gone to seed,' said Jean-Charles. 'Welcome back, Number Six.'

'Jean . . . Jean, I thought . . .' He couldn't get another word out. His throat felt raw and smokey and there was a cindery taste in his mouth.

'Next time I invite you to dinner, Daniel, I'd be grateful if you'd leave the place in one piece.'

A beep-beep-beep sounded and the nurse checked her pager. 'I'll be back in a while,' she said to Jacquot. 'Get some rest. If you're a good boy, we'll let you out in the morning.' And with that she turned on her heel, stepped through the curtain and was gone.

'I'm in hospital?'

'You and Nathalie. *Les deux.*'

'She was hurt?'

Jean-Charles chuckled. 'She said it was painful, but she'd do it again.'

Jacquot tried to shake his head, to clear it, to work out what Jean-Charles was saying. How could he be standing there? How could they have survived that blast? It didn't make sense.

'. . . don't understand . . .' Jacquot managed.

'*Je suis un papa*. A little girl. Four point three kilos.' He looked at his watch. 'Two hours and twenty-three minutes ago. It's why we weren't at the house to greet you. Nathalie was putting the *gigot* in the oven when her waters broke.' Jean-Charles chuckled. 'Just like that. In the kitchen, would you believe? I didn't have a number for you, so I left a note on the door. "Baby arriving. Key under the pot. Help yourself." Left the place at a run and reckoned you could take care of yourself. I was going to phone to let you know where we were.'

'You know what happened? Your house?'

Jean-Charles nodded. 'Hey, you win some, you lose some. I'm only glad it went when it did. A couple of hours earlier and we'd have been toast. And, by the sound of it, a couple more minutes and you'd have gone with it.'

'How did you know? About me? The house?'

'Our neighbour. Jeannette Descourts. Old lady. She came with you in the ambulance. She saw it all. Said she watched you get out of the car and start up the lawn. Said you looked very suspicious. The ponytail, probably. And then, just as you start across the front lawn, the place just erupts. According to Madame Descourts, you took off backwards, clean through the air – very stylish move, Daniel. Very stylish. Landed on the grass, but another metre and you'd have dented your car.'

'*Merde* . . .'

'You caused a bit of a stir, I can tell you,' Jean-Charles continued, pulling up a chair. 'The first thing Madame sees when she gets to you is your gun. So what with the ponytail, you've just got to be *Milieu*, the Mafia. Some kind of hit-man or bomber. Five minutes after the place goes up, there's ambulance, police, fire brigade, and the local SWAT team. If they hadn't found your badge, you'd be cuffed to that bed and there'd be a couple of *flics* keeping you company.'

And then Jacquot remembered. Everything seemed to surge back. The team. The killings. The reason he'd come to see Jean-Charles in the first place. Not for dinner. But to warn him. And if it hadn't been for Nathalie going into labour, if it hadn't been for his empty fuel tank and the stop at that garage, they'd all be dead.

A sense of urgency suddenly gripped Jacquot and his head began to throb, his cheeks to burn.

'. . . Something you need to know, Jean. Something . . .'

There was a swish of curtains and the nurse was back, a plastic cup of water and a pill dispenser in her hands. She gave both men a stern look.

'For a new father, Monsieur Rains, I think you'll find you're sitting at the wrong bed. You two may be old friends, but he's not the one who just gave birth. If you don't mind my saying it, you need to be with your wife, monsieur. And your daughter. One floor down, in case you'd forgotten.'

It was as if Jean-Charles hadn't registered the urgency in Jacquot's voice. Or if he had, the thought of his wife and new daughter had him out of his chair and heading for the curtain before Jacquot could manage another word. It was hopeless.

'I'll come back later . . .'

'No you won't,' scolded the nurse, raising the cup and pills. 'This man is going to take a nap whether he likes it or not.'

'Tomorrow morning, then?'

'Not until after Rounds,' said the nurse briskly. 'Eight-thirty earliest. *Et maintenant, allez-vous-en. Vite, monsieur. Vot' femme, vot' bébé.*'

Behind her back, Jean-Charles swung up an extravagant salute, gave Jacquot a great beam of a smile, and disappeared through the curtains.

'I need to speak to my boss,' said Jacquot as the nurse leant forward with the pill and water.

She shook her head. 'No you don't.'

And that was that.

50

'*Jésu . . . Jé-su . . .*' whispered Jacquot. He was standing in front of a mirror and he couldn't believe his blood-shot eyes.

Someone should have warned him. He hadn't thought about it. What he looked like. After the Rounds doctor had signed him off earlier that morning with instructions to go home and take it easy for a few days, Jacquot had struggled out of bed and was looking for his clothes when he realised he desperately wanted to pee. The mirror was in the bathroom. The moment he switched on the light he saw himself. One sock, a pair of pants, a swathe of bandaging around his chest and a face that looked as though he'd fallen asleep on the beach and been rewarded with a bad case of sunburn.

His forehead and cheeks were as shiny as a polished

apple, there was a curling peel of skin on the tip of his reddened nose and on his chin, and his eyebrows had black crumbs in them where once there had been hair. It was the same with his eyelashes, still there but clearly shorter than they once had been. He couldn't believe it. Where was the face he knew?

'Not a pretty sight, is it?' said the nurse, appearing behind him in the bathroom door. 'But it's better than last night, I can tell you. Swelling's gone and it's starting to peel. More *saumon cru* than *saumon fumé*, if you'll pardon the description.'

'How long will I look . . . ?' he managed to croak.

'Like Geronimo on the warpath? Why? You got a date?' The nurse smiled. She was tubby around the belt of her uniform, her arms bulged out of her short sleeves, but her smile was warm and caring and gave an attractive slant to features bare of make-up. 'Let's just say you'll look like a tourist for a couple of days and your face may sting in a cold wind. But you'll just have to live with it. Here, I brought you your prescription. Cream for the night-time, plenty of it, and painkillers for the rib, no more than six a day. And these,' she said, rattling a brown bottle, 'are for your throat. Dissolve and gargle, twice a day. Also, the less you use your voice, the quicker you'll get it back.'

Well, that's good to know, thought Jacquot. 'Thank you, madame. You've been very kind.'

'So you want me to send up your friend? His wife and daughter are sleeping and he's desperate to go and take a look at what you did to his house.'

Without thinking, Jacquot smiled.

'Ouch,' he cried as his lips cracked and his cheeks smarted enough to bring tears to his eyes.

'Oh yes,' said the nurse. 'I forgot to say – not too many facial expressions for a while. You'll soon learn what you can and can't do.'

'You look like a traffic light and smell like a fireplace,' said Jean-Charles as they drove away from the hospital.

'Thanks for that,' growled Jacquot, who'd already noticed a few looks from passers-by – either surprised or sympathetic, both equally embarrassing.

'Under normal circumstances,' continued Jean-Charles, 'I'd be happy to offer you a shower, or loan you some clothes, but right now I'm afraid that's not an option.' After stopping at the local gendarmerie where Jacquot picked up his gun and badge – his rank was high enough to ensure no comment from the local *flics* – Jean-Charles headed out to Domaine de la Côte.

On the way, keeping it simple, sparing his voice as much as he could, Jacquot filled Jean-Charles in about what had been happening. The team. The deaths. His suspicions.

As they passed through the Domaine's main gate, Jean-Charles started to shake his head. 'I can't believe it,' he said. 'I mean, I don't doubt either your suspicions or your conclusions, Daniel – all of this happening – but who would do such a thing? Why?' And then, as they turned into Jean-Charles's road, '*Merde alors*. It really has gone!'

Parking as close as he could get, the entire property cordoned off like a crime scene, Jean-Charles got out of the car and stared up at what had once been his home, but was now just a blackened shell. The roof had gone and most of the top floor. Smoke billowing from the ground-floor windows had left a line of matching black eyebrows on those sections of wall still standing, the lawn was littered with charred debris and blackened roof tiles, while the grass within three metres of the blast was a belt of scorched black. All that was left of the palm trees on the far side of the house were splintered stumps and the cypress trees looked like blackened candles.

Lifting the security tape so that Jacquot didn't have to bend down and jar the rib, Jean-Charles nodded at the two gas vans parked up ahead.

'We've been telling them for months,' he said, his careless jokey manner now hardening. 'Five, maybe six times they've been around – Madame Descourts, the Valenciens. We've all smelt it. The gas. And every time they come out to look,' said Jean-Charles, 'they tell us everything's fine. Not a problem.'

'Gas?' asked Jacquot. 'So you're saying the explosion was caused by a gas leak?'

'You thought it was a bomb? Someone tinkering with the gas?'

Making a murder look like an accident, thought Jacquot. He nodded. 'Something like that.'

'*Non, non, non,*' said Jean-Charles, shaking his head as he took in the scene of devastation. 'This was an accident. An accident waiting to happen. There have been problems with the supply since the day we moved in.' As they walked up the slope, the lawn squelched under foot. 'Hell, they must have emptied a ton of water on the place.'

'When was that? The move?' asked Jacquot, trying to pitch his voice so he didn't hurt his throat.

'Two or three months ago. Before that we were living with Nathalie's mother. Which reminds me, I'd better give her a call and tell her to expect us back.'

The two men reached the top of the slope and stood looking at the front of the house, the porch and front steps sagging from the wall, the open doorway criss-crossed with charred beams, the distant heights of Roquefort now visible behind the house. The chill morning air smelt of burnt wood and blasted stone, lubricated with the heady, sinuous scent of gas.

'Just as well I'm a lazy bastard,' mused Jean-Charles, working a stiffness out of his shoulder. 'Nathalie's been telling me for weeks to get our stuff out of storage. I just didn't get round to it.'

Jacquot smiled carefully at his friend.

From the side of the house, two overalled gas inspectors appeared. They wore blue hard-hats and carried clipboards. When they saw Jacquot and Jean-Charles one of them came over with his arms spread, as though to herd them away. 'Messieurs, you shouldn't be here. It's private property.'

'My private property,' replied Jean-Charles coolly. 'Or what's left of it, thanks to you lot.'

The man didn't know what to say. He was thin and scrawny, the overalls one size too large for him. He looked at Jacquot and Rains – two hefty national squad rugby players who, given the slope of the land, towered above him – and giving them both an uncertain smile he headed back to his friend.

With a final forlorn look at what had once been his home, Jean-Charles turned away and he and Jacquot followed the inspectors down to the roadside, Jacquot looking around to see if he could remember anything from the night before – getting out of his car, starting up the lawn. Was it the top row of shuttered windows that had bulged first and exploded out towards him, driven by a boiling blast of orange flame, or the lower floor? All he could really recall was that terrifying sound, that hollow *whumph*, and the rush of hot air that had lifted him off his feet and seared away his eyebrows, eyelashes and what felt like a dozen layers of skin.

And the pram, of course, spinning and wheeling through the air, surfing on that billowing flame.

They found it by Jacquot's Peugeot, on its side, its struts bent, its plastic hood and seating burnt away. Jean-Charles picked it up, examined it and then lobbed it on to the lawn.

'Some dinner,' said Jean-Charles, pushing his hands into his jacket pockets.

51

It wasn't just the pram that had taken a pounding. And nor was it just Jacquot's scorched features that attracted attention after he and Jean-Charles Rains parted company. At least four roof tiles had landed on Jacquot's Peugeot after the explosion, leaving its roof and bonnet badly dented, the entire car coated in a water-streaked soot-black skin. As he drove through Rouret and on to the garage outside Roquefort that had saved his life, he could see people turning to watch the car pass. At the garage – a lifetime ago, he'd stood there – he bought a token and put the Peugeot through the car wash, sitting behind the wheel and watching the sudsy rollers sweep down on to his blackened windscreen.

Given the ongoing problem with Jean-Charles's gas supply and his conviction that the explosion really was an accident, Jacquot was forced to admit that on this occasion what appeared to be an accident might actually have been just that.

Not that Jean-Charles had discounted Jacquot's concerns, or dismissed his suspicions. Despite his disbelief that such a thing could happen, he was prepared to accept that Jacquot might be right, and before Jacquot drove away Jean-Charles had promised to keep an eye open, and to keep in touch.

'You must come and see Nathalie, and our baby,' said Jean-Charles, hugging Jacquot. 'We've called her Alba.'

'When I get my face back,' replied Jacquot. 'I wouldn't want to frighten them.'

Jean-Charles laughed.

'And remember,' Jacquot continued, 'just because this was an accident, it doesn't mean there won't be another. Just be careful, my old friend.'

Forty minutes later, Jacquot checked in at the Hôtel Bon Accueil in Villefranche-sur-Mer, apologising for arriving a day late and not calling ahead to warn them. The lady behind the reception desk couldn't have been more understanding. 'You have been on holiday, monsieur?' she asked, as he filled in the registration form. He knew at once she was referring to the state of his face, unable to resist a comment.

'*Oui*, Guadeloupe,' he replied, his voice hoarse and whispered.

'My mother swears by aloe,' she continued, handing Jacquot his key. 'I'll ask her to drop some by.'

The pleasantries over, Jacquot asked where he might find the bar and was pointed across the tiled reception area. Sitting in the Monday morning sunshine, he ordered a *grande crème et calva* and looked in his bag for his pills. The side of his chest had started to hurt and, just as his nurse had warned, the fresh breeze off the harbour had made his face sting.

'*Voilà, monsieur. Une crème, et calva*,' said the barman setting down a large cup of coffee and a *ballon* of calvados, the sun sparkling through its caramel depths. He slipped the bill under the ashtray and then gave Jacquot a sympathetic grin. '*Permettez-moi*, monsieur. But you look as if you need it.' And with that he was gone.

Reaching for his calva, Jacquot decided he'd better get used to being greeted in this manner – whether he liked it or not – and without thinking he tossed back a slug of the calva. It didn't take more than a split second to realise his mistake, the back and sides of his throat shrieking as the calva scorched its way down.

Merde, merde, merde . . . Even thinking the words hurt.

* * *

It was growing dark when Jacquot left his room. He'd stayed there all day like a wounded animal licking its wounds. He'd bagged his smokey clothes for the hotel's laundry, unwound the bandaging from his chest and then drawn a steaming hot bath. Thirty minutes after sliding into its scented warmth he'd hauled himself out and, dizzy with the heat, worked the cream into his face. Closing the shutters, he'd lain on the bed and listened to the chink-and-clink of boats in the harbour beyond his room and dozed gently through the afternoon. At four, he applied more cream (his face seemed to soak it up), gargled as instructed and tried unsuccessfully to rewind the bandage round his chest. In the end he gave up and dressed carefully in fresh clothes, just an occasional wince of complaint from his cracked rib. Apart from the scorched face and croaky voice, it was a pain he was used to from the field of play and the mean streets of Marseilles. For the first time in twenty-four hours, he felt human.

Jacquot had no idea where to start looking for the fisherman Sidi Carassin but his friendly receptionist did.

'Right outside our front door, monsieur. Across the road there.' She pointed to a stone jetty, then glanced at her watch. 'But I think you may have missed him.'

Outside, the lights of St-Jean-Cap-Ferrat glimmered across the bay and, rattling across distant points, the

Nice-Menton train rolled eastwards, windows lit, tiny fluorescent squares blinking out as the train entered a tunnel. Carefully, beneath the hotel canopy, Jacquot drew in a deep breath of crisp sea air and was pleased to note the gargling seemed to have done some good. He let out his breath equally carefully, and then tried inhaling through his nose. Even easier. A couple, arm in arm, walked past, glanced at him, but seemed not to notice his scorched face. But then it was dark, and he was backlit by the hotel. Wrapping the scarf round his neck, he crossed the road to the quay and stepped down on to the jetty.

The receptionist was right. The only vessels moored there were an old trawler that had been converted into a floating Dive School, its deck hung with drying wet-suits, and a pair of Zephyrs moored alongside. But no *pointus*. Out on the darkening bay, beyond the far quay, Jacquot could faintly hear the distant chortling splutter of a *pointu* heading out to the fishing grounds and could make out a bobbing set of lights. He could only guess it was Sidi.

Returning to the quay and wondering what to do next, Jacquot noticed a white Renault van parked outside the Bureau du Port. The van's sliding side door was open and a figure was leaning into its darkened interior. There was something immediately familiar about the fall of hair but the yellow Wellington boots, jeans and sailor's pea-jacket were a million miles from the low-cut dress she'd been wearing the last time Jacquot had seen her.

'Mathilde? *C'est toi?* Mathilde Carassin?'

The figure pushed away from the van and turned to Jacquot.

'*Oui, c'est moi. Qui . . . ?*' She peered through the gloom.

Jacquot turned his head and pulled his ponytail through his hand.

She spotted the movement. 'Daniel? Daniel Jacquot?'

'*Exacte*. It's good to see you. *Ça va? Ça marche?*' They kissed three times and stepped back as though to get a better look at each other.

'Monsieur *Flic* has been in the wars, *n'est-ce pas*?' She stepped forward and gently touched her fingertips to Jacquot's cheek. 'They say aloe is good.'

'So I'm told.'

'But what a surprise. To see you here.' She looked puzzled. 'You live up-country don't you? Carpentras? Cavaillon?'

'Cavaillon, that's right. I was just down here on business and I thought I'd drop by, say hello.'

Mathilde sat in the van's door space, shucked off her Wellington boots, and reached for a pair of shoes. 'Well, I'm afraid you've missed Sidi.' She gestured out to sea.

'But if you're here in the morning, around seven, he'll be back then.'

She stood, shuffled on her shoes and stowed the boots. She caught hold of the door handle and swung the door closed with a sound that reminded Jacquot of the *whumph* that had accompanied the previous night's explosion.

'Well, what are you up to?' asked Jacquot. 'If you're free, what about a drink. Dinner?' He pointed to the brasseries that lined the quay.

Mathilde gave a surprised but delighted chuckle. 'How wonderful. I'd love to . . .' She hesitated. 'And it's not every night I get invitations like that. But I can't, Daniel. I'd love to, *vraiment*. But I have to get to work.'

Jacquot frowned.

'Airport limousine service,' explained Mathilde. 'I start in precisely' – she cuffed back her sleeve and looked at the time – 'forty-seven minutes. I'm so sorry, truly.'

'Well, I'm staying at the Bon Accueil. Maybe we can meet up tomorrow. It would be nice to see Sidi. Maybe lunch?'

'Sidi'd love that. And so would I.'

'Here? Midday?'

'If I have to carry him kicking and screaming.'

* * *

Two hours later, after a solitary dinner at La Mère Germaine, the restaurant where Olivier and Claude Lorraine had dined together on the night of their 'crash', Jacquot pushed his hands in his pockets and wandered back along the quay to his hotel. Normally, he would have taken serious note of a menu that declared: '*Notre Chef et son équipe vous proposent* . . . ; *Le Sommelier vous conseille* . . . ; *Le Chef Patissier vous régale avec* . . . ; and *Le Barman vous présente* . . .' and heeded the warning. But if Olivier had chosen this place for dinner, reasoned Jacquot, then there were surely redeeming features. Which, happily, there had been: a thick fish soup that, lukewarm and without the croutons, slid down painlessly, followed by a pearl-flakey *cabillaud roti*, its crisped skin reluctantly put aside. Splashing out on a bottle of Pibarnon '90, and managing to smoke three cigarettes without a single cough, Jacquot felt a deep, satisfied warmth as he pushed through the front door of the Hôtel Bon Accueil and headed for the lift.

'Monsieur? Monsieur Jacquot?' came a voice from behind the reception desk.

Jacquot turned.

The receptionist held out a bag. 'My mother dropped in the aloe for you.'

52

Daniel Jacquot's room was five floors above the street, a metre or so below the illuminated letter 'n' of 'Hôtel Bon Accueil'. And while the balcony was easily wide enough for a table and chair, and the railing easily high enough, Jacquot still felt uncomfortable. For a man who didn't like heights, a fifth-floor bedroom was easily three floors too high. If the building burnt down, he'd tell anyone who asked, he wanted to be close enough to the ground to be able to jump if neccesary, and survive. He'd already had a word with the receptionist and been told that, *malheureusement*, a room on the floors below would not be available until the end of the following week at the earliest. Now that the season was over the rooms on the first four floors were being refurbished. He would have to make do for the time being.

It was for this reason, at a little after seven the following morning, that he peered so carefully over the balcony railing. For Jacquot, high balconies were a little like horses. He didn't like either very much, but he liked to make out that he wasn't too bothered. He could handle them – *pas un problème*.

Far, far below, the small jetty opposite the hotel that had been boatless and deserted the evening before was now packed with *pointus*, two and three abreast, the fishermen passing up the last of their catches. Parked beside the jetty was Mathilde's Renault van and there, jumping from one *pointu* to another, was Sidi, balancing a styrofoam container filled with iced silvery fish.

Jacquot looked at his watch. He'd have breakfast first and then wander across and say 'hi'. He could see that the two of them, Mathilde and Sidi, were busy and that he'd just be in the way. But he mis-timed it. As he poured his first coffee in the small conservatory *Salle du Matin* he heard the Renault's sliding door slam shut and saw the white van make an illegal turn and head out of town.

He'd have to wait for lunch.

In the meantime there were four possible options. He could either visit Gilles Millet in Grasse or the *notaire* Val Caloux in Théoule, call in at Cap Corsaire or drive out to the slip road between the Corniche Moyenne and La Turbie where Olivier and Claude had had their 'accident'. Since Gilles Millet and Val Caloux were both a good hour's drive away, and since Pierre Dombasle would not be home until the following day, a 'look-see' on the La Turbie slip road seemed the most sensible alternative.

This connecting road between the Moyenne and Grande Corniche roads was no more than three or four kilometres but, as Jacquot soon discovered, its numerous hairpins made it seem far, far longer, every twist and turn set with road signs warning of *Lacets* and *Virages Dangereux*.

The real problem, of course, was parking. The road might be wide enough for two lanes of traffic at a pinch, but there was no room for parked cars as well. Unless you had your own driveway, there was nowhere safe to pull in. Before he knew it, Jacquot was up on the Grande Corniche and having to turn round to come back down. Taking a bit of a liberty he pulled in at the first driveway that afforded some space off the edge of the road and started down on foot. If he was blocking someone in, he'd hear their horn and be back in a flash. So sorry, broken down . . . whatever.

It was not, however, the most comfortable walk. The road between the Grande and Moyenne Corniches offered a drop on its seaward side that was almost as vertiginous as Jacquot's balcony, and he was hard pressed to walk along its low-walled edge without letting his eyes stray. Far below, when he dared look, was a glittering Mediterranean bracketed by pine-clad headlands and directly below him, what looked like a vertical drop dotted with sharp rock outcrops, prickly-pear cactus and blade-leafed aloe. Two hundred, three hundred metres? Jacquot thought it best not to consider how high he was and tried to keep his eyes on the road.

It was too soon to expect a bouquet of flowers to mark the spot where Olivier and Claude had plunged off the road, so Jacquot looked out for a scar or skid mark in the gravel edging of the road, a broken stretch of stone balustrade, or a likely-looking swimming pool and broken branches on the slope below him. He found what he was looking for soon enough. No bouquet, but a single line of black rubber that led straight to the low stone wall. The top-most edge of this wall was newly chipped and, twenty metres below, Jacquot could clearly see a patch of blue, a square of terrace tiles, and broken branches. He had no doubt that this was the spot where Olivier and Claude Lorraine had left the road.

Walking on a few more metres, Jacquot found a section of wall on a sharp corner that afforded a clear view of the road in both directions. He made himself as comfortable as he could, vividly aware of the drop at his back, lit up a cigarette and watched as a lorry ground its way uphill and a car towing a caravan came down. Because of the bend neither driver could see the other until the very last moment, almost where Jacquot sat. With a ferocious clanging of gears and a cloud of blue exhaust, the lorry changed gears and blasted its klaxon, the car with its caravan, suitably warned, slowing down, drawing into the side of the hill and hugging it tight. With what looked like just centimetres to spare the two vehicles passed each other and continued on their way.

After his drive with Olivier not a week before, on much the same kind of road, it was easy to see how Olivier's 'accident' might have happened. If the car and caravan had not drawn into the side of the road, and if the lorry had not given a warning blast on its klaxon, the two of them could easily have crashed. Of course at night, neither the lorry nor the car would have needed to sound a horn, the beam of approaching headlights would be clearly visible. So how, Jacquot wondered, was Olivier forced off the road as he came powering up from Villefranche and the Corniche Moyenne? The only possible explanation, as far as Jacquot could see, was that Olivier and Claude had been followed by the killer. And given that motorbikes were faster and more manoeuvrable on these kinds of roads than cars, it seemed likely to Jacquot that the killer had also been riding a bike, coming up fast behind them, drawing alongside before ramming them off the road. It would have been a tricky and dangerous piece of riding but it was definitely possible – and on this particular stretch, about the only way to manage it. So, a woman who knew this road, who knew how to handle a motorbike, and ride it as well as Olivier.

Back at the car, Jacquot checked the time. It was closing on 11.30 and there seemed little point in doing anything else but heading back to Villefranche for lunch. Afterwards, he'd call Val and Gilles to set up a meeting, and the following day drive out to Cap Corsaire for a chat with Pierre Dombasle.

Jacquot had a feeling as he released the handbrake and headed back down to the coast that he would have all he needed after that.

One way or the other.

53

Sidi and Mathilde Carassin were waiting on the quayside when Jacquot pulled in at his hotel at a little after twelve o'clock. Even in November the Corniche roads were busy and it had taken longer than he'd expected to make it back to Villefranche.

As soon as she saw him, Mathilde waved and she and Sidi came over. Both had dressed for the occasion, Mathilde in loose linen trousers, blouse and boots, Sidi in a sun-faded blue denim shirt, cotton chinos and espadrilles, and both looked fit and tanned and freshly showered.

'I thought for a while there you were going to stand me up,' said Mathilde, leaning down at the driver's window and displaying a generous expanse of cleavage, 'but Sidi said only a fool would do that to me and, according to him, you're not a fool.'

But that was as far she got. Her husband seemed to tuck in under her arm and push his way in through the window, embracing Jacquot as he sat at the wheel.

'I'm assuming,' said Jacquot when he could manage it, 'that you'd prefer to eat somewhere other than the home stretch?'

'*Pas de tout*,' replied Sidi. 'They all buy my fish along here so they must be good, *hein*? Worth a try, wouldn't you say?'

And so, after squeezing his car in beside the Carassins' van, the three of them set off along the quay. Fifteen minutes later they were sitting at a table outside a restaurant called Hameçon and studying the menu. The waiter who had brought the menus and water and aperitifs was clearly new and did not know Sidi, but as soon as the *patron* spotted them he came out to greet them, hugging Sidi and Mathilde like long-lost friends and shaking Jacquot enthusiastically by the hand.

'They say the fish is good here,' said Sidi, his teeth a gash of white in his nut-brown face. 'Maybe I should try it.'

The *patron* turned down his mouth, as though that was a bad idea. 'If monsieur wishes, of course,' he said. 'But I should tell you that our supplier is not of the first order. If I were you, I would order the chicken or the beef or the lamb. Anything but the fish. Very, very poor,' he added, shaking his head.

There was a moment's silence and then laughter. Yet, to Jacquot's astonishment, meat was exactly what Sidi and Mathilde ordered, a fat wedge of entrecôte and a prettily stacked pile of pink *côtelettes d'agneau*.

It was, reflected Jacquot, impossible to dislike Sidi Carassin. Despite the hard-earned lines that gouged his thin cheeks and brow, his rough hands and thinning black curls, there was something engagingly gentle and boyish about him. Jacquot had met him first at a training session at the Parc des Princes ground in Paris. He knew the winger from TV and had felt a real thrill when Sidi came over in the team changing room and introduced himself.

Sidi, as Jacquot learned, had come up the hard way. After his family fled Algeria in the fifties, his parents had settled in St-Jean-de-Luz where his father worked with the fishing fleet. Sidi had followed in his father's footsteps, earning enough money to buy his first *pointu* at about the same time he started playing with Biarritz. After just two seasons with Biarritz he was selected for the national squad and the *pointu* was taken from the water and put under canvas. By the time Jacquot met Sidi in that locker room at Parc des Princes he had thirty caps to his name and an awesome reputation. He had a way of high-kicking his legs as he ran that made it near impossible for anyone to get a decent hold on him, as slippery a customer as the *colinots* he took from the deep. Get the ball to Sidi out on the wing and it was a good bet he'd score. Which he did, time and time again.

But success on the pitch had not translated into success after it. Unlike Valadier, Souze and Savry, Lorraine, Peyrot and Touche, his sporting prowess had failed to provide when he hung up his boots. He was *arabe*, after all, a *pied noir*, and life off the pitch was never going to be easy for such a man. After an honourable retirement from the national squad and a reasonably attended testimonial match, Sidi had played two more seasons with Biarritz then pulled the canvas off his *pointu* and, in the absence of anything more promising, gone back to fishing.

It was at Dombasle's reunion that Jacquot had learned the rest of the story from Olivier. A year after retiring, Sidi had married Mathilde, a *Basquaise* whose father had worked the same boats as Sidi's father, and they'd had a daughter. Everything had been fine until the girl was five when, according to Olivier, she'd contracted meningitis. By the time it was spotted, it was too late. The child died. And that was the end of Biarritz. Within six months, Sidi and Mathilde had sold their home, the *pointu*, and swapped the Atlantic for the Mediterranean. For the last seven years the Carassins had worked the fishing grounds from that tiny jetty along the Villefranche quay.

'Mathilde said you were down here on business,' said Sidi, cutting a slice from his steak and smearing it with mustard. 'You chasing the bad guys? Is that where you got the face?'

Jacquot nodded. 'Sometimes it goes with the turf,' he replied. 'You know how it is.'

'So what's the case? Can you tell us?'

It was just how Jacquot wanted it to begin, Sidi asking the questions and Jacquot answering them – the hit-and-run in Paris, the wine rack in Bordeaux, the 'tryst' killing in Toulouse, and Savry's 'suicide'.

'His hands were clean?' asked Mathilde, frowning. 'I don't understand . . .'

'He'd wedged an oily towel into the back window to seal it, and he'd used quick-drying fire cement to secure the hose to the exhaust pipe. But there wasn't a scrap of dirt on his hands.'

'You noticed something as small as that?' said Sidi in a wondering tone. 'No wonder you're a *flic*.'

'Anything since then?' asked Mathilde, leaning back in her chair.

'You haven't heard?' Jacquot looked at their faces. They shook their heads. 'Well, it's one of the reasons I'm here. To warn you. Since Savry's so-called suicide, there have been a few more incidents,' he continued, failing to point out that it looked as though only the wealthier team members were being targeted. One by one, Jacquot ticked the names off his fingers: Peyrot drowning, Olivier's bike crash on the La Turbie link road, and the explosion at the Rains's house.

'That's how I got this,' said Jacquot, gesturing at his face.

'His house exploded? Someone blew up his house?' asked Mathilde in astonishment.

'The investigators are saying it's a gas leak,' replied Jacquot, noting Mathilde's reaction. 'But I'm not so sure. It's just too much of a coincidence, wouldn't you say?'

'And Jean-Charles?' asked Sidi, a forkful of steak halfway to his mouth, dripping *jus* on to the plate. 'He's OK? His wife?'

'They were at the hospital. His wife Nathalie was having a baby.'

'*Mais c'est vrai*,' exclaimed Mathilde. 'She was pregnant. At the party. I remember. Of course.' And with that she set to work on one of her *côtelettes*, delicately stripping the meat from the curving bone.

'I read about Marc, of course,' said Sidi, 'but I didn't know about the others till the reunion. Luc and Patric. And then Bernard. But the police said it was suicide.

There was a story in the paper the following week. According to them, Bernard committed suicide.'

'Sometimes we get it wrong,' said Jacquot.

'So you think there's a killer down here?' asked Mathilde.

'I'm not sure,' replied Jacquot carefully. 'Just a feeling, more than anything. Apart from Luc up in Paris and Patric in Bordeaux, the others have all been down south – Antoine, Bernard, Claude, Marc.' Once more he failed to mention the fact that they were all well-off.

'Well that's not surprising,' said Mathilde. 'This is the Côte d'Azur, after all. You can make a lot of enemies down here. And a lot of money.' Mathilde flashed Jacquot a look. 'Take that lobster you're eating. There's a fifteen-franc mark-up on that for us. In Biarritz we'd have been lucky to make eight.'

'Nine, nine at least,' chipped in Sidi with a grin.

'Now that's interesting,' said Jacquot smoothly. 'So you think it might have something to do with money? So far I haven't been able to establish a motive for the killings. Maybe you're right.'

'You think he'll try again?' asked Sidi.

'Who said it's a "he"?' replied Jacquot, reaching for his wine.

'You think it could be a woman?' asked Mathilde, with a hint of surprise in her voice.

'If it wasn't for Marc Fastin, I wouldn't be so sure. But numbers don't lie. He arrives at the club with one woman, but ends up dead with another. So where's the lady he arrived with?'

Putting down his wine glass, Jacquot reached for his napkin and dabbed carefully at his lips. Sunlight glanced off the glasses and sparkled through the wine.

Across the table, Mathilde narrowed her eyes. 'Daniel Jacquot,' she began sternly, 'you have to be kidding?'

Jacquot frowned. 'I don't understand.'

Mathilde gave him a look, and said with a kind of shocked disbelief, 'You're checking me out, aren't you? Go on, aren't you? You want to tick me off your list.'

Beside her, Sidi chuckled, not altogether sure what was going on.

Mathilde smiled deliciously. She looked pleased with her detective work, and seemed delighted to think she might be considered a suspect. Perhaps it intrigued her, thought Jacquot, even excited her. Jacquot had seen the same look many times.

'Because,' continued Mathilde, 'if Bernard *was* murdered, and if the killer's a *woman*, then she must be one of the women at Pierre Dombasle's party. It stands to reason. And I'm one of them.'

'I should have known you would be as clever as you

are beautiful, Madame Carassin,' said Jacquot with a smile and a nod. 'You have me fair and square.'

She clapped her hands with delight. 'And all this time I thought we were having lunch because we were old friends,' she teased.

'What,' cried Sidi, finally catching on, 'he thinks you're the killer? You?'

'Well, you can see his point,' said Mathilde. 'I mean, he is investigating a murder. He's got to be thorough. He's got to cover all the bases. That's why he's a policeman.' Then she turned back to Jacquot. 'So, Daniel, come on. Don't you want to know where I was on the night of . . . ? And can I account for my whereabouts? In short, do I have an alibi?'

Jacquot shrugged, scooping up the last of his lobster risotto. Two days on from the blast he was pleased to note that swallowing had become easier, his voice a little less croaky. All he had to do now was watch out for any sudden movements with his left arm. If he forgot, his cracked rib was quick to remind him. The nurse was right. Cracked ribs bite.

'Well, let's see,' continued Mathilde. 'I was with Sidi when Bernard died. And when was the explosion – two nights ago? Well now, two nights ago I was with my friend, Babette. A movie. *Roméo et Juliette*. Let me tell you, that boy, the one who played Romeo, Leo something. That boy is going to be big. Di Caprio. That's it.'

'And the others, Mathilde?' asked Jacquot. 'Luc, Patric, Antoine, Marc and Claude?'

'The others? Well, I wasn't at the movies, and I wasn't with Sidi. So I killed them, of course. What else was there to do?'

Jacquot was the first to laugh. She was a remarkable woman, Mathilde Carassin. Sharp, fast and very beautiful in a hard, considered way. There was no doubt that Sidi Carassin had found himself a fine wife, even if he'd had the cards stacked against him everywhere else.

'But why aren't the police down here handling it?' asked Mathilde. Coffee was served, sugar lumps dropped into cups and cigarettes lit. Both Sidi and Mathilde smoked.

'They don't think there's anything suspicious. Or if they do, they're not admitting it. Why give themselves more work than they want or need. As far as they're concerned, Antoine was drowned, Claude Lorraine was killed in a road crash, and Bernard committed suicide. And they're not particularly interested in what happened in Paris, Bordeaux or Toulouse. Too much leg-work. Too many problems. And, of course, there's Pierre Dombasle.'

'You've lost me,' said Sidi.

Jacquot smiled, sipped his coffee carefully. 'Bernard

died at Dombasle's home. And it wouldn't do to upset someone like Monsieur Dombasle, now would it?'

'So how long are you going to be down here?' asked Sidi, after thinking this over.

'Three or four days. I need to see Val and Gilles and Dombasle. Let them know what's happening. Tell them what I *think* is happening.'

'Val Caloux,' said Sidi, with a grin. 'Well, you'll enjoy meeting up with him again. One of your big fans, *n'est-ce pas*?'

54

As Sidi had said, it was never going to be an easy meeting with Val Caloux. But Jacquot knew there was no avoiding it. The two men may have had little fondness for one another, but if there was a potential threat to Caloux's life, then Jacquot was duty-bound as a police officer, if not a friend, to warn him.

After bidding farewell to Sidi and Mathilde on the quay, Jacquot had called the Calouxs from his hotel room. Corinne had answered warmly, as though she'd been expecting someone else, but her voice became cool and clipped when she realised it was Jacquot and what he wanted.

'Could we make it another day, Daniel? We're absolutely so busy right now. We have a reception at the Mairie tonight for Les Vieux d'Antibes, the annual

Confédération des Notaires Publiques lunch tomorrow . . .'

'It really is very important, Corinne. It will only take a few moments of your time. I promise.'

There was an icy silence and then, 'Can you be here at five? Promptly? Val should be able to manage a few minutes then.'

'*Très bien*,' replied Jacquot, gritting his teeth but keeping it friendly. It was the 'promptly' that did it. And Val 'managing' to find time for him. 'I'm over at the Bon Accueil in Villefranche,' he told her, 'so I should be able to make it by five. I look forward to seeing you.'

When he hung up, and without thinking, Jacquot raised his arm to check his watch and felt a jab of pain. He should have learned by now – every time he forgot that cracked rib, he received a sharp reminder. Wincing, he decided it was time for a couple of painkillers, a soothing gargle and a quick call to Brunet in Cavaillon to see how his assistant was getting on with the other suspects.

'I think I might have something,' said Brunet, when Jacquot put his call through to Cavaillon. 'Maryvonne Pelerain. Lives outside Perpignan. Her husband's a postman, works at the local *Poste*, and she supplements the income with a rep job.'

Maryvonne Pelerain. Théo's wife. Jacquot saw the face immediately – sharp blue eyes that narrowed when she smoked, the way she tipped back her head when she exhaled. Her hair was wavy but dressed close to the head and there was a certain presence about her – challenging, opinionated and undoubtedly sexy in an earthy, lipsticky way – and at Dombasle's party just a little tipsy. Too tipsy too handle Savry?

'A rep job?'

'Some beauty product company. Door to door, that kind of thing. Only she's an area manager. Oversees pretty much the whole of the south-west. In the last year or so she's clocked up several thousand kilometres . . .'

'And how exactly did you find all this out? Do I want to know . . . ?'

'I have a friend at the local tax office down there. We used to ride together. Superb pace-cyclist, he is. You should see him on a hill climb. Just *formidable*.'

'And how exactly does your friend in the tax office come into the picture?'

'A query on Madame Pelerain's tax returns, of course. A query regarding her claim for driving expenses in the last fifteen months – fuel, mileage, wear and tear. Apparently she was very helpful when my friend called her up. Canny, too, if you ask me. Right on the nail, she said she was in a meeting and could she call him back?

What was his name, again? And his telephone number? She must have checked him out because half an hour later she was back on the blower, being as helpful as you like.'

'And?' asked Jacquot, smiling as much at Brunet's ingenuity as at the range and scope of his contacts. Maybe all that competition cycling at weekends was the way to build up your address book.

'Well, she gets around, does our Madame Pelerain. To be precise, a little over thirty-eight thousand kilometres at the wheel in the last twelve months, not to mention the trains.'

There was a slight emphasis on the word 'trains' that Jacquot couldn't miss. 'Trains?'

'Paris, Bordeaux, Toulouse. Three days in each. Two area-manager meetings, and a conference. That was the trip to Paris.'

'I'm not sure I'm going to believe what you're about to tell me.'

Down the line came one of Brunet's delighted insider chuckles.

'I think you will, boss. I think you will.'

'J'écoute, j'écoute. Dites-moi.'

'The dates for all three trips . . .'

'. . . Match the dates for Valadier, Souze and Fastin?' interrupted Jacquot. 'You're kidding me?'

'Not me, boss. She even confirmed the dates in writing. Sent my friend a fax for his files. And then, of course, there's Savry. And she was at the party.'

Jacquot felt a quiet surge of excitement. The more he thought about Maryvonne Pelerain, the more she seemed to fit the profile.

Means – tick.

Opportunity – tick.

Motive? Jealousy? Her victims richer than she and her husband? Was Claudine right? Or was there another reason they hadn't come up with yet? Some other link?

'Of course we've haven't been able to establish her movements yet for Peyrot or Lorraine,' continued Brunet.

And Jean-Charles too, thought Jacquot, if the explosion *hadn't* been an accident.

'My friend at the tax office decided it would look a little suspicious wanting details for the last couple of months.'

'I'd say he's right,' said Jacquot.

'Of course, if she's got an alibi for either,' Brunet continued, 'I'd guess she'll be out of the frame.'

'But right now it's looking good,' said Jacquot. 'Three cities, three murders, and three matching dates. And Savry too. Good work. Thanks, Jean.'

55

The *notaire* Valentine Caloux and his wife Corinne lived in a stuccoed Empire-style villa in the hills above Théoule-sur-Mer. The house was square and compact and set behind a white, pillared wall, its open balustrading backed by green panelling so that no part of the front garden or ground floor could be seen from the road. Only the top floor with its balconied windows was visible, and the crowns of a half-dozen palm trees clustered around the front and sides of the house, their fronds within stroking distance of the walls.

As Jacquot approached the gate and checked the number, he made a swift calculation. In a resort like Théoule, just a few miles west of Cannes and Antibes, a house like this, with a view along the coast and what looked like fifty metres of frontage, you had to be looking at what? Eight? Nine million francs? Not bad for a *notaire*. Unless, of course, Caloux was shouldering a massive mortgage just to look good. It was the kind of thing a man like Caloux might do to endorse his credentials, or to make them appear better than they were. He was always a man concerned with appearances, Jacquot remembered. Sharp suits, colourful ties, always the longest at the locker room mirror – getting his hair right, shooting his cuffs. Or maybe it was family money – Corinne's? Valentine's? Jacquot made a mental note to have Brunet check out the books.

For once Jacquot remembered the rib as he checked the time and was rewarded with only the tiniest wince as he pushed back his cuff. As requested, it was exactly five o'clock. Maybe a minute or two past. But so what? Seeing the entryphone grill in the left-hand gate post he pressed the button and waited to be let in.

The voice he heard over the entry phone – '*Oui? Qui est là?*' – was a voice he didn't recognise. Neither Corinne's nor Val's.

'Daniel Jacquot,' he answered. 'Chief Inspector Daniel Jacquot.' He was out of his jurisdiction but he didn't think a little bit of rank-pulling would hurt with the Calouxs.

'*Un moment, monsieur.*' And then, '*Entrez, s'il vous plaît.*'

As the last word disintegrated into a squeak of static, the high green-panelled gates started to swing open and Jacquot stepped into a gravelled courtyard just large enough to accommodate not only Caloux's brand new BMW but a smart little Mercedes soft-top. Not bad for a public servant, thought Jacquot. So *notaires* clearly *could* make good money.

As he reached the front steps, he saw a figure loom the other side of the opaque glass-panelled door and a young girl opened it, bobbing what seemed very like a curtsey to usher him in. Val Caloux, thought Jacquot, would just love that.

'I'm expected,' said Jacquot with a friendly smile.

The girl glanced at him and then lowered her eyes, stood back for him to pass. 'Of course, monsieur. Madame Caloux said to expect a visitor.'

Closing the front door the girl hurried ahead of him, into a large hallway with a tessellated floor and wide terrace windows overlooking the coast. Already, promenade lights were sparkling distantly in the dusk.

From the first floor, a sharp, flinty voice floated down. 'Adèle? Would you show monsieur downstairs. My husband is in the gym.'

'Hi, Corinne. It's Daniel.'

There was the minutest delay in replying. But if she must . . . 'Daniel. *Bonsoir*. I'm sorry, I'm getting ready . . .' She sounded put out, as though she'd done someone a favour and now regretted it. Somewhere upstairs a door clicked shut and there was silence.

As though covering for someone's rudeness, Jacquot smiled at Adèle who gave a brief, pinched smile back. 'If you'll follow me, monsieur . . .'

Like Souze's house near St Selve, the Caloux residence had more floors than it showed to the world. On the front there were just the two floors and maybe a cramped couple of attic rooms behind the single mansard window in the roof, but from the hallway a flight of stairs led down into a sun-lounge that ran the length of the property. Sliding open a glass terrace door, Adèle pointed to a long, low building that had been built out to the left of the house.

'The gym's over there, monsieur. You'll find Monsieur Caloux there.'

Jacquot thanked her and crossed the terrace, looking up at the back of the house – a long balconied terrace on the ground floor and a set of shuttered windows on the first. Out of the corner of his eye, Jacquot noticed a lace curtain stir when all the others remained still. He guessed he was being watched.

The gym smelt of warm sweat and cool linament, and as he slid the glass door closed behind him, Jacquot could hear a rhythmic padding and panting. At the end of a narrow passage, Jacquot stepped into a fully equipped gym – a range of Nautilus machines, a rack of chrome weights, a rowing machine and rubber mats. On the walls was a mass of framed team photos and a glass-fronted cabinet lined with caps, the caps that Sophie had said Caloux would happily surrender in exchange for that one single try that Jacquot had scored so many years before.

The man himself was toiling on a Walkmaster in the corner of the room. He was wearing a sleeveless exercise top, shorts and plimsolls, his socks drawn up to his knees, his upper legs covered in a pelt of black hair, as were the backs of his arms and shoulders. It was a black strangely at odds with the head of steel-grey hair that shot up from his scalp as though charged with static.

'If it isn't my old friend Daniel Jacquot,' said Caloux, hands gripping the handlebars in front of him, legs pummelling away but getting him nowhere, sweat dripping off his brow.

'And good to see you again,' lied Jacquot. 'Nice place you've got.'

'We don't all rest on our laurels,' replied Caloux shortly, as much for the breath available as to underline what he really meant. A policeman. A *notaire*. For Caloux, there was a world of difference. And he didn't intend to let it go unnoticed, unremarked upon.

Making himself comfortable on a plastic-covered bench, Jacquot took out his cigarettes.

'Jesus Christ, man. What do you think you're doing?' cried Caloux, his rhythm faltering on the Walkmaster, almost stumbling as the moving rubber belt maintained its speed, Caloux's attention now directed at the cigarette that Jacquot had placed between his lips as he patted down his jacket for a light. The *notaire* looked horrified. 'You can't smoke in here, man. What the . . . ?' he reached for the control panel and switched off the Walkmaster. As the turning mat slowed he leapt from the machine and squared up to Jacquot. 'Good God, man . . .'

'Oh,' said Jacquot, his eyes as wide and as innocent as a choirboy. He took the cigarette from his mouth, slid it back into the packet and returned the pack to his pocket. 'Sorry, Val. I didn't think . . .'

Bristling with indignation, Caloux reached for a towel and rubbed it over his face, his shoulders, the black body hair slicked down with sweat, the grey hair on his head springing back into place. 'As Corinne told you on the phone,' said Caloux, 'we're a little pressed for time.'

So pressed that you can manage a work-out, thought Jacquot, but he said nothing.

'Now what exactly can I do for you, Jacquot? Corinne

said it was important – whatever it is.' Throwing the towel aside, he settled himself into one of the Nautilus machines and gripped the handles. He sucked in a breath of air and his cheeks ballooned. With a swell of the shoulders, he brought the handles together, a pack of weights the size of a small car rising up behind him. With an 'oufff' of release, he eased his arms back and repeated the move.

Jacquot had a fair idea that the whole performance was exactly that, Caloux's horror at the possibility of Jacquot smoking a cigarette while he worked out meant to reinforce the fact that here were two totally different men – one of them an athlete determined to keep his body up to scratch, the other a layabout cop with a ponytail who'd been lucky enough to fumble a ball, make a run and score a try that no one would ever forget. Jacquot could feel the role that Caloux had given him settle comfortably on his shoulders. He was in his element.

'They'll kill you . . . those . . . faster than . . . any bullet,' said Caloux, the words spoken when his timed breathing allowed.

'Not quite as fast,' said Jacquot, who'd known his fair share of bullets.

'Whatever . . .' said Caloux, as though he didn't give a damn. 'Your body, your life.' Closing his eyes he increased the rhythm as though to further stress the difference between them.

With no cigarette to occupy him, Jacquot got up from the bench and walked around the room, looking at the framed team photos, the framed muddy shirt, the framed testimonials, the framed newspaper reports.

'I read a piece in a magazine the other day that said more middle-aged men die on their exercise bikes than they do on the road, or on their wives.' Jacquot turned and smiled.

'Girly mag . . . ? Or fashion mag . . . ?' asked Caloux, straining, relaxing; straining, relaxing. 'I certainly . . . didn't see anything . . . in *Le Monde* about it.'

Jacquot came back to the bench and sat down again, watching Caloux disengage himself from the weight machine. The *notaire* picked up the towel again and wiped himself down. A 'V' of sweat stood out on the chest of his tank top.

'So, time's short. What can I do for you?' Caloux went to a water container and poured himself a cup. As he drank, the up-turned water container bubbled and burped.

'I wanted to know if you see anything of the team. Apart from the reunion. Work. Social.'

'And this is important?' Caloux dropped the cup in a wastebasket.

'It could be.'

'How so, exactly?'

'Well, six of them are dead and a seventh, Olivier Touche, is in intensive care at Hôpital Saint-Saëns.'

'And?'

'You don't sound surprised?'

'Should I? We're not young any more, Jacquot. Unless you keep in shape, you have to pay the price.'

'I'm not sure it's just a case of—'

'Look, Jacquot. They drink, they smoke, they eat too much. Probably taking drugs, for all I know. You were at the reunion; you saw it. They've let themselves go. Savry? A great scrum-half in his time, no question, and a fair-to-middling journalist. But he was a drunk. Just couldn't handle it, that's all. Peyrot too.'

'And Luc Valadier? A surgeon?'

'Hey, he was run over, I heard. And Touche? What can I say? That motorbike was way too powerful for him, and Claude – who did make an effort – paid the price for his tomfoolery. As for Souze?' Caloux waved his hand around the room. 'Souze had a wine cellar. I've got a gym. Does that tell you something?'

Jacquot was starting to get annoyed. 'Sounds as though you've got it all worked out.'

'Yeah. I have. I'm not stupid.'

'What would you say if I told you they were murdered? All six of them.'

Caloux looked hard at Jacquot. Then smiled. 'I'd say you're heading the same way.'

Jacquot tensed. 'Meaning?'

Caloux, who'd taken a seat on another of the benches, leaned forward. 'Letting yourself go, old buddy. I mean . . . you smell of drink, you look like you've just been rolled in an alleyway, and for all I know you're popping drugs – or whatever it is they do.'

Jacquot held himself back, even smiled, then took a slow, easy breath and got to his feet.

'Listen, Val. I really don't care if you believe me or not. The fact is these deaths are not "accidents". Someone killed those men. And that someone hasn't finished yet. I'm just here to tell you what's going on.'

'Don't worry about me, Jacquot. I've still got my eye on the ball, even if it looks like the rest of you haven't. I know how to look after myself.'

'I'm sure you do. I'm sure you do. Outside centres, if I recall, aren't selected for their delicacy. I just thought you should know, that's all.'

Jacquot turned to the door, but as he did so, Caloux came off his bench and caught Jacquot's sleeve.

'Listen, laddie,' said Caloux, coming up close, still holding on to Jacquot's sleeve. If Caloux could smell drink on him, Jacquot could smell a sour mix of peppermint breath and sweat on Caloux. 'Just because we played in the same team once – just the one time, as I remember – well, that doesn't mean to say I have to like you. Or take your advice for that matter. *Compris?*' If Caloux had nodded over his shoulder at that moment to the caps in the cabinet, Jacquot wouldn't have been in the least surprised. What did surprise him was Caloux's directness – Jacquot couldn't quite believe it. The man was actually squaring up for a fight. All that exercise seemed to have pumped him up. He seemed to swell with aggression.

'I'll see myself out, then,' said Jacquot and looked at Caloux's hand on his sleeve.

Caloux grunted, then let him go.

Jacquot got as far as the sliding glass door, before he turned and spoke.

'Just for the record, Val, I don't much like you either.'

A minute later, crossing the garden, Jacquot wished he'd said nothing. It felt like a cheap shot and he regretted it. Even if he had meant it. People like Val Caloux, well . . .

Back in the house, taking the stairs to the ground floor two at a time, Jacquot swung into the hall in time to see Corinne leaning towards a mirror on the wall and applying lipstick.

'Oh, Daniel. I thought you'd gone already,' she exclaimed, as though embarrassed at being caught with her lipstick. She screwed it closed and dropped it into a clutch bag. She was wearing a black cocktail dress, her gold-coloured hair was caught in a glittering butterfly clasp, and the stones in her ears and on her fingers sparkled against her tanned skin. She turned to him, straightened her shoulders, and switched on a bright little smile.

'On my way now,' he replied. 'Nice car, by the way. The Merc?'

'Oh that,' she said following him to the door. 'Getting a little old, I'm afraid.'

'If I had a car like that,' said Jacquot, pausing on the top step, looking down at the neat little convertible, 'I'd pull down the hood and take her for a spin. Up on the Corniches, maybe, all those twists and turns. Now there would be some driving.'

Corinne smiled like her husband, mean and thin. 'Now why on earth would I want to do something as foolhardy as that?' she said.

'You're only young once,' replied Jacquot.

Corinne gave a brittle little laugh. 'What a charming idea,' she said.

56

Duty done, Jacquot spun the wheel of his Peugeot through the bends that led back down to Théoule's pocket-sized promenade. Opening the window, he drew in a sharp, chill breath of sea air without any rasp to his throat. Ahead, a double strand of coloured lights stretched away from La Napoule to the lighthouse at Cap d'Antibes, strung like a necklace round the bay between a shifting black sea and a darkening night sky. It pointed the way to Villefranche, and the patient at Hôpital Saint-Saëns, and Jacquot followed it, arm out of the window, Ladysmith Black Mambazo in the cassette deck.

As he slid down the rise to La Napoule, he sorted out his schedule. Check in on Olivier, find himself somewhere for dinner, call Claudine and get an early night.

Tomorrow he'd phone Mageot to set up a meeting with Dombasle – as a matter of urgency – and, while he was waiting, he'd drive out to Grasse to see Gilles Millet. After that, as far as he could see, there was only one thing left to do: check those train times for Perpignan and call on Maryvonne Pelerain. Five days, Rochet had given him. And only three left to find a killer, or prove a murder.

When Jacquot finally arrived at Saint-Saëns, he took the lift to the fourth floor and headed towards the nursing station. There was a soft underlying smell of warm old fruit and antiseptic in the air, and a gentle electric hum.

'Monsieur Touche has moved,' said the nurse behind the desk. 'He's on Recovery, one floor up. You won't be able to visit, I'm afraid, but I know his son's up there and one of his friends. There's a small visitors' area on the landing. You'll find them there. On the right as you get out of the lift.'

Jacquot thanked her and a few minutes later came out of the lift on the fifth floor. On the right was the waiting room she'd told him about, set behind a glass screen, with various seating areas separated by walls of indoor plants. There was a TV high up on the far wall – sound off, a news anchorman interviewing someone. It looked a little like an airline's Executive Lounge – without the bar and the waiter service.

It was years since Jacquot had last seen Olivier's son, Pascal, and if it hadn't been for his father's height and build and the man Pascal was talking to, Jacquot would never have recognised him.

'Pascal, Daniel Jacquot. I'm a friend . . .' began Jacquot, reaching out a hand.

'*Mais bien sûr*,' Pascal interrupted, leaping to his feet and shaking Jacquot's hand. 'I remember you, of course. And my father is always talking about you.'

Jacquot turned to the older man, who'd also got to his feet.

'Danny, good to see you again. Even if . . .' Gilles Millet shrugged, looked around as though their surroundings said all that he could say and more.

'Gilles. *Et toi, et toi aussi, ami*,' replied Jacquot, shaking Gilles's hand. 'But how is the patient? Have they operated already?'

'This morning,' said Pascal. The three men sat down and Pascal leaned forward, elbows on knees, hands clasped. He looked as though he was giving a team talk. 'Five hours on the table. It's still too early to know for sure, but they say he's probably through the worst. There may be some memory loss, slurred speech, possibly a weakness on his left side – like he'd had a stroke or something. But they say it's recoverable.'

Jacquot nodded, put on an encouraging expression,

not sure whether 'recoverable' was good news or bad. How 'recoverable'? All of it? Or just some? And which?

'He's a tough bugger,' said Jacquot. 'And Sophie? How's your mother bearing up?'

Pascal's face split into a grin. 'Cursing you out, Monsieur Jacquot. Said you got her drunk. Said you had no scruples. Thank you. She needed a break and it did her the world of good. Even if she says it didn't.'

'It was a pleasure, as always, to be of assistance. Give her my love when you see her, and tell her a *café-calva* always works for me.' Jacquot got to his feet. 'So. I'll try and call by tomorrow sometime. Can't say when, I'm afraid.'

'It's good of you to drop by. And you, too, Gilles. Thank you.'

Gilles had also risen to his feet and was reaching for his coat. Pascal saw them to the lifts, telling them he'd be staying on an hour or two longer, in case his father regained consciousness.

'He's a good lad,' said Jacquot, on the way down in the lift.

'My godson. A great boy. And his sister the same,' said Gilles. Like the rest of them, Gilles Millet had aged, but there remained something coiled, anxious and flighty about him, as though he was waiting for a signal to break into a sprint. Just how a right wing should be, reflected Jacquot.

'Just really nice kids, you know,' continued Gilles, as the lift doors opened and they stepped out into the entrance hall. 'Olivier and Sophie have done a great job. You got kids?'

Jacquot shook his head. 'Not yet, but the clock's ticking. You?'

'Two girls. Nine and three. Scorpio and Leo, so they've both got mouths on them. Like their mother – she's a Scorpio too.'

The two men followed each other through the revolving doors and paused on the top step.

'Thirsty work, hospitals,' said Gilles, rubbing his hands together and glancing uncertainly at Jacquot. 'Fancy a drink?'

'Sure,' replied Jacquot. 'Sounds good.'

57

'Olivier called me before the accident. Said you'd spoken to him.'

They'd found a bar and ordered their pastis when Gilles said this. 'It all seemed a bit unlikely at first,' he continued. 'But now . . . well, after what happened to Olivier, I don't really know what to think.'

'At least you're prepared to consider it a possibility.'

The pastis arrived, they added their water, and dug at a bowl of olives without using the toothpicks provided.

'With Claude dead and Olivier where he is, it would be a fool who didn't stop and think.'

'You're quite right,' said Jacquot, thinking of Caloux and Murier.

'Olivier suggested it might be the wealthier members of the team who are being targeted?'

'The choice of victim so far certainly points in that direction. But it is by no means a certainty. For all I know, it's the ones standing that'll get it next.'

Gilles frowned and Jacquot explained about the team photo. 'Maybe it's just another coincidence, who knows?' he said.

Gilles splashed more water into his pastis, and offered the jug to Jacquot who shook his head. 'I mentioned it to Fabienne, my wife,' he said. 'It seemed sensible in the circumstances. And she agrees with you. It's all just too . . . tight.' Gilles shook his head. 'But who would do such a thing? And why? After all this time.'

'Maybe that's the reason,' said Jacquot. 'Those eighteen years. And all that's happened in them. There we all were, young guys, sharing the glory . . . and now. Real life. Some of us were lucky, others not. Maybe it's someone trying to juggle the bubble in the spirit level.'

'You think all this is down to money? Who's got what?' Gilles shook his head. '*Non, non.* It has to be more than that, surely?'

'Jealous people do the strangest things, Gilles. You'd be surprised.'

It was as if Gilles hadn't heard him. He looked down at his drink. 'The problem is, the kids. Do you think they could be at risk?'

Jacquot spread his hands. 'That I cannot say. So far, the killer has concentrated on the team.'

Gilles took a breath, as though embarrassed by what he was about to say. 'But that doesn't mean he won't, does it? If he feels like it. If he gets a chance. Which is why, Daniel, we're going away. I thought you should know. Fabienne is not happy. We took the kids out of school yesterday and we're off to the States on Thursday.'

'I can't say I blame you,' said Jacquot, knowing for certain that Fabienne could no longer be considered a suspect. In his opinion, opting to leave the country because the police were now investigating simply did not fit in with his take on the murders. As well as passion, it seemed to Jacquot that there was an added attraction for the killer in hiding tracks, fooling the police. It had become a macabre game, as much as a bloody settling of scores. That suddenly the killer was being pursued by the police would be of no account. There was a job to do and there was nothing that would stand in the killer's way. No, Fabienne was clearly out of the frame.

'I feel bad about it, you know,' said Gilles. 'But like I say, it's the wife and the kids first. It just all feels like it's getting very close. And we don't want to be around.' Gilles gave Jacquot a furtive look, waiting for a nod of approval.

Jacquot gave it. 'I would do the same if I were in your

shoes. Give me an address, or a phone number and it's fine. Another pastis?'

'Sure. Why not?' Gilles's relief was palpable. 'But my turn,' he said, signalling the waiter.

Digging into his coat pocket, Jacquot pulled out his cigarettes. He held the pack up to Gilles who shook his head.

'Tell me,' said Jacquot, a cigarette between his lips, the lighter flaring, 'do you ever bump into Val Caloux, or his wife Corinne?'

'Grasse's dangerously close, but no, thank God, we don't.'

'I thought you two were friends. Back when we were playing. Out on the line.'

'With all due respect, Daniel, you really weren't with the team long enough to be familiar with the personal dynamics. Sure Val and I played well together. He passed clean and fast, and I had good hands and fast legs. Also, he was devious as a snake, always drawing the opposition away from me. A feint, you know, a switch of direction. And I would be clear.' Gilles shrugged. 'But friends? Off the pitch? Then? Now?' Gilles shook his head.

The pastis arrived. The ritual followed, pistachios instead of olives this time.

'And why was that? Any reason?'

'He was the one team member you wished was not on the team. Because then you had to get on with him. You know what I mean? It was difficult.'

'And Caloux was that man?'

'Caloux was that man. Like I said, he was a great player – a superb outside centre, ruthlessly competitive – but also a bully and a bigot. And a pompous, vain little *crapaud* as well. Always checking himself in the mirror – a shop window even; making sure he looked OK. There was something . . . unhealthy about him. It's difficult to explain.'

'And Corinne?'

'If you think the All Blacks are frightening, they've got nothing on Corinne Caloux. She's like a . . . like a Geiger counter,' said Gilles, putting aside any reserve, and warming to his subject. 'She homes in on you, waves her wealth detector as I call it, and she knows in an instant whether or not you're going to be useful to her. If you pass the test, she's all over you like a rash. If not. Fuck off. Siberia. No time to waste.'

For a brief moment Jacquot saw again the chic little cocktail dress, the neat cap of hair, the glistening red lips and eyes as chill as icicles.

'When she discovered that I was an architect and Fabienne was an interior designer, well that was it,' continued Gilles. 'Instant best friends. But it didn't last.

Corinne's big problem, according to Fabienne, was not so much design, but position – where the house was, rather than the house itself. Corinne couldn't make up her mind whether Théoule was fashionable or not. Always going on about it. Was it too Esterel, if you understand, or was it Côte? She drove Fabienne mad with her ceaseless bleating, her . . . *snobisme.*' Gilles chuckled. 'And the house is very beautiful. *Très, très chic.* Exquisitely proportioned. A real jewel. But Corinne seemed not to appreciate that.'

Gilles took up a pistachio and cracked its shell, winkled out the greening nut and popped it into his mouth. It was clear to Jacquot that since he'd got it off his chest about going off to the States, Gilles had relaxed considerably.

'For me, Daniel, a beautiful house is a beautiful house wherever it happens to be, and a delight and a privilege to live in. And a beautiful house with a history – what could be a finer thing?'

'It has a history?' asked Jacquot.

Gilles nodded enthusiastically. 'Shall I tell you something? A month after she first visited the property, Fabienne discovered that the house had been built by Leopold II of the Belgians, for a mistress. He went there many times, apparently, and Fabienne actually traced love letters written by the king to this mistress at that address. Can you imagine? Such history. How wonderful. But you know what? When Fabienne told Corinne this marvellous piece of information, the woman was devastated. Swore Fabienne to secrecy.'

'But why?' asked Jacquot.

'*Mais, c'est clair, non?* It was the house of a mistress. A whore. Corinne was living in the house of a woman of ill-repute. *Quelle horreur*. And you know, there was nothing that Fabienne could say to make it better. Corinne simply didn't understand what she had.'

'So you haven't seen much of them recently?'

Gilles shook his head. 'We went to the wedding. A couple of dinner parties early on, while Fabienne was working on the house. But after Fabienne told her about the mistress . . . well, it was as if Fabienne had something on her, knew something that Corinne didn't want anyone else to know about. And that was it. *Finis*.'

58

It was a little past midnight when Claudine Eddé put down the phone to Jacquot.

He sounds tired, she thought, finishing her wine. She'd been pouring it when the phone rang and when she heard his voice, she'd brought both phone and wine to bed with her, made herself comfortable, curled up with his voice. She could have talked to him all night, but she'd sensed his tiredness, noted the low raspy voice, his disinclination to talk much and she'd finally let him go with a gentle 'miss you'. Now he was gone and she was alone again.

It was Claudine who had told Jacquot about the hotel in Villefranche. Halfway between Cap Corsaire and Nice it was an easy drive to the Calouxs, the Dombasles, Jean-Charles and Nathalie, Gilles and Fabienne Millet in

Grasse. And probably no more than a stroll to see the Carassins if Sidi berthed along Quay Amiral Courbet and not at the Darse marina.

Claudine had stayed there herself. Years earlier. She had gone with her first husband to visit the chapel of St Pierre which Jean Cocteau had decorated. While he worked on the chapel, Cocteau had stayed at the Bon Accueil and this proximity, this sense of living art history, had thrilled Claudine, to feel so close to the artist whose sculpted head watched the comings and goings of the *quai* from a plinth beside the Bureau du Port. It had been more than twenty years but she remembered the foyer and the mosaic in the floor and the fish tank and the pictures of famous visitors that lined the walls. And that view from her balcony – the sun rising over the headland of Cap Ferrat, the great liners that moored in the harbour, the moon paving a line of silver across the deep-water bay, the little boys with their hand-lines fishing between the rocks.

And that's where he was now, preparing for bed. She wondered what floor his room was on – not too high, she hoped; in only the short time they had been together, she knew how he hated heights. If they put him too high, he was sure to ask for a lower floor, and even then he'd likely check the diagram on the back of the door to see where the fire escape was. Yet like everyone who professed a fear of heights, Claudine also knew his compulsion to confront them, or test them, by going to the very edge. The look on his face . . .

He'd be naked too, she guessed. Even in November. Sliding now into his lonely bed, or maybe cleaning his teeth. Those big feet of his planted on the bathroom floor, the long legs and cheeked buttocks, the narrow cleft of his spine rising into a wide, muscled back, his black hair loose. From behind he reminded her of a Red Indian warrior, the way that long, waving hair brushed his tanned shoulders.

Unlike her first two husbands, she recalled, Daniel had not the least embarrassment about his body – something that had surprised her. Sometimes he wrapped a towel round his waist, which made the stomach look somehow harder, leaner; and sometimes he padded around in a nightshirt – bringing her breakfast in bed, tucking the material between his legs as he settled next to her. But most of the time, getting ready for bed, he would be naked, as though it was the most natural thing in the world. Completely unconcerned.

Once, from the bath, she'd seen his reflection in a mirror. Bare feet to the top of his head. He'd gone to close a bedroom window and when it was secured, he'd just stood there, with his back to her, looking out at the night. And then, without thinking, he'd palmed his hands down over his buttocks and stretched back and laced his fingers behind his neck, through his hair. That was as far as he'd got before she was out of the bath and on him, creeping up from behind and taking him in her arms, wrapping her warm wet body around his. It had been irresistible. And slowly he'd turned and pulled her to him . . .

Somewhere in the dark, beyond the house, a lone owl hooted and cooed. And without any warning Claudine felt a wave of unease slide over her, stroke her thighs and settle with an ache in her belly, fingertipping its shivery way into the small hairs at the back of her neck.

She wished now that he was home, there with her, safe.

So this was what it would be like, she thought, living with a policeman.

him, something that had been landlocked in the Lubéron since his dismissal the year before from Marseilles.

At the turning for St-Jean-Cap-Ferrat and with time to spare, Jacquot indicated right and set off on a brief tour of the headland to savour the beauty of the morning – the pine-needle paths, the high gates, and the glimpsed stuccoed fronts of some of the most valuable real estate in the world. According to Olivier, Pierre Dombasle had lived on Cap Ferrat when he first came down to the coast. After just twelve months, he'd pocketed a ten-million franc profit on the sale of his property and moved to Cap Corsaire. Apparently he'd told Olivier that he found Cap Ferrat just a little 'suburban' for his tastes.

After a ten-minute wander through this 'surburban' enclave, pausing by the chapel of St Hospice to look across the gulf to where Pierre Dombasle now lived, Jacquot glanced carefully at his watch, feeling only the lightest jab from his rib (he was learning). A little after ten, another twenty minutes until his appointment at Cap Corsaire.

At this time of year there wasn't much problem with traffic, but when Jacquot dropped down into Beaulieu after his tour round the narrow lanes of the Cap, what traffic there was was slowed by a section of cordoned-off promenade. Outside the casino, a gang of council workers were giving the palm trees their annual trim, and the road was littered with chopped fronds. Soon enough, though, he was out of Beaulieu and following the train tracks to Eze, watching for the tunnel mouth and then turning up to the right on the unpaved, gravelly side road that led to Dombasle's estate.

Easing the car to a stop in front of the gates, Jacquot waited for them to open. On top of the right-hand pillar the camera that Claudine had spotted on that last visit stared down blankly. Thirty seconds . . . a minute passed, and the gates remained closed. Maybe there was no one manning the camera, no one to see his car waiting there. With a sigh, Jacquot got out and walked over to the speaker grill on the left-hand pillar. He was five or six steps from it when the gates began to swing open. Cursing lightly, Jacquot returned to his car, slipped it into gear and drove through them.

The grounds of Cap Corsaire were as impressive as they had been the last time he'd visited, the walled hairpins switching down between terraces of olive, fig, agave and cactus, the seashell-gravelled drive curving between tightly cropped grass borders, twin lines of cypress and the darker, wilder ground beyond thrown into cool shade by pine, aleppo and eucalyptus.

And the house . . . Jacquot remembered that Claudine had whistled when she saw it, and it was easy to see why. If ever there was a house that Jacquot would love to own, it was this one. Move it a few kilometres along the coast, say somewhere between Cassis and Marseilles, and it would be just perfect.

As he drew closer, Jacquot saw that the house had changed since the reunion – the length of blue runner that had covered the front steps was gone, louvred panels had been fitted to the open sides of the loggia and the blue awnings that had shaded the upper terraces had been wound back in. A month earlier, every window on the top two floors had been flung open. Now they were closed and shuttered. It was as if the house had been mothballed for winter, a house not a home. This was where someone lived occasionally, rather than constantly. It made Jacquot a little sad.

Pulling up in the forecourt, Jacquot saw the front door push open and a familiar figure appear on the loggia, then trot down the steps.

'Looks like you've been in the wars,' said Guy Mageot, taking in Jacquot's ravaged features as the two men shook hands. 'Not sure which is worse, you or the car.'

'You should have seen me a couple of days ago. I looked as though I'd fallen asleep in the sun.'

'Nothing worse than looking like a tourist.'

'Tell me about it,' said Jacquot, surprised at the apparent friendliness of the welcome. When he'd called to set up the meeting, Jacquot had caught Mageot in the middle of something – he could hear voices in the background – and their exchange had been brief. A time agreed, and that was it. Of course, there had never been that much warmth between the two of them in their playing days – Mageot preferring the company of Souze and Druart – but it struck Jacquot that his old teammate was pleased to see him. At the reunion they'd exchanged greetings, said a few words to each other, and that was it – until Savry's body was discovered when, it seemed to Jacquot, Mageot had rather enjoyed his run-in with Chief Inspector Murier. And Jacquot had no difficulty recalling the sense of gentle menace he'd felt when Mageot took him up to Dombasle's study.

But now the man was hospitality itself, as if the house was his, he the owner in Dombasle's absence. 'Come on in,' he said, leading Jacquot up the steps and ushering him into the house. 'What can I get you. Coffee?' Mageot glanced at his watch. 'A drink?'

60

Crossing the main salon, past the loggia terrace where fifteen tables had been set out for the reunion dinner, Mageot led Jacquot to the back of the house where the louvred panels had not yet been set up, a wide avenue of lawn sweeping down between the pines to the sea. As they settled themselves in plushly upholstered terrace chairs, a white-jacketed houseboy appeared. Jacquot recognised him immediately, one of the two lads who'd carried their bags to their *cabane*.

'If it makes it any easier for you, Danny, I'm going to have a pastis,' said Mageot. He was wearing a pair of tight jeans, black loafers and a white polo neck that seemed to make his cauliflower ears appear even larger and redder.

'Since it wouldn't be polite to let a man drink alone,' said Jacquot, 'a pastis sounds just right.'

The houseboy disappeared and Mageot settled a pair of smiling blue eyes on Jacquot.

'So. It looks like you might have a point,' Mageot conceded. 'After Antoine, Claude and Olivier. I assume that's why you called, why you wanted to see the skipper?'

'You're right, it is why I wanted to see Pierre. And you. And anyone who played in that team, whether they were reserves or not. It could be you next as easily as me or Pierre.'

'You really believe that?'

The houseboy reappeared with the pastis and Jacquot waited until they were alone again before answering. 'Right now, I'd say Pierre is more at risk than you and I.'

'How so?' said Mageot.

'So far, it's the wealthier members of the team who are being targeted. And apart from Bernard, all the victims seem to have had some business arrangement with Pierre.'

Mageot frowned.

'Luc's clinic, Olivier's restaurant, the deal Antoine was hatching with him . . .'

'You've been doing your homework,' said Mageot. 'And you're right. They did all have dealings with the skipper. But why shouldn't they? You've got a good idea, you need some funding, it's natural you'd come to him. Friends, old team-mates. That's what it's all about.'

'Well, I have a feeling that someone doesn't like it. Maybe someone asked Pierre for funding and he said "no".'

'Could be,' conceded Mageot with a shrug. 'But if they had asked for something and the skipper'd said "no", I would've known about it.'

Jacquot sipped his pastis – cool, clear, icy aniseed – and took this in. 'You don't mind my asking, I hope, but it seems like you know a lot about Pierre's business dealings.'

'Danny, I'm head of security. I have to know what's going on, who he's seeing. And if he doesn't tell me himself, I find out. I wouldn't be doing my job if I didn't.'

'So how come you're not with him now?'

For the first time Mageot looked uncomfortable. 'It's a personal matter. He's in Marseilles. Left last night and will be back in time for lunch.'

'And Madame Dombasle?'

'She and Nonie have been up in Forcalquier at the country house. A new pool is being put in and they wanted to make sure that everything is as it should be.'

'So the whole family is off somewhere and you're sitting here with me?'

Mageot chuckled. 'I'm head of security, Danny, not a foot-soldier. I plan. I make things happen. So they're safe. At all times. Wherever they go. But always discreetly. *Par example . . .*' Mageot glanced at his watch. 'Nearly twenty-six minutes ago, while you were still driving out here, Lydie and Nonie called in at a shop called Bonheur in Forcalquier. According to their driver – a karate black belt, by the way – Bonheur sells soaps, scented candles, pot-pourris.' Mageot's tone was dismissive. He waved a hand. 'All that bathroom stuff – accessories. And since I haven't heard anything, I'd guess they're still there. As for the skipper, he has left his meeting and is even now on his way back.'

Jacquot nodded. He was impressed. 'In the flying boat?'

Mageot smiled. 'Sold it two weeks after the party. But it served its purpose, wouldn't you say?'

Jacquot shook his head. 'It's a way of life I can't imagine.'

'I don't have to imagine it. I see it every day. But he's worked for it, Danny, I'll give him that. While the rest of us were hanging around picking our noses, the skipper was out there – doing deals, networking, making friends.'

'How long have you been with him?'

'Last ten years, give or take. Before that I was a club

doorman. God knows where I'd be now, if it wasn't for Pierre.'

Mageot suddenly fell silent, as though he'd said too much and regretted it. 'You never really got to know him, did you?'

'Four months in the squad. Just the one game.'

'But what a game, eh?' said Mageot. 'And you scoring what has to be one of the most beautiful tries I have ever seen. That run . . .' Mageot gazed past Jacquot and smiled. He was back there at Twickenham. 'There we were, all trampled down in the mud on our own line, and suddenly, by the time I lift out of that last scrum, you've got the ball in your arms and you're through their line. I just stood there watching, not believing. I remember thinking the Ref was sure to blow his whistle, call you back for some infringement. But he didn't. And you kept running, with just the one *anglais* anywhere near you.'

'Courtney. He was a solicitor.'

'The winger. That's right. Another ten metres and he'd have caught you up, brought you down for sure.'

'He clipped my heel . . .'

'But he did it too late, didn't he? Wasn't quite fast enough.'

'I caught him on the hop, left-footed. Had a few metres on him before he came after me.'

'And that little swerve you did, at the halfway line.' Mageot shook his head. 'Like a dance step it was, dainty as you please. But effective. Gave you an extra metre when you needed it. Very smart. And running like your life depended on it . . .'

Jacquot chuckled. 'It probably did!'

'Your head was up, shoulders back and your legs were pumping. And the crowd. That roar when they saw you two sprinting down the field. Realised what was happening. English and French both. "Get the bastard," screamed *les Anglais*. And "Run! Run. Run!" go the French.' Mageot was chuckling now.

'I'll never forget it,' said Jacquot.

'Jesus, what a try. You know what the skipper said? When you dived over?'

Jacquot shook his head.

'You were getting to your feet by the time we got to you. Touche had hauled you out of the mud, Sidi was on your back and Jean-Charles was hugging you. That's when the skipper turned to me and said—'

A soft voice came from behind them.

'Monsieur. *Je m'excuse.*'

It was the houseboy.

'Yes, Geralde?'

'Monsieur Dombasle . . . *il arrive*.'

61

There was no sound from Pierre Dombasle's Bentley as it turned into the forecourt, save a soft crunch from its tyres as they passed over the sea-shell gravel. Jacquot, standing just behind Mageot on the front steps, was also fairly certain that it was impossible to tell when Pierre Dombasle's driver switched off the engine. If indeed he had. The Bentley just crunched towards them – and then silence descended when it came to a halt at the bottom of the steps.

It was exactly then that Jacquot noticed the long, deep, wavering scratch to the bodywork, running from the front wing on the driver's side to the rear passenger door. Someone had keyed the Bentley with a vicious intent. Where the key had first touched the car, the metal was dented; where the line finished it finished with an upward curve, like a flourish.

'*Merde*,' he heard Mageot whisper.

Then the back passenger door opened before the chauffeur could get to it and out stepped Dombasle.

'They got me again, Guy.'

There was a clear sense of blame being directed. As though it was Mageot's fault. Which, Jacquot supposed, it could well be.

'I can see. You know where?'

'Overnight. Roucas Blanc. The car was in the drive, behind the gates . . . Daniel. Danny,' said Dombasle, breaking off to smile and reach past Mageot for Jacquot's hand, as if noticing him for the first time. 'Good to see you. And thank you for coming out. As you can see,' continued Dombasle, turning to the car, gesturing to the scratch, 'another *billet-doux*.'

He tossed his briefcase to the driver, a heavy-set man in a lightweight double-breasted suit. It looked a size too big. Room for movement, wondered Jacquot? Another of Mageot's black belts?

'This has happened before?' asked Jacquot.

Dombasle turned to Mageot. 'What is it now? Three times?'

'Four, if you count the smashed headlight on the

Ferrari. Five, the passenger window. Six, the bonnet emblem, the flying "B".'

Dombasle turned back to Jacquot. 'Can you believe it? The price we have to pay to live in paradise, eh? But let's go inside,' he continued. 'We can talk over lunch. I'm starved.' And Dombasle was up the steps and pushing through the doors into the house with Jacquot and Mageot bringing up the rear.

Over his shoulder, directed at Mageot, came a litany of questions.

'Has Lydie called?'

'Are they still at Forcalquier?'

'What time are they back?'

'Did you speak to Manolo about the heating?'

'Have you called the pool people?'

Lunch was served in the dining room, on the east side of the house, its open windows framing a view, down yet another alley of trees, of sheer limestone cliffs and a narrow band of blue water. Dombasle sat at one end of a long refectory table, Mageot and Jacquot either side of him and facing each other. Within seconds of taking their seats, the houseboy, Geralde, and two other jacketed staff, entered with their first course – a *salade tiède* of mixed red leaves, croutons and *gésiers*. A two-year-old Fleurie was poured, still water offered. Inside, Jacquot smiled.

'I thought you quite mad,' said Dombasle, taking up a fork and spearing the salad, pushing the leaves into his mouth. His voice became crowded, dropped a tone. 'It simply didn't make sense. Bernard, I mean. Clean hands? Dirty hands? And Luc and Patric murdered? *Non, non, non.*' The first mouthful was swallowed and another followed. Jacquot was surprised at how quickly Dombasle ate, cramming it in like a hungry schoolboy before the bell rings. But maybe that was how billionaire businessmen, with an empire or two to run, had to live. The best that money could buy, but no time to savour it – or, indeed, to notice it. Just food – fuel.

'But now it appears you were right after all,' continued Dombasle, scooping up the last of the leaves. 'I mean, Luc, Patric, Marc . . .'

'Twice is coincidence, three times and it's criminal,' said Jacquot.

'. . . and then Bernard, Antoine, Claude. And poor Olivier . . . how is he, by the way?' asked Dombasle, turning to Mageot.

'I spoke to Pascal this morning. Olivier is conscious and smiling.'

'Does he know about the leg?'

'Pascal told him. Apparently he nodded and said "I thought so."'

'A tragedy,' said Dombasle, then turned back to

Jacquot. 'Gilles tells me you warned him? Olivier, I mean.'

'I said he should take care. I don't know whether he believed me or not,' said Jacquot, leaning back as the salad plates were removed, replaced almost immediately with what looked like a ravioli of langoustes, a pair of crossed pink claws laid over a single pasta parcel. A Pouilly-fumé was added to the Fleurie and fresh glasses put in place.

'He believed you enough to phone us and pass on the message,' said Dombasle. 'To be frank, it was only after Olivier's crash that I took your warning seriously. But you knew from the start. Remarkable.'

'It is my job, Pierre.'

'I suppose it is. It's also Murier's.'

'You know as well as I why Murier behaved the way he did.' Jacquot hoped he sounded more loyal than he felt.

'Really?' Dombasle quizzed him. 'Do I?'

Jacquot picked up his fork and smiled. 'Oh I think so, don't you?'

The ravioli was exquisite. Jacquot closed his eyes at the first mouthful.

'So how do you see it, Daniel? What's your take on this?'

'Well, to start with, the damage to your cars is significant. Six scratches, six deaths. They must be linked, surely? But I'm not so certain it's the killer doing it. I suspect there's an accomplice involved, that someone will have been paid to leave you these . . . messages.'

'Messages or warnings?' asked Dombasle, pushing idly at his pasta.

'Almost certainly the latter.'

Dombasle glanced at Mageot, then looked at Jacquot. 'But why? What's the point of it all – the motive? What have any of us ever done to end up like this, being stalked by some psychopathic killer?'

At this stage, Jacquot was not prepared to share his suspicions with either of these men. God alone knew where they would run with it. The game could be blown. But there was nothing wrong, he decided, with bringing in a new angle to see how they both responded. It was the scratches on the car that had done it, that alerted him.

'Frankly, I don't believe the killer is interested in Olivier and the others,' said Jacquot, scooping up a pink speckled claw with the last of the ravioli and hard-pressed not to stop talking and simply savour this glorious food. 'It's like those scratches on your Bentley. A way to get at you. To draw out the misery, the pain. Because what the killer really wants is you, Pierre. Whoever's doing all this is doing it to make you suffer. All the things you hold dear. Friends. Possessions.'

Dombasle didn't seem convinced. 'So the motive is what? Revenge? Some pissed-off businessman who came a cropper and blames me? Someone trying to get their own back?'

And what's so surprising about that? thought Jacquot. Someone like Chantal Valadier, say. If the way Pierre had treated her was any indication of how he behaved in business, then there must have been people queuing round the block for a shot at him.

Dombasle gave Jacquot a knowing wink. 'They all say they will, you know, but they never do.'

'Until now, perhaps,' replied Jacquot, suddenly wanting to unsettle Dombasle, shock him out of his complacency. 'Which is why I called Guy. I wanted to warn you.'

'Which I appreciate,' said Dombasle, pushing his plate away and getting to his feet. 'Don't get me wrong.' He strode over to a matching refectory buffet and brought back a decanter of red wine. Standing behind Jacquot and then Mageot, he filled their glasses, silent, deep in thought. To cover the silence Jacquot swirled the wine in his glass, tipped it to his nose, then took a sip. By his reckoning they'd tasted no more than a glass each of the Fleurie and Pouilly-fumé. He hoped they made more time for this third wine. He might not have been able to identify the château or vintage but he knew it was a Bordeaux and he knew it was sublime.

By the time Dombasle had retaken his seat, a *pavé* of beef was being served, thick as a rich man's wallet, its caramel hide weeping juices. Four fat golden *frites*, scattered with rock salt, appeared on side plates.

Oh yes, thought Jacquot, slicing into his steak. Just perfect. He glanced across the table at Mageot. Dombasle's head of security had clearly been watching him. Mageot raised his glass, and eyebrows, in a single swift movement, and his lips slid into a knowing grin. Jacquot smiled back. Somehow, their earlier chat about the game, the scoring of that long-ago try, seemed to have established some kind of bond between them, brought them close. Just as Jacquot's wonder at such glorious excess at Dombasle's table further bound them.

'But how sure are you?' Dombasle asked, chewing his second mouthful of steak before Jacquot had even started on his first.

'Right now it's supposition, just gut instinct,' Jacquot admitted. 'It can be nothing else. But I'd say it's a good one, worth pursuing. To begin with, all the victims were wealthy and all of them, to some extent, owed that wealth to you. Your investment in them. Luc, Marc, Olivier. The clinic, the restaurant, Marc's legal practice . . .'

If Dombasle was surprised to discover just how much Jacquot had found out, he covered it well, waving his fork dismissively. 'But these are small things, Daniel.

Tiny ventures. It's just a way to help old friends, to stay in touch.'

And in control, thought Jacquot. 'So who haven't you invested in?' he pressed. 'How many friends haven't you helped?'

Dombasle looked thoughtful. When he spoke, it was as though he hadn't heard the question. 'It's an established business wisdom,' he began, 'that you never invest what you *can't* afford to lose. You've got to be covered, they'll tell you. But me, I've always gone and done the opposite. I've always gone for the big bet, do you know what I'm saying?' Dombasle settled his eyes on Jacquot.

Jacquot nodded, not altogether certain where this was headed.

'And fortunately for me,' continued Dombasle, 'it's always paid off. Royally. Until now. But you know what?' He rapped the table with his knuckles and looked at the two of them. 'Money's one thing, friends are another. So, what do we do? How do we stop all this?'

Jacquot swallowed a mouthful of pavé and wanted to groan with pleasure. But he didn't. Instead he said: 'As soon as I can convince the authorities to take this seriously, one police jurisdiction will start talking to another, the case files will be reopened, and investigations will be set in motion. It takes time. A few days, maybe even weeks.' Time for me to get down to Perpignan, thought

Jacquot, and have a word with Maryvonne Pelerain. And Olivier.

Dombasle picked up one of the *frites* with his fingers and dunked it into a tub of mustard. The steak had disappeared. Dombasle grinned. 'It's already started,' he said, waving the chip at Jacquot. 'I had a word with my good friend Gaspard Blois at the *Ministère de la Justice* and he's promised me they're on to it.'

'An investigation?'

Dombasle nodded. 'And protection. I thought Murier would have called you?'

'Not yet,' said Jacquot, selecting the mayonnaise for his *frite*. Even given this Gaspard Blois contact, he was not at all surprised that he hadn't heard from Murier.

'Well, I'm sure he will,' continued Dombasle, wiping his lips with a corner of his napkin and glancing at his watch. 'I took the liberty of letting him know that you were down here and having lunch with me. Apparently he's sending out one of his best men. He should be here any minute.'

62

When Detective Inspector Christine Ambert arrived, the three men had left the dining room and were sitting in the salon. All three rose to their feet when she was announced, Jacquot as surprised as the others at her appearance.

'You look like you've been in the wars, Chief Inspector,' she said by way of greeting. 'Must be rough up there in Cavaillon.'

'Just a winter bonfire, detective. A change in the wind caught me by surprise.'

'You know each other?' asked Dombasle, clearly not happy that Murier's top man should turn out to be a woman, not to mention lower in rank. Jacquot could see that he didn't like it.

'After Olivier's crash I shared my concerns with

Detective Inspector Ambert,' replied Jacquot. 'She was kind enough to pass them on to Chief Inspector Murier.'

'Who sends his apologies,' said Ambert to Dombasle and Mageot. 'He has to be in court this afternoon and asked me to take his place.'

Geralde appeared. Dombasle saw him and asked the detective if she would like anything. Coffee? Tisane? A drink?

She shook her head. 'Nothing thank you. I'm just here to let you know that your concerns are being taken very seriously, and that an investigation is under way.'

'That is most gratifying to hear,' observed Dombasle. 'One police jurisdiction talking to another, case files being reopened, and investigations set in motion,' he said drily, repeating almost word for word what Jacquot had told him earlier. 'Perhaps if Chief Inspector Murier had taken more care over Bernard Savry's "suicide" we might be further along than we are right now. Still, at least things are moving.'

'They are indeed, monsieur. And to that end I was wondering if I could ask you some questions?'

'Not me, I'm afraid, Detective Inspector. I have calls to make and a busy schedule.' Dombasle rose to his feet and gestured to Mageot. 'However, Guy here, my head of security, will be happy to help in any way he can.'

With a nod to Jacquot and Mageot, and a more

pronounced bow to Ambert, Dombasle left the salon, closing the door behind him.

'So, Detective Inspector Ambert. How can I be of assistance?' said Mageot.

And so the questions began, Ambert referring to a notebook every now and again, and glancing at Jacquot as though to assure herself that she was asking the right ones, starting with Savry's death and the party.

How well did Dombasle know Monsieur Savry?

How many guests at the reunion?

Who stayed and who didn't?

Would it be possible to have names and addresses?

And what about staff?

When she asked whether Mageot could think of any possible business rivals or enemies who might hold a grudge or wish to embarrass Dombasle, he threw up his arms.

'Where to begin, Inspector? SportÉquipe is a global business with an active acquisitions programme. There could be any number of people out there who might feel ill-served, vengeful. It is the nature of the game. A score to settle, *n'est-ce pas*? But as Monsieur Dombasle will tell you, they may threaten, but they never follow through.'

Ambert smiled. 'Tell me, monsieur, did Monsieur Savry have any business dealings with Monsieur Dombasle?'

Smart girl, thought Jacquot.

Mageot returned the smile. 'Not exactly business dealings, but Monsieur Dombasle helped Bernard on a number of occasions.'

'Helped?' asked Ambert.

'Through SportÉquipe, Monsieur Dombasle was able to provide Bernard with access to the people he wanted to write about. Some of his big features.' Mageot glanced at Jacquot. 'Bernard also wanted to write a book. An official Dombasle biography. But Monsieur Dombasle declined.'

'Declined?'

'It was felt not to be appropriate. Monsieur Dombasle does not actively pursue such kinds of personal self-promotion.'

'And was Savry upset by this?'

'I would say so, yes. But they still remained friends. It was all very *amical*.'

'So otherwise their relationship was good?'

'That's correct.'

'And what about the other victims? Messieurs Valadier, Fastin . . .'

'They too had dealings with Monsieur Dombasle. But only on a very minor level, you understand. Financial backing, loan guarantees – that sort of thing. A gentle opening of doors, if you like . . .'

'And do any others in the team have similar arrangements?'

'Jean-Charles Rains up in Rouret, Gilles Millet in Grasse. And myself, I suppose.'

And so it went – questions and answers – with Mageot undertaking to fax a list of reunion party guests to Christine Ambert's office, and offering to be on hand to help in any way he could.

It was dark outside when Christine Ambert finally tucked away her notebook and the two men walked her to the front door.

'Can I offer you a lift back to town, Chief Inspector?' she asked, pulling on her coat, a scarf and blue beret.

'That's very kind, Inspector, but I have my own car,' replied Jacquot with a small bow.

Ambert nodded and smiled, then shook their hands. She thanked Mageot for his help, told him to call her at any time, whatever she could do to help, and then bid them both *adieu*.

'Now I know why you joined the police,' said Mageot as her tail-lights disappeared down the drive.

63

From the moment he'd left Mageot and Dombasle at Cap Corsaire, Jacquot had been expecting it. He had even spotted a car, parked in a works lay-by, lights out, a few hundred metres from Dombasle's front gate. He hoped he'd been mistaken, but the flash of headlights in his rearview mirror told him he wasn't.

On the outskirts of Beaulieu he pulled in and got out of his car. She'd unwound her window by the time he reached her.

'Please don't tell me you have to get back to Cavaillon, because I know you're staying at the Bon Accueil in Villefranche,' she said to him sweetly. 'And I really do need a drink, even if I said "no" back at Dombasle's. And we do need to talk, don't we?'

'Official business?'

'Correct.' She smiled.

Jacquot couldn't think how to get out of it. 'One drink only. I have calls to make.'

'I know just the place,' she said. 'Follow me.'

Five minutes later they were pulling in to St-Jean, down by the marina. She found a place to park immediately, but it took Jacquot a few minutes more to find somewhere for himself. She was waiting for him by her car.

'Maybe it would be better if you called me Christine, rather than Detective Inspector or Ambert,' she suggested, sliding her arm into his and leading the way.

'Is this what you call official business?' he asked lightly, nodding at their linked arms, noticing the same scent he'd smelt in the lift down from Arbuthepas's office. He wondered if she'd reached for her make-up bag while she waited for him in that lay-by at Cap Corsaire. He had a feeling she had. The beret had gone and her hair looked somehow fuller than it had in Dombasle's salon. Her lipstick looked fresh too, there was a soft tan blush to her cheeks, and beneath the perfume he could smell mint on her breath.

'In order to exchange confidential information and debate a current police investigation in a public place,' she replied with a smile, 'I would suggest it is important to establish a suitable cover, wouldn't you say?'

'Inspector . . .' Jacquot began.

'Christine,' she said, hugging his arm.

Before he could say anything more, she had reached forward and pushed open the door of a marina brasserie, just a tiny bar squeezed into a corner. There were only two stools, a single sofa and a bar top wide enough to accommodate an ice bucket and three coasters. Shrugging off her coat and dropping it on to the sofa, Christine Ambert hauled herself easily on to the stool and reached into her bag for a pack of cigarettes.

Jacquot pulled the second stool away from the bar and, at a respectable distance from Christine, eased himself on to it, keeping his eyes off the sharp, nyloned angles of her knees and the lip of her tight skirt, made even tighter by the stool.

There was no barman evident, just a waiter taking orders at one of the half-dozen tables in this dimly lit brasserie. Jacquot wondered whether Christine had deliberately chosen this venue and decided she had. There was a warm, hushed intimacy about it, a place for lovers.

'So tell me,' asked Jacquot, rubbing his ring finger as though there was a ring there, 'how is my good friend Chief Inspector Murier?'

'Not very happy,' said Christine. 'He got a call from the boss saying drop everything and find out what

Dombasle's going on about. Full co-operation. Do whatever.'

Jacquot nodded. 'I bet he loved that.'

'Not as much as you do,' she replied, sliding a cigarette from her pack and passing the lighter to Jacquot. As he flicked it alight, she cupped her hands round his and drew on the cigarette as though she hadn't smoked for a month, sucking the flame towards the tip. When she was done, she offered the pack to Jacquot.

Jacquot took one. Like his brand, it had no filter. He tapped an end on the bar, put it between his lips and lit up.

'I have to confess,' he said, passing the lighter back to Christine, 'I can think of nothing nicer than watching Murier squirm.'

'Really?' she asked, and gave him a look. 'Well, I certainly can.'

Jacquot was saved by the barman.

'*Bonsoir, monsieur, mademoiselle. Ça va?* Can I get you something to drink? Something to eat. Dinner perhaps?'

'Well, that sounds just perfect,' replied Christine, before Jacquot had a chance to say anything. 'Dinner it is, then.' And she slid from her stool, picked up her coat from the sofa, and followed the barman into the restaurant. He showed her a table in the middle of the room but she shook her head, looked around, and pointed to another, almost hidden in the corner of the room, beyond the spill of the downlighters, with just a candle to light the table.

She is a piece of work, thought Jacquot, as he took his seat and made himself comfortable. He knew exactly what she was up to, what she wanted, what would probably happen if he let it, but he was also confident that he could handle it. If pulling rank didn't work – and he didn't think it would – he was still certain he could steer his way through safely. When the time came, here at the table or later, out by their cars, he would let her down gently, apologise if he had misled her in any way, given her the wrong idea, as though it was his fault. In the meantime, he had to admit he was warmed by her interest in him and he knew that their evening together would be fun. Better than eating alone at La Mère Germaine or Hameçon, or going back to a lonely hotel room, he thought to himself.

'So what did you do to your face?' asked Christine, calling back the waiter for an ashtray. 'It certainly wasn't a bonfire.'

'I was visiting a friend. Jean-Charles Rains. His house exploded as I walked across the lawn.'

Christine was startled from her flirting, just as Jacquot had hoped.

'Jean-Charles Rains. One of the team?'

'*Exacte*. Right now they're saying it's an accident. A gas leak. But who knows?'

'What do you think?'

'For now, it's an accident, as they say. A coincidence. We'll have to see what happens.'

Menus were brought, wine ordered. Jacquot looked for something light and settled for a simple omelette and green salad. Christine ordered the same.

'Don't tell me you're on a diet?' she asked.

'I had lunch with Dombasle, remember?'

'It was good?'

'Spectacular.'

'I should have come earlier.'

'You wouldn't have enjoyed it. Boys' talk.'

'But I love boys' talk,' she said, with a twinkle in her eye. 'So down and dirty. All that bluffing and puffing-up and testosterone just . . . going to waste.'

Jacquot smiled. 'So what did you think of Pierre Dombasle?'

'Well, he's still alive, I suppose. So that's good.'

Jacquot laughed. 'And?'

'And I love his house. Can you imagine living somewhere like that? *C'est ravissante. C'est sans pareil.*'

'He has four just like it.'

'Well, he can keep the other three. I want that one,'

she said, putting out her cigarette. 'That'll do just fine.'

The omelettes arrived, the *frites*, the side salads. White wine was poured.

'So what's your next move?' she asked. And then, a second later, 'So we can put dinner on expenses.'

'Like I said,' replied Jacquot, choosing not to acknowledge the intended message, 'I think Dombasle's the target – the men closest to him being selected, killed one by one, death on his own doorstep. It's all been planned, meticulously. The only swerve in the whole thing, the only time the killer's made a mistake, is Savry's "suicide". I have no doubt the killer came to that party with an intent to kill, and came equipped – hose, fire cement – but I suspect a target hadn't been identified. The killer was just going to hang out, see what was on offer. You ask me, it could as easily have been any of us, but opportunity presented itself in the form of Bernard Savry, and the killer didn't hesitate.'

'And he was alone, no wife to get in the way.'

'He wasn't the only one. There was Jean-Baptiste, remember. The curé.'

'Maybe the killer's Catholic?'

'Then there's Guy Mageot, Dombasle's head of security.'

'And you?'

'I was with someone.'

As he said the words Jacquot felt a weight lifted from his shoulders. She'd asked, and he'd told her. He'd said what needed to be said, lightly, gently. He might not have a ring, but . . .

And then she paused, frowned, toyed a moment with her omelette. Then she raised wide blue eyes and looked at Jacquot. 'So what you're saying is that the killer was a guest at Dombasle's party.'

Jacquot held her look. 'It has to be, surely. If it wasn't a suicide – and it wasn't – the killer was either a guest, a member of staff, or someone breaking into the property. Which one would you go for?'

'And the killer's a woman.'

'Is that a question?'

'No, it's not. It can only be a woman.'

'Savry was gay, did you know that? Could have been a man, or one of Dombasle's houseboys? You saw Geralde.'

Christine pushed her plate away and reached for her wine. 'It makes no difference. A man couldn't have killed Fastin.'

'Why not?'

'Because the killer had to go to that club with a partner. It's how those places work. And where's the partner, excuse me? There's only Jean-Claude Rives hanging around when the police arrive, wondering where his wife is. It wouldn't surprise me if it was the killer who called them.' Christine shook her head. 'If you ask me, there's someone missing in all the deaths. Souze, Fastin, possibly Valadier – I'd have to see scene-of-crime for that – Peyrot almost certainly. Lorraine and Touche? Another "hit-and-run"?'

'Bravo. You have been doing your homework.' Jacquot was surprised, and impressed. He'd become so intent on Christine as a woman – the sexiness, the company, the harmless flirting – that he'd forgotten she was a policewoman too. And clearly a very smart one. Murier would do well to watch his back, thought Jacquot.

'Take Souze,' she continued. 'A flirt if ever there was one. Five personal assistants in the last three years. His son in hospital, his wife staying over in a company flat . . . come on . . . he took someone home with him – someone he did or didn't know, but a killer all the same. And a woman. And don't try to tell me Souze was a closet gay.'

'Not as far as I know.'

'And then there's Peyrot. Tripping over his laces? No, no, no . . . he's a top-rate sailor – did you know that? Anyway, there's a bar at the Vauban, Les Vagues, like a clubhouse. Peyrot was there with clients – they were the last to see him. He'd been drinking, they said, but not a huge amount. According to these clients, he decided to stay on after they left. He'd just seen someone he recognised, he told them. Some time later he was spotted leaving with a woman.'

'Any description?'

She shook her head.

The waiter returned, took their plates, and they asked for coffee.

'So how many party girls do you have on your list?'

'Thirteen.'

'And you've narrowed it down to?'

'Six.'

Christine Ambert leaned her elbows on the table and rested her chin on clasped fingers. 'You're not telling me the truth, Chief Inspector.'

'You know as much as me, I promise,' said Jacquot. As with Dombasle, he didn't want to show his hand quite yet. 'Ah, except . . . I'd almost forgotten. All the victims were wealthy, and all of them had business dealings with Dombasle.'

Christine nodded, took this in. 'So how many of you rich ones are left?'

'Excluding me . . . Three, maybe four. Jean-Charles Rains, whose house blew up. Gilles Millet who lives in Grasse. And Pierre Dombasle, of course. Also, possibly, Val Caloux.'

'Valentine Caloux. In Théoule? The *notaire*?'

'You know him?'

Christine laughed. 'How extraordinary. What a small world. Of course I know him. Or, more accurately, his wife . . . I forget her name . . .'

'Corinne.'

'That's her. That's the one. Last summer she was arrested for shoplifting. Denied everything, of course; threatened everyone in the store with lawsuits, but we had to bring her in. Two hours later her husband comes to headquarters and she's out. And charges are dropped. But she was with us long enough for someone to call up Records. She has one, you know? Four years ago, she was arrested for beating a girl she had working in the house. A Filipino. The Filipino made a complaint and Madame Caloux was arrested. This time all her husband could do was get bail. But two weeks after bail was granted the Filipino was found drowned. Accidental death. No witnesses. No charges. Case dismissed. Except the investigating officer was suspicious enough to keep her sheet on file. No charges, it should have been wiped. But he kept it on.' Christine reached for her coffee, took a sip, holding his eyes over the cup. 'You never know. Maybe the killer's Corinne Caloux?'

As Jacquot had suspected, their evening together didn't stop at the one coffee. Two more were ordered. And a Bas Armagnac for mademoiselle and a calva for monsieur. By the time they left the restaurant the night was dark and chill, stars glittering, a half-moon riding in the sky.

Jacquot was trying to remember where they had parked their cars when an arm slid around his neck and her mouth was on his, her lips sliding, brushing, across his.

But it wasn't a kiss that was going anywhere . . . and she knew it.

Because that was how she wanted it.

Just a taster, Jacquot, that's all you're getting for now . . .

As they broke from the embrace, Christine caught hold of his lapels and thrust her mouth to his ear. He could feel her breath on his skin and smell the perfume in her hair.

The words were hurried and whispered, as though she was afraid to speak them out loud: 'I'm going to be in your life, Jacquot. One way or the other. Whether you like it or not. Until you are mine. You may be taken right now, but there *will* come a time . . . and I *will* be waiting for you. But for now . . .' She let go his lapels, pecked him on the lips, and stroked her fingers down his cheek. 'For now, I forgive you.' Then she reached out and straightened his jacket. 'There. That's better.'

With that single movement, the reaching forward, the

patting his lapels into place, Jacquot felt an overpowering urge to respond.

'Call me,' she said, pushing him away. 'Anything I can do.' And she crossed to her car.

Jacquot watched her start up, drive off and then turn up ahead. As she came back past him and drew level, she slowed and wound down her window.

'You know the way?' she asked.

'I know the way,' he replied.

'And you can't be tempted?'

Jacquot shook his head.

'This time,' she replied, and with a wave she accelerated away.

64

That is one hell of a determined young lady, thought Jacquot as he swung down into Villefranche. He could still feel the slight, teasing push of her fingertips against his chest as she stepped back from him, and the touch of her hair on his cheek, her lips on his, her mouth whispering in his ear. He couldn't remember the last time he'd been hit on so intently. And so confidently. This woman, Christine Ambert, she was . . . well, quite something.

Parking his car below the Villefranche citadel, Jacquot walked back to his hotel, going over his encounter with Detective Inspector Ambert. In the lobby there was no one at the desk so he reached over and helped himself to his room key. There was a folded note that fluttered out with the key, a phone message.

It was timed at around 10 p.m., when he and Christine Ambert were still swapping speculations in the St-Jean brasserie. 'Miss you, Claudine' was all the note said. Jacquot read it twice, wondering if it was too late to call her back – yes, it probably was – lingering over the words and feeling just a quiet shading of guilt as the lift doors opened.

Up in his room, Jacquot crossed to the terrace windows, unlocked them and opened the shutters. Tonight, he decided, he would sleep with the slap of the sea against the rocks below. But first, he thought to himself, I'm going to step out there and have a final cigarette before turning in. And if there's a calva in the mini-bar, I'll have one of those too. I reckon I deserve it.

To his great delight there was, indeed, a calva in the mini-bar. Tipping the liqueur into a glass, he took it out to the balcony and, keeping close to the wall, put the glass down on the table. Across the bay the lights of Cap Ferrat glinted like scattered chips of ivory and the breeze carried a soft vanilla scent from some of the most pampered gardens in the country. Before sitting down, however, a familiar compulsion made him go to the balcony railings. It was like a dare, a test, and he couldn't resist it. Slowly, cautiously, he inched forward, gripped the rail and, dropping his eyes from the distant lights of the Cap, he looked down at the cobbled quay five floors below.

He took a deep breath, felt just the slightest rawness in his throat, and pushed back from the rail. It was then, as he was about to step away from the edge and sit at the table with his drink and his cigarettes, that he caught a shadowy movement in the corner of his eye, something behind him, coming at him, even sensed perhaps, a wave of air, a subtle disturbance in the space behind him.

Something not as it should be.

Jacquot had no time to protect himself. Before he could do anything – turn, side-step, cower – he heard a pig-like grunt and felt hands push against his back with enough force to send him stumbling forward, the side rail of the balcony catching and pressing against his left hip, its hard, cold edge acting as a deadly fulcrum point, his weight cruelly off-balance.

He heard the table crash over, and his glass of calva shatter. For a moment he thought he must be imagining it all. But then his feet were suddenly in the air, and the upper half of his body was toppling over the railing.

As quickly, and as finally as that.

He was over. And falling.

In thin air. Five floors above the street. Sea and sky and stars and lights flipping over.

And just seconds to live.

There was no room, no time for panic, but he felt his

heart start to thump and his blood turn cold and his limbs seemed not to answer, hands flailing wildly and uselessly for something to grab hold of.

But there was nothing.

Jesus, I'm going to die, he thought.

I'm going to die.

C'est finis . . .

65

It was the flagpole, jutting out at an angle from the wall of the hotel, to the left of his balcony and two metres below, that broke Jacquot's fall, smashing into his belly and folding his body in two like a gymnast's on the asymmetric bars, his forehead almost smacking against his knees. The breath was crushed from his chest, his cracked rib screamed, and for a moment he hung there like a piece of washing on the line.

But gravity hadn't finished with him, his weight not equally distributed. The lower half of his body, from the ribs down, was heavier than the top half, and before he could adjust his position he felt himself start to slide, slipping backwards, over the pole. Very quickly.

From somewhere a scrap of sense and a preposterous will to survive leapt into action, telling Jacquot's arms and elbows and hands and fingers to scrabble for some kind of hold before it was too late. He'd been given a chance, hitting that flagpole. He couldn't afford to ignore it.

It was the rope that held the flag – Italian or German, Jacquot could never tell the difference – that, at the very last moment, the fingers of one hand latched on to, gripped tightly.

There was a split-second of intense relief, and then an icy dread. Would the weight of his falling body be held by this cord? Was the cord good and strong, or old and tired and ready to shred? Was it properly secured at the end of the flagpole? And if it broke, but he managed to hang on, would it swing him further into thin air, dangling him from the tip of the flagpole? Or bring him crashing in against the wall of the hotel?

And what of the flagpole? Was the flagpole secure? Was the bracket that held it to the wall firmly screwed in? Or rusted? Ready to snap?

Jacquot was aware of all these questions – and none of them. There was simply no time, no space for conjecture. It was either life, or death. Nothing else.

Everything depended on the rope.

And the rope held, and his fingers didn't let go, and the next instant his falling body was pulled up short, another stab of molten pain scorching through the side of his chest from his cracked rib.

So sharp and sudden was this pain that, on reflex, Jacquot almost let go of the rope. But he didn't. He held on to it, the soft pads of his fingers burning from the cut of it, the weight they were carrying.

But he'd stopped falling. He'd stopped falling.

It was then that he realised he had a right hand, and he brought it up to grab another section of the rope. Two hands, now he had two hands on the rope, and a dizzy delight spun through him. But it didn't last long. He was still hanging four floors above the pavement. And swinging helplessly.

It was probably this swinging, as much as his weight, that finally snapped the rope. One minute he was holding on like grim death, wondering what to do, the next he was falling again, straight down, until the rope played out, stretched tight and jerked him back towards the wall of the hotel, slamming him into it with a mighty crunch that he felt in his elbow and shoulder.

Yet still it wasn't over. He had managed to keep a burning, blistering hold on the rope, and to have the comfort of the wall at his shoulder rather than dangling helplessly over the street, but that was all.

Frantically, feet scrabbling for a toehold but finding none, Jacquot took swift stock of his situation. He was hanging at the end of a rope midway down the front of the hotel, somewhere between the fourth and third floors. A metre above him, and a metre on either side, were two fourth-floor balconies. Tantalisingly out of reach. Below him, maybe a metre from his outstretched toes, were the side-railings on two third-floor balconies. Since there was no way he could reach the fourth-floor balconies, his only option was to try and launch himself at one of the two balconies below. If he hadn't been so scared he would have laughed at such a prospect.

It was then, dangling from the end of the rope, that he heard a car drum past on the cobbles below. Looking down he saw it disappear under his armpit, out of his field of vision, just the sound of it now, climbing up out of town.

And in that instant Jacquot remembered that he had a voice. And though he could see no one on the street below, he knew that if he shouted loud enough someone – the hotel receptionist, another guest, a waiter from one of the restaurants trudging home – was sure to hear him.

So that's what he did, drawing in breath to scream out for help.

Of course the scream would have been a great deal more effective if Jacquot had managed to see it through. But as the first word hit his throat the rawness he had fondly hoped was just a memory made its presence felt. He might have been able to eat and drink and smoke and talk, albeit a little hoarsely, but screaming was altogether different. It felt as though he had peeled away the lining of his throat with his fingernails, and the words '*aidez-moi*' came out as a wounded bleat.

Jacquot closed his weeping eyes and tried to think.

Who had pushed him?

Who would do such a thing?

And why?

Those were the thoughts that flooded into his panic-filled brain. But he knew as quickly as they lodged there that they were no use to him. If he wanted to live, this was neither the time nor the place to speculate on the who and the why. Survival was all. Later, if he lived, he could play policeman.

But not now. Not here.

And then he remembered what he'd been thinking about before he heard the car. The swing. The jump.

It was all he could do. His only chance.

If the rope continued to hold and he could set up a swing, launch himself properly, he might just make it to one of the third-floor balconies below, the top of their side-railings only a metre or so from his feet. But he had to act fast, do it before the rope started to slide through his numbed fingers, or finally pulled away from the cleat that held it.

Cautiously, pushing his shoulder against the wall,

Jacquot swung out his legs and felt the rope follow with a menacing creak – a movement, a rudimentary swing. He tried it again, building on the momentum. Then another swing, and another, stronger now, back and forth like a pendulum, the rope starting to twist and squeak, his shoulder, hip and shoes scuffing against the wall. With any luck, another three, maybe four swings would give him enough impetus and momentum to let the rope go and try for the balcony.

So long as his luck held . . .

So long as the rope didn't break first . . .

So long as there was enough feeling left in his fingers to let go . . .

Shaking away these doubts, hanging on with every ounce of his strength, Jacquot gradually built up his swing, increased his speed and planned the leap.

The right-hand balcony . . .

The top of its side railing . . .

No more than a metre below him and, with each swing, coming closer, closer. Within reach.

If he could just manage one more swing . . .

Yessss . . .

And maybe another . . .

Yeesssss . . .

It was at the end of this last swing, just as Jacquot was about to let go of the rope, that it finally snapped away from its mooring above his head, the extra weight he'd put into the swing too much for it to bear. The next instant he was falling again, and reaching out for the balcony . . . reaching out desperately while the rope fell away from him, snaking down through the air to slap on to the pavement far below.

But due to the rope failing, Jacquot's forward momentum was no longer as great as he'd anticipated, and because of this his feet missed the lip of the balcony, and his shins scraped painfully down its edge. But his fingers, scrabbling at the side-rails, somehow managed to get hold of two of them and close tight, the cold metal sliding through his fists until friction dried the sweat off his palms.

And suddenly Jacquot wasn't falling any more, and there was something more substantial than a rope to cling on to. But Jacquot knew without looking that he was still too far from the ground, that he'd die or, at best, sustain serious injuries, if he jumped or fell.

He wasn't out of the woods yet.

Unable to look down, all Jacquot could see was the tiled floor of the balcony whose side-railings he was hanging from and, no more than a metre away, at the terrace door, three tins of paint and a roller tray left by the painters – so close, so safe. So far.

It was then, without any bidding, that the thought

struck him that had he accepted Christine Ambert's invitation he would not be where he was now, clinging to the railings of a hotel balcony with every ounce of his strength. There was a lesson to be learned there, he thought wryly.

But this was neither the time nor the place to think such things.

With fingers burning and spears of pain jabbing at his rib, Jacquot had to come up with something that would get him out of this jam. And get him out of it fast. Since there was no chance he could haul himself up and over the balcony, or swing a foot on to the ledge, the only alternative was to move, hand by hand, rail by rail, around it. Because, Jacquot suddenly realised, he was now only a dozen or so handholds away from the far side of the balcony which, if he remembered correctly, was only a single floor above the breakfast-room awning.

Maybe a three-metre drop, nothing more. At the very least it would break his fall. He'd survive. All he had to do was haul himself around the balcony before the strength in his arms gave out. Or the palms of his hands started smoking.

Keeping his eyes on the pots of paint, concentrating on their shape and size and position, Jacquot began the journey, cold sweat streaming into his eyes, shafts of red-hot pain slicing into his side whenever his left hand took the full weight of his body while his right hand reached along for the next rail.

Gritting his teeth, his breath searing his throat, Jacquot inched around the corner of the balcony, then along its front until finally, five hand-burning, muscle-screaming minutes later, he reached the far corner and squinted over his shoulder.

And there it was. The awning over the breakfast room. A beckoning scoop of blue canvas that would surely hold his weight on just a three-metre drop. So long as he didn't land on one of the metal struts that supported it. That would be painful.

Closing his eyes, squeezing them shut, he whispered a prayer and opened his fists, let go of the railings. Two seconds later, he hit the awning on his back, bounced, rolled with the slope, and clattered over the guttering into the street. Landing miraculously, fair and square, if a little wobbly, on both feet.

Terra firma.

He had made it down.

66

In the dream he was falling. Somewhere black and chill with only the sound of air rushing past him. Just falling, endlessly, endlessly plummeting downwards, arms and legs scrabbling nervily like the limbs of a sleeping dog. And sooner or later, if he didn't do something, he was going to come to a stop, hit something. With deadly results.

Jacquot sprang awake, blinking in the bands of sunlight streaming through the shuttered terrace doors. For a second or more, he was still falling, every nerve alert, but the dream receded and, with a wave of relief, he saw where he was. The bed he was lying in, the TV, the fridge. Familiar objects that, thankfully, were where they should be, firmly planted, not falling with him.

But it was no dream. He had been falling. The night before someone had tried to kill him, someone had pushed him from his fifth-floor balcony. The dirt on his hands, the burning skin of his palms, the scrape marks on his shins and the aching rib – all attested to his late-night spill. Even his throat was complaining, a dry swallow doing nothing to comfort the rawness. Only somehow he'd managed to survive. Never, ever again, he swore to himself, would he set foot on a hotel balcony higher than the first floor.

Jacquot was in the shower when the phone rang, the hot water stinging his face and hands and grazed shins. Switching it off and stepping through the plastic curtains, he reached for a towel and went through to the bedroom.

'*Oui?* Jacquot.'

'Sound a bit rough, boss. Hard night?' It was Brunet in Cavaillon.

'You could say,' was all Jacquot could manage.

'I thought I'd catch you early. Let you know what's going on.'

'Tell me,' said Jacquot, reaching for his cigarettes, lighting up the first of the day without a coffee to introduce it. His throat burnt as much as the tip. After a couple of puffs he stubbed it out, head spinning, throat screaming.

'First – Madame Druart. She could probably have killed every one of them. But not Patric Souze.'

'And why not?'

'Because she's never been to Bordeaux.'

'And how exactly did you find that out?' asked Jacquot, not entirely sure that he wanted to know what ruse Brunet had employed to secure this information.

Brunet chuckled down the line. 'I told her I was calling from the Tourist Office in Bordeaux and was delighted to tell her she'd won a competition. A Wine Tour in Bordeaux, with a long weekend in the *Ville Rose*, Toulouse, thrown in. She was thrilled. Said she'd never been to either city. I know it's thin,' admitted Brunet, 'but she said it so quickly, so enthusiastically.'

'And what will she think when her prize tickets don't arrive?'

'Regrettably, Madame Druart failed to answer all my questions correctly.'

Brunet had also played this same game with Pierrette Cabezac, the teacher's wife in Pau. 'She may have got all the answers right, but she can't take the holiday because she's injured her foot. Slipped off a kerb and twisted her ankle. Been laid up a month or more.'

'And Florence Talaud?' Somehow Jacquot found this conversation oddly soothing.

'She could have killed every one of them,' said Brunet quietly, then paused.

Jacquot knew how much his assistant loved these moments, the holding back of crucial information –

whatever it was he had managed to dig up. Leaving Jacquot to ask the inevitable and equally crucial question.

'But . . . ?'

'She's left-handed – and Fastin's throat and genitals were cut left to right.'

'And how did you find that out? I mean, you were on the phone to her? And you've never met her, right?'

'That was the last of my three competition questions,' said Brunet. 'Are you left-handed or right-handed?'

'And the other two questions?'

'Can you drive? And, have you ever been to Bordeaux or Toulouse?'

'*Jé-su*, Jean. You are something.'

67

With Mesdames Druart, Cabezac and Talaud crossed off his list of suspects thanks to Brunet's ingenious game, and since Fabienne Millet would be leaving for the States that day with her husband and children, Jacquot was down to just three names: Maryvonne Pelerain, Corinne Caloux and Mathilde Carassin.

Fifteen minutes after putting down the phone to Brunet, at approximately seven-forty-five, Jacquot was dressed and working on a Room Service breakfast. When he'd finished, he lay back on the bed, reached for his notebook and picked up the phone. His plan was simple. All he had to do was establish the whereabouts of all three women when he was pushed from his balcony. He was certain that the grunt he'd heard behind him, seconds before he was pushed, belonged to a woman, and if one of these three suspects had any trouble accounting for their movements, Jacquot might be one step closer to finding the killer and hitting Rochet's deadline.

The first number he called rang and rang. At last it was answered and a sleepy voice came on the line.

'*Allô? Allô?*'

It was a woman speaking.

'Maryvonne? Maryvonne Pelerain?'

'*Oui. C'est moi. J'écoute. Oufff. Alors . . .*'

'*C'est* Daniel. Daniel Jacquot.'

There was a long pause and then, summoning some energy from somewhere, the voice perked up. 'Daniel? Danny? Hello, how are you? Why, we were only talking about you last night. At dinner.'

'Dinner?'

'Why, Théo's birthday. Isn't that why you're calling? Here, hold on, *ne quitte pas*, he wants to have a word. And don't leave it so long next time, you hear? Come and stay, why don't you, with that gorgeous wife of yours?'

And then the phone was taken from her and a big voice boomed down the line. 'Eighteen birthdays I've had since we played together, Daniel Jacquot, and this is the first time you call to wish me Happy Birthday? Either you're pissed or you want to borrow money.'

'Neither. I just want to know why I wasn't invited?'

There was a moment's silence down the line as the big man considered this. 'It was Maryvonne arranged it all. Blame her. Only do me a favour and leave it till tomorrow so she can get rid of her hangover. She may sound good on the phone, but right now she looks like death. And don't call so bloody early next time.'

'I thought postmen got up early?'

'Not on bloody holiday, they don't.'

After hearing at length about the previous evening's birthday party and accepting Théo's invitation to visit – 'some time soon, you hear?' – Jacquot broke the connection, laid the phone on his chest, and dialled up the next number.

This time the phone was picked up on the third ring.

'*Oui?* Résidence Caloux.'

It was the voice of the girl who'd opened the door to him two days earlier. Young, a little hesistant, fearful almost. Jacquot thought of the Filipino girl and wondered what it might be like to have Corinne Caloux as a boss.

'*Bonjour, mademoiselle.* This is Daniel Jacquot. I hope I haven't called too early?'

'*Non, non. Pas de tout*, Monsieur, Monsieur . . . ?'

'Jacquot. Daniel Jacquot. Of the *judiciaire*,' he added for good measure. 'I was at the house a couple of days ago, Tuesday, seeing Monsieur and Madame Caloux. Maybe you remember?'

'*Ah, oui. Bien sûr,*' said the voice. 'And how can I be of help?'

'I wanted to speak to Madame Caloux, if that is possible? If she is at home?'

'*Je regrette*, Monsieur Jacquot. I am afraid Monsieur and Madame Caloux are away at the moment. They will not be back until the weekend.'

'Do you have a number where I can reach them?' asked Jacquot, his interest piqued.

'For Monsieur Caloux, *oui*. Just a moment. Ah, yes . . . here it is. He is staying at the Dacia Luxembourg Hotel, in Paris. Boulevard St-Michel. I have the number if you want it?'

Jacquot took the number just in case. 'And Madame Caloux? She is with her husband?'

'*Non*, monsieur. I believe she was visiting her sister, or maybe her mother. She didn't leave a number. She said she would call if she needed anything.'

'And when did they leave?'

'Monsieur Caloux yesterday afternoon. Madame, by car, a little later.'

'You've been very kind, thank you.'

'*De rien, Monsieur Jacquot. De rien.*'

Since there was no point making a third call – he

would see the Carassins soon enough, down on the quay – Jacquot put the phone back on the bedside table, clasped his hands across his stomach, and let his mind wander.

Someone had tried to kill him.

Down here in Villefranche.

Why?

To put an end to his snooping around?

To stop any possibility of further investigation into the murders?

To clear the way ahead?

That seemed the likeliest bet to Jacquot.

But then maybe he'd got it wrong. Or rather, maybe Claudine had got it wrong. Could it really all come down to money, that only the rich team members were being targeted? Could it really be because some of them had made it big, and others not?

Or was there something else?

Something he hadn't yet considered?

For all he knew, he'd simply been the next in line, his fall from a fifth-floor balcony so easily explained away as an accident. He'd been drinking, he didn't like heights, he must have tripped, lost his balance . . .

One thing he did know for certain was that Maryvonne Pelerain was off his list of suspects. She might have been in Paris, Bordeaux and Toulouse on the dates when Luc and Patric and Marc had been killed, and she might have had the kind of job that provided all the cover and opportunity she needed, but right now she was down there in Perpignan nursing a hangover, after what sounded like a riotous dinner party to celebrate her husband's birthday. There was no way she could be involved.

It had all looked so promising when Brunet had called him up and briefed him on her movements. But last night's attempted murder surely put her out of the frame. As far as Jacquot was concerned, she could only continue to feature as a suspect if last night's shove over the balcony was nothing more than a burglary gone wrong. And since nothing had been taken from his room – his gun, wallet, or car keys – and since, in his experience, hotel burglaries rarely involved murder, Jacquot didn't believe that for one moment.

And did Maryvonne really have a motive anyway? Why would she want to kill off her husband's old teammates? Had any one of them ever done either of them any kind of harm? Judging by Théo's popularity at the reunion, it seemed unlikely. All through that evening, Jacquot had seen him in close and friendly dialogue with all the players, and in all the time he'd known him, Jacquot had never heard a bad word said about dear old Théo. Too innocent to understand – let alone take part in, or profit from – the politics of high-level sport, Théo was just a big, lumbering lump of a man who loved his wife and his children and his country almost as much as he loved his rugby.

But if Maryvonne Pelerain was off the list, there was still Corinne Caloux to consider, with her nasty little temper and her 'unofficial' police record. And just the previous afternoon she had left home, leaving no contact details, ostensibly to visit with a mother or a sister. Until he had Brunet tell him otherwise, Madame Caloux was still a contender. And definitely staying on his list.

As was Mathilde Carassin, at that very moment probably down on the *quai*, helping Sidi with his catch. If he'd wanted to, Jacquot could have stepped on to the balcony and he would probably have seen her.

But he didn't. Instead, Jacquot got up from his bed, went into the bathroom, gargled, swallowed a double dose of painkillers, and smoothed into his cheeks the aloe oil that the hotel's receptionist had given him. As soon as the shine of the oil had soaked into his scorched skin, Jacquot left his room and took the lift to the lobby.

68

The first thing that Jacquot did when he came out of the hotel was turn and look up at its pastel-wash façade. There, beneath the hotel sign, on the top floor, almost in the middle of the building, was his room and the balcony. It seemed impossibly high, and he wondered how he had ever managed to pull through. Even the third-floor balcony he'd managed to reach and, hand-over-hand, work his way round, looked quite high enough. It also struck Jacquot that last night he had felt like the only man in the world, entirely alone, hanging on up there for dear life, yet this morning the quay was alive with people and traffic.

Crossing the road, Jacquot headed for the *quai*. At the far end, among a crowd of *pointu* fishermen in their faded *bleus*, he could see Sidi swinging his plastic catch crates up on to the jetty from the bow of his boat, a low sun sparkling off the mounds of ice and the silvery scales of the fish.

'Et bonjour, Sidi. Ça va?'

'Hey, Daniel. How's it going?' called Sidi, hopping up on to the jetty, his dark berry eyes dancing with delight at seeing his old friend, his teeth a dazzling white in a net of mahogany wrinkles.

'So you're working alone this morning? No Mathilde?'

'Oh, she'll be along any time now. She probably finished late, so she's maybe overslept a little.'

'How late's late?' asked Jacquot, as though he was simply making conversation.

'Ten, eleven. Sometime around then. Hey, *elle arrive maintenant. Regarde.*'

Jacquot looked back along the jetty and saw the white Renault van pull into its usual space outside the Bureau du Port. The driver's door opened and Mathilde jumped out, waved to them both, and slid open the side door. Then she hurried towards them, apologising as she drew near for being late. She looked tired and drawn, Jacquot thought, her eyes still soft and unfocused from sleep. It was as if she hadn't quite woken up.

'The traffic, you wouldn't believe. And it's November.' She leaned forward and kissed Sidi – 'How was it? Good night? Certainly looks like it' – and then she turned to Jacquot and smiled the widest smile, gave him a hug that made him wince. 'Third time this week, Daniel. How lovely. Or have you come to arrest me?'

'Not yet, Mathilde, you're still in the clear,' he told her and the three of them laughed, Sidi, as though he hadn't quite understood the joke, a second or two behind Mathilde and Jacquot.

'You want some coffee? Or soup?' asked Mathilde.

'Soup?'

'Tomato and basil. I make it myself. After a night out there, Sidi likes soup when he gets back in. Me, I'm coffee. What about you, Daniel?'

'If you let me help carry the catch to the van, I'll try some of that soup.'

And so the three of them set to, carrying a dozen loaded crates from the end of the jetty to the van. More than a little hampered by the pain from his rib and hands, Jacquot managed only two crates, during which time Sidi and Mathilde handled the rest. Sidi appeared not to notice the weight, almost running from *pointu* to van and back again, dancing over the ropes that snaked across the jetty and swerving past the various mooring bollards without seeming to look. And Mathilde was never far behind him, dropping on to her haunches, gripping a crate and rising straight-backed like a weightlifter, the mounds of ice sparkling beneath her chin.

When the job was finally done, heart beating with the effort, Jacquot accepted his mug of steaming tomato soup, poured with a steady hand by Mathilde, and toasted the pair of them.

'I've been sitting at a desk too long,' he admitted, savouring the rich tomato flavour. Each mouthful slid painlessly down his throat and he could feel it warming its way into his belly. No wonder Sidi liked soup after a night out alone at sea.

'The tomato's my favourite,' said Sidi, draining his mug, wiping his mouth with his sleeve. Mathilde offered the Thermos to refill his mug, but Sidi pointed to Jacquot. 'My friend first. He may only have carried the two crates but it probably felt like fifty.'

'You're right, they did. But no more, thank you. Sidi's the one who deserves it.'

'Oh go on,' said Mathilde, pouring the soup into his mug despite his objections. 'There's another Thermos flask in the van. There's easily enough.'

By the time Jacquot had finished the second mug, Sidi had gone back to the *pointu* to store his gear and secure the boat.

'So what now?' asked Jacquot.

'Place St-François for the last of the market and then

home to bed. Twelve till five, if we're lucky, then Sidi's up out for the night again. But tomorrow we're off. All day, all night.'

'And you? You working late again?'

'Why the interest? You planning on asking me out?' She gave him a teasing, squinty look, raised her eyebrows. 'What would my husband think?'

'He'd think I was a man of taste and discernment,' teased Jacquot back. 'Wouldn't you?' asked Jacquot as Sidi, rolling down his sleeves, came back to the van.

'What's that? I missed it.'

'I said that if I asked your wife out for dinner, you'd say I was a man of taste and discernment.'

'Yes, I would,' replied Sidi, as Mathilde pulled the side door closed. 'But knowing you, Daniel, I'd give it serious thought beforehand. So, are you staying much longer?' Sidi nodded over the bonnet of the van at the Bon Accueil.

'Another day or two, perhaps.'

'So we'll see you before you go?'

'I'm sure of it.'

'*Eh bien*,' said Sidi, clasping Jacquot's hand so hard that Jacquot nearly screamed out loud. '*À la prochaine, mon ami.* And keep out of the sun, hein?'

'Daniel. It was good to see you again,' said Mathilde stepping forward as Sidi hoisted himself into the driving seat and started up the engine. She planted a hand on his shoulder and leaned forward to peck his cheeks. 'And thanks for the help.'

'Thanks for the soup. I didn't deserve it.'

'Oh I think you did,' she replied. 'Don't you?'

69

The trouble with suspects, mused Jacquot as he watched the Carassins' van turn into the traffic and, with a wave from Mathilde, drive off, was that they rarely behaved as you expected – or hoped.

Take Mathilde. If she was the woman who had pushed him off that balcony the night before, and if she was the woman who was killing his team-mates one by one and scratching the score on Dombasle's fleet of cars, then she was playing the game of her life, cool as an iced pastis, behaving as if nothing had happened, as if she had nothing to hide.

And yet, that last remark about the soup? Almost a taunt. Did she really mean, as Jacquot imagined, that he deserved it for his mountain-climbing the night before and surviving her attempted murder? Or did she mean

– in all innocence – that he deserved it for helping with the crates of fish?

Surely she wouldn't tease him like that, almost challenging him? It would be absurd to take such a chance. Either she really was innocent, or she knew she had absolute control, and knew exactly what she was doing.

Rounding the first bend, a hundred metres away, the van gave off a plume of blue exhaust smoke as Sidi selected a lower gear at the start of the hill out of Villefranche.

Flexing his shoulders and working his back after his stint with the crates, Jacquot watched it disappear then crossed to the hotel.

The friendly receptionist was on duty. 'I see the aloe's working,' she told him. 'It looks much better, monsieur.'

'Thank you. Do you mind if I use the phone?'

'Long distance or local?'

'Cavaillon.'

'Then please help yourself.'

As he'd hoped, he caught Brunet at home.

'A little job, Jean. Shouldn't take you long. I want you to track down a Madame Corinne Caloux. Lives in Théoule. She might be visiting her mother or her sister. I don't have names for them, I'm afraid.'

'I'll get on to it, and call you back.'

'If I'm not here, leave a message with reception.'

'*T'as pigé*. You got it.'

After speaking to Brunet, Jacquot stepped back out of the hotel and wandered along the *quai* looking for a suitable spot for a reviving *grande crème et calva*. It was closing on eleven and the sun, streaming down out of a clear blue sky, made sitting outside a pleasant option. He found himself a table two doors down from Hameçon and, keeping his face in the shadow of the awning, lit a cigarette and stretched out his legs.

He had just taken his first sips of coffee and calva and was lighting up another cigarette when his attention was drawn to a sleek black Ferrari making its way down the *quai* as if the driver was looking for someone. Its progress was slow enough for other cars behind it to beep impatiently and overtake extravagantly when space allowed on the narrow harbourside road. Jacquot tried to make out who was driving – a man or a woman – but sunlight splashed across the raked windscreen. Fifteen metres away, he heard the first warbling chortle of its engine.

And then, directly opposite him, the Ferrari pulled in and the driver's window slid down.

Jacquot blinked. It was Mageot.

Tossing back his calva, Jacquot left some money on the table and, making sure the road was clear, crossed to the Ferrari. He bent down to the window, a warm smell of cool leather and hot oil drifting up at him.

Mageot leaned across the passenger seat and opened the door.

'Get in. The skipper wants a word.'

70

On the drive to Cap Corsaire Mageot did little more than grunt a 'you'll see', or a 'I'd prefer the skipper to tell you' in answer to his questions and Jacquot quickly realised that there wasn't going to be much conversation on the journey. So he sat back and enjoyed the curious pleasure of a Ferrari, a car he had never once sat in, but a car with which Mageot was clearly familiar. He drove like a pro, shifting through the gears to accommodate the bends and the straights between Villefranche and Cap Corsaire, the straights eliciting a powerful skull-numbing roar from behind their heads when Mageot put his foot down. It was a fabulously exhilarating drive and when they arrived, Jacquot felt a tiny worm of disappointment when Mageot stopped in front of the house and switched off the engine, sorry that the trip was over so soon. At least he'd get a lift back in it, he thought to himself, as Mageot led him up the front steps and into the house.

'You'll find Monsieur Dombasle in the study, sir,' said Manolo, standing at the bottom of the stairs.

'Thanks, Manolo,' replied Mageot and he led Jacquot up the stairs and down the long corridor to the louvred doors at the end. When they entered the study, Dombasle was standing at his glass-topped desk.

'Daniel. Good, good. At last,' said Dombasle without preamble. 'Here, look.' He tapped his foot against a cardboard box placed on the floor beside the desk. 'Guy, show him.'

Dombasle turned his back on the box as Mageot bent down and lifted the lid. There was a rustle of tissue paper and then he stood aside. Jacquot stepped forward and looked into the box. At first it looked like a cushion, white and fluffy, but then Jacquot saw the two pink mouths and the lolling tongues and the two lengths of pink ribbon knotted tightly around the necks of Lydie's treasured bichons frises. He didn't need to see anything more. Someone had strangled the two dogs and wrapped them up in tissue paper as though they were a gift.

Dombasle had turned and was looking squarely at Jacquot. His eyes were cold and his scarred, battered face seemed to throb with anger. From nowhere, Jacquot remembered what Olivier had once told him about Dombasle. The boys were in Paris playing the South Africans and at half-time the Springboks were a converted try up after a sub for Jean-Charles had fumbled a ball, tried to kick it into touch only to see the Springbok scrum-half scoop it up and score under the posts. According to Olivier, Dombasle's face had literally bulged with fury. 'It was as if the face had a life of its own,' Olivier had told him. 'It . . . it kind of ballooned . . . a big red pulsing balloon – there's no other way to describe it. It was as though every muscle in his face was receiving electric shocks. And his voice, Daniel, soft as velvet.'

That was the voice Jacquot heard now as he drew away from the box. A low, drawling whisper, each word honeyed with a wish for revenge. 'This time the bastard's gone too far,' snarled Dombasle. 'I want him, Daniel. And I want him now. Today,' holding Jacquot's eye as though Jacquot was the man to carry out his wishes.

'And Lydie? Does she know?'

Dombasle did not reply. Instead he leaned forward to his desk and pressed the 'Play' button on a tape recorder.

The voice was distant and muffled, impossible to tell if it belonged to a man or woman.

'A little gift sent, not with love, but with hate. Your wife watched as the little doggies died, and her daughter

too. Count yourself fortunate that there are dogs in the box and nothing else. Be assured, however, that this will happen if you do not do what I ask. I will call this afternoon. And no police.'

Dombasle switched off the tape and looked out across the garden to the sea. 'They're missing,' he said finally. 'We called the *appartement* in Nice immediately, but there was no answer. Guy, here, drove in to town to see what he could find. Picked you up on the way back.'

Jacquot turned to Mageot. 'And?'

'No sign of a struggle. None at all.'

'Note?'

'No note I could find.'

'Beds slept in?'

Mageot nodded. 'Carlo, the driver, dropped them off last night, when they got back from Forcalquier.'

Dombasle broke in. 'There was some film "do" that Lydie wanted to go to at the Victorine Studios. I was busy, so she took Nonie.'

'And Lydie was staying overnight? At the *appartement*?'

'That's right,' said Dombasle. 'It's Nonie's place, but it's big enough for all of us, if we want to stay over – after a party, the theatre, dinner with friends. Lydie uses it more than I do – shopping, that sort of thing.'

'And Lydie was due back today?'

'For lunch. Carlo was going to pick her up' – Dombasle glanced at his watch – 'about now.'

'When did the box arrive?' asked Jacquot.

'At breakfast,' replied Mageot. 'A van drew up at the gates. It was there just a moment. When it drove off, there was the box.'

'You have this on the security camera?'

Mageot nodded. 'But no shot of the registration number, or the driver.'

'And the van?'

'No trade name. White, a Renault.'

Jacquot turned down his mouth in an effort to conceal a shiver of excitement. The Carassins's van was white and a Renault. And bore no trade name or signs on its sides or doors. And that very morning Mathilde had been late at the jetty.

'When the van drove off, was there heavy smoke from the exhaust?' asked Jacquot. It was a long shot, but . . .

Mageot frowned. 'I don't think so,' he replied quietly, clearly not pleased to be shown off the ball in front of Dombasle. 'Certainly nothing that showed.'

'And apart from this taped message, and the dogs, there has been no attempt to make further contact?'

'None,' replied Dombasle.

'*Rien*,' added Mageot, glancing at Dombasle.

Jacquot caught the look.

'And?'

'When Carlo returned last night,' began Mageot, 'there were two scratches on the car. Two. Across the boot.'

'Is that when he noticed them? After coming back from Nice?'

'This morning,' replied Mageot. 'Said it must have happened while he was seeing Madame Dombasle and Nonie to the *appartement*.'

'And what time would this have been? Last night, when Carlo dropped off Lydie and Nonie?'

'Around seven, seven-thirty,' replied Mageot. 'Carlo said he was back here about nine.'

Jacquot nodded. Took this in.

'So,' said Dombasle, 'what do you suggest we do?'

Jacquot smiled. 'I suggest we wait for a phone call.'

71

'We wait?' Dombasle's voice had risen a fraction. A rack of frown lines creased across his forehead. 'Is that all?'

'Is there anything else?'

'What about the police?'

'You sent for me,' replied Jacquot. 'Which means, I assume, that you don't want the *judiciaire* involved and that they have not yet been told.'

'That's correct,' Dombasle confirmed. 'But do you think we should?'

'You have been told not to contact them. The kidnapper would expect a man in your position, Pierre, to keep quiet and go along with such demands. For now. Certainly at this early stage.'

'But?'

'I'm a policeman, Pierre. And I'm sure that Guy, as head of your security, will have told you that police involvement is a sensible precaution in cases like this.'

'Yes, he did. So should we call? Bring them in on it? What do you think?'

Jacquot sighed. 'Frankly, it can do no harm. So long as you don't let Chief Inspector Murier become involved.'

'You don't rate him?' asked Dombasle.

'Do you?'

'Well, who else then? What about that girl of his? The one who was here yesterday. His assistant. The pretty one.'

'Detective Inspector Ambert.'

'Is she any good? Do you think she could handle it? Discreetly.'

'She would be put in a very difficult position,' said Jacquot, 'if you told her what was happening and asked her not to pass on the information. She would be obliged to report it to her boss, Murier, and bring him up to speed. If you make that call, it's a risk you would have to take. And if Murier's involved . . .'

'What do you think?'

'I think she would help, for the time being.' If only to get one over on Murier, thought Jacquot, and maybe start making a name for herself. It was a risk, but he reckoned it was a risk she would take. For now.

The call that they had been waiting for came shortly after Mageot phoned the Nice *judiciaire* and spoke to Detective Inspector Ambert, asking her to drop by. By this time the three men had left the study and made their way to the salon, Mageot carrying the box with the dogs and leaving it with Manolo. Twenty minutes later, Manolo reappeared. He went to Mageot and whispered in his ear.

'Skipper. It's a phone call. For you.'

Jumping to his feet, Dombasle went to the phone and picked it up. '*Oui?* Dombasle.' For the next thirty seconds, he didn't say a word, just listened. And then, 'No, I haven't.' And then a few moments later. 'Yes, I understand.'

Slowly, Dombasle replaced the receiver.

'She wants the Kaminski Parure.'

Mageot whistled.

'It was a woman's voice?' asked Jacquot.

'Sounded like a woman. Muffled, like the tape, but yes, I'd say a woman.'

'And the . . . what did you call it?'

'The Kaminski Parure,' explained Mageot. 'A suite of matching jewellery. Madame Dombasle's diamond and ruby tiara, necklace, bracelet and earrings.'

'I bought it for my wife, for our tenth anniversary,' said Dombasle proudly.

'And its worth?'

Dombasle blew out his cheeks. 'I paid fifty million francs. Part of a private business deal, you understand. On the open market? At auction? According to my good friend, Monsieur Nigel Milne, an expert jeweller in London's Jermyn Street, such a valuable and historic suite of jewels could easily reach as high as seventy million. Maybe more.'

Seventy million francs for five pieces of jewellery, thought Jacquot. It really was a different world. There he'd been thinking cash or wire transfers and here was a demand for jewellery. Easily transportable and, out of its settings, easily convertible. Into any currency. Very clever.

'And this jewellery is at the bank?'

'Here, in the vault,' said Mageot, nodding at the floor and somewhere below them.

Jacquot thought about this for a moment. 'So who would know of this Kaminski Parure?' he asked. 'Its value. The fact that you own it. That you keep it here. How could anyone know such a thing except close friends? Staff?'

Dombasle looked embarrassed. 'For our tenth anniversary, and on a whim of my wife's, a magazine called *Regarde Sud* was invited to Cap Corsaire. It was a big spread. You may have seen it. I had just bought the

Kaminski jewels for my wife and of course they featured in the story. Anyone who saw that issue of *Regarde Sud* would know who owned the jewels and where they could be found.'

Jacquot nodded. 'The press can be a dangerous bedfellow, *n'est-ce pas*?' was all he said. And then, 'Tell me about the pick-up. What are your instructions?'

'Midnight tonight,' replied Dombasle. 'On the Peille road out of La Turbie. I'm to bring the jewels in exchange for Lydie and Nonie.'

'They will be there?'

'No, I get an address where they can be found.'

'She specified you, as the driver?' asked Mageot, who was clearly trying to work something out, come up with a plan.

'Yes,' said Dombasle. 'I'm to go alone.'

Jacquot nodded. 'Did she give any directions? Exactly where the exchange will take place?'

'Somewhere between La Turbie and St-Martin. That's all she said. Apparently, I will be flagged down.'

Smart, thought Jacquot. No chance to set something up in advance. The Peille road, as Jacquot knew from his ride with Olivier, was far too long to patrol effectively, with any number of potential drops and cut-offs. And setting up blocks at either end or surveillance teams would mean Lydie and Nonie could come to harm.

Wherever they were. Jacquot wondered again if there was an accomplice involved.

Mathilde Carassin and her husband?

Or Corinne and Valentine Caloux?

Or maybe the two women were working together?

'I wonder if I could make a quick call,' asked Jacquot, reaching for the phone. 'It's a local number,' he added with certain emphasis and a gentle smile.

'Call the man in the moon if it'll help,' said Dombasle anxiously. 'Right now I feel like we're two points down and playing injury time.' And then Dombasle managed a grin. 'Just the kind of conditions you favour, Daniel, if I remember correctly?'

72

Less than five minutes later, Jacquot put down the phone. Mageot and Dombasle looked at him.

'Well?' said Dombasle.

Jacquot settled himself back in his chair, went over what Brunet had just told him, but decided to keep his cards close to his chest.

'As you both know,' he began, 'I have been carrying out an unofficial investigation since the reunion party and Bernard's "suicide". You will remember I was not happy with Chief Inspector Murier's findings – or lack of them,' he added gently. 'I had no doubt that the "suicide" was murder. A very adeptly arranged *mise-en-scène* set up to cover the killer's tracks. In much the same way that the deaths of Luc, Patric, Marc, Antoine and Claude were "arranged" – murder as accident. Case closed. Just as you saw Murier do with Bernard.'

Neither Dombasle nor Mageot saw fit to say anything.

'In the course of this investigation I have narrowed down my list of suspects. A simple process of elimination, based more on opportunity than motive. Apart from believing that every death is aimed at you, Pierre—'

'But why?' interrupted Mageot. 'Why bother? Why not hit the skipper first, if he's the target?'

'Like I said, to cause him pain, Guy. I mean, seventy million francs? Now, that hurts.' Jacquot paused and turned to Dombasle.

'And let's not forget, Pierre, the deep and lasting affection you have for your team. Or certain members of that team. An affection that has – Savry excluded – persuaded you to back them in various business endeavours. Is that not so?'

Dombasle gazed at the floor. 'As I said at our last meeting, each death hurts, each death is a terrible loss. And each time, a scratch on my cars to remind me of the score.'

'Which is what all this is about,' continued Jacquot. 'The killer wants to hurt you. Frighten you. Damage you.'

He glanced at the two men. Neither looked like they wanted to say anything.

'So, getting back to my suspects . . . as of this morning,

I had three names left on my list. For one reason or another all the others have been crossed off one by one. The three suspects who remained were all women. Just before Guy picked me up, I had narrowed it down to two.'

'Two,' exclaimed Dombasle. 'Then we have them. They should be brought in for questioning, surely. Maybe they are working together?'

Jacquot shook his head 'As of that phone call, my list of suspects has been narrowed down to just one name. And she lives just a few kilometres from here.'

'Jesus, Jacquot, you know how to string it out, don't you? But let's cut to the chase. The name? The name?'

Jacquot held up his hand. 'In a moment. In a moment. First, perhaps you could tell me what you know about Corinne Caloux.'

Abruptly, as though he hadn't heard the question, Dombasle swung round to Mageot. 'Guy, a moment please?'

'Sure, skipper,' replied Mageot and he withdrew, leaving Dombasle and Jacquot together. The light was gone from the sky and the first stars were flickering out at sea. A gust of chill wind blew in and the fronds of an indoor palm rattled.

'Corinne? Is she the one?'

'You tell me.'

73

'Corinne Caloux is a bitch,' said Dombasle. 'And I regret to say that her husband's not much better. They live down the coast in Théoule-sur-Mer.' Dombasle paused.

'And?' Jacquot said at last.

'Five years ago, I began a brief affair with Corinne. It was a mistake, but she was, is, a very sexy woman. There is something dark and dangerous about her. You have met her. You will know what I mean.'

Jacquot nodded, remembering the slim figure, the hungry eyes, the cap of creamy hair. Sexy, yes. And dangerous too, he had no doubt. For some it was an irresistible combination.

'We met first a few weeks before her marriage to Val. They were living in Paris back then. I knew immediately that one day we would be lovers. And I was right. Shortly after their marriage they moved down here and we met again at a big charity gala. Corinne was on the committee and had persuaded me to play the auctioneer. You know the sort of thing – there's a lot of it down here. Celebrities parting with large sums of money in a blaze of publicity for any one of a dozen good causes. A holiday for two in Mauritius. A case of Le Pin 1962. The loan of a super-yacht on the *quai* at St Tropez. People pay crazy money for such trifles. And, at Corinne's insistence, I was the man with the hammer. That evening, after announcing that SportÉquipe would match each of the ten winning bids, Corinne's charity made more money than they had taken in the previous two years. It was a phenomenal success. The following day she phoned me, ostensibly to thank me for my generosity at the auction. I told her that we should meet up and I invited her to dinner, at my home in Marseilles.'

Now Jacquot knew where Dombasle had been two nights earlier, while his wife was in Forcalquier. In Marseilles, Roucas Blanc, with whoever was his latest conquest.

'We knew what we were going to do without a word being said,' continued Dombasle. 'The moment she walked through the door. And she was mesmerising . . . *si aventureuse*, *si ingénieuse*.' Dombasle shook his head as if at the wonder of it, and chuckled. 'You wouldn't believe . . .'

'And this affair lasted how long?'

'Three years,' replied Dombasle, gathering himself, looking Jacquot squarely in the eye.

'And how did it end?'

'She asked me for money. Not for a charity, but for her husband. Val had a scheme, she said, he needed backing – and she had heard that I sometimes helped "worthy causes", that other old team-mates had benefited from my own good fortune in business.' He held up his hands, as if in surrender. 'But you know that already. And why not, for God's sake?'

'And the scheme?'

'Let's just say it was suspect, possibly criminal. And I never cross that line.'

'So you said "no".'

Dombasle nodded. 'And Corinne was not happy. When she realised I could not be persuaded by any means, she threatened me. Told me some of the money raised at her auction had been "lost" and that if she leaked the story to the press, SportÉquipe and I would end up on the front page and not look good.'

Dombasle smiled. 'I took a gamble. I told her to do as she pleased. I never heard another word. But at least some good has come of it. Val is still a *notaire*, *n'est-ce pas*? And not in jail, where he would probably have ended up had he gone ahead with his "venture". As things turned out, I did them a favour after all. So there you are.'

'And Mathilde Carassin?'

At that name Dombasle started. 'She is the other suspect?'

Jacquot said nothing.

Dombasle blew out his cheeks, looked up at the ceiling. 'So she gets her revenge,' he whispered, almost to himself. 'After all this time . . .'

'Revenge?'

Dombasle said nothing for a moment, then caught and held Jacquot's eye. 'A few months after that debut match of yours in London,' he began, 'Sidi Carassin announced that he was going to get married. The little monkey had found a mate.' Dombasle said this with a smile, as though inviting Jacquot to share in his prejudice. It was typical locker-room talk and when he realised that Jacquot disapproved of both the sentiment and invitation, Dombasle softened, changed direction. 'Anyway, Sidi brought her along to a team party – some end-of-season do. And she was just the most beautiful young woman, a body to die for. Every man in the team was thinking just one thing. What I wouldn't give . . .'

Dombasle gave a sigh. 'That night, the first time I met

her, I behaved badly. I had drunk too much, I'd just pulled off my first big sponsorship deal, I was skipper, I was king of the castle . . . you know how it is, Daniel?' Another invitation to be complicit. Jacquot kept still and silent.

Dombasle took a deep breath and let it out in a slow, regretful sigh. 'I took advantage, Daniel. I suppose you could say I . . . raped her.' He chuckled lightly at the word, as though it was an overstatement, too strong, too emotive, to properly describe what he had done. 'I admit she was not willing. She made that quite clear. But I persisted, I didn't stop. I couldn't stop . . .' Dombasle gave Jacquot another sharing look, man to man . . . we understand these things . . .

'But it was all so long ago,' said Dombasle, as though time should have healed any wound, any damage.

'Some memories go back a long way, Pierre. Some people survive on the prospect of some future revenge. It keeps them sane, nourishes them. And since then, you have done well, very well. So add a little pinch of jealousy to the brew and you have a potent adversary, *n'est-ce pas*?'

'So it's Mathilde? You think it's her?'

But Jacquot did not reply. Over Dombasle's shoulder, he saw the salon door open and Mageot reappear, ushering Detective Inspector Christine Ambert into the room.

74

'Monsieur Dombasle,' said Christine Ambert, reaching forward to shake his hand, holding on to her shoulder bag to stop it from swinging between them. 'It is good to see you again.' Her deep blue eyes flicked from Dombasle to Jacquot. '*Et vous aussi*, Chief Inspector. How nice to see you, too.' Her grip was dry and firm and carried no message beyond simple professional courtesy. Just as it should be. Though Jacquot knew differently.

With greetings completed, Mageot brought another chair to the table and held it while Christine Ambert settled herself. She was dressed in jeans, with a check jacket over a polo-neck sweater. She was wearing boots with a low heel and no jewellery beyond an expandable strap watch that looked, Jacquot suspected, more expensive than it was.

'So, messieurs. I believe you have a problem? How can the *judiciaire* be of help?'

'Detective Inspector,' began Dombasle, taking the lead, 'before I start, I want your undertaking that what I tell you goes no further . . .'

Ambert gave Dombasle a patient, understanding smile, but shook her head. Just as Jacquot had known she would. 'I'm afraid I can't do that, monsieur. Whatever you say to me in my capacity as a police officer must, of course, be reported back to my superiors.'

'All I'm suggesting, Detective Inspector, is a little leeway,' Dombasle persisted, a man used to getting his own way. 'It is a delicate matter that brings you here, and it is your help, as a member of the *judiciaire*, rather than your immediate boss's, Chief Inspector Murier, that I am particularly requesting. On a matter pertaining to our discussions yesterday. By the way,' he asked, 'have you mentioned our meeting to Murier?'

'Not yet, monsieur.'

Dombasle beamed. 'Exactly, Detective Inspector. And that is all I am asking. A little leeway. A little discretion. Just for now.'

'I have to tell you, monsieur, that I am not comfortable with this.'

Jacquot was pleased to see Christine Ambert make no bones about her professional responsibilities. Her duty as a member of the *judiciaire*. Even if a senior officer – Jacquot himself – appeared to be involved.

'And so you should be. So you should be,' replied Dombasle suavely. 'But also be assured, Detective Inspector, that my good friend, Gaspard Blois, at the *Ministère de la Justice*, will be properly advised of your assistance in this matter.'

The implication hung in the air. There was silence around the table. And then, with an almost imperceptible nod of the head, Detective Inspector Ambert joined the team, and Dombasle told her all they knew: a box containing two dead dogs delivered to the house; the scratches on his cars; his wife and stepdaughter apparently kidnapped; the tape-recorded message and the phone call stating demands and exchange details.

After asking much the same questions as Jacquot, she settled on the ransom demands. 'So, as I understand it, you have been asked to deliver these jewels to a particular place, and at a particular time – in exchange for your wife and stepdaughter?'

'Midnight tonight. On the road to Peille. The D53. After the La Turbie turning, I am to switch from main headlights to fog lights. At some point on the road I will be flagged down. The jewels will be exchanged for the whereabouts of Lydie and Nonie.'

'Their whereabouts? You mean they won't physically be there? For exchange? You'll hand over the jewels without actually seeing them?'

'That is so,' admitted Dombasle.

'And we have absolutely no information regarding who might be involved?' continued Christine Ambert. 'Apart, that is, from staff, friends and the readers of *Regarde Sud*?'

Dombasle and Mageot shook their heads. But then Dombasle shot a look at Jacquot. 'I think the Chief Inspector might have an idea,' he said.

Christine Ambert turned to Jacquot and raised an eyebrow. 'Chief Inspector?'

Jacquot held the look. Eventually he asked, 'Is there anyone at HQ that you can call up?'

'You mean without Murier finding out?'

Jacquot nodded, smiled.

'Well, there's Christophe at the *judiciaire*. Sergeant Christophe Haddonet. He's a good lad and will do anything I ask.'

Jacquot wondered if this Haddonet was like his own Brunet back in Cavaillon. Somehow Jacquot suspected he was. Every good detective needs a Brunet or, in this case, a Haddonet.

'Then tell him', said Jacquot, glancing at his watch, 'to get down to the St-Pierre harbour in Villefranche – St-Pierre, not the Darse – and to look out for a white Renault van. It'll be driven by a woman, Mathilde Carassin, tall, blonde, in her late thirties. Sometime in the next hour she'll be dropping off her husband down by the jetty.'

Christine Ambert wasted not a moment. A call was put through to Nice *judiciaire* and Sergeant Haddonet was asked for.

The conversation that followed was brisk and to the point. 'Christophe, get one of the boys and set up a watch on a possible suspect, Mathilde Carassin.' She passed on Jacquot's description and the make of the van. 'Whatever you do,' she continued, 'don't get spotted and be prepared to move fast. And use our usual frequency, OK?' She put down the phone. 'It's done,' she said, and her eyes suddenly gleamed with excitement.

'So you think she's the one?' asked Dombasle, turning to Jacquot.

'It would appear so,' replied Jacquot. 'According to my assistant, Madame Corinne Caloux is currently enjoying a few days with her sister and mother in Brittany.'

And then, suddenly, for no reason that he could

identify, Jacquot felt a fleeting, shadowy sensation that he'd missed something. Something . . . not quite fitting.

Or rather, fitting so well, so tightly, that it was not immediately apparent.

75

The next hour was spent poring over detailed maps of the three Corniche roads and making plans. How useful, how straightforward it would all have been, mused Jacquot, if the kidnapper's ransom demand had been written on the back of a supermarket till receipt, as the dog-napper in Lourmarin had done. Instead, here they were working out distances, likely-looking drop-offs, and possible escape routes.

The only respite came at a little after seven when Manolo came into the salon to let them know that a light supper had been prepared and was awaiting them in the dining room. As light suppers went, Jacquot decided he couldn't fault it. A long buffet table had been set with enough choices to satisfy the most demanding of palates or *arrivistes*. Here a glistening mound of large-grain

Beluga caviar swaddled in a bowl of shaved ice; beside it, cold lobster and crab, platters of foie gras *cru et cuit*, juniper-smoked salmon from Norway, tureens of soup both hot and cold, and cold cuts of beef, pork and lamb. As they helped themselves from the buffet, Jacquot caught Christine Ambert's eye and he knew she was as stunned as he was by the display.

An hour or so later, Jacquot was lingering over the last forkful of a truffled-cream pappardelle when Dombasle leaned across to Mageot and whispered in his ear. Mageot nodded, left the room and returned nearly ten minutes later with a slim leather box about the size of an attaché case. Retaking his chair, he made room for the case on the dining table, flipped the catch and lifted the lid. In a swift, practised manner he swung the open case into the centre of the table so that Jacquot and Ambert could see for themselves. Beside him, Christine Ambert gasped.

There, bedded in cream velvet, lay the Kaminski jewels, the candlelight sparkling off the rubies and diamonds, amply proportioned gemstones intricately worked into a tiara, a four-tier necklace alternating diamonds and rubies, a pair of similarly stranded bracelets, and extravagantly clustered earrings, long enough, reckoned Jacquot, to reach the shoulders and brush the skin of whoever wore them.

'Ooh là là,' said Christine slowly, *'quelle parure. C'est magnifique.'* She looked across at Dombasle. 'May I?'

Dombasle indicated that she should help herself and she lifted the necklace from its velvet bed. 'So heavy,' she almost laughed.

'Seven hundred and twenty carats in total,' said Dombasle. 'Three hundred and forty carats in rubies, three hundred and eighty in diamonds, the difference due to the single diamond drops on the earrings.'

The three men at the table watched Christine Ambert hold the necklace up to the light from the candles, then lay the twinkling stones against her wrist.

'It is said that the diamonds were mined in India, on the Kollur fields near Hyderabad,' continued Dombasle, as Christine Ambert replaced the necklace and took up one of the earrings, laying it in the palm of her hand. 'And the rubies in Burma's Moguk Valley. The stones you see here were apparently cut from four single nuggets – two diamond, two ruby – that had once belonged to Babar, the first of India's Mogul Dynasty. After Babar's death the stones disappeared for almost two hundred years, until they turned up in Amsterdam, where they were bought by a Russian nobleman – Kaminski – on behalf of the Empress Catherine of Russia. They were taken back to St Petersburg and it was there that the court jeweller, Lazarev, recut the stones and set them as you see them now.'

'So beautiful,' said Ambert, spinning the earring with a finger, candlelight winking off the stones.

'But not so beautiful,' said Dombasle, 'is the manner in which they were transported from Amsterdam to St Petersburg. In order to avoid border taxes, or the possibility that the stones might be stolen on the long journey home, Kaminski had the four nuggets cut into sixteen pieces. He then had his surgeon slice open the sides of his legs, conceal the eight rubies and eight diamonds therein and then sew up the wound. When Kaminski returned to Russia, his legs were opened up and the stones retrieved. They say it was impossible to tell which stones were rubies and which were the diamonds – the blood, you understand.'

'Some things you need to know. Some things you don't,' said Ambert, placing the earring back in its case. 'Tell me, will the jewels remain in the box for the hand-over? Or will they be loose?'

'I hadn't thought,' said Dombasle. He looked at Mageot who shook his head, shrugged. 'But why do you ask?'

'It would be useful to attach a tracking device,' explained Ambert.

Which made Dombasle smile. 'Already done, Inspector. The insurance company demanded it when I said that the jewels would be kept at my various homes and not in a bank. Either that, or the premium would have shot through the roof.'

Jacquot noticed Mageot's jaw clench. It was clear that he had not been informed of this detail and equally clear that he was not happy about being kept out of the loop. As Head of Security, it was only right that he should have known, been confided in. Jacquot felt a little sorry for him.

Dombasle reached for bracelet and, handling it with an easy familiarity, pointed to the clasp. 'Each of the pieces has a microchip here, in the clasp. Small enough not to be noticed, but strong enough to send out a powerful signal. I have already alerted the insurance company, and they will be able to trace the stones before they are parted from their settings.'

Ambert smiled. 'Well, at least I don't have to set something up at the last minute. We could have done it, of course, but I would've had to clear it through Chief Inspector Murier.'

'Then let us be thankful for small mercies,' said Dombasle.

76

At a little before eleven, Pierre Dombasle's Bentley and the black Ferrari were brought to the front of the house. As they had agreed during their planning session, Dombasle would drive the Bentley with Mageot hunkered down in the back seat, while Jacquot and Ambert would follow at a discreet distance in the Ferrari.

It was the only part of their plan that Jacquot had not been altogether happy about.

'You should know that I have never driven such a car before,' he told them. 'I am not used to it. If it came to a chase, if good driving was required, there might be a problem.'

'Same with me,' admitted Ambert. 'But I'm happy to give it a go,' she said. 'If you don't give something a try, you're never going to know, are you?' And she'd accepted the keys to the Ferrari with the same delight that she had handled the jewels.

Of the four of them, only Dombasle was unarmed. Jacquot and Ambert had their service pistols and Mageot a 9mm Smith & Wesson automatic. When Jacquot saw it, he'd immediately asked to see a *permis* for the weapon. Mageot had promptly produced one and now, at the bottom of the front steps, they paired off towards their cars. The jewels had been transferred to a briefcase and Dombasle placed it in the well of the passenger seat while Mageot stowed himself away in the back. Behind them, Jacquot lowered himself into the Ferrari's passenger seat while Ambert, coat buttoned and hair tucked under a beret, slid elegantly in behind the wheel.

It was then that a muffled blaze of static came from Ambert's handbag. It was her police radio, a report from Sergeant Christophe Haddonet. Ambert pulled it out and listened, her fingers tapping the wheel of the car.

'Sorry, boss, we lost her,' Jacquot heard Haddonet say. 'We started the tail at St-Pierre, like you said, and we followed her back to Nice. She stopped at a bar in the old town, had a drink and something to eat, then got back into the van and started driving around. No pattern to it. Which was when she must have spotted us. She jumped a set of lights on Riquier and by the time we were through she was gone. We've been quartering the district for the last forty minutes but there's no sign of her.'

'Don't worry. It's not your fault,' said Ambert. 'Just head for the Grande Corniche, and park up at La Turbie. If Madame Carassin was on Riquier the chances are she's heading in this direction.' With that she signed off and dropped the radio back in her bag.

Up ahead the Bentley had moved off, swinging round the forecourt and turning down the drive, its headlights blazing a path between the borders of cypress, aleppo and eucalyptus.

In the Ferrari, Ambert leaned forward, inserted the key and fired up the engine. 'Oh, will you listen to that,' she said softly, licking her lips and pedalling some revs into the mix. 'It's just not fair . . .' Then she released the clutch, but dropped the revs too low and the engine promptly stalled.

'*Merde alors*,' she swore and restarted the engine. This time she kept up the revs as the clutch was released, but the timing wasn't right and the car lurched forward, its rear end fishtailing wildly, its tyres spitting up gravel.

'Don't you dare say a word, Chief Inspector,' said

more than just the jewels, Mageot would let off a couple of shots to confuse the killer and summon armed assistance from Jacquot and Ambert in the back-up car. Otherwise, once Dombasle had been given the address, and since the jewels were tagged, the kidnapper was free to go. With the tracking device in play he or she would be picked up soon enough.

They had also agreed that the kidnapper would need to find a spot on this isolated stretch of road where the Bentley could be safely flagged down. Since the road was too narrow to stop and park on the verge – if there even was such a thing – it seemed likely that the Bentley would be taken off road. Using Mageot's most detailed and up-to-date *Cartes de Randonnée* showing footpaths and hiking trails along the fifteen-kilometre drive to Peille, they had discounted private driveways, lay-bys or overtaking points and identified just half a dozen possible sites where an exchange could take place. The first two were between the settlements of Le Gavan and Figourn – the entrance to a forestry track and a hiker's shelter across the valley from the quarries of Le Castéou. The other four were further on, along an even more isolated stretch of the road between Les Lacs and La Paran. It would be somewhere here, they all agreed, furthest away from habitation, that the drop would be made.

But plans – no matter how thorough or sensible –

have a dreadful habit of going wrong. Huddled around Dombasle's dining table the four of them had reckoned on a fair amount of light from a half-moon in a clear sky so that Jacquot and Ambert could cruise up close with their headlights off. But as Jacquot and Ambert reached the turning for La Turbie on the Corniche Moyenne, fat pellets of rain started smacking down on the Ferrari's windscreen.

But it wasn't just the rain that was going to skew their plan.

78

'I've made a mistake, haven't I?' said Christine Ambert at last.

She and Jacquot had just swung off the Grande Corniche at La Turbie and up along the narrower route to Peille, not a word exchanged since leaving Cap Corsaire.

Jacquot knew at once that Christine Ambert wasn't talking about her driving.

'Yes, I think you have,' he replied, and without letting her see he slipped his gun from his holster and rested it in his lap, pointing at her.

'I knew I must have done something,' she said quietly. 'You suddenly changed. Back at the house. I could feel it.' Playing the wheel on the first of the steep curves leading out of town, she glanced across at him. 'Was it something to do with the jewels?'

Just over a kilometre ahead the Bentley's tail-lights blazed as it slowed for the next bend.

'*En effet*, this fine car,' replied Jacquot. 'Just before Dombasle handed you the keys.'

Approaching the bend that the Bentley had just negotiated, Ambert touched the Ferrari's brakes. Working the gated gearbox with more expertise than she'd started with, Christine Ambert double de-clutched on the turn, the engine surged and the pools of the Ferrari's headlights swept across an empty void.

'How? What mistake?' she asked, straightening the wheel and increasing their speed. Once more the Bentley was visible up ahead.

'"If you don't try, you die". Or words to that effect,' replied Jacquot, gripping the hand rest as the Ferrari slithered on a patch of roadside gravel.

Ambert was shaking her head. 'I don't understand.'

'Marc Fastin? Club Xéro? It was a favourite saying of his.'

Ambert said nothing, just kept her eyes on the road ahead. Jacquot wondered if she'd spotted the gun in his lap. He didn't think so.

'You knew him, didn't you? And you killed him that night in the club.'

Ambert said nothing now, but Jacquot could see her

features harden, the lights from the dash glowing on her face.

'And the beret,' continued Jacquot, suddenly remembering. 'Let's not forget your beret.' He might also have mentioned the white wine, come to think of it.

'My beret?'

'It was Mademoiselle Talleyran who told me about the beret.'

'Talleyran?'

'She was Fastin's girlfriend before you. The one he dumped when you came along. She saw the two of you once, from her office window. When I asked her for a description all she could remember was that you were tall. And wore a beret.'

Jacquot was surprised at how calm, how composed Ambert appeared to be. She kept her eyes on the road, her handling of the Ferrari seemed to be improving with every passing kilometre, and what looked like a smile was starting to crease her cheeks. It was as if she knew something that he didn't, as if she still had an ace up her sleeve. This sense of being toyed with was unsettling. But Jacquot carried on, his hand tightening on the gun.

'And it was you who pushed me from my balcony, wasn't it?'

Ambert sighed. 'You were getting too close, Chief Inspector. As simple as that. Like Savry writing those reports in the newspaper. Sooner or later he was going to make enough noise for someone to take him seriously. It was the same with you.'

Jacquot nodded in the darkness, eyes flicking between Ambert and the road ahead. There was something wrong, he was sure of it, something he hadn't quite prepared himself for. And he knew that time was running out.

'So what are we going to do now, Chief Inspector?' she asked.

'We're going to do exactly what we planned – follow the Bentley and arrest your accomplice.'

'*Comme tu veux*,' she replied and, with a wicked grin, she put her foot down.

79

As far as Jacquot could see there was no flagging down, no swinging torch in the night. Just the sudden twin red glare of the Bentley's tail-lights and the pulsing orange beat of its hazard lights, no more than a kilometre ahead on one of the straightest stretches of the route, at the entrance to the forestry track, the first of the possible drops that they had identified in Dombasle's dining room. Since their headlights would have been clearly visible to the kidnapper, Jacquot instructed Ambert to keep them on and keep driving. When they reached the Bentley and saw what was happening, they could either drive on – just another car headed for home – or stop to help.

Twenty metres from the Bentley, the rain lashing down through the headlights, the wipers thump-thumping across the windscreen, Jacquot saw the Bentley's front passenger door open and Mageot step into the road, the briefcase with the jewels held over his head to protect him from the rain. As soon as Ambert saw him she flashed around the Bentley and spun the Ferrari in the wood-chip entrance to the forestry track. Seconds later she had turned the car and pulled up behind the Bentley, the Ferrari now pointing back to La Turbie.

Putting the car out of gear, she turned to Jacquot, smiled and held out her hand for his gun.

'You won't be needing that now, Chief Inspector.'

Before Jacquot could say a word, there was a sharp tap on his window. He turned and found himself looking at the muzzle of Mageot's 9mm automatic. Mageot stood back and gestured with the gun that Jacquot should get out of the car. There was nothing Jacquot could possibly do. He felt Christine Ambert's hand prise his gun from his fingers, then jab it into his arm. 'Out. Now.'

The rain was hard and cold, drenching Jacquot in seconds. Stepping past him, Mageot slung the briefcase into the Ferrari's back seat and, keeping the gun on Jacquot at all times, he slid into the passenger seat.

Whether Christine Ambert realised it or not, Jacquot knew that her accomplice Mageot was going to pull the trigger. The cold eyes, the smile. Jacquot was just seconds away from taking a 9mm bullet in the head or chest. His reaction was pure instinct, the kind of intuition that had once told him where the ball was going, where the opposition was weakest, and when to exploit it. Tipping backwards on his left foot, he lifted his right leg and kicked out hard at the Ferrari's passenger door. The contact was as sure and true as the instinct that generated it and the door slammed back against Mageot's wrist, the fingers splaying out with the pain, the gun clattering to the ground. As Jacquot reached for it, the Ferrari's tyres dug into the tarmac and the car shot forward, its rear wheels catching on the barrel of the gun and sending it spinning backwards to clang against the Bentley's rear bumper.

By the time Jacquot retrieved it, the Ferrari was roaring off down the road, back to La Turbie, its tail-lights glaring as it slowed for the first bend.

Gun in hand, Jacquot ran round to the Bentley's driver's door. Through the rain-smeared window he could see Dombasle slumped against the steering wheel. He pulled open the door and felt for a pulse in the neck.

'Shot me,' said Dombasle. 'Shot me . . .' The voice was weak, but it was strong enough to express a sense of astonishment, even muted outrage. That Mageot, his Head of Security, his old team-mate, had actually and deliberately shot him.

'Can you sit up?' asked Jacquot.

'Help me . . . I'm . . .'

Tossing the gun onto the back seat, Jacquot eased Dombasle away from the wheel and examined the injury. The left side of his jacket and shirt was soaked in blood. Judging by the ragged tear Jacquot had seen in the back of the driver's seat and a matching hole in the door frame, it was clear that the bullet had gone straight through. What it might have broken, punctured or otherwise damaged on its journey, Jacquot had no way of telling. What he did know was that Mageot would have pulled that trigger to kill, not just wound. He would have to get Dombasle to a hospital fast.

'I'm going to try to lift you into the passenger seat. Can you push up with your legs?' shouted Jacquot over the rain drumming like hoofbeats on the roof of the car.

'*Oui, oui. C'est . . .*' With a groan Dombasle pushed himself up and Jacquot, grasping him under the arms, heaved him across on to the passenger seat. Dashing around to the passenger side door, he straightened Dombasle up, then reached across for his legs, freeing them from beneath the steering wheel.

'What about Lydie? Nonie?' gasped Dombasle, the breath hissing through his teeth.

'Don't worry about that. I know where to find them,' replied Jacquot, pretty certain they'd be tied up in Ambert's apartment. Pulling down the seat-belt strap, he secured Dombasle then ran round to the driver's side and dropped in behind the wheel. He looked at the array of knobs, dials and switches in front of him and groaned. Oh, for his faithful old Peugeot in the car park at Villefranche.

Putting it all out of his mind, Jacquot felt for the ignition key and found it. Either unable to reach it with Dombasle slumped over the wheel, or imagining that neither Dombasle nor Jacquot would be in any fit state to drive, Mageot had left the key in the ignition. With a grateful twist, Jacquot turned it and winced at the bitter screech from the starter motor. The engine was already running. Cursing lightly, Jacquot released the hand-brake, pushed the gear lever to 'Drive', and felt the two-ton Bentley slide forward.

80

Since he was facing the wrong way, the first thing Jacquot had to do was turn the Bentley. Spinning the wheel, he slung its nose across the road and up into the entrance to the forestry track, crumpling the front wing on a large boulder. *Merde!* Engaging reverse he then sent the car surging backwards, until its back bumper smashed into the low retaining wall on the far side of the road, jolting the two of them in their seats.

'*Merde alors*,' whispered Dombasle beside him. 'That's a hundred thousand francs you've cost me . . .'

'Sorry, Pierre, it's a little bit bigger than I'm used to,' said Jacquot, wincing at the screeching rasp from the Bentley's rear end as the bumper scraped clear of the wall.

'It doesn't matter. *C'est rien.* Just get after that *conard*.'

'*Conards*,' corrected Jacquot. Easing the car forward, he straightened up the bonnet which seemed to stretch ahead of him like the landing deck of an aircraft carrier and pressed down on the accelerator, thanking the gods for an automatic transmission and trying to get some sense of the play in the steering as he powered off down the road in pursuit of the Ferrari. With some hair-raising bends up ahead it would be useful to know what he could do with this monstrous machine, how far he could push her.

Dombasle roused himself, using the seat belt to pull himself upright. 'The girl too? They're together?'

Jacquot didn't have time to answer. The first bend, a sharp left-hander, was coming up fast, a sprinkling of distant lights across the valley in front of him and a sheer drop between them. Judge the corner wrong and two tons of finely tuned British engineering, lacquered coach-work and hand-tooled leather would go blasting through the wall and sail out into space.

'Drop off the gas, touch the brake, then push down hard as you turn into the corner,' said Dombasle, as though reading Jacquot's mind and not being too comforted by the contents. 'There're no headlights ahead, so use the whole road,' he added.

Aha, thought Jacquot, the Olivier Touche School of driving. But he did as he was told, basically because he didn't know what else to do – foot off the gas, a tentative dab at the brake, and then, against all his instincts, he piled on the power as he turned into the bend.

For a millisecond Jacquot was convinced he'd left it too late, misjudged his approach, failed to take proper account of the rain-slicked surface. But the wheels held, the car seemed to crouch down over the tarmac and, save a nervous little wobble as he straightened up in preparation for the next bend, Jacquot had taken his first corner at speed in a car that cost more than four times his salary. At what speed he couldn't say, since he hadn't taken his eyes off the road for a single second.

But it was fast. He knew that.

So was the second bend, negotiated with another nervous wobble.

'Stamp your foot down, for Christ's sake, or we'll both be done for . . .' warned Dombasle, managing to get some volume into the words, clinging now with both hands to the seat-belt strap.

A third and a fourth bend followed, equally sharp but far more cleanly negotiated. The car was a dream to drive, Jacquot was relieved to find. It seemed to sense the road ahead and take it on full and square – and survive. Taking the driver with it.

It was possibly this belief in the car's ability to drive without him, as much as his growing yet ill-founded confidence in his ability to control it, that accounted for what happened next, a lapse in concentration on the first real switchback down into La Turbie. As he pulled out into the middle of what was only a narrow road, he glimpsed a set of headlights coming up and around at him. At exactly the same moment the off-side back wheel slid into the dip of a camber with only gravel to grip on to. Jacquot felt the pull and loss of control an instant before Dombasle and desperately tugged at the wheel.

'À *gauche, à gauche*,' hissed Dombasle. 'Left, left, and then hard to the right, hammer the gas.'

Because Dombasle's instructions came a second too late, the back end of the Bentley skidded on the camber, swung even further round and pushed the bonnet back out into the road, into the path of the oncoming car.

It was a Peugeot, much like Jacquot's own, a little younger maybe, with a driver who could see – if not altogether believe – what was about to happen and had the presence of mind to take avoiding action. With just seconds to spare, the Peugeot turned into the slope, sent a line of trash bins spinning high into the air, and received a hefty thump across its rear wing from the passing Bentley as it finally straightened up and powered away.

After such reckless, skin-of-the-teeth driving it seemed

somehow ridiculous to Jacquot to come to a halt at a set of red lights fifty metres further on. He even indicated.

'What the hell are you doing?' growled Dombasle. 'Where the hell do you think you're going?'

'Getting you to a hospital,' Jacquot told him, his hands sticky on the steering wheel with Dombasle's blood.

'Christ's sake, man, that can wait. Get after them. The other way, dammit. They'll have turned left, down to Menton and the border. It's the quickest way out of the country and the Ferrari's got Italian plates. And don't forget.'

'What? Don't forget what?' said Jacquot, mounting the kerb as he made the turn then bouncing off it. They both rose in their seats and then dropped back into them.

'The clasps,' said Dombasle. 'The clasps.'

81

Pierre Dombasle wasn't the only one nursing a wound.

In the orange glow from the Ferrari's dashboard, Guy Mageot's face was pale and drawn, the skin glistening with a thin sheen of sweat, his left hand cradling his right arm against his shoulder. He had heard the wrist bones break when Jacquot kicked the passenger door shut and he'd been nursing it ever since, groaning like Dombasle with every bump and swerve as the Ferrari roared down into La Turbie, spinning to the left on to the Grande Corniche, heading east for Menton and the border. It was just as well he had had the forethought to give Christine three practice sessions with the Ferrari to cover such contingencies. With his wrist broken there was no way he was going to be able to handle the Ferrari himself.

'Did you take the keys?' she asked as they flashed beneath the last streetlight in La Turbie and headed out of town. 'The Bentley?'

Mageot shook his head mournfully. 'I didn't think they'd be driving anywhere,' he grunted.

'Well, that's just great,' she replied bitterly, skidding to a stop at a set of temporary traffic lights. Beyond it, fifty metres of repair work on the retaining wall had closed one half of the road. With a clear line of sight, Ambert would have ignored the red signal had it not been for a laden cattle-truck lumbering along the single lane towards them. 'But before we do anything,' she said, 'before we go another kilometre, we get rid of those clasps.'

The truck passed them, red turned to green and the Ferrari pulled out and roared off.

'And how exactly do you plan on doing that?' asked Mageot.

Reaching into her shoulder bag, Ambert pulled out a lighter and handed it to Mageot. 'Turn up the gas to full, put the flame to the clasps and melt the chips.'

'With a broken wrist?' spat Mageot.

Ambert's lips tightened. '*Merde . . .*' Seconds later, she braked hard and pulled into a driveway on the outskirts of Roquebrune. 'Get me the briefcase,' she said, and as

Mageot leaned back with his good hand, she leaned down to pick up the radio.

She flicked the transmit switch. 'Christophe? You there?'

82

Sergeant Christophe Haddonet had not had a good evening. It had started out well enough at Villefranche, his *deputé* Lascarre quickly marking the suspect at the jetty and the two of them trailing her van back to Nice. It had been easy enough for the next two hours, parked outside a bar in St-Jacques, but within ten minutes of her driving off they'd somehow managed to lose her in the old town's tangle of streets. Whether she knew she was being tailed, whether she'd given them the slip deliberately, or simply done it by chance, he could not say. Not wanting to call it in immediately, Haddonet and Lascarre had spent the next half-hour trawling up and down every street within six blocks of the port looking for that white van. Finally, reluctantly, Haddonet had radioed his boss. Now, as per instructions, he and Lascarre were parked outside a row of darkened restaurants on La Turbie's main *place*, engine off, Thermos out and the rain hammering down on the roof of their car.

'Christophe? You there?'

Spilling coffee in his lap, Haddonet grabbed for the radio. He listened intently, nodding with every '*oui, Inspecteur*' as though Christine Ambert could actually see him. With a final volley of '*oui*'s and a '*C'est compris, Inspecteur*,' he turned to Lascarre.

'There's been a shooting up near Figourn. Getaway car's a silver-grey Bentley. She wants an 'all points' out on it, and if we see it we're to show them the lights and pull them over.'

It was only minutes later that a silver-grey Bentley skidded to a halt at the lights across the *place*, on the road from Figourn.

Haddonet nudged Lascarre and smiled.

Maybe he'd be able to make up for losing the van after all.

83

Leaving La Turbie for Roquebrune and Menton, the Grande Corniche soon narrows, a thin ribbon of coiling highway clinging to sheer slopes above the balconied skyscrapers of Monte Carlo. From here, in a series of swooping straights and stomach-churning blind corners, it drops down to sea level, a little over four hundred metres in less than eight kilometres. It is always an exhilarating drive, never more so than at the wheel of someone else's valuable car, in hot pursuit of another high-performance, high-value automobile, at night, in the pouring rain.

'How do I make the wipers go faster?' asked Jacquot, peering through the rain-smeared windscreen as the Bentley roared out of La Turbie. 'I can't see a thing through the rain.'

Dombasle reached forward and turned up the speed on the wiper controls.

'You're doing fine,' said Dombasle, almost choking on the last word as a cattle truck lumbered round a blind corner taking up more than half the road. '*Mehhhh . . . rrrr . . . duhhhhhh . . .*'

Praying that the Bentley was strong enough to withstand contact with the rocky face of the slope, Jacquot wrenched the wheel to the left and was deafened by the shrieking, spark-flying scream of metal on stone and the ear-splitting blast of the lorry's klaxon as they somehow slid past each other.

'I don't know what is worse,' whispered Dombasle. 'Letting you destroy this car or losing the jewels.'

'We haven't lost them yet,' said Jacquot and, up ahead, no more than a kilometre or so in front of them, he spotted a pair of red tail-lights disappearing round a bend. The lights were low to the ground and only occasionally showed above the retaining wall. It had to be the Ferrari. At almost the same instant Jacquot became aware of a flashing blue light in his rear-view mirror and the start-up whoop-whoop howl of a police siren.

Smart girl, thought Jacquot, remembering the police radio. There was not a doubt in his mind that she radio'ed her friendly sergeant and given him a description of the Bentley.

'Keep driving,' ordered Dombasle, 'they'll never be able to overtake.'

But that didn't mean they didn't try at every possible opportunity.

'They're crazy,' cried Jacquot as he swung the Bentley from side to side, trying to block them, his eyes flicking from the rear-view mirror to the route ahead and what he could now clearly see was the Ferrari.

With a roar of engines and the frantic wailing of a police siren, the three cars powered down the Grand Corniche into the Vistaero curve and raced over the cross-roads, only Haddonet's Renault unable to avoid a slide on the bend. With a screech of tyres, it skidded round the turn and, bouncing off a grass verge, set off after the Bentley.

84

The end came suddenly. And unexpectedly.

In the Ferrari, Ambert and Mageot reduced their speed as they dropped down into Menton, its late-night streets deserted, its shop windows caged and darkened, its streetlights shawled in haloes of orange rain. The Italian border was the other side of town, just a few kilometres away along the Promenade du Soleil.

In the Bentley, Jacquot had caught up with the Ferrari, now dawdling just a few metres ahead, the fall of Ambert's hair and the bulk of Mageot's shoulder visible through the tiny back windscreen. Since the police had obviously been alerted to keep an eye out for a silver-grey Bentley, all Ambert had to do was keep in front of him and motor round Menton until the police car that had chased them from La Turbie caught up with them, or the local Mentonnais gendarmerie took an interest in the battered Bentley and pulled it over. Or maybe they'd try to lose the Bentley in the snarl of narrow streets of the old town. In the next few minutes, if he didn't do something about it, Jacquot knew that Ambert, Mageot and the jewels would be free and clear. And no one at the border would notice anything more than a black Ferrari with Italian plates driven by a pretty blonde returning home.

Or would they simply stop, wondered Jacquot, on a quiet stretch of road, and use their guns to end it? Mageot might have lost his Smith & Wesson, now out-of-reach somewhere in the back of the Bentley, but Ambert had her own and Jacquot's service pistols. It would be over in a moment.

As the Ferrari crossed a *rondpoint* and headed sedately down Avenue Carnot, its engine burbling happily, Jacquot knew what he had to do. Before it was too late.

As the blue flashing lights of the police car reappeared in his rear-view mirror and closed on them fast, Jacquot stamped his foot on to the accelerator and the Bentley surged forward.

'*Jésu*, Daniel . . .' cried Dombasle when he realised what Jacquot was going to do.

Up ahead, trapped like a rabbit in the Bentley's

headlights, the Ferrari jerked forward, jinked to the left and then to the right. But it was too late. The Bentley ploughed into the Ferrari with an explosive crunch of metal and the popping tinkle of broken glass, its bonnet climbing up on to its rear end like a dog on a bitch, shunting the Ferrari forward, its trapped tyres and buckling bodywork screeching along the metalled road, smoke billowing from its crumpled engine vents, rain misting over its raked roof and bonnet.

Jacquot saw the driver's window open and a gun appear, a lash of flame spurting from its tip. The first bullet went wide, the sound of the shot sharper, louder than the screaming metal, echoing along the empty street. But the second and third bullets came closer to home, shattering the windscreen and sending a shower of glass over Jacquot and Dombasle.

Ducking behind the wheel, Jacquot pushed down even harder on the accelerator, praying the engine wouldn't stall, steering the locked cars towards the gates of the Jardins Biovès. As the tangled mess of metal mounted the kerb and hit a streetlight, the Ferrari jerked round one final time and the Bentley rose monumentally above it.

Beside him, Dombasle chuckled hoarsely. 'Wasn't the Bentley enough?' he asked.

her eyes were fixed on Jacquot. Impatiently she pushed back a strand of hair from her face.

'Few killers ever see fit to explain everything,' began Jacquot, taking another bite of his toast and tapenade. 'Particularly the "why". Once they've been caught, they'll either deny the crime or, sooner or later, they will confess. If you're lucky they will tell you who and where and when and how. They will sign a statement, maybe, and make their pleas in court. But – ' Jacquot licked his lips and chuckled, '– they will rarely tell you "why".

'You see, many killers derive a kind of perverse satisfaction from keeping something back, refusing to tell the whole story. Once caught, once they're sitting in a cell, they realise it's the one thing that they have that the police can't get at. It makes them feel special, superior. They're still ahead of the game. Or so they imagine.'

Jacquot took a sip of his pastis, thinking of Ambert and Mageot the last time he'd seen them, sitting stubbornly silent in their lonely tiled cells in Nice's Maison d'Arrêt; of Olivier and Pierre recovering slowly in their hospital beds in Saint-Saëns; of Lydie and Nonie bound, gagged and weeping with relief when he found them in Ambert's apartment. It had been a week since that wild, headlong chase down the Grande Corniche – a week of interview rooms and hospital visits and witness statements – and Jacquot was happy to be home at last.

'And this Christine Ambert, and her brother Guy?' Claudine's eyes were wide, like a child listening to a fairy story.

Jacquot shook his head. 'Half-brother. They had the same mother but different fathers.'

'OK, OK. And?'

'As you know they have confessed to the murders – Guy first, Christine Ambert eventually. She was the toughest to crack. According to Guy, Ambert dealt with Souze, Fastin and Peyrot while he was responsible for Valadier, Lorraine and Savry. They shared the honours.'

'So what do you think? Claudine persisted.

'Since they haven't seen fit to tell us why they did it, I must make an educated guess. First their background. Their mother was a working girl in Marseilles, but neither Guy nor Christine knew their fathers.'

'That's no excuse,' Claudine butted in.

Jacquot held up a hand. 'When their mother died, Guy was nineteen and Christine six. He brought her up himself. I have a very dim memory of a young girl at one of the training sessions but I can't be sure. Anyway, rugby was the making of Guy, offered him a way out. After a tough upbringing, with very little money, he suddenly had enough from playing and work to keep them both. And things looked good. By the time he hung up his boots, he had saved enough to start himself off, and help Christine through college, joining the police of all things.

'But things don't always go to plan. Eventually Mageot got through his money, lost one job after another and saw his prospects dwindle away, ending up as a night-club bouncer while some of his team-mates grew ever more wealthy and more successful. In the end, of all possible indignities, he ends up working for his old skipper, being told to do this and do that without, I'd imagine, too many *mercis* or *s'il vous plaîts*. As for Christine Ambert, well, she's stalled at every turn. A woman in a man's world. According to her file she was an exceptional police officer, but time and time again promotion went to the men – on a number of occasions to men far less able than her.

'And all this time, the two of them stayed in touch. Until Inspector Ambert decided to take matters into her own hands. If she couldn't get what she wanted professionally, then she'd get it another way. According to Mageot, Ambert was the brains behind it, the one who made it all happen – he just went along with it . . .'

'Well, he would say that, wouldn't he?' said Claudine with a snort, reaching for the wine and refilling her glass.

Jacquot shrugged. 'Maybe, maybe. Anyway, she goes to her half-brother, equally disenchanted with the cards life has dealt him, and together they hatch a plot. A sweet revenge on all those old team-mates who did better than him, and on all the third-rate police officers who took her promotions – ending up with enough money to keep them comfortable for the rest of their lives.'

'But murder? Why all those murders? If they wanted to get Pierre, why not just kidnap Lydie and Nonie and have done with it?'

'Because, I suspect, it wouldn't have been enough. Killers, my darling, especially killers like Mageot and Ambert, are often grotesquely self-obsessed, and unusually arrogant. It was probably important to them that they inflicted as much pain and fear and damage as they could along the way – and still get away with it; something to establish their cleverness, their superiority.

'It was like a game, you see, a chance to prolong the pleasure of their revenge, to show just how much smarter they were than the rest of us. And both were ideally placed – Ambert transferred to the Nice *judiciaire*, Mageot working for Dombasle, knowing everything that was going on. They set up the deaths to fool us all, making them look like accidents. But leaving clues, the scratches on Dombasle's cars, to see if anyone would pick up on it. And to begin with no one did. Which would have delighted them even more, made them bolder.'

Jacquot paused, contemplating his empty glass and

the last smudges of tapenade in the bowl. He was suddenly aware how late it was, and tried to remember how many pastis he'd put away since driving out to Claudine's house after his return to Cavaillon, wondering whether he could make it back to his small apartment on the Cours Bournissac, wondering, hopefully, if he would even have to.

'It's time I was going,' he said uncertainly.

Claudine's eyes were on him and she smiled.

'There's no rush,' she said. 'And anyway, I have a gift for you.' She reached down into the pocket of her painter's smock. 'I've been thinking about it. While you've been away.'

Jacquot frowned.

'Just a tiny thing,' Claudine continued, blushing slightly, and her hand slid across the table towards him, hiding something. 'But I think it's time, don't you?'

Slowly, she lifted her hand and a key glinted in the candlelight.

Jacquot and the Angel

Martin O'Brien

A shotgun fired repeatedly at close range and a wealthy German family living in Provence is wiped out. Chief Inspector Daniel Jacquot's murder investigation is one of the most baffling – and personal – cases of his career.

Many of the villagers in the region remember only too well the atrocities committed during World War Two. But Jacquot soon finds that some memories are less reliable than others . . .

When a mysterious young woman arrives claiming a special insight, her presence could be a breakthrough. But the trail takes ever-darker turns into a story of love, betrayal, hatred and blackmail that goes back more than half a century . . .

Praise for Martin O'Brien:

'Well-drawn, strongly flavoured setting in Marseilles . . . with grisly forensics. Rich, spicy and served up with unmistakable relish' *Literary Review*

'O'Brien's evocation of the hot, vibrant and seedy French port is as masterly as Ian Rankin's depiction of Edinburgh' *Daily Mail*

'A strikingly different detective, Jacquot walks off the page effortlessly' *Good Book Guide*

978 0 7553 2287 9

headline

Jacquot and the Master

Martin O'Brien

Provence, a sensual landscape of golden light, rich contrasts and striking colour, is an artist's dream. But sometimes dreams can turn into nightmares.

Chief Inspector Daniel Jacquot of the Cavaillon Regional Crime Squad is called to an artist's retreat, a luxury hill-top hotel. A young woman is missing. There are blood-stains, but no body . . .

Among the guests under suspicion are those who have both means and motive, with personal secrets and their own dangerous liaisons to conceal.

Looming over them all is a celebrated and reclusive artist whose masterworks are priceless. And when a summer storm isolates the hotel, and not one but two bodies are found, passions start to run high . . .

Praise for Martin O'Brien:

'Only an Englishman could set his detective fiction in France and infuse it with such passion for the place and its people . . . well-written and compelling . . . tight plotting, excellent characterisation and lyrical descriptions mean Jacquot is here to stay' *Daily Mail*

'A wonderfully inventive and involving detective story with vivid French locales creating the perfect backdrop. *Jacquot is top of le cops' Daily Express*

978 0 7553 3505 3

headline